Praise for Maegan Beaumont

Carved in Darkness

Named a Best Debut of 2013 by *Suspense Magazine*

"Prepare to be overwhelmed by the tension and moodiness that permeates this edgy thriller. Beaumont's ability to keep the twists coming even when the answer seems obvious is quite potent."—*Library Journal* starred review and Debut of the Month

"Pulse-pounding terror, graphic violence, and a loathsome killer."—*Kirkus Reviews*

"Beaumont knows how to keep you on the edge of your seat … Buckle up for the ride of a lifetime."—*Suspense Magazine*

"Maegan Beaumont might be new to thriller scene, but her debut thriller, *Carved in Darkness,* promises to be the first in a long line of novels. Be warned, however, this novel isn't for those who jump a mile every time they hear something go bump in the night. But for anyone who's ever dreamed about enacting a just revenge, this book is for you. Beaumont knows how to cook up and serve a dish called revenge, but she doesn't serve it cold. She serves it sizzling hot."—Vincent Zandri, Bestselling Author of *The Remains* and *Murder by Moonlight*

PROMISES TO KEEP

A NOVEL

MAEGAN BEAUMONT

MIDNIGHT INK
WOODBURY, MINNESOTA

FIRST EDITION
First Printing, 2015
Published in association with MacGregor Literary, Inc. of Hillsboro, OR

Book design by Bob Gaul
Cover design by Kevin R. Brown
Cover images: iStockphoto.com/26969505/©sundrawalex
              iStockphoto.com/21669021/©Andrey_Kuzmin
Editing by Nicole Nugent

Midnight Ink, an imprint of Llewellyn Worldwide Ltd.

Library of Congress Cataloging-in-Publication Data
Beaumont, Maegan, 1975–
  Promises to keep/Maegan Beaumont.—First edition.
     pages; cm.—(A Sabrina Vaughn novel; #3)
  ISBN 978-0-7387-4450-6
  I. Title.
  PS3602.E2635P76 2015
  813'.6—dc23
                                    2015017139

Midnight Ink
Llewellyn Worldwide Ltd.
2143 Wooddale Drive
Woodbury, MN 55125-2989
www.midnightinkbooks.com

Printed in the United States of America

For Goofy: who loves ya?
Goose does, and don't you ever forget it.

The woods are lovely, dark and deep,
But I have promises to keep,
And miles to go before I sleep,
And miles to go before I sleep.
—Robert Frost

ONE

THERE WAS BLOOD ON Michael's boot.

Not a lot—just a drop or two—but it bothered him. He licked the pad of his thumb and rubbed.

Should've bought the black pair…

"I'm sorry, am I boring you?"

Looking up, he found Alberto Reyes staring at him from behind his desk with the small glittering eyes of a snake.

He shrugged and kept rubbing. Reyes continued to stare. After a few moments the spot came clean and he dropped his foot to the floor, giving the man his full attention.

"As I was saying…I'm a fan of your work, *Cartero*. I find your brutality quite beautiful." Reyes studied the pictures he had fanned across his desk as if he were trying to choose his favorite among them. He picked up one and held it close to his face, tilting his head to the side. "You're knife work is exceptional—absolutely no hesitation, just … exquisite." Reyes placed the photo on top of the pile and got back to watching him.

Michael folded his arms across his chest and made himself smile. "I don't get paid to hesitate, Reyes. I get paid to deliver messages, and I've delivered yours, so …" He stood and pinned the smaller man with a look that said he'd rather not discuss his knife skills.

"Ah, yes, so, you have," Reyes said. He opened a side drawer on his massive desk and pulled out a large manila envelope. It bulged from all sides, its contents barely leaving room to seal it. "Your payment, as agreed." Reyes placed it on the desk and set his hands on top of it, barring Michael from taking it. "But first, I have a matter I'd like to discuss …"

Michael stifled an eye roll. Taking a trip to the window, he looked out across the compound. The helicopter that had brought him here sat on its pad, waiting to take him back to the mainland. A small fleet of speedboats bobbed along the surface of the distant ocean. In front of them, a long stretch of white sand seemed to mold itself to the water's edge.

He'd never been to the beach in anything but fatigues. Never laid in the sand without his eye pressed to a scope, finger resting on a trigger. He now felt the weight of the life he'd chosen pressing down on him, rooting him in place. He dug his hands into the pockets of his fatigues, brushing a finger across the photograph he kept there, and took a few deep breaths. He missed his parents. He missed his sister.

But his parents were long dead, and Frankie? Well, she was better off without him.

Thinking of the man behind him, Michael let go of the picture. Alberto Reyes always had a matter to discuss, business to conduct. A year ago he'd been nothing more than a lieutenant in his cousin's cartel. It was his single-mindedness that allowed him to climb to the top of Colombia's drug trade in a matter of months. That, and the fact that Reyes had hired Michael O'Shea to kill every rival he had, starting with his own cousin—the one kill Michael would've made for free.

"I don't think there's anyone left, Reyes. Pretty sure I killed 'em all."

"So you have." Reyes chuckled. "I admire your work ethic, *Cartero*—so few of our generation understand the dedication required to not only obtain power, but to keep it." Reyes stood and joined him at the window.

"I don't want power." Michael wanted his money so he could get the hell out of here.

"Any other man I'd call a liar, but you ... you, I believe." Reyes wagged a finger at him. "I take pride in finding a man's weaknesses. Yours are few and far between. Your fees are outrageous, but I've seen the way you live. You care little for money. You kill for drug dealers but abhor drugs. You take women, but never the same one more than a few times, so no attachment is ever made."

He thought of Reyes's cousin, Mateo Moreno. His blood and brains sprayed across the courthouse steps. The kick of his rifle against his shoulder a split second after he'd taken the shot. "I got what I wanted."

"Revenge is a powerful motivator, but for a man like you ... Killing my cousin was more of a *need* than an actual *want*. You *needed* to kill Mateo—to put right what he'd done to the Ramos woman and your brethren. Your *wants* are much ... softer."

Michael could practically see the forked tongue peeking out from behind his teeth. "Is that so?" he said, a trace of East Texas creeping into his drawl. "Right now, what I'm wanting ... it don't feel too soft."

Reyes laughed. "This is why I like you, *Cartero*. You have no fear. I made a study of you—of what you wanted. It became an obsession of sorts." Reyes smiled like they were friends. "I almost gave up. But then I realized that it isn't about what you want; it's about what you can't have."

For some reason, Michael's thoughts turned toward the photo in his pocket. The baby sister he'd probably never see again. Frankie.

"I want you to work for me. Exclusively."

Michael's hands curled into fists. He was like a cheerleader with too many dates to the prom. They all wanted exclusivity. To keep him as a pet. "No thanks. I'm a free spirit."

Reyes laughed again, clapping him on the shoulder like they were lifelong friends. "But aren't you curious? You don't even know what I have in mind for you."

He'd heard it all before: *Come, be my personal* sicario. *Stand at my right hand and slit the throats of my enemies ... blah, blah, blah ...* He shrugged and returned his attention to the faraway ocean. "Doesn't matter. I don't do exclusive."

"I want you to protect my daughter, Christina."

He turned his face from the window. "Excuse me?"

Reyes's handsome face split in a grin reserved for putting people at ease. Michael had seen him use it on rivals and underlings—usually right before he had them fitted for a Colombian necktie. "This is a dangerous life, my friend—one I've chosen, but Christina is innocent in all this. She has no choice. I would never be able to live with myself if the decisions I've made caused her death."

4

Reyes was saying the right things, making the appropriate gestures of concern for his only daughter, but Michael didn't buy it for a second. Reyes cared for no one but himself. Providing for his daughter's safety was a means to an end, nothing more.

"So you hire an assassin to play babysitter?" He eased his shoulder from beneath Reyes's hand. *Well, aren't you Ward friggin' Cleaver…*

"Who could be better? My business takes me away from home more often than I'd like. Those who would seek to harm her would never dare—not if it were *El Cartero* who guarded her," Reyes said, leaning in and speaking softly. "You are the only thing they fear."

He tipped his head toward the window, a *nice try, asshole* smile on his face. "You built this fortress on an island, fifty miles from the mainland. I think she's safe."

Just then the study doors flung open and in ran a little girl, no more than four or five. She clambered at her father's feet, black pigtails bouncing wildly in a jumble of corkscrew curls. The little girl climbed up Reyes's leg and he lifted her into his arms, settling her against his side.

"Christina, what have I told you about barging into my office when I'm with friends?" He chided her gently, but Michael had a feeling that it was all for show. An act.

The little girl looked confused. "Not to. But you said—"

"It is no matter. Since you are here, I'd like you to meet a friend. His name is Michael," Reyes said, turning the girl in his arms so that Michael could get a good look at her. Chubby cheeks framed by those riotous curls. A pair of chocolate brown eyes stared back at him. She reminded him of Frankie. The Frankie he knew, not the one who'd grown up without him.

"I'm Christina." The little girl held out her hand and he took it, giving it a gentle shake.

He looked past the girl to her father, who watched the exchange with the satisfied smile of someone who knew he'd won.

TWO

Barcelona, Spain
August 2015

MICHAEL LOOKED AT THE woman sitting next to him. Her name was Pia Cordova and he was going to kill her father.

"What's the matter, baby?" Pia said in his ear, relying on proximity rather than volume to make herself heard over the frantic pulse of music that flooded the club's VIP lounge. "Don't you like me?" She gave the front of his shirt a light rake with her manicured nails. He imagined she was trying to turn him on, but she was doing a piss-poor job of it. He made himself look at her, forced a leering smile onto his face. She was beautiful, in a bleach-blond, fake-breast sort of way. The only child of one of Europe's premier arms dealers. She'd have been his type a couple of years ago—eager to please and easy to forget.

These days he'd rather stick his dick in a bear trap.

As it was, he could barely look at her, let alone do what came next. A sharp kick was delivered to the bottom of his foot. He shot a glare at his partner. Ben had a woman in his lap and his tongue down her throat and still managed to give him a *hey, asshole—get with the program* look. Time to nut up and do his job.

He leaned into Pia and smiled. "*Like* isn't really the word I'd use to describe how I'm feeling," he said in heavily accented English. Nuzzling her neck, he pressed his lips to the tender spot behind her earlobe. "Let me get you a drink. Vodka?" He tilted his chin at her empty glass.

Her lips curved into a predatory smile as she took his hand, running it up her smooth, naked leg, pushing his fingers beyond her skirt's too-short-to-be-decent hemline while she licked at his earlobe. "Getting me drunk isn't necessary," she purred.

With Ben still giving him the stink-eye, Michael forced his hand higher. "I want to take care of you…" His other hand caught her chin as he lowered his lips onto her open mouth, kissing her until she was splayed against the black leather couch they sat on, panting.

Standing, he grinned down at her for a moment before he turned and headed for the VIP's private bar, shouldering his way in. He got the attention of the same bartender he'd been using all night—a petite blonde with a pixie cut and sly brown eyes—and held up two fingers. As soon as she saw him she nodded, continuing to mix the drink for the waitress who was waiting next to him.

"I thought it was you, but I was unsure."

Michael secured a puzzled look on his face before turning. "Do I know you?" he said in the same thick German accent he'd been using all night, giving the man behind him a remote smile, his gaze straying to the long raised scar that slid down the side of his face into a hook near the corner of his mouth. It gave him a perverse satisfaction to know that the mark hadn't faded over time.

The smile returned, causing the scar to crinkle. "Come on, I won't ruin your game. I just wanted to say hello," the man said. "It's been too long."

Not nearly long enough.

Michael looked past the young man in front of him. Two armed guards were standing a few yards away, and he smirked. "I see Daddy still won't let you cross the street by yourself," Michael said, sufficiently knocking the smug look off the man's face. "What are you doing here, Estefan?"

"My father's businesses have grown in your absence, *Cartero*," Estefan said with another self-satisfied smile. "I am his second-in-command these days."

"Good for you," he said with a disinterested shrug—as if he hadn't been keeping tabs on Alberto Reyes and his ever-growing reach. As if the idea of killing both Estefan and his goons wasn't fighting to take precedence over the job he was currently working.

His bartender slid two drinks across the bar. A Kettle One and a water, both on the rocks. The water was marked with a lime wedge, but she tapped a manicured finger against its rim, just in case, and he smiled at her. Pia's vodka had enough Rohypnol in it to tranquilize a horse.

Michael reached into the breast pocket of his suit to pull out a thick stack of bills held together with a wide silver clip. He peeled off a few hundred Euros. "Pour Mr. Second-in-Command whatever he wants—the rest is for you," he said, picking up his drinks before he turned and looked Estefan full in the face and gave him a wink. "See you around, kid."

THREE

HIS CELL PHONE, SET to vibrate, rattled on the plush carpeted floor of Pia's bedroom. Michael reached down and found it without looking. It was a text.

Finished?

He looked at the woman sleeping next to him. She wasn't just sleeping; she was totally zonked by the sedative slipped into her drink at the club. He'd taken her to bed and joined her—played along until the drugs took effect. He felt a twinge. He always did when the job involved women, but he buried it. Twinges caused hesitation. Hesitation wasn't something he could afford.

Almost. Done in ten.

Michael sat up, pulled on his pants, and got to work. He cloned her cell phone and her computer, collected a DNA sample, and scanned her fingerprints and retinas. Jorge Cordova lived in a fortress with state-of-the-art security that only he and his daughter were coded for.

He didn't bother to wipe down his prints when he left. They weren't in any system or database he needed to worry about. He even tossed a business card on her nightstand before he left—tonight he was Gregor Ehrlichmann, an investment banker from Berlin.

Cordova was due back in Barcelona the next night. Michael would gain access to his home using the samples he'd collected and put a bullet in his brain. The clones he'd made of Pia's computer and cell would be used to generate a trail of evidence that would prove she hired a hit man to take out Daddy because he froze her thirty-million-dollar trust fund.

Poor Pia was about to have a very bad day.

———

"So?" Ben said when Michael walked in a few hours later. The kid was sitting on the couch of their suite playing *Call of Duty: Ghosts* and eating nachos. Sometimes he wished he was the boss's son ... and then he remembered that the boss, Livingston Shaw, made Charles Manson look like a door-to-door Bible salesman.

He took off his suit jacket and tossed it in the general direction of the chair. "Samples are collected and handed over to tech. They'll use them to do what they do. We'll be ready to roll tomorrow night."

Ben rolled his eyes at the television screen. "I wasn't asking for an operational debrief, Major Stick-Up-the-Ass. How was *she*? Did the infamous Pia Cordova live up to the hype?"

"Pure magic. Best night of my life." He sat down and stared at the television screen, watching the kid kill a couple dozen insurgents. "You wanna explain to me why I get stuck with all the shit jobs?"

"We flipped for it. Besides, *shit job*—really? That chick was bangin' hot, and she wanted it—*bad*." The kid cocked his head to the side and worked the controller double time.

"Yeah, well, next time feel free to be the one to give it to her." He needed a shower.

Ben cut him a look. "You didn't sleep with her." He shook his head in disgust. "Do you even *have* testicles?"

"Ask your mom, she'd know." He reached for the nachos. They were cold, but whatever.

Ben laughed. "The only way she'd notice your balls is if they were bright white and shaped like Vicodin." He paused the game and tossed the controller onto the table. It landed in the nachos. "Seriously, how are you gonna get over that chick if you won't *let* yourself get over her?"

"Careful, kid." It'd been over a year since he'd seen Sabrina, if you didn't count every time he closed his eyes. Forget about her? He'd have better luck forgetting how to breathe.

Ben just laughed. "First off, I'm not a kid. I'm only three years younger than you are. Second—"

The cell on the coffee table let out a beep. Ben picked it up and rolled his eyes before flipping it open. "It's the asshole," he said in a stage whisper before he spoke in the phone. "Hey, Dad, what's up?"

FOUR

HE AND BEN HAD been called into the FSS Barcelona office at three a.m. By Livingston Shaw. Whatever was about to go down couldn't be good.

Michael thought of the last time he'd been called into a private audience with Shaw. He'd been told that the implant in his back wasn't just a tracking device used to keep tabs on him; it was also there to kill him if he got out of line.

He reached for the base of his spine. It was still there. It would always be there—a capsule, the size of a dime. Inside was enough military-grade biotoxin to wipe out a small town. It was rigged with a detonation chip that responded to a phone number. Once the number was dialed, voice-recognition software would take over. A one-word code plus a seven-digit code was all it would take to kill him.

He looked at Ben. He and his father were the only two who could detonate the capsule. One was his boss; the other was his partner. Ben looked at him and smiled. Michael dropped his hand and stared at the floor.

First Security Solutions had offices all over the world. On the surface, they were a private firm that provided protection to visiting US dignitaries and supplemental security to American Embassies worldwide. But that was a bunch of bullshit.

In reality, FSS was a privatized military organization that specialized in government-sanctioned covert ops. They were wolves in sheep's clothing. They went places that'd give the CIA a case of the flop sweats and did things that'd make a SEAL hide in his mother's skirts. Michael had been on board for three years now, and he'd hated every single second of it.

They took the elevator to the thirty-second floor. The doors slid open, revealing an expansive office—blood-red carpet surrounded by endless banks of bulletproof windows. He didn't have to see it to know what it looked like. Eleven offices in as many countries and they all looked the same, right down to the throw pillows and drink coasters.

"Shit," Ben said under his breath. Michael looked up to see Brian Lark standing next to the boss's desk, poised like a pet dog. Which was exactly what he was.

He felt the rage—years old and bone deep—rear its ugly head. Their eyes met, and Lark's dimples popped out as the smirk deepened to an actual smile. Heavily muscled arms covered in coffee-colored skin crossed over his massive chest. Lark knew exactly what he was thinking, could read his *bring it on, asshole* expression from across the room. Michael's hand fell to the grip of his Kimber .45 and began to lift it off his hip.

Ben stepped in front of him, suddenly all business. "Don't do it," he said in a low voice. Michael looked at him; the *I'm just a fuck-up* vibe he usually threw off was gone in favor of something closer to the truth.

"Michael, Benjamin, please join us," Livingston Shaw said from his desk. His tone and words were warm, welcoming even, but Michael knew better. Livingston Shaw was Genghis Khan in a ten-thousand-dollar suit. He didn't do warm or welcoming unless it served a purpose.

The kid nailed him with a hard look. "Keep it together," Ben said in that same low voice before he turned to his father and flashed him a smile. "I'd rather be playing Xbox," he said as he strolled across the room. Michael stayed where he was, taking a few seconds to get himself under control. Lark just kept grinning.

"Michael…" Shaw let the word trail off, but its meaning was clear. *Get your ass in here—now.* He left the elevator and made himself follow the kid. Stopping a safe distance away, he stood, feet planted shoulder width apart, hands behind his back to hide the fact that they were balled into fists. Shaw smiled up at him, his guileless blue eyes alert and sharp despite the fact that it was the middle of the night. "I just received confirmation that the first phase of the Cordova operation is complete."

"Yes, sir," he said in a barely controlled tone while staring at the spot just above Shaw's head. "Cordova is due back in Barcelona later today. I'll be ready to move after dark."

"Good. After which, the two of you will be without assignment," Shaw said. "I have a private matter that needs your attention."

Ben's head snapped up from studying his fingernails. "What? Oh, *hell* no. A month between jobs, that's the deal," he said. "I'm going—"

"Benjamin." Shaw's tone said that anyone else would be dead by now.

"—to Vegas." Ben sighed. "I had tickets to see Celine."

"What do you need done, sir?" Michael said. The sooner they got their assignment, the sooner he could get the hell out of here.

Every second counted when you were fighting a losing battle against a homicidal urge to kill the man who betrayed you.

"I knew I could count on you, Michael." Shaw smiled and gestured past them, to the reception area they'd passed on their way in. Sitting there quietly was an older gentleman in a suit slightly less expensive than Shaw's, with a full head of silver hair and sharp brown eyes. Michael guessed him to be in his early seventies. He looked haggard, worn down—like he was trapped in hell and couldn't find his way out. He knew that look. He'd seen it in the mirror.

Shaw stood and circled the desk. "Michael, Benjamin, I'd like you to meet Senator Leon Maddox. His grandson is missing, and you're going to find him."

FIVE

Missing.

Michael cut his partner a sidelong glance. His usual smartass grin had given way to an expression that left little question as to how he felt about the implication that word offered.

"You were right to come to me, Leon. I only wish you'd done so sooner," Shaw said, sitting next to the Senator before looking up at the small cluster of men. "I assure you, my son and Mr. O'Shea are the best FSS has to offer. Both have extensive experience when it comes to rescue and recovery." Shaw gave him a slight smile that caused the muscle in Michael's jaw to clench tight.

Leon Maddox swept a skeptical gaze over him, one that said he knew exactly who he was and exactly what he'd done, and that he was not to be trusted. "Thank you, Livingston. In the interest of foreign relations, I foolishly agreed to allow the Spanish authorities to handle the situation. I regret it." He settled his gaze on Ben. "I understand you're quite the tracker."

"I'm the best," Ben said, shooting a hostile glare at his father. "But green-lighting an off-the-books black op to find junior is a bit overkill, don't ya think?"

"Benjamin—"

"No, Livingston. The boy's right." Maddox looked at the man sitting next to him. "It's a total abuse of my power and our friendship that I should even be here asking for help." He looked up at the kid. "But I am. And I'm not ashamed to say I'll use you and your friend here, along with whoever and whatever is necessary, to see my grandson returned," Maddox said as he stood. He held his hand out to Ben, who shook it. Maddox turned to Michael and gave him a long quiet look. "I don't trust you."

"I don't blame you." He looked the old man in the eye.

Maddox issued a quiet bark of laughter before holding out his hand. "I want my grandson home, and I want the bastards that took him dead. Every last one of them. I want it understood that they've messed with the wrong man. Am I clear?"

"As a bell, sir." He took the hand offered and gave it a firm shake before moving to the side, letting the Senator pass on his way to the elevator.

———

"They were visiting family friends—an old boarding school roommate of Senator Maddox's son, Jon." Shaw used a discreet button panel on his desk to activate the large LED screen behind his desk. "It was to be a quick trip before school started for their children—Claire, age nine, and Leo, age six." The screen behind Shaw flipped through various family photos. The Maddox family on the steps of the Alhambra palace in Granada. Leo and Claire sitting in the stands at the Plaza de Toros Monumental. The screen flashed to a close-up of Leo. "He and his mother took an early-morning trip to Mercat Del Encants. She became distracted by a merchant, and when she turned back around, Leo was gone." Shaw dropped his hands onto his desk.

"No ransom demands?" Michael said.

"No," Shaw said.

"Surveillance?"

His boss nodded and hit another button. Leo's picture was replaced by surprisingly clear security footage. The camera was aimed directly at a string of high-priced booths. To the left of the screen, a well-dressed blonde strolled the aisle with a small boy in tow. The blonde was stopped in the middle of the thoroughfare by a young girl peddling scarves. The boy pulled away, eager to use his mother's distraction to his best advantage. She turned her head for a few seconds—five at best—but it was enough. The instant her back was turned, a man swept into the frame, ball cap pulled low to hide his face, and scooped the boy into his arms. He clamped a hand over Leo's mouth and was gone before the blonde even manages to tell the girl *no thanks*.

Shaw paused the feed. "That's it. Ten seconds of tape. Less than helpful, I'm afraid."

The guy on the screen kept his face turned away. He seemed to know that the camera was there, so it was safe to assume that whoever he was, he'd planned the abduction. Michael studied the frozen images on the screen and tried not to let the look of absolute terror on the boy's face bother him.

"Where was their security detail?"

Shaw inclined his head and shrugged. "Jon Maddox is an up and comer—his father is pinning presidential hopes on his chest, but his wife, Sara, is…less than cooperative. She'd been expressly forbidden from taking Leo from the hotel without his detail, and she agreed not to do so."

"But she did it anyway," Ben said, shooting Michael a sidelong glance.

"Any chance she's involved?" Michael said.

Shaw shook his head. "No. She's completely beside herself. Leon said she's been under heavy sedation since the abduction."

Michael said nothing. He wasn't counting anyone out—not even the old man. Leon Maddox played the part of bereaved grandfather to a T, but if he'd learned anything it was that the face most people showed the world was a lie.

"What about her?" He tipped his chin at the screen, indicating the young woman with the scarves. "Anyone talk to her? Ask her what she saw?"

"Spanish authorities haven't been able to find her."

"Bullshit. They can't find one girl?" This came from Lark, who until now had been content to sit quietly. He crossed his arms over his chest, shooting a pointed look Michael's way. "Either they don't care or they've been paid not to look," he said.

"My guess is both," Michael said, studying the frozen video. The girl looked scared, that's for sure, but she didn't look surprised by what was happening. "I guess we have our square one." Michael stood, ready to get started, but his partner had different ideas.

"I have a question," Ben said, his clear blue eyes gone ice cold. "Why the hell do you care about some kid that got snatched from a flea market?"

"Leon Maddox is my friend." Shaw folded his hands on his blotter and pinned his son with a glare.

"You don't have friends; you have chess pieces." Ben shook his head. "There's always something in it for you. So what is it?"

"Believe it or not, Benjamin, I happen to care a great deal about what happens to Leo Maddox—"

"You *care*?" Ben shot to his feet. "Well, look at you ... all magnanimous and shit," he said with a laugh. "I'd like to know where your nobility was the day Mason and Emily—"

"That's enough, Benjamin."

Ben went still. "That's where you're wrong, Dad. It'll never be enough," he said, and Michael was sure he was seconds away from launching himself across the desk at his father. Instead, he turned and stalked his way toward the elevator. They watched him go in silence.

"Benjamin has always had a flair for the dramatic, I'm afraid," Shaw said, turning his attention to Michael. "Despite his suspicions as to where my motives lie, it's imperative that Leo Maddox be found. So much so that I'm willing to offer you a deal: I'm giving you one week. If you can find and bring the Maddox boy home within that time, I'll set you free."

SIX

WHEN MICHAEL GOT BACK to their suite, he looked around the room and shook his head. The wall was now wearing the congealed nachos Ben had been eating before their meeting with his father, and the coffee table that held them looked like it had exploded into kindling and strewn itself around the room.

"Like what you've done with the place," he said, letting his gaze settle on his partner, sitting on the couch, playing Xbox.

Ben shrugged while working the controller. This time he was killing zombies by the dozen.

"Who're Mason and Emily?" Michael said.

Ben was quiet for a few seconds, like he wasn't going to answer. "Mason was my brother." He shifted the rest of the words around like he was having trouble making them leave his mouth. "Emily was his wife."

Michael rubbed the back of his neck and winced at what he was about to say. "Wanna talk about it?"

"Nothing to talk about, Dr. Phil. They're dead."

"Fair enough." Michael looked at his watch. It was just after five in the morning. The marketplace where the Maddox kid disappeared would be up and running, the vendors and peddlers setting up for the day. If they were going to find the girl, now was the best time to do it. "Come on, let's go find the girl in the surveillance video, see what we can get out of her."

Ben shook his head, let out a brief bark of laughter. "Don't you ever get tired of asking how high when he says to jump?"

Now it was Michael's turn to laugh. "Really? I don't have the luxury of saying no," he said. "What I *have* is a goddamn dirty bomb in my back and a boss just looking for an excuse to blow me the fuck up, so you can take your little pity party or whatever the hell this is and shove it up your ass."

Ben cut him a look. "He's not the only one who's got your number, you know." It was a reminder that, if he wanted to, Ben could make him just as dead as his father could.

"You aren't gonna kill me." Michael sounded more sure than he actually felt. "No one else will work with you."

Ben smiled. "True. Besides, you owe me a favor. I can't kill you until I collect."

It was a reminder of exactly what Ben had done for him twenty-two months ago. He'd been shanghaied into another job. Taken away from Sabrina at the precise moment she needed him most. Ben had given him a small reprieve. Somehow he'd used his status as the boss's son to his advantage and gotten Michael back to Sabrina in time to save her life. She'd be dead if not for Ben. He hadn't forgotten that, nor had he forgotten that Ben's help had come at a price.

"I know."

Ben shrugged and changed the subject. "Let me guess. My father told you that if you find this kid, he'll cut you loose, right?" Ben's glare was steady and fixed on the screen full of flesh-eating mutants.

"Yes." Michael leaned against the wall and crossed his arms over his chest in an effort to keep his fingers from finding the capsule embedded in the small of his back.

Ben finally paused the game. "He'll never do it. He'll never let you go. That's not how my father is built. He'd kill you in a heartbeat if he thought you'd outlived your purpose, but let you go? No way."

He shrugged. Ben was right; Livingston Shaw kept his word only when it suited him. "I know, but that's a pretty hefty carrot to dangle, which means finding the Maddox kid isn't just about looking out for an old friend. There's a reason he's helping Maddox. If I can figure out why, I might be able to use it as leverage somehow. The only way to do that is to find the boy."

Ben un-paused the game only to let his on-screen icon be overtaken by the undead. He watched the carnage for a few seconds before shifting his gaze back to Michael. "Do you miss her?"

The shift in conversation topic was abrupt. Michael didn't understand the correlation between his feelings for Sabrina and Shaw's motivations in finding Leo Maddox, but he knew he'd need Ben's help if he had any hope of succeeding.

"Every second of every day."

"What would you be willing to do to get back to her? To be able to stay with her?" Ben's face had taken on a strange gravity, as if the weight of the world rested in this one question.

"Anything."

The answer must have been the right one, because Ben tossed the game controller on the floor where the coffee table had once been. He stood. "Good to know. Give me a few minutes to change and we'll go." Ben left the room, leaving Michael to wonder exactly what kind of debt he owed and what kind of man he owed it to.

SEVEN

MICHAEL STEPPED AROUND AN old man spreading out a tattered blanket before dumping a box out onto it. Matchbox cars and antique lighters tumbled out along with bootleg DVDs and kitchen gadgets. "*Perdóneme, señor,*" he said. The old-timer shot him a glare as he passed, which he returned with a wry smile. He tended to have that effect on people.

Midmorning at Mercat Del Encants. People were everywhere, young and old, every shape and size. Ben blended perfectly. The kid played Hapless College Student to a T. Having changed into a pair of cargo shorts and a ratty AC/DC concert shirt, he flitted from booth to booth, smiling and chatting his way around the flea market.

Michael followed at a safe distance, trailing a sting of Pips, as he called FSS lackeys, behind him. Junior's outburst must've rattled Shaw more than he let on if he sent a pack of his specially trained lapdogs to make sure they didn't screw up. He began to wonder, same as Ben, what the boss was hoping to gain by recovering Leo

Maddox. What had the Senator promised him in exchange for his grandson's safe return?

Finally, after about an hour of fishing, they got a bite. Ben asked about the scarf girl, described her to an old woman surrounded by several boxes of VHS tapes. He said he'd seen her around a few days ago and he'd thought she was pretty. He confided in the old woman that he'd been hoping to find her so he could ask her out for coffee. The old woman gave him a wide gap-toothed smile.

Bingo.

"Let me handle it, okay? Her name's Eliza," Ben said as they wound their way through the market, heading toward the long low row of wooden structures that housed the food and more high-priced shops. "She takes one look at you, dude, she's gonna rabbit."

Michael looked down at himself and saw nothing out of the ordinary. Faded jeans and an old navy blue Hanes shirt. "What's wrong with the way I look?"

"It's not your clothes," Ben said. "It's *this*." He waved his hand in Michael's direction. "You. All of you. The whole thing. Everything about you is hostile. You need to relax."

"Relax?"

"Yeah, relax." Ben hitched the backpack he carried up on one shoulder. "Do some yoga. Kill a Pip. Take the stick out of your ass—*something*. Just do it before I get back with the girl," he said before disappearing into the crowd, leaving Michael alone with a couple hundred people and a half dozen of Shaw's walking, talking insurance policies.

Relax? Every breath he took, every second he lived, was because someone else had decided to allow it. How in the hell was he supposed to relax?

27

Michael took a few turns around the market, keeping a close eye on the dark maze of shops and lean-tos that Ben had disappeared into and then suddenly, there he was. Talking and laughing with a pretty young woman with large dark eyes and a shy smile. It was the girl from the surveillance video, and she was gazing up at Ben with a star-struck look as he led her though the marketplace toward a small outdoor café.

They took a seat and placed their order with the waiter. Michael did another lap around the tables and booths. The Pips followed. He watched Ben and the girl. Coffee and *buñuelos* made an appearance. Ben smiled and charmed the girl for several minutes, putting her at ease before signaling Michael by looking at his watch.

The girl looked up as he approached, and the smile perched on her face wobbled and fell. She shot a hurried glance at Ben before she started to shove herself away from the table. Ben's hand shot out and gripped hers across the table. "*Eliza ... esta bien. Nadie va a danarte. Queremos preguntarte algo. Solo unas preguntas. Nada más, te prometo.*" He gave her a reassuring smile. "*Hablas inglés?*"

The girl nodded slowly. "Yes, I speak English." She looked up at Michael and shook her head. "But I know nothing worth telling. I sell scarves. I am no one."

Michael took a seat next to her and leaned forward just a bit, dropping his voice to keep the conversation private. He could tell she was lying. "There was an American boy here with his mother a few weeks ago. He was small—blond with hazel eyes. You spoke to his mother, distracted her while your partner in the Yankees cap snatched him. We have it all on tape," he said.

Her eyes widened just a bit, and she started to shake her head. "No. I don't know what you are saying. I—"

"Stop. Just stop." Michael used his fingertip to turn her face toward the crowd. "Do you see them? The men in suits, circling like vultures?" He paused, waited for her to nod. "They're here for you. To make sure you tell us what we need to know. And when they start asking questions, I can assure you, it won't be over coffee and doughnuts." He watched the tears well up in her eyes as understanding took root.

She turned her face away from the crowd. "I can't. You don't understand. These men are very dangerous."

"Who are they?" Ben said.

The girl shrugged, looked miserable. "I don't know." She swallowed hard, eyes full of tears again. "They took my brother first. Told me that if I helped them, they would bring him back, but . . . it's been a very long time."

"How long?" Ben said.

"Eight months."

Eight months? Leo Maddox was taken only three weeks ago. A sick feeling began to form in the pit of Michael's stomach. "Was the American boy the only one you helped abduct?"

Her eyes flooded with tears. She shook her head. "No. But he was the last. There has been no one since."

Michael looked across the table at his partner. How many children could be taken in eight months?

"Eliza, where is he? Where do they take the children?" Ben said.

"I don't know," she said quietly, staring at the tabletop. She was scared, couldn't look him in the eye. She knew more than she was letting on.

Michael leaned back in his seat. "You're lying."

She looked up at him. "I don't know. But . . . the man who took the boy—the one you are looking for—he was not the man that usually comes." She chewed her lower lip. She seemed to be deciding if she could trust them with the truth. "The man that usually comes is shorter, heavier. This man was taller, thin. He had a scar."

"Where?" he said, the skin on the back of his neck going tight. He knew before she even answered him.

"Here," she said, running her finger along her cheek. "It was long—from his temple to the corner of his mouth. I saw him once, in the street. He was getting into a big black car with an older man in a suit."

"How do you know for sure it was him?" Ben said.

She looked at Ben. "I recognized the scar, and—"

The sudden impact of the bullet snapped the girl's head back, its exit making a hole the size of a fist in the back of her skull. Blood sprayed across the plate of pastries, soaked into the white cloth that covered the table. Brain matter and even more blood splattered onto the bricks beneath their feet.

Ben and Michael stood and moved swiftly, away from the cafe, for the cover of a narrow easement between the café and neighboring bookstore.

Screams and shouts sounded from the café behind them, but neither one of them turned around. They kept walking—there was nothing they could do. The girl was dead.

"Fuck," Ben muttered under his breath, shaking his head almost in time with his quick stride. "Someone didn't want her talking."

"I know who," Michael said, stepping out of the alley where they'd parked there car. He gestured for Ben to stay in the shadows while he surveyed windows and rooftops for possible blinds. It was instinctual, the need he felt to protect his team. Ben ignored him and stepped out in the road alongside him.

"Well, Michael, are you going to share your answer with the rest of the class?" his partner chimed brightly while skirting the bumper to his side of the car.

"Reyes." Just saying the name out loud made it almost too real to deal with. He should have taken him out a year ago, when he first found out that Alberto was targeting him.

"Reyes doesn't strike me as the down-and-dirty type." Ben pulled his door open before cutting him a doubtful look across the roof of the car. Sirens wailed in the distance, getting closer. "Besides, Reyes doesn't have a scar."

Michael thought about killing. Heard the crinkle of plastic sheeting beneath his boots. Felt the resistant tug of skin and muscle against his blade. Reyes, his lizard eyes flat and distant, watching as he got what he wanted. He yanked his door open and returned his partner's gaze. "He's not and he doesn't—but his son does." *And is.*

Now Ben smiled, but there was no humor in it. The sirens were close, but it mattered little to either of them. "How do you know?"

Michael shrugged and tried to unearth himself from the avalanche of memories he was suddenly buried under. "Because I'm the one who gave it to him."

EIGHT

Cofre del Tesoro, Colombia
March 2008

THE TIDE WAS LEAVING, the shards of light scattered across the blue-green surface of the water losing their luster in the setting sun, growing dimmer and dimmer with every push and pull of the ocean.

He looked down at the little girl playing in the sand a few feet away. "Time to go," he said before casting an appraising look down the length of the private beach. It was deserted. Always was, but he scanned the trees just the same. Looking for the flash a scope, the sudden scatter of birds. He'd been hired to keep Reyes's daughter safe, and that's what he'd do. Even if all he was protecting her from was hermit crabs and sunburns.

It'd been four months since he'd stood at the window in Reyes's office, seeing the water in the distance. Four months since he realized that he'd never been to the beach without a gun on his back or a target to neutralize. Now a day didn't go by without him dumping sand out of his boots.

He was living the dream.

Looking down, he wasn't at all surprised to find that the little girl was still loading sand into a bucket in careful measured scoops, giving each a pat with the flat of her pink plastic shovel before adding another. He sighed. "Christina."

"Why won't you wear swim trunks?" she said. Ignoring the warning tone in his voice, she lifted her head just enough to eye the leg of his dark cargo pants. "I know you have some."

"Because they'd look funny with my lace-ups." He wiggled the toe of his boot, and she cracked a smile. "I'm serious—the tide's out. Time to pack up."

The smile died, and she allowed her gaze to travel upward until it hit his face. "You're always serious." Her dark eyes, the way they held his without wavering, were sharp. Too sharp to belong to a child. Sometimes it was difficult for him to believe she was only four. Correction: she was five. Her birthday had been last week. No party. No cake and pony rides with her friends. Christina wasn't allowed to have friends. Aside from breakfast with her mother every morning and the occasional visit from her father, all she had was him.

Squinting behind his sunglasses, Michael looked away, pretending to do another visual sweep. He ignored the twinge—a mixture of guilt and pity. "I'm not your playmate, Christina. I'm your protector."

She picked up the bucket and turned it over, giving it a wiggle. "I liked the last one better," she said, lifting the bucket to reveal a perfectly formed tower. "He had a funny moustache and told knock-knock jokes."

"Well, I hate to disappoint." He smirked at her sass. "Knock, knock."

She looked up at him again. "Who's there?"

"Get your stuff, it's time to go."

She narrowed her eyes, pitching her pink shovel in the direction of her beach tote. "Make me."

Michael took a deep breath, let it out slowly. "I'm warning you …" He let the rest of the sentence go, looking down at her with what he hoped was an appropriate amount of severity.

"*I'm warning you*," she mimicked him, dropping her hands to her hips. "You can't do anything to me. I'll tell my—"

He didn't wait for her to finish her sentence, just took a step forward and hooked an arm around her waist, lifting her out of the sand to sling her over his shoulder. She screamed, her tiny feet kicking against his chest, her equally tiny fists beating against his back. "You can't leave my stuff here! Put me down!"

He ignored her, heading for the black H2 parked in the sand twenty yards away. A sudden flutter of birds took to the sky, bursting from the dense stand of trees, a breathless scatter that stopped him in his tracks. It was likely the girl's screams that sent them flying, nothing more. But the skin on the back of his neck went tight, telling him something entirely different.

Without thinking he dropped to one knee, slinging Christina off his shoulder. "Hush," he breathed, pinning her with a look that instantly killed her protests. The little girl went still. Eyes wide, she nodded, understanding perfectly. "Good. Now," he said, pulling a set of keys from his pocket, "when I tell you to run, that's what you'll do."

Something moved, a deeper shadow, crouched within the dense canopy of trees. Something that didn't belong there. He looked down at the girl again. To whoever was watching, it would look like he was giving her a stern talking to over her behavior. "Just like we practiced, okay?"

Tears welled up in her eyes. "I'm scared."

"Me too, but it's gonna be okay. Do you trust me?"

She nodded. "Yes. Michael, I'm sorry I was so—"

"Shhh, I know. Ready?"

She nodded again, watched him as he pulled his Kimber .45 off his hip, keeping it low and tight against his thigh. "Run," he said, breathing the word softly, relieved when she turned without hesitation, her bare feet digging into the sand as she pushed herself into motion.

As soon as she was clear, Michael brought the gun up. Levelling it at the trees, he squeezed off three shots in rapid succession, aiming into the canopy. If he was wrong—if it was an animal or one of the maids trying to sneak onto the private beach—they'd come out running. The silhouette startled but didn't bolt ... and it didn't return fire either.

He cut a fast glance at Christina. She was almost to the H2, legs pumping fast and hard against the soft give of the sand. He used the key fob to unlock the SUV's rear hatch—it popped open just as she reached it. Christina shot him a fleeting look before she scrambled inside and shut the hatch behind her.

Good girl.

As soon as she was inside, he locked the SUV, relying on its armored body and bulletproof windows to keep her safe. He stood, making his way toward the stand of trees quickly. His vision zeroed in on the shadow huddled against the thick trunk of a tree. *"Los tres primeros fuero ndirigidos alto intenciona damente. Los tres siguientes no habrá."*

The first three were aimed high intentionally. The next three won't be.

The shadow shifted mere seconds before it lost its courage and bolted deeper into the trees. He followed, dodging branches and clumps of bushes. "Stop," he bellowed loudly, raising his gun, aiming it into the center of the shadow. He wasn't sure if it was the tone or the actual word that did it, but the figure did as he said, stopping short.

It was a woman.

The cartels weren't above using women and children as decoys and assassins. Her hands went out and up, fingers splayed wide.

"*Date la vuelta. Despacio.*"

She did as he said, turning slowly. As soon as he got a good look at her face, he dropped the gun. It was Lydia Reyes, Christina's mother. "Goddamn it," he swore softly. "Mrs. Reyes, what are you doing here?" It felt strange calling her *Mrs.* Anything—she was hardly older than his baby sister, Frankie.

"I just wanted to see her. Please, please don't tell him," she said, her eyes darting wildly from his face to the SUV behind him. "I just—he won't let me see her."

"You had breakfast with her this morning." Michael ignored the twinge of guilt he felt when he said it. It was true—Lydia and Christina had breakfast together every morning, but they were under constant supervision. Reyes claimed that his wife was unstable. Michael was pretty sure it was all about control.

"I know, but I never get to see *her*," she said, struggling for an explanation. It was unnecessary; he understood what she meant. Christina was like a living, breathing doll when her father was around. A pint-sized Stepford Wife. It was unsettling.

Still he shook his head, shifting from side to side. "Mrs. Reyes—"

"Lydia. Please, call me Lydia." She took a step forward, her dark eyes wild with desperation. "I know you care for—" She must've thought better of her words because she stopped and changed direction. "Please. Can I just talk to her?"

Bad idea.

36

He crossed his arms over his chest. "It's late. We're getting ready to head back to the compound."

"Oh, okay. I understand." She dropped her hands to her sides and turned to leave. "Could you just . . . " she said, turning her face in his direction. "Could you tell her that I miss her?"

He nodded, and she turned to walk away.

"Wait."

She stopped again, turning fully to face him, hope etched plainly on her face.

He was going to regret this.

"We're here every day; usually get here right after lunch." He said it fast, before he could change his mind. "Approach from this spot so I can see you coming. And come alone."

Her breath caught, hands fluttered at her sides, clutching at her skirt. "Thank you. Thank you, *Cartero*."

"Don't call me that." The frown that settled onto his face must've frightened her, because she took a step back.

"I'm sorry, it's what I hear Alberto and his men call you, so I thought—"

He cleared his throat and looked away. "It's not my name. My name is Michael."

"Thank you, Michael," she said, a small smile trembling on her lips. "Tomorrow?"

He nodded and watched her walk into the trees, waiting until she was gone before he turned and made his way back to the H2 where Christina hid.

Using the key fob, he popped the hatch. "Christina, it's safe to come out now."

The lump under the ballistics blanket didn't move.

"*Christina*."

"You have to say the magic words. I can't come out unless you say them," she said, her voice muffled beneath the cover.

The magic words. The code they'd worked out to let her know that he wasn't coaxing her from hiding under duress. "Pink pony," he said.

Christina tossed the blanket away and launched herself at his chest, her little arms winding tightly around his neck, legs wrapped around his middle. His throat, suddenly hot and dry, worked itself against the well of emotion he usually kept in check. Without thinking, he lifted his hands to hug her back.

"Who was it?" she said into his neck. "Did you kill them?"

He kept a running list of bad ideas, and getting close to this kid was at the top of it. Instead of holding her, he wedged his hands between them and set her away. "It was no one." He lifted her over the seat. "Get buckled up. It's time to go."

NINE

Livingston Shaw glared at Michael from across the gleaming expanse of his polished desk. "Are you certain that it was one of Reyes's men that took the Maddox boy?" Shaw said, somehow managing to make him feel as if he were personally responsible for the abduction of the Senator's grandson.

Michael stared at the spot directly above Shaw's head—his favorite—and took a deep breath before answering. "Yes. I recognize the tattoo on his neck from the surveillance footage." All of Reyes's men were branded with the same tattoo, a common practice within the cartels. He'd decided to keep the rest—that not only was it one of Reyes's men but his son—to himself. The scar was unique to Estefan; the tattoo wasn't. If Ben objected to him lying to his father, he didn't say a word. Of course, that might have something to do with the fact that he was currently sleeping on his father's sofa.

"Reyes is based in Colombia. He's a little far from home, isn't he?" Lark said, from his position beside Shaw's chair.

Michael made himself look at Lark. "Trust me, he's here," he said, thinking of his run-in with Estefan a few nights ago. "He's been pushing his way into Cordova's territory for a while now."

"You think this has something to do with the Cordova op?" Shaw said, his interest obviously piqued.

The thought turned Michael's stomach. Knowing that he'd had a part in making such a thing possible tightened his jaw. "He's had his eye on Cordova's trafficking operation for a while now."

Shaw arched an eyebrow. "And you know this because … ?"

Michael shrugged. "Because I've had my eye on *him*."

"So why didn't you make the connection sooner?" Lark said. Another accusation.

Michael shot his former partner a warning look. He had to take Shaw's shit but not Lark's.

"I think you're missing the point my partner's trying to make here, Jolly Green." They both turned to find Ben still stretched out on the couch behind them, eyes still closed. He cracked a lid and aimed one sky-blue eye at his father. "Reyes is behind the snatch and grab of Leon Maddox's grandkid." Ben smiled. "Which means we might have a chance of getting him back."

"Okay, fine. Reyes has a daughter, right?" Lark shrugged. "I say we snatch her and demand a trade."

"No," Michael said.

"Why? Easiest way to—"

"I said no." His tone closed the subject.

Lark tipped his head back and let out a loud crack of laughter. "You slay me, man. Really? Like you're some kinda saint. You killed more people than cancer and you get twisted over one little kidnapping?" He shook his head. "What the fuck did that crazy cop bitch do to you?"

Michael's heart stopped. Time slowed to a crawl. His stomach clenched like he'd been kicked in the gut. He looked at Shaw and saw he was watching the exchange with avid interest—and not one ounce of bewilderment.

He was suddenly sure that Lark had told Livingston Shaw everything there was to know about Sabrina. Who she was. How he knew her. That she mattered. Shaw's knowledge of her made her a tool to be used against him or, worse, a liability to FSS.

In the space of a second, he weighed his options and decided on a course of action. He'd have to be fast. Take Shaw out first. Two to the head, then—

"Hey."

He turned to see Ben standing in front of him.

"Probably not a good idea." Ben tipped his chin down and he followed with his eyes to find his Kimber gripped in his fist, finger on the trigger. He didn't even remember pulling it.

He shot Lark a look over the kid's shoulder before looking back to Shaw. He sat leaning back in his chair with a wry smirk on his face, cell phone in hand, finger poised to dial. Michael remembered the capsule in his back and holstered his gun. He was good to no one dead. The need to find Leo Maddox had just been suddenly and precisely balanced by his need to warn Sabrina that she was no longer safe—and probably never had been.

"Well … that was awkward," Ben said to no one in particular, careful to keep himself between Michael and Lark.

Michael ignored him and focused on what had to be done now. He looked at Shaw. "We need to get stateside, interview the family. There could be things the mother saw that she's not even aware of. We need to question her and the kid's nanny. Whoever had access to him over the past few weeks. There's a good chance Reyes had inside help."

Shaw seemed to be weighing his words, testing their validity before making up his mind. He shook his head. "You still have business here to attend to. Cordova is scheduled to arrive—"

"We'll leave as soon as it's done." Michael was getting himself stateside, one way or another.

Shaw smiled. "Very well, Michael. The family is convalescing at Leon's estate, just outside Helena. I'll alert him that you and your team will be arriving shortly."

Team? He didn't have a team. He had Ben. He shook his head. "I don't need Pips—I mean, a team—sir. Ben and I work best alone."

Shaw's smile faded. "Of that I'm certain, but I'm not sending a security detail, Michael. I'm sending Mr. Lark. He's going with you."

TEN

Michael crossed the dark lawn with confident, long-legged strides, approaching the guard stationed there as if he belonged. The man, hearing his approach, turned but didn't raise his gun. Didn't seem worried about him at all. Michael gave him a reassuring smile as he closed the distance, and the guard returned it with a look of annoyance.

"Volver a tu puesto, idiota," the man hissed, but Michael kept coming, closing the distance between them, the smile firmly fixed in place. The man realized Michael was an intruder seconds before he grabbed him, clasping his chin and the back of his head, giving his neck a violent jerk that snapped it in two.

The guard dropped, and Michael stepped over him to mount the marble steps that led to the front door. Cordova slept in a third-floor interior suite. No windows. No outside access. Getting to him would've been nearly impossible without the samples he'd collected from his daughter. Armed with Pia's prints, his knife, and a few dozen rounds of ammo, the task was almost mundane.

He approached the screen and scanner fixed to the wall and leaned forward. The retina and fingerprint scan had to be done simultaneously or it would trigger a silent alarm that would send every available guard his way. Timing was everything.

He aimed his eye over the scanner just as he began to roll his index finger across the screen. The gloves he wore were outfitted with neoprene tips embedded with Pia's prints, and the contact in his eye was coded with her retinal signature. The door lock released.

Piece of cake.

He stepped into the dark foyer and his earpiece crackled. "You've got one coming toward you—ten yards and closing," Ben said. Hijacking Cordova's security feed had taken him less time that it'd taken Michael to kill the guard. From where he was, not only did Ben have eyes on almost every square inch of Cordova's estate, he was also able to manipulate the feed. Anyone else monitoring the surveillance footage would see nothing out of the ordinary. The kid certainly gave Lark a run for his money for Geek Squad status.

There were two guards per floor. Any who saw Michael had to be dealt with. He ducked into an alcove under the stairs and drew his knife, waiting for the second guard to pass before stepping back into the hall, directly behind him. He held the black ceramic blade tight against his forearm while he slipped the other around the guard's neck and across his chest. Michael shoved the guard's shoulder into the wall, pinning his arm at his side while he lifted the other away from his body, driving the blade several times between his ribs, a vicious tattoo into his heart and lungs. He was dead before he even knew he was in trouble. Michael dragged him into the vestibule, out of sight, before dropping him on the floor.

"Where's the other first-floor guard?" he said quietly, wiping his knife off on the dead guy's shirt.

"Stationed at the back of the house. He shouldn't be an issue," Ben said.

"The second floor?" He tucked his knife away but within easy reach. Ben still hadn't answered him. "Kid?"

"They just followed Pia Cordova into a second-floor bathroom."

Shit. What the hell was *she* doing here? "Can you see them?"

"No, the bathroom is blind, but I'm pretty sure they weren't heading in there to hold her purse while she pees." Ben paused. "If she sees you, you're gonna have to kill her. This is supposed to be a clean sweep. No witnesses."

Michael ignored him. He'd been assigned to kill Cordova and to tell the truth, he didn't feel bad about doing it. But killing his daughter was not on the books. Not unless absolutely necessary. Michael lifted a silencer-equipped 9mm from his leg holster.

"You've got a clear shot to the top," Ben said. "Wait … Cordova's on the move. He's heading toward you."

Good. He could get this over with and get out without having to deal with Pia. Michael stepped into the hall and took the stairs two at a time, rounding the second-floor landing. He mounted the third flight and was five steps from the top when Cordova appeared at the head of the stairs, his wide girth swaddled in a silk robe, a cut crystal tumbler in his hand.

His muddy brown eyes widened in shock even as his mouth yanked open to sound the alarm. Michael leveled the 9mm at Cordova's face and pulled the trigger twice in rapid succession—*ssk, ssk*—drilling twin holes in the man's forehead. He lowered the gun before Cordova could make a sound. The glass slipped out of the fat man's hand as he fell back and bounced down the stairs to smash on the tile below. The sound echoed through the silent house.

"Shit. You've got incoming."

A split-second decision had Michael flying down the stairs the way he'd come. He holstered his gun and reached for his knife as he took the stairs downward. He could hear the third-floor guards running in the direction of their fallen boss, shouting frantically. One of them would try radioing for help. He didn't have much time before they realized their frequency was jammed and came after him.

He could hear the remaining first-floor guard pound his way toward him. Michael stopped on the staircase and waited for his head to pop up over the shared railing between the two sets of stairs. Seconds later, head and shoulders appeared. Michael gripped the railing and swung toward the guard, driving forward with the blade of his knife. The guard was ready, turning swiftly and taking aim. He got a shot off that slammed into the wall mere inches from Michael's head. The roar of it echoed in his ear, heat searing the side of his face. He sliced the blade across the guard's throat, severing his jugular in one clean sweep. The guy tumbled backward down the stairs, and Michael vaulted the banister, landing in the first-floor stairwell in a crouch.

"Move your ass," Ben barked into his ear.

Adrenaline dumped into his system. He pulled a SIG P238 from the small of his back. The door directly across from him swung open and a pair of guards tumbled out, shirtless, yanking up their pants as they did. Using the darkened stairway as cover, Michael fired. The first guard took three bullets center mass. Blood bloomed across his chest while the other guard took aim. Wild shots drilled into the wall and floor, but one of them found its mark, mushrooming against Michael's Kevlar-covered chest. The impact knocked him off his feet and he tumbled down the stairs, landing on top of the guard he'd just bled out.

He flipped over and covered the staircase despite the fact that he felt like he'd just been hit in the midsection by a semi. The second guard appeared at the top of the stairs. Michael pulled the trigger again and again, hitting the man in the neck and face. He fell, revealing a half-naked Pia cowering behind him.

Shit.

"You gotta do it," Ben said in his ear.

He holstered the gun and stood. The third-floor guards were pounding down the stairs, but it didn't matter. They'd see safeguarding Pia as more important than chasing him down. He hit the door as fast as he could and did what he did best.

He disappeared.

ELEVEN

San Francisco, California
That morning

SABRINA DIDN'T WANT TO get of bed. In fact, she seriously considered calling in sick and staying there all day. She played with the thought for a few minutes, imagined letting the day waste away. As tempting as it sounded, she knew herself well enough to be certain that she'd be climbing the walls by noon. Beside, today was her first day back on Homicide. Mathews would love it if she didn't show.

She reached over and gave the body next to her a poke. "If I'm getting up, so are you," she said, swinging her legs over the side of her bed. Standing, she made her way to the bathroom. She looked over her shoulder. The covers were still pulled up tight. "You better be up by the time I'm ready to go or your ass is getting left here," she said before disappearing into the bathroom.

She came out fifteen minutes later to find Avasa, her two-year-old Rhodesian Ridgeback, waiting for her outside the door. She smiled. "Thought so," she said, giving the dog's floppy ears a ruffle. She dressed quickly and grabbed her shoes, sitting down to put them on. "Let's get out of here before—"

The baby monitor next to the clock came to life. Avasa whined.

"Relax. It'll just take a few minutes." She headed for the door, not at all surprised when the dog hopped back on the bed and burrowed her way under the covers.

Sabrina made her way downstairs, taking the hall as quietly as she could. Pushing her way into the nursery, she couldn't help but smile. She always smiled when she saw her. The baby was on her back, rolling from side to side, happily trying to eat her own toes. Sabrina leaned over the side of the crib, and the baby broke into a wide happy grin at the sight of the face that hovered above her. Reaching down, Sabrina lifted the sleep-warmed bundle from her crib, giving her a slight bounce. She was rewarded with a giggle. The sound was her new favorite.

The baby leaned away from her chest and gazed up at her with eyes that were the tawny brown of a good shooting whiskey. Her smile crinkled them at the corners, and for a moment she looked just like her daddy.

"Hey, thought you'd be gone by now," he said from the doorway, and Sabrina turned to see Devon Nickels, light brown hair rumpled from sleep, flannel pajama pants slung low on narrow hips, his broad chest bare except for the burp cloth tossed over his shoulder. He had a bottle in one hand and a picture book in the other, *Good night Moon*.

"Late start. Go back to bed, I've got her," she said, reaching for the bottle, reluctant to hand the baby over. Nickels laughed and shook his head, pulling the baby out of her arms.

"No, *you* go back to bed. It's my turn," he said with a grin, making shooing motions with the book. The baby's smile widened even more at the sight of her daddy, and she clapped chubby fingers against his cheek so he'd look at her and smile back. "Good morning, beautiful girl," he whispered, dropping a soft kiss on her cheek before turning toward Sabrina, who lingered nearby. "Out," he said and laughed when she heaved a sigh and stomped across the room.

Turning in the doorway, she watched father and daughter settle into the rocker next to the crib. He handed her the bottle and she popped it into her mouth. He fit her into the crook of his arm before cracking the book to read its pages, his soft low voice reaching out to her, soothing her.

"Going for a run?" he said in the same voice he used to read to his daughter.

"Yeah. Want me to wait?" She liked his company when she ran, preferring it to being alone these days.

"Can't today. Got SWAT re-cert at eight o'clock." He looked up at her and smiled.

She gave a low whistle. "Lucky you."

He chuckled softly. "Quit playin'—it's just you and me here, so you can admit it. We both know you're gonna miss it."

He was right. She *was* going to miss it, but she shrugged that off. After spending fifteen months loaned out to SWAT, she'd finally been able to make her way back to Homicide. Her time away had proved to her that Homicide was where she belonged, Mathews be damned. Besides, SWAT was out of the question for her now. One cowboy in the family was enough.

She smiled. "Want me to take over so you can get ready?" she said hopefully, and he laughed.

"No, I want you to stop hovering."

"Hey, I don't hover."

"You do. You're a hoverer," he said. "But I forgive you. Actually, I think it's kinda cute."

"*Cute*?" She scoffed and pushed away from the door. "Now you're just being mean."

"Sabrina."

She looked back to see his face had gone serious. "Hmm?"

"Take the dog."

"Like she'd let me leave without her."

"And your backup piece."

"And I'm the hoverer?" she said and rolled her eyes. "Hello pot, meet kettle."

"I'm just—" He looked down at the baby zoning out in his arms, her lips slack around the bottle in her mouth, soft black curls framing her face. He looked back up at her but didn't finish what he was going to say. Didn't have to. He worried about her. They all did—Val, the twins, Strickland. Their worry was like the aftershocks of an earthquake, rippling out to touch her when she least expected it, tipping her off balance. Shaking her with its reminder of everything that had happened over the past two years. Wade. David.

They worried because they loved her. Because, as her family, it was their job.

"Okay, okay," she said with a nod and lifted her pant leg to show him the .380 LCP strapped to her ankle. "Never leave home without it."

"Thank you." Nickels pulled the bottle from the baby's mouth and placed her gently on his shoulder. He began to rub and pat her back. "You know, if you want to skip the run altogether and make me pancakes, I wouldn't mind in the slightest."

She laughed. "That's what I love about you, Nick—forever the optimist," she said before turning to make her way back to her room.

By the time she tied her shoes and tossed her hair into a ponytail, Avasa was up and waiting at the door, ready to go.

———

They ran the trail. Her feet pounded down the dirt, even and steady despite the twinge that shot through her thigh every time her foot made contact with the ground. It would always hurt. Would always remind her of what had happened to her, how close she'd come to dying. That it had been her half-brother who'd been the one to hurt her. The tight, puckered flesh that marred her leg had finally healed. She'd finally let it. She'd battled her way through rehab—and this time she hadn't stopped until it was done.

These days the agonizing pain had faded to nothing more than a dull ache. But she welcomed the discomfort—relished it in a strange way. The pain in her thigh reminded her that she'd made it through. It was the fact that she still suffered, just a little, that proved to her it was real.

She'd survived.

Without even thinking, her feet and legs began to slow until she was walking along the trail. She was close. The dog, used to it by now, trotted the few remaining yards and sat in the dirt to wait.

Stopping, Sabrina faced the woods where she'd found a dead girl two years before. She stared into the trees. It was like staring into the face of a monster.

What's wrong, Melissa ... miss me?

Wade's voice echoed in her head, little more than a whisper. He'd crept up on her over the past few days, growing louder and louder. Soon the faint murmur in her head would become a howling scream. She'd put it off too long, managed to fool herself into believing that this time Wade was gone for good.

Gone for good? Ain't no such thing, darlin'…

She'd have to go see Phillip later. It was the only way, the only thing she'd found that could quiet the voice in her head, but for now she did the only thing she could—she ignored him. Focused on the space between the trees where she'd found the girl. It was hard but she made herself do it. Instead of listening, she forced herself to remember the way the girl looked. The empty sockets where her eyes should've been. The lime-green polish on her toes. The red ribbon tied around her wrist. The word stabbed into her stomach.

R U N

You keep bringing us back to this place, darlin'. You even understand why?

He'd asked her that once, staring down at her, a sickening grin stretched across his ruined face. Yeah, she understood why. She felt the calm steady beat of her heart. Reminded herself that not only had she survived, she'd won.

Are you sure about that, darlin'?

Her cell let out a chirp, and she plucked it off her hip.

"Vaughn."

"Hey, Little Miss Sunshine, I hear you're my new partner." It was Christopher Strickland. Hearing his voice made her smile. Made it easier to push Wade's relentless whisper from her mind.

"That's what they told me," she said, her smile turning to a full-fledged grin. Yeah, she'd miss SWAT, but this is where she belonged.

He laughed. "Well then, you better get your ass in gear—we caught a case."

She turned away from the clearing and snapped her fingers. Avasa's ears picked up and she trotted over to where Sabrina stood, looking up at her expectantly. "Text me the address. I'll meet you there in an hour," she said before closing her phone and heading for home, her dog at her side.

TWELVE

Sabrina crossed the street, approaching the cluster of badges that milled around the front yard belonging to the address Strickland had sent her. The uniform stationed at the perimeter gave her a head nod but not much more. No smile. No black-humored commentary on what was going on inside. He barely looked at her as she ducked under the tape. She straightened and looked around. More of the same. Somber faces and hushed voices. It was like someone had turned the volume down on the entire crime scene. Only one thing could do that. Turn a crew of hardened cops into a bunch of dour-faced librarians.

The murder victim was a child.

She made her way up the front walk, forcing her feet to move faster than they wanted to go. No one wanted to work a child murder. Those were the ones you couldn't shake loose. They stuck with you. Haunted you. She pushed her way inside and found another uniform standing just inside the door. She gave him a questioning glance, and he tipped his head in the direction of the hallway.

The house was empty, the floor littered with fast-food wrappers and old newspapers. Windows were painted over so the morning sun was defused down to little more than a reddish glow as it struggled to push its way through the glass. Another pale-faced uniform was stationed just outside one of the rooms off the hallway.

She stepped into the room to find Strickland crouched over a body so little all she could see was the top of a blond head and small bare feet. She dug a pair of latex gloves out of her jacket pocket and pulled them on. "Hey."

He looked over his shoulder and jerked his chin at her. "Hey. Hell of a welcome back, huh?" he said, watching her circle around the body to stand opposite him. She looked down, steeling herself for what waited at her feet. It was a boy. No obvious cause of death, his body pale and still. Naked.

She blew out a sigh and hunkered down to get a better look. She glanced at her partner. Strickland rubbed his hand across his mouth and shook his head. "He can't be more than six or seven."

He was small. She'd have guessed younger, but she didn't say anything. "Any witnesses?"

"No." Strickland dropped his gloved hand and brushed his fingers along the ligature marks that marred the boy's wrist. "Anonymous 911 call from a burner cell. I got a couple of uniforms doing a walk-through, but so far—"

"Hey, you guys are gonna want to see this." She and Strickland looked up to see a uniformed officer. His head poked into the room, like the rest of his body had refused to make the trip. His gaze drifted down to the body stretched out on the floor between them before bouncing back up. "Some pretty weird shit in the basement," he said before retreating back down the hall.

She tried not to let her frustration get the best of her. But it was hard—really hard—to let Strickland take the lead. Especially when he led like an old lady.

"You want to move a little faster, Grandma?" she said from where she was, stuck behind him on the basement stairs.

"Your leg *must* be better, huh? A year and some change on SWAT and you're ready to kick down doors," he said. He clicked his flashlight on and swept it across the interior before taking a few more steps into the gloom. "Not sure if you remember, but we take a more civilized approach here in the land of suits and ties."

"More like the land of dentures and bingo," Sabrina said under her breath as she followed, moving farther down the stairs. That's when the smell hit her.

"Busted sewer line," Strickland said, but he was wrong. She knew that smell. Had been trapped in the dark with it for eighty-three days. The smell told her that this is where the boy had been kept. That he'd been held against his will, confined somewhere that didn't offer the luxury of a toilet.

The single bare bulb that hung in the middle of the room did little except create a small circle of watery light; the rest of the room was dark. Strickland shuffled forward a few more steps, doing his best to keep her on the stairs until he knew it was completely safe. She could already see a habit forming, an irritating one that annoyed her. "Strickland, I swear to God..."

He shot her a look over his shoulder. "Better safe than—"

"You're being ridiculous." She shouldered her way past him, pulling her Mini-Mag from her pocket. She clicked it on. "I think I've proved it takes a lot more than a dark basement to kill me."

Liar, liar…

"Nice, Vaughn—real nice." Strickland shook his head. He hated being reminded of what'd happened to her. That he hadn't been there to help her.

"You been doing those deep-breathing exercises I taught you?" She was teasing him now, making light of a situation neither one of them could change. And even if she could, she wouldn't.

He aimed his light in the opposite direction. "Fuck you, Vaughn," he said with no real heat behind it.

She scanned the opposite side of the room, her beam passing over a large wrought-iron cage. Then another. And another. And another. Whatever she'd been about to say died in her throat. "Oh…" She let the word out on an expulsion of breath, too soft to sound like anything but a sigh. There were leashes clipped to the outside of each of them. Buckets full of shit and piss next to bowls that'd probably held food and water. There were four of them, which meant that the dead boy upstairs wasn't the only one who'd been held here. So where were the rest of them? It wasn't something she wanted to consider, but the body upstairs might not be the only one they found.

Home sweet home…

"Take a look over here," Strickland said.

She turned in the direction of his voice, and her flashlight found the back of his head. His was pointed at a video camera set on a tripod. "This just keeps getting better by the second," he said in a disgusted mutter.

She aimed her light at the ground and crossed the room to the camera. "No tape. But we'll get CSU down here, have them dust every square inch. No way this freak wore gloves the whole time. We'll catch him," she said, sounding more sure than she actually felt. She knew better than anyone that monsters weren't always that easy to catch. Sometimes they were more than just dumb animals; sometimes they roamed free.

She ran her flashlight along the floor, looking for something, anything that might point her in the direction of the sick bastard who thought keeping little kids in cages was an okay thing to do. Her light caught the edge of a curtain. She watched it flutter as if touched by a breeze. But there was no breeze. Not down here. It fluttered again.

She motioned for Strickland to be quiet and aimed her light at the edge of the curtain. She saw movement, something shifting slowly along the floor.

There was someone there.

THIRTEEN

SABRINA'S HEART SLAMMED INTO her throat. She unsnapped her holster as quietly as she could and shot a look over her shoulder. Strickland had seen it too. He drew his weapon and nodded. She lifted her SIG P220 off her hip and took aim at the curtain.

"SFPD. I know you're back there. Come out with your hands where I can see them," she said in a tone that gave little doubt as to her intent if her command wasn't followed.

No response, just the slight flutter of the curtain that told her that who or whatever was behind it was still there.

"I said, SFPD. Come out—"

A pair of feet appeared, nothing more than the tops and toes. They were small and pale in the steady beam of her flashlight.

Holy shit. It was a kid.

She changed tactics, softening her tone but still holding firm. "It's okay, you're safe. I'm a police officer. It's okay to come out now," she said but didn't lower her gun. There was a chance the child behind the curtain wasn't alone.

Small feet shuffled closer and a hand peeked out from the split between the curtains. The opening was pulled wider to reveal dark vacant eyes and a sharp nose set in a face that was painfully thin. Equally thin shoulders and torso appeared as the kid moved forward slowly. Just like the dead boy upstairs, he was naked.

"Are you alone back there?" she said. The kid didn't answer, just stared at her with those empty eyes. She motioned the child closer. "Come here, it's okay." She looked at Strickland and tipped her head in the direction of the curtain. He nodded and moved forward, gun raised.

Sabrina reached out and latched onto the boy's arm, pulling him toward her. The second her fingers made contact, he went crazy, swinging and shouting in a language she didn't understand.

She dragged the boy clear of the curtain. He fought against her grip, screaming and flailing, while Strickland did a sweep of the room behind it. He came out a few seconds later. "Nothing. Just a mattress, a TV, and another camcorder," he said over the din of the boy's screaming. "What the hell is he saying?"

She shook her head and looked at the boy, saw his face, white and stretched thin with terror. He wasn't speaking English, but his fear was obvious. "Shhh, shhh—it's okay. We're here to help," she said, hoping her tone would convey the message her words couldn't.

The boy darted away from her, nothing but a pale blur as he bolted toward freedom. She started after him, pounding up the steps, Strickland two strides behind her. She reached the top of the stairs and saw him running down the darkened hallway, darting this way and that.

"Stop him," she shouted, hoping the uniform at the front door would be quick enough to catch him.

The boy cut to the left, and she followed through the living room doorway. He saw the uniformed figure blocking his way out and darted to the left again, cutting across the room to the other side of the house—toward the room where the dead boy probably still lay stretched out on the floor.

"Don't go in there!" she shouted, even though he didn't understand her. He disappeared through the doorway seconds before she reached it. She skidded to a stop. Coroner Mandy Black was hunkered down next to the body on the floor, but the whole of her attention was concentrated on the boy who'd just burst into the room. He was crouching in the corner farthest away from the doorway, knees drawn tight against his chest by arms so thin and pale they looked like twigs, bleached white by the sun.

He started rambling again, eyes, like miniature black holes aimed at the body on the floor. She started to cross the threshold, but Mandy threw up a hand and shook her head. Sabrina stalled out mid-stride and watched as Mandy stood, crossing the room on slow and steady feet. She said something in what sounded like the same language the boy was speaking and as if Mandy had thrown a switch, he stopped talking.

Sabrina watched and listened. Mandy got closer and closer, still speaking the strange language in a low easy tone that seemed to sooth the boy. It sounded Slavic, maybe Russian. Strange coming from the woman crouched on the floor. She must've asked him a question because the boy nodded, eyes suddenly flooded with tears. He started to speak again, but his speech had lost its hysterical edge. Mandy got close enough to reach out and touch him, but she didn't. She kept her hands at her sides, shaking her head as she crouched low and slow in front of him. She kept talking. The boy kept listening.

"What. The. Fuck," Strickland said behind her. "Coroner Barbie speaks gibberish."

"It's not gibberish, dickhead. It's Russian," Mandy said without looking up.

Sabrina felt a prickle, like electricity dancing along her skin. What was a Russian boy doing in an abandoned house in San Francisco?

She looked away from the boy crouched in the corner to the one dead on the floor.

"Ask him if he knows the victim," Sabrina said.

Mandy spoke quietly and the boy answered, shaking his head. "No. He said he's never seen him before."

Sabrina studied the boy on the floor. He was small and blond. She entered the room and squatted down next to the body. She peeled back a lid and looked at his eyes. They were milky, but she could see enough of the iris to know they were hazel.

She stood. "I need some air," she said, brushing past Strickland on her way out the door. She could feel him watching her, and she silently urged him not to follow.

She didn't need air; she needed to call Ben Shaw, because there was a very real chance that she'd just found Leo Maddox.

FOURTEEN

Ben met him on the tarmac a few hours later. "What part of *clean sweep* did you not understand?"

The part where it entailed shooting an unarmed woman. "Relax. It's gonna be fine," he said, dropping his duffle at his feet. "The gun used to do the guards has her prints all over it, and I used different calibers and kill methods. Once you plant the evidence in her computer that points the way to her hiring a hit squad, no one is gonna believe her lone-gunman theory."

"She saw you." Ben shook his head. "What if she recognized you from the club?"

"Please. The last time she saw me, she was blitzed out on booze and roofies," he said, despite the doubt that nagged him. "That whole night is a big black hole as far as she's concerned."

Ben was as unconvinced as he was. "You should've killed her. Leaving her alive was sloppy."

Michael eyes narrowed just a twinge. "Would you've killed her?" he said. Ben looked away, and he scoffed. "Didn't think so.

It's bad enough she's gonna spend the rest of her life in prison for multiple murders she had nothing to do with. Just let it go."

"Easy for you to say—" Ben's phone let out a chirp. He dug it out of his pocket and glanced at the screen. "Meet you on the plane," he said, turning his back on him and walking toward the tail of the plane before answering. Michael watched him go, caught the smile on his face that appeared after he said hello. The grin faded quickly, replaced by a look that said he was all business now. After only thirty seconds, he snapped his phone closed and dropped it in his pocket. He walked back toward the front of the plane. "Change of plans. We're making a pit stop before heading to Helena," Ben said, and he moved past Michael up the steps to the interior of the Lear.

"Where?" Michael said, picking up his duffle and following.

His partner shot him a look over his shoulder. "San Francisco."

———

San Francisco.

As soon as Michael boarded the plane, he dropped his duffle and stretched out on the couch, closed his eyes, and willed himself into oblivion. But it was useless. No way was he sleeping. Not when all he could think about was Sabrina.

It looked like fate had finally decided to stop being such a bitch and throw him a bone. He'd been wracking his brain, trying to figure out a way to slip his collar and find a way to see her, but suddenly his way was clear ...

He looked across the interior of the Lear to where Lark had set up shop and felt the skin on the back of his neck draw tight once more before closing his eyes again. At least it was clearer than it had been a few hours ago. He still had to figure out how in the hell he was going to get rid of Lark and the kid—

"We need to talk."

He cracked a lid to see Ben sitting cross-legged in the middle of the aisle, three feet from his face. He looked worried. It was never a good sign when Ben looked worried.

"So talk." He closed his eyes again and waited for the kid to start in with whatever was bothering him, but all he heard was the constant tapping that told him Lark was on his computer.

He opened his eyes. Ben was still there. The worry was too. "Look, getting shot makes me tired, so if you're just gonna—"

"It wasn't Lark. It was me . . . sort of. I'm the reason my father knows about Sabrina."

He shot a glare in Lark's direction. He was sitting at the table. The same table they'd been sitting at that last time they'd all been together on this plane. They'd been having a conversation much like this one. He'd trusted Lark, and Lark had betrayed him. Now it seemed to be Ben's turn to fuck him over. When was he gonna learn?

He shifted his glare back to Ben and settled on his face. "You have two minutes."

"My dad knew something was up with you. After finding your sister's killer, you came back wrong, and he wanted to know why." Ben scrubbed a hand over his face and shook his head. "He kept at me, bugging me. Reminding me that my duty was, first and foremost, to my family. To him," he said with barely contained disgust. "I repeatedly and quite emphatically told him to go fuck himself."

Michael narrowed his eyes on the kid's face. "Skip to the part where I get screwed over. It's always my favorite."

"I knew it was only a matter of time before Green Mile back there started flapping his yap and guaranteed, nothing he had to say would've been favorable." He jerked his head toward Lark, who was listening. He hadn't turned around, but his tapping had stopped. "But I kept my mouth shut and an eye out. Helped her get her job back. Tried to get her to rehab her leg." Now he looked serious. Serious Ben was also never a good thing. "I did what I could—for her and for you."

It took him a second to understand what Ben was saying, but then the realization hit. "You recruited her."

Ben shrugged. "It was either recruit her or kill her," he said, shaking his head. "You're the one that brought her into this mess, man. I was just trying to make sure she stayed in one piece."

"By turning her into an assassin?" His stomach clenched at the thought of Sabrina doing what he did, going the places he went. He thought of her standing over a mark like Cordova and pulling the trigger.

"She isn't an asset; she's a spotter. She sees a hard-to-locate target cross her desk or catches on to something that might interest us during surveillance, she calls me. That's it."

"What does any of this have to do with your father? You could've turned her without handing her over."

"I did. She's the one—she handed *herself* over. For you." Ben swiped a rough hand over his face. "I mean, Jesus, didn't you ever wonder how she got you out of there? You *and* her friend? She's badass, but she's not a miracle worker."

"She called your father." It wasn't a question. He could almost see her doing it. He'd been in bad shape, poisoned by whatever David Song had been using to incapacitate his victims. He'd felt himself dying, and he hadn't cared—not when it meant dying for her. And in the end it had been her sacrifice, not his, that'd saved them both.

Defeat and anger: he felt them both, struggled with them as they pulled his in every possible direction. "She's the one who called you just now from San Francisco. She's your contact there."

Ben hesitated then nodded. "One of them, yeah."

"How long? How long has she been working for you?"

Ben hesitated again, this time a bit longer. "I approached her while she was still in that hospital in Texas."

All along. Ben had been in contact with Sabrina all along and he hadn't said a word. Something crawled along the nape of his neck and trickled down his spine. "Is she chipped?"

"No. I convinced my father it wasn't necessary," Ben said.

"How?"

Ben shrugged. "Does it matter?"

Michael felt a dull pounding start up in the back of his skull, and he had to make himself unclench his fists. "Yeah. It does. It matters a lot."

"I might've ... *liberated* certain evidence from the SFPD that could've been used to prosecute her in a few murders," Ben said.

He was talking about the bat she'd used nearly twenty years ago to defend herself from being raped by her mother's boyfriend. The same bat Wade Bauer had used to kill a police officer in order to frame Sabrina for murder. If Livingston Shaw had it, he'd be able to make Sabrina do anything he wanted. "Where is it now?"

"My dad has it," Ben said, but he cut his eyes in Lark's direction for a split second and gave him an almost imperceptible shake of his head. He was lying. Wherever the bat was, Shaw didn't have it.

"Why? Why are you protecting her?" he said. Ben's motives mattered, and the wrong ones would get him killed.

Ben got that look again. That serious look that showed you just who he really was. "Because my father has stolen enough from you. Don't get me wrong—you made your bed all by yourself, but as far as I'm concerned, your debt to him is cleared."

Michael looked away, out the window at the blue and white that whipped by so fast it looked like it was standing still.

The kid was wrong. His debt would never be cleared. Not until Reyes was dead and buried.

FIFTEEN

AFTER BEN CAME CLEAN about Sabrina's involvement with FSS, Michael didn't even try to pretend to sleep. He cleaned his weapons instead.

Laid out on the table in front of him, the muted gleam of gunmetal was familiar. Comforting even, in a strange sort of way. This was what he knew. What he did. Who he was. The person he'd been after Frankie's death, the one who fell in love with Sabrina—that wasn't him. Never had been.

He could hope and wish all he wanted. For a different life. To find a way clear of the two tons of shit he'd buried himself under. It didn't matter. Not when faced with the reality of what he really was. Not when he admitted that he would probably never be free of Livingston Shaw. He ran the bulk patch through the barrel of his gun and gave it a few twists before pulling it clear. It came out clean.

Besides, did he really think he'd been made to settle down? Fall in love, lead an average existence? Pancakes and crossword puzzles on lazy Sunday mornings. Walks in the park and neighborhood barbeques. He thought about Tom Onewolf, the only normal guy he knew. He had a wife and daughter and ran his uncle's diner. For a moment, despite everything Michael knew about himself, he wished he could trade places with him. Be average. Be stable.

Be someone else.

Lark was right. Sabrina had done something to him. Made him want things he couldn't have. To be a man he couldn't even imagine. He tried to be angry at her, but it was no use. He'd decided a long time ago that whatever his problems were, she wasn't to blame. He let her get too close; he had no one to blame but himself.

He swiped the bulk patch over the slide, clearing away imaginary debris before adding a few drops of gun oil here and there.

But it was possible now. She was in as deep as he was. He could finally have something, someone, he wanted. They could be together…

As soon as the thought came to him, he rejected it. She deserved better—a lot better—than him. He thought of the cop who'd had the hots for her. Nickels. Yeah, he'd be good for her. He was clean. Capable. And just the thought of Sabrina with him made Michael want to kill something.

He passed the bulk patch over the body of the gun, careful to clear the rails, and ran it over the lip of the magazine. A shadow fell over the table and he looked up, not at all surprised by who he saw standing over him.

Michael smirked and dropped his eyes back down to the gun in his hand. "Did you fall down and hit your head or something, asshole?" he said.

"Maybe, but I got enough wits to hear what Junior told you about your girl," Lark said, still standing over him and still staring.

Michael didn't answer. He reached for his gun cloth and started rubbing away the fluid residue left on his dismantled gun. He got busy ignoring Lark; it didn't matter, he just kept talking.

"He's the one who told the boss about her, not me."

"Technically, she turned herself in." *For me.* His jaw clenched tight as he shot Lark a look. "Is this going somewhere, or are you looking for a shoulder to cry on?" He'd never been able to stomach Lark's bitchy little girl routine for long; time had done nothing to stretch his patience. He fixed the slide back into place and racked it back to ensure it rode the rails without catching.

"What I'm looking for is an apology."

Michael laughed. Tipped his head back and let loose. "Yeah? Well, keep looking because you won't find one here." He popped a fresh magazine into the grip of the gun and racked a bullet into the chamber before laying it on the table. He looked up at Lark. "You're just pissy because she beat you to the punch. I'm sure you would've loved to be the one to offer up that little gem to Shaw."

"But I didn't." Lark jabbed a finger over his shoulder at Ben. "He *turned* her, and he gets a pass? What's up with that?"

"He did it to save her. What you did, you did to save yourself." Michael stood, forcing Lark back a few steps away from the table.

"I did what I did to save us both."

"Remind me to send a thank you card." He looked down at the gun on the table.

Lark read his mind. "Shooting me won't change anything. You can't have what you want. None of us can. We walked away from nine-to-five and minivans a long time ago. No use callin' bullshit now."

Michael kept his expression neutral. "Has anyone ever told you that you have this annoying habit of repeating yourself?"

"Yeah, well, here's another repeat, just so we're clear: I'm here to make sure you don't get any silly ideas about riding off into the sunset with your Lady Cop—"

"Funny, I thought that's what the dirty bomb attached to my spine was for."

"—so, just remember: She's a hell of a lot more expendable than you are."

Michael holstered his gun and curled his hands into fists, squeezing them so hard he felt his knuckles crack. "Pushing me . . . it's a stupid move."

"I'm not the one being stupid," Lark nearly growled at him, and Michael laughed again. Lark had him there. When it came to Sabrina, *Stupid* was his middle name.

SIXTEEN

Cofre del Tesoro, Colombia
July 2008

"What is it?"

Christina stood at the edge of the grass, small fingers worrying against the seams of her pale pink dress. She looked up at him.

"It's a tire swing," Michael said, jamming his hands into the pockets of his fatigues.

"What's it for?"

"It's for fun." What seemed like a good idea this morning now felt silly. He grimaced at the old jeep tire and rope he'd found in the garage. He hadn't even thought to wipe it down before stringing it up. Jesus, he was bad at this. "Never mind. You want to go back inside?"

"No." She said it quickly, her pigtails bouncing wildly with the forceful head shake she gave him. "I'm tired of inside."

He smiled down at her. "Me too. Want to give it a try?" he said, cocking his head at the swing.

"Yes, please." She smiled back, looking at him like he'd just offered her something priceless. The smile faded a bit and her fingers started to worry again. "What am I supposed to do?"

He took her by the hand and led her onto the grass. When he'd first found the tree a few months ago, he'd hardly been able to believe it. An oak tree growing on an island off the coast of Colombia. He'd been so curious that he'd asked one of the other guards about it.

"When Mrs. Reyes was pregnant, *Hefe* had it shipped all the way here, fully grown from America and had it planted so that his son would have a good, sturdy tree to climb," the guard had told him. "*Hefe* is still waiting for his son."

He hadn't said it, but the implication was clear: Christina was a disappointment to her father. The tire swing had been an impulsive reaction to what the guard had told him. A *fuck you* to Reyes for discarding his only daughter like a broken toy. For treating her like a thing instead of a child.

They stood in front of it now, and he gave it a push so she could watch it swing gently back and forth. "You put your legs through the hole and sit on the edge," he said to her, brushing the black smudges touching it left on his fingertips off on his dark pants.

"I'm going to get dirty."

"Probably," he answered, ready to take her back into the house.

Christina watched the tire sway for a few moments, doubt slowly being replaced by determination. She lifted her arms, looking up at him, this time with expectation, and it took him a second to realize what she was asking. Lifting her, he held her up so she could thread her legs through the hole in the tire. "Hold on here," he said gruffly, suddenly attacked by the memory of doing almost the exact same thing for Frankie when she was little. He moved her hands to the base of the rope. "Don't let go," he said just before giving her a gentle push, sending the tire away from him.

She came back and he pushed her again, a little bit harder this time, and she spun around on the return trip, her eyes wide with worry but also something more. Excitement—the kind of terrified joy that makes you believe you can do anything. That you are not a disappointment. That you are perfect, even if your hair is loose and your dress is smudged with grease and road dust.

He pushed again and this time she squealed, "Higher!"

He pushed her until he could barely lift his arms and her dress was ringed in black. Neither of them noticed. "Did you have a tire swing when you were my age?" she said to him, taking hold of his hand on the walk back from to the house. He didn't pull away.

"No. I didn't live in a place that had trees." How could he explain to her that when he'd been her age he'd live in a shitty rent-by-the-week with his heroin-addicted mother? That he didn't even remember *seeing* a tree until he'd been taken to Sophia and Sean for fostering after his mother died. "But I did when I was older."

He still remembered sitting in the front seat of his social worker's ancient VW Beetle staring out the window at the place that would eventually become his home. The tire swing looked like it was there just waiting for him, and he wanted to swing on it so bad he could taste it. He hadn't been there a week before he found a hacksaw in Sean's tool chest and cut the rope from the branch, the tire hitting the ground with a dull thud.

"Did you love it?" Her eyes were wide, cheeks still flushed by wind and exhilaration.

"I did love it," he said. When he'd woken up the next morning after cutting it down, it'd been strung back up, as if he'd never touched it. It became a sort of game between him and his new father. He'd cut it down and then Sean would string it back up. Him telling Sean to give up. That he was hopeless and would never allow himself to be loved. Sean telling him that no matter what he said or did, he would never give up. He would never stop trying. "My sister loved it too."

"You have a sister?" Christina stopped, her hand jerking in his. "What does she look like?"

He looked at her. She had the same curly dark hair and smooth olive skin as Frankie, who looked so much like Sophia. On impulse, Michael pulled the photo of a twelve-year-old Frankie from the pocket where he always carried it and held it out to her.

Christina's gaze latched on to the photo along with her fingers. "She has curly hair too." She traced the crazy tangle that surrounded Frankie's face with the tip of her finger. "Does she like the beach?" she said, searching for something that would connect her to the wild-looking girl in the picture.

"She does, but she's older now. In high school, but that's how I think of her." *That's how she looked the last time I saw her.*

She handed the photo back and resumed walking. "Thank you," she said as they stepped into the looming shadows of the house.

"You're welcome," he said, giving her hand a small squeeze before he pulled away. "Sorry about your dress."

"It's okay," she said, giving him a smile, wildness playing at the corners of her mouth and for the first time, she looked like what she was: a child. "I never liked it anyway."

SEVENTEEN

THEY LANDED AT MOFFETT Federal Airfield a few hours later and climbed into the standard-issue black Land Rover that waited for them inside the hangar. Michael took the back seat without protest. He preferred it actually; that way he was not only able to keep Lark in sight, he could laugh at him every time he took an uneasy look over his shoulder.

He barely paid attention until they drove by Mount Davidson Park toward the quiet neighborhoods tucked around it. One of those neighborhoods belonged to Sabrina. Michael sat up in his seat and looked at the rearview mirror, trying to catch Ben's eye, but the kid wouldn't look at him.

"The hell are we doing way over here? The FSS field office is twenty miles that way," Lark said, jabbing a thumb out the window.

"I have other plans," Ben said, taking a quick glance in the rearview mirror, straight at Michael. Michael didn't like what he saw.

They rolled past Sabrina's street and hooked a right to head up the hill. When they stopped in front of the stately Victorian painted a creamy white with French blue gingerbread detail, he stared out the window and felt like throwing up. Time had done nothing to change it. The same rosebushes with their heavy-headed blooms. The same porch swing with its deep red cushions. He hadn't been back, hadn't called. Not like he used to.

Just then, Miss Ettie, the elderly woman who owned and ran the B&B, stepped out onto the porch. He could see her wide smile and snappy brown eyes from where he was. She waved them in, but it wasn't *them* she was waving in. It was Ben.

Michael watched him lean across the seat into Lark's space to wave back before he put the Rover into park. "What are we doing here?" Michael said.

The kid cut him a look, an unreadable expression on his boyish face. "Checking in," he said before climbing out of the SUV and making his way toward the house.

Michael retrieved his duffle and case from the cargo area of the Rover as slowly as he could. He watched Ben stride up the front walk, Lark lagging behind, and wondered again what the kid was up to. This was San Francisco; you couldn't swing a dead cat without hitting a hotel. Not to mention that it was mandatory for all FSS employees to report immediately to the field office upon arrival. He learned a long time ago that the rules rarely applied to Ben, but they were on a case. This wasn't a social call. Why were they here?

Ben took a step forward and captured the old woman's hand in his before he leaned in and dropped a kiss on her cheek. Watching them, Michael felt his gut clench. Ben knew her.

He thought of all the times the kid had taken off on his own after a job. It suddenly became clear where Ben had been spending his downtime and why he'd stopped asking Michael to tag along.

He couldn't help but think of Sabrina. She lived one street over, directly behind the B&B. It's what made staying here two years ago so convenient.

Michael watched from the cover of the Land Rover's trunk as Miss Ettie reached out her hand and allowed Lark to shake it. It was a sight, seeing that massive hand swallow her tiny fingers in a handshake that was meant to be dainty but ended up looking awkward. Seeing Lark standing so close to the old woman reminded him of Sabrina's grandmother. Reminded him that Lark was responsible for her death. He'd killed Lucy Walker as sure as if he'd point a gun at her and pulled the trigger.

Michael slammed the hatch and stepped onto the curb, feeling exposed and out of place when the small cluster of people in front of him turned and looked his way. Miss Ettie moved away from the men in front of her, and her face broke into a grin that grew wider and wider with each step she took toward him.

She stopped in front of him. "I've been worried about you," she said, shaming him whether she meant to or not.

He dropped his duffle and case on the front walk, stunned when she wrapped her arms around his middle and pressed her head into his rapidly tightening chest.

"I'm sorry." He didn't know what else to say.

"You better be. You left quite the mess behind, and you sure as hell better be sorry about that too," she said to him before she turned and walked toward the house, expecting the men behind her to follow in her wake.

EIGHTEEN

SABRINA SAT IN THE chair next to the hospital bed and watched the boy sleep. According to Mandy, his name was Alex Kotko. He'd been kidnapped from St. Petersburg, where he'd lived on the streets, abandoned by his father after his mother died. He had no idea how long he'd been in captivity and could tell them nothing that might help lead them to the man who'd held him.

There was a soft rap on the door before it was opened. "Hey." She looked up to see Mandy standing just inside the doorway.

Sabrina gave her a smile that waned quickly. "Hey," she said, sitting up a bit. Strickland wasn't the only one who called Mandy Black *Coroner Barbie*. With her bright blond ponytail, pert freckled nose, and dark-green eyes, she looked more like a cheerleader late for math class than an assistant chief medical examiner. It was an apt nickname, but Sabrina never used it. She knew how much Mandy hated it.

"How's he doing this morning?" Mandy said, shutting the door behind her.

"As well as can be expected, I suppose." She glanced at the boy. He was still asleep.

Mandy read her perfectly. "It had to be done."

Sabrina nodded. "I know. I just…"

It'd taken well over an hour for Mandy to coax the boy out of the corner and another thirty minutes before she was able to drape the blanket Strickland had brought in from his trunk around his shoulders. She wasn't sure what Mandy had said to him, but whatever it was, it was enough for him to allow her to lead him through the house and out into the yard.

People had gathered. Neighbors crowding around the tape barrier. Uniforms pushing them back. They all went quiet when they saw the boy. He pressed himself into Mandy's side, her hand shielding his eyes from the sun and his face from the people who stared at him. Mandy pushed the boy into the back of Strickland's unmarked, following him in. Sabrina had gotten in the back as well, hemming him into the middle of the bench seat—the coroner on one side, her on the other. She said nothing, just listened to Mandy talk to the boy in a low comforting tone, trying not to think about what she knew had probably happened to him in that basement.

The hospital. The boy was a victim who needed medical treatment, but he was also evidence that needed to be processed. She knew from experience that the medical exam after rape was nearly as traumatic as the assault itself. If there was any way she could avoid putting him through it, she would. But there wasn't.

The second he saw the doctors, he went wild again. Shoved Mandy into the wall and ran, but he didn't get far. It'd taken three orderlies to restrain him while the nurse gave him an IM injection full of something that turned his bones to jelly. They wheeled him down the hall, leaving her feeling like shit, but Mandy was right. It had to be done. She looked at the paper bag the nurse had brought her an hour ago. Fingernail scrapings and various swabs—hopefully everything she needed to find the man responsible and nail him to the wall.

"What are you doing here?" she said, changing the subject. Nothing good would come from re-opening old wounds.

Mandy looked at the sleeping boy. "I thought I'd come hang around until Social Services showed up. They were having a hard time scrounging up an interpreter. I'd hate for him to wake up and have no way to communicate. Besides..." Mandy cut Sabrina a wicked look. "I don't think he likes you very much."

"Yeah? What was your first clue? Was it when he tried to bite my hand off or when he called me a *government whore* in Russian?" She'd insisted that Mandy translate everything he said, in addition to catching it on the voice recorder app on her cell.

Mandy winced. "The Russian people hate and fear their government. Criminals and murderers are held in higher esteem."

"I wish I spoke a foreign language. All I can do is swear in Spanish, and that's just because Val cusses me out on a regular basis." She laughed. This time it felt a bit easier. "Where'd you learn to speak Russian?" Sabrina said, more out of curiosity than anything else, but when Mandy's face went still, she was sorry she asked. "Look, I'm sorry. It's not any of my business, I just—"

Mandy shook her head. "No. It's okay. My parents were fluent. They taught me." She looked at the boy again. "Some things you just don't forget."

There was another knock. A uniformed officer pushed the door open. "I'm here for...this." He picked up the bag and signed the piece of paper attached to it to maintain chain of custody. "You need a lift, Doc?"

Mandy shook her head. "No, but thanks. I'm waiting for the Inspector."

The uniform headed out, bag in hand. They were quiet for a while, both of them absorbing the events of the previous twenty-four hours that led them to the hospital bedside of a boy neither one of them knew.

Finally, Sabrina spoke. "Strickland asked you to come by, didn't he?" she said, and she took Mandy's silence for confirmation. She sighed. "He's like Mother Hen on steroids."

"He's your partner. Give the guy a break," Mandy said, easing into the chair next to her.

"Oh, I'd like to sometimes, believe me." She took a breath and blew out a sigh. "I don't need a babysitter."

"I'm not your babysitter. I'm your friend."

That's what she liked best about Mandy. There was no bullshit to sift through when you talked to her. She said what she meant. Still ...

"Don't you need to get to—"

"Relax. I called Randell in to transport the body back to the morgue after we left yesterday. It should be there now."

She shook her head. "I don't want Randell to perform the autopsy. I want you." Mandy was the best. She cared about the people that hit her table. Not just their bodies, but who they were before they died. That was important to her.

"Don't worry, the case is still mine. I scheduled a room for later this morning," Mandy said. "Between you, me, and Mother Hen, that sick son of a bitch is as good as caught."

Before she could answer, her phone buzzed in her pocket. "Speak of the hen ..." she said as she pulled it out and glanced at the screen. "Hey, how's it going?" she said into the phone.

"Less than great. Mathews just left. He's playing your song," Strickland said before barking out a few orders to the gaggle of uniforms he was undoubtedly trying to organize.

"The *Where-the-fuck-is-Vaughn* song?" She sighed. "I haven't heard it in so long, I actually miss it."

"Further evidence that you need your head examined," Strickland said. "Anyway, he wants us both to get to the station ASAP."

She looked at the sleeping boy. He was pale, frail-looking. Like he'd been dragged through hell again and again until he was so spent, so worn, that he'd begun to fade away.

You remember what that's like, don't you, darlin'? The good ol' days …

Sabrina stood, somehow managing to push Wade from her mind, at least for the time being. "I'll see you there in an hour."

NINETEEN

SHE'D BOUGHT CURTAINS.

It was all Michael could think, standing at the window of his room, looking out across the yard toward the back of Sabrina's house. She hated curtains; they blocked out the light. He glanced at the little writing desk tucked into the corner of his room. Saw the chair he used to sit in while he watched her—

The knock on his door pushed him away from the window, like he'd been caught doing something wrong. Ben poked his head in. "Housekeeping," he said before pushing his way in. He tossed a dry-cleaning bag across the back of the leather armchair just inside the door. "Better suit up."

Michael glanced at the bag but didn't move. "What are we doing here, Ben?"

The kid gave a long-suffering sigh. "I told you: she found a body that matches the description of the Maddox boy along with a live witness that might be able to lead us to the who, how, and why."

"No. What are we doing *here?* In this house." The words came through gritted teeth. "And please bear in mind that I have absolutely zero patience for your bullshit right now."

Ben gave up with a lazy shrug. "Alright. I just figured you'd want to see her. Tryin' to do you a solid."

He wanted to see Sabrina more than he'd wanted anything in his whole life. "You thought wrong. We don't have time for this crap. We've got a kid to find, so—"

Ben glanced at the window. "A few days ago you were ready to chew off your arm to get to her. Quit flip-flopping—you're making me dizzy."

"Why in the hell are you so interested in my feelings?" he said quietly.

Ben shrugged. "Because you have them. For her. I find it … encouraging."

Unease settled against his skin and for some reason Michael thought of the debt he owed to the man in front of him. Rather than pursue it, he changed the subject altogether. "What's in the bag?"

Now the kid smiled. "Cheap suit, FBI badge—the usual."

He began to wonder, not for the first time, if his partner was on drugs. "You want me to play Fed? *Here?* You *were* paying attention when I explained to you the pile of shit I had to slog through just to make it out with my neck intact the last time I got involved in one of her investigations, right?"

"Quit your bitching. No one's going to remember you. Not with that mob on your head." Ben grinned.

"Don't remind me," Michael said, running a hand over his head. He'd grown it out for the Cordova job and hadn't had a chance to cut it. He thought of Sabrina's partner, Strickland. From a distance the guy had looked like your typical cop. Rumpled. A bit dopey. Up close was a different story. Christopher Strickland was going to remember him, no doubt about it. Michael shook his head. "You go."

"Can't. I get to go to the hospital and play diplomat from Russian Embassy," Ben said in a thick Russian accent. "And no, we can't switch. Your Ruskie sucks."

"*Eto luchshe chem vash, mudak.*" It's better than yours, asshole.

When he still didn't move, Ben crossed his arms over his chest and gave him a hard look. "Look, this is how the job gets done, you know that. The sooner we get in, the sooner we can get out. So quit being a pussy and put on the suit."

TWENTY

MICHAEL HIT THE STATION lobby and flashed his fake badge at the desk sergeant. The guy bounced a sharp look from the badge to his face and back again. His lip curled up a bit and he chuffed a harsh, one-note laugh. "I'll phone it up. Homicide's on three," he said before slapping the desk phone out of its cradle.

Feds always got the ticker tape parades when they came to town. It was enough to give him a case of the warm fuzzies, but he understood. He'd never been a fan of law enforcement himself. Michael stowed the badge in his breast pocket and nodded his thanks before making his way to the elevator, feeling like he was on display every step of the way.

He kept his face turned away from the surveillance cameras mounted in every corner, more out of habit than actual need. Lark had wanted to come with him, but that had earned him nothing more than a round of belly laughs in the face. Instead he'd been left behind, reduced to maintaining and manipulating security feeds from both the station and the hospital. Michael could just see him, surrounded by computers in Miss Ettie's sunroom, scowling at the monitors. He'd been pissed beyond belief that he was getting the big freeze, but what could he do? Run and tattle that the other kids wouldn't play with him? Fat chance. Admitting to Livingston Shaw that you couldn't handle the task at hand was like chumming shark-infested waters. Lark would rather eat the crap sandwich Ben was feeding him than disappoint the boss.

The door slid open on the third floor and he shouldered his way past the silent patrol officer, feeling his eyes drilling into his back until they slid closed again, but he didn't turn around. Instead he asked the closest cop to point him in Captain Mathews's direction.

He made it about halfway across the room when he happened across it. Sabrina's desk. Clean. Uncluttered. The desk butted up to it was disgusting—and occupied.

Strickland sat with his feet kicked up on his cluttered work-space, nose buried in a stack of files resting in his lap. Michael walked by without slowing, heading for Mathews's office. Strickland never looked up.

A couple of sharp knuckle raps earned him a terse bark that sound like *come in*. Michael pushed the door open, fixing his best *I'm just here to help* smile on his face. Behind the desk was a man in his early forties, sandy hair cut high and tight and small dark eyes that looked like they were already counting the days until retirement. "You the fed?" Mathews said.

Michael nodded. "Yes. Special Agent Marcus Payne, sir." The word *sir* stuck in his throat, but he took a few steps into the room and leaned across the worn desktop to offer his hand. It was taken and given a few disgruntled pumps before being all but thrown back at him.

"Got a call from your field office. Told me you'd be coming in," Mathews said, managing to make it sound like he'd caught Michael taking a piss on his prize tulips. "Have a seat. Inspector Vaughn was just about to get down to the debrief."

Michael looked at the pair of chairs to his right. The one offered was empty. Sabrina sat in the other, less than two feet away.

TWENTY-ONE

ONE OF SABRINA'S MOST valued attributes was her ability to compartmentalize. She could divide herself into sections—mother, cop, friend, partner. One section rarely bled into another. It was how she had survived eight-three days of rape and torture. How she'd been able to pull the trigger and blow her half-brother's face away when she'd learned what he'd done to her. It was her ability to operate in sections that allowed her to sit in Mathews's office next to Michael without totally losing it.

She'd been called into Mathews's office for what she assumed would be the reboot of her weekly reminder of how much he hated her. Before her transfer, he used to call her in and sit her down just so he could go over all the ways she wasn't fit to carry a badge. She was impulsive, insubordinate, noncompliant with department policy...oh, and despite evidence to the contrary, he was convinced that she'd had a fellow officer murdered a few years ago. He'd warn her that he was watching her, that one screwup was all he needed to give her the boot. She'd let him rant at her for a while and when he ran out of steam, she'd thank him for his time and leave. It was kinda their thing.

She picked her favorite water spot on the wall—the one shaped like Florida, to the left of his head—and started staring, waiting for the diatribe. It never came.

Instead he said, "A fed is on his way up here to stick his nose in the kiddie murder you and Pigpen picked up today. Try not to embarrass the shit out of me, will ya?"

A few knocks sounded behind her, but she didn't bother to turn around. *You meet one fed, you've met them all.* Then she heard his voice and she *couldn't* turn around.

Michael. Michael was here.

Taking a deep breath, she turned and held out her hand, formed her mouth into a courteous smile. "It's nice to meet you, Agent Payne. I'm Inspector Vaughn." She looked down at the hand she held out in front of her. As steady as you please. He took it and gave it a shake while saying something about how nice it was to meet her. Her eyes touched his for a moment—the quiet gray of them seemed a bit darker than she remembered but just as beautiful. His hair was longer and styled. His face was calm, passive even. It was a look she remembered well.

The part of her that wanted to bolt from the room reared its ugly head for just a moment, but she walled it off. Pulling her hand back, she dropped it in to her lap and looked at her captain. "Shall I start?" Mathews grunted at her; she took that as an affirmative. She started talking, filling them both in on the case. They listened. Michael asked a few questions and she answered him, surprised at the tremor-free sound of her own voice.

When finished, Sabrina sat back in her seat and let the two of them talk it out. She was too busy concentrating on keeping herself in her seat to participate in what they were saying. The creak of Mathews's desk chair drew her attention. He sat up in his chair and placed his hands, folded, on top of his desk. A sure sign that he was about to say something that would piss her off.

Instinctively, she clamped down on her temper in an attempt to cut Mathews's mouth off at the pass.

Looking at Michael, he said, "I feel I should mention that I have deep reservations concerning Inspector Vaughn's ability to lead an investigation of this magnitude. Not only is she newly returned from a fifteen-month stint on SWAT, she's rash and unpredictable." Mathews looked at her, and she saw herself lunging across the desk to bitch-slap him silly. "Vaughn's been instructed to provide you with full cooperation and to assist you in all matters of this investigation," he said, even though he'd informed her of no such thing. "But in the interest of transparency, I'll admit that she's not the inspector I'd have chosen for this assignment. If at any time, you feel like you would prefer a different liaison, don't hesitate to say so."

Never one to disappoint, Mathews hit every nerve Sabrina had and it took everything she had to keep her mouth shut. *Egotistical, overblown son of a—*

"I've been fully briefed on what you view as Inspector Vaughn's shortcomings, Captain Mathews. I'm also aware that, despite where she's been for the past fifteen months, she's the best investigator you've got." Michael/Agent Payne stood, looking down at Mathews with a mix of amusement and contempt. "As for her being expected to comply—if I wanted someone to follow me around and lick my shoes, I would've asked for a dog. Inspector Vaughn is expected to speak her mind, ask questions, and follow the evidence. If that leads her in a different direction than the one I'm heading, I'll welcome and appreciate any insight she can provide." He delivered the last of his statement directly to her.

Mathews turned and gave her a look that would've killed her if looks were capable. "Get out."

"Yes, sir," she said quietly, unable to scrape away the smirk that'd plastered itself to her face. Easing herself from the chair, she stood and managed to get through the door without giving voice to the myriad smartass comments that were doing the Super Bowl Shuffle around her head.

She started toward the bullpen but pulled up short. Strickland was sitting at his desk, going over witness statements to make sure they hadn't missed anything from the canvass. Michael was less than twenty yards away. More than a year and he'd finally come back—but as usual, he hadn't come for her.

On impulse, she grabbed her jacket off the back of her chair and pulled it on.

Suddenly this was the last place she wanted to be.

TWENTY-TWO

MICHAEL SHOULDN'T HAVE OPENED his mouth. He should've listened to the crap Mathews spewed, nodded, thanked him for his time, and left. That's what he was getting ready to do, but then he made the mistake of looking at her. The look of quiet resignation on Sabrina's face told him that this was something she'd heard before. Something she was long used to. And that didn't sit well with him at all.

So he stood, towering over that self-important piece of shit, and let loose. He didn't regret what he said or the shouting match that had ensued behind closed doors, with Mathews threatening to call his superior and him laughing in his face. No—what he regretted was that he'd allowed Sabrina out of his sight for the two minutes it took him to tell Mathews to shove it up his ass. He should've remembered that she had a habit of taking off when the situation at hand promised to be emotionally messy.

The light coat that had been on her chair was gone, which meant she'd left the building. Glancing at Strickland, he saw that he'd traded the files in his lap for his keyboard. He was peering at his computer screen, painfully pecking at the keys with an excruciating lack of skill or speed. "Where'd your partner go?" Michael said, yanking open one of her desk drawers to rifle through it. Not because he thought it would offer him any answers but because his messing it up would make her angry.

"Better not do that. She gets testy when assholes touch her stuff," Strickland said, glancing up from the screen with a frown. Sabrina's partner looked at him as if he'd known Michael was here all along, which went to show that no matter how impressive Michael found him, he continually underestimated the man.

Slamming the drawer shut, he went for another one, scattering colored paperclips and perfectly sharpened pencils everywhere. "Where'd she go?"

"Home. Spelunking. Around the world in eighty days. How should I know? She was here and now she's not," Strickland said, his tone gaining edge as he sat back from his computer to look at Michael.

"You just let her go?" he said, slamming yet another drawer.

"Let her? I'm sorry, are we talking about the same woman?" Strickland said, his voice thick with sarcasm. "No one *lets* her do anything. You of all people should know that."

Michael ignored Strickland's last comment. "If you see her, tell her I need to talk to her," he said, pulling a business card from his breast pocket. He flipped it at Strickland, who stared at him while it sailed over his desk and onto the floor next to his chair. Without even looking at it, Strickland turned back to his computer and resumed his hunt-and-peck routine. "Yeah, I'll be sure to do that for you. Have a good day," he said.

Clenching his jaw with enough force to make his teeth ache, Michael walked away before he did something he probably wouldn't regret.

He walked to the lot that housed officer parking. Her car was nowhere to be seen. She was in the wind, and he had no idea where she'd gone.

———

The boy was awake, although he was pretending not to be. Sabrina pulled up a chair and prepared to wait him out. If at all possible, he was even paler than she remembered, the dark shock of hair that fell across his forehead standing out in stark relief against the impossible white of his skin. She glanced at the tray of untouched food on the nearby overbed table. How long had it been since he ate?

The social worker was long gone. As horrific as the circumstances were, she was "doubtful that his case took any kind of precedence." There were children everywhere in need of social services. Sabrina assumed it went down as it always did—they came in, took a report, tried to ask the kid some general questions, and talked to the doctors about his condition. Not much they could do, really; he was the Russian Embassy's problem now.

A brief conversation with the charge nurse when she arrived told her that Ben had come and gone. The business card he left at the station was embossed with the insignia for the Russian Consulate. It looked official—just like the badge Michael had been flashing around the station earlier. A quick peek in the waiting room reassured her that Ben had taken precautions before he'd left. The Pip pretending to watch *Maury* barely glanced at her, but he knew she was there. His kind didn't miss much.

She glanced at her watch. It was just after three o'clock. How long did she think she could hide out here before she had to face Michael? Just the thought of him tied her stomach in knots.

The door pushed open, letting a young female nurse in with a soft *hiss* and *click*. "How's our boy?" she said, checking the level on the bag of fluid hanging from the pole.

"Playing possum." Sabrina watched as she made sure the leather restraint cuffs that kept him in bed were secure.

"Can't say I blame him. He's been through a lot," the nurse said, brushing hair off the boy's forehead. He flinched but managed to keep his eyes closed. "The doctor will be by in a few minutes to give you a full report."

The phone in Sabrina's pocket buzzed against her rib cage. She smiled the nurse out the door before she reached for it. "This is Vaughn."

"Hey, if it isn't my long-lost partner," Strickland said.

Sighing, she closed her eyes for a moment. She'd known this was coming. "Hey, Strick. What's up?"

"Oh, nothing much…just trying to solve this pesky murder." His voice had that nasty bite to it that set her teeth on edge. "Were you planning on coming out of hiding anytime soon, or am I gonna have to do it on my own?"

"I'm not hiding. I'm at the hospital; the boy's awake." She was still able to lie like a pro. Years of practice made sure of that.

"Uh huh…right." Strickland wasn't buying it. He never did. "He left about an hour ago, so it's safe to come back."

She didn't bother to ask who he was talking about. It would be an insult to her partner's intelligence. Of course he'd recognize Michael, there was no use denying it. "Was there a reason you called?"

"Actually, yes. The house our victim was found in was a fore-closed property. I traced the paperwork back to a local bank. It hit the auction block about six months ago and was bought by a shell company. Among their list of business expenses are quarterly trips to Thailand, Cambodia, and Colombia. It's a bit of a tangle, but I think I traced ownership back to a private investor. Walter Elm."

All of the countries he listed were well-known as sex tourism des-tinations, but the last one snagged her attention. "Colombia? When was the last time Elm went to Colombia?"

"Less than a month about. I'm heading to his office now. Wanna go?"

The *hiss* and *click* of the door told her that the promised doctor had arrived. "Yeah. Give me thirty to get back to the station. Look, the doctor is here. I'm gonna get the rundown from him and then I'm on my way."

Dropping the phone in her pocket, she looked up with a smile, but it died within seconds of realizing that, despite the white coat and stethoscope, the man in front of her wasn't in the habit of saving lives.

He was in the habit of taking them.

TWENTY-THREE

In spite of the nagging knot in the pit of his stomach, Michael forced himself through Sabrina's front gate and up the walk. He knocked on the door and waited, even though he knew she wasn't home. Her car was nowhere to be seen ... but there *was* a black Nissan Titan parked in the driveway like it belonged there.

He told himself it was perfectly reasonable for him to be here. He was on an assignment and Sabrina was a part of it. He had every right to establish that whoever was here was supposed to be. It was professional courtesy that had him standing on her front porch—nothing more.

He was full of shit.

The door opened and he suddenly felt like he was sucking wind. Devon Nickels stood in the doorway. His bare feet and rumpled hair told Michael more in two seconds than a long-winded explanation ever could. He was comfortable and relaxed. He was exactly where he should be. He was at home, and Michael was intruding.

Nickels stared at him for a moment before speaking. "You've got to be fucking kidding me."

"Where is she?" he said, trying his best to ignore the intense urge to grab the man in front of him and break his neck. The baby on Nickels's hip made it marginally easier to keep his hands to himself.

She let out a squeal, her chubby fingers curled around the collar of Nickels's navy blue SWAT T-shirt. A gold band glinted on the hand that anchored the baby to his side. She grinned, crinkling the corners of her whiskey-colored eyes. Michael tried not to look at her. Tried not to think about what she meant.

"Not here. I'll forget to tell her you stopped by." Nickels moved to shut the door, but Michael was faster. His hand shot out and gripped the doorframe. At the same time, he jammed his foot in its path. Nickels's expression went from annoyed to angry in the blink of an eye. "*Honey*," he shouted over his shoulder before turning his carefully guarded expression back in Michael's direction.

Sabrina's friend Valerie appeared a moment later, wiping her hands on a dish towel. "What is it?" She looked through the open door, her expression turning from puzzled to something more difficult to define. "Michael." She whispered his name a moment before she stepped through the doorway and wrapped her arms around him, resting her head on his shoulder.

He went stiff, looking at Nickels in hopes of finding some help, but there was none to be had. The cop watched the two of them, his expression softening slightly as he held on to the baby in his arms just a bit tighter.

It was suddenly clear but before he could comment, Val raised her face from his shoulder and looked at him. He envisioned her as she was the last time he'd seen her—small and naked, being dragged along a dirt path by a man who intended to kill them both.

"No scar?" she said, studying the side of his face where David Song had sliced him with a scalpel.

"No. I got lucky," he lied. It'd taken a few surgeries for FSS's plastic surgeon to repair the damage Song had done, but the result was worth it. It was as if his confrontation with the man who'd stalked and murdered three women before turning his attention toward Sabrina and Val had never happened.

Almost.

"I'm glad. You're way too pretty for a scar." She smiled at him, taking a step back. "Sabrina called a while ago. She's at the hospital, following up on a case she's working."

"Thanks," he said, lifting his gaze to look at Nickels for just a moment. "And congratulations. Both of you."

Val gave him another smile. "Thank you," she said, pulling the baby from Nickels's grasp and into her arms. "For everything." She turned and said something to her husband before disappearing back into the house.

TWENTY-FOUR

Cofre del Tesoro, Colombia
January 2009

MICHAEL LOOKED AT THE young woman sitting beside him. Lydia had taken her shoes off as soon as she sat down, her brown toes digging into the pale sand, face turned up to the sun. Just beyond them, Christina played tag with the waves, running after the water only to turn and scurry away from it the moment it returned, giggling all the while.

"You should smile more often."

He turned to find Lydia watching him. "If I did, people would know the truth."

"What?" Lydia said, grinning at him. "That you're human?"

He laughed, shaking his head. The girl had gotten bold in the months she'd been sneaking down to the beach to join them. Her initial fear had evaporated quickly, leaving an intensely curious nature.

There was nothing she wouldn't ask, and he'd found that there was little he felt uncomfortable telling her. "Yeah, something like that."

The laughter died between them, fading slowly until there was nothing by silence. "What *is* the truth, Michael? Why are you here?"

He looked away from her, watched Christina zigzag back and forth across the sand, her peals of laughter tinkling like bells. "There's nowhere else for me to go." He hadn't meant to say it, but once the truth escaped him, more followed. "I can't go home and what I was doing…"

"The killing." She said it softly, her face tipped down to catch his line of sight.

He finally turned to her, looked her in the eye. "Yeah. The killing… it was killing *me*." He nodded. "So instead, I let your husband pay me an obscene amount of money to play on the beach and read bedtime stories."

"Do you miss it?" she said, genuinely curious.

"Miss what?"

"Home," she whispered the word, transforming it into nothing more than a wistful sigh.

He thought of Frankie—the only home he had left. "Yes, I do. What about you, Lydia? Why are you here?"

She cut him a sidelong glance. "I live here."

He laughed in spite of himself. "Okay, smartass. Maybe what I mean is, *how* did you get here?"

She lifted her shoulder in a halfhearted shrug, her mouth quirking into a smile that did nothing to hide the tears that glittered in her eyes. "I don't know. This isn't where I'm supposed to be. I was very young when Alberto found me working in my father's coffee fields. He was charming. Said the right things. He was so polished. Even as nothing more than his cousin's gofer, you could see he wanted *more*. He paid my father three hundred dollars—before I knew what had happened, I was married and taken away."

"Your parents *sold* you?"

Her lips pursed, her dark eyes clouding just a bit. "Colombia is not like America. Here, choice is a luxury. Men like Alberto are not the kind of men you say no to."

He looked away. "I'm sorry."

"For what? None of this is your fault," she said. She looked at her daughter, now building one of her sandcastles a few yards away, and suddenly her smile became genuine. "Besides, without Alberto, there would be no Christina. For that alone, I have no regrets."

"Do you love him?"

She thought quietly for a long moment—so long that he was starting to regret asking—before she finally answered. "There was a time, in the beginning, when I hoped that I would learn to. But no, I don't. I can't," she said, looking up at him. "What about you? Was there ever someone special?"

Now it was his turn to think. "Yes."

Lydia drew her knees to her chest, hugging them tightly. "Tell me about her?"

Michael looked out across the ocean, seeing not the water but the small East Texas town he grew up in. "She was a few years younger than me. I didn't see her very often—usually when my parents dragged me to church or when I stopped into the diner where she worked. They had this video game—*Millipede*—I used to play it all day just so I could see her." He grinned in spite of himself. "I don't want to even think about the amount of money I wasted on that stupid game."

She smiled at the memory he'd shared with her as if it were her own. "You must have liked her very much."

His grin faded away, memories taking root. "I did, but she had a boyfriend and I was"—he struggled to find the right words for what he'd been back then—"not someone she took much notice of."

Lydia frowned. "Did you love her?"

It was the same question he'd posed to her only minutes before and it gave him pause, just as it did her. "I wanted to be good enough for her."

She gave him a look that said she understood full well that he'd managed to avoid answering the question. "Were you? Good enough for her?"

He shook his head. "I tried but could never quite manage it."

She gave him a sympathetic look. "Perhaps when you finally leave here, you can find her again."

He looked away, casting his gaze across the ocean. "She was murdered a few years after I joined the Army."

Her eyes went wide. "Oh … I'm sorry."

"Don't be. It happened a long time ago," he said, shutting the door between himself and a past he couldn't change, even though just thinking about it, what Melissa must have gone through, twisted his insides. He looked up, his gaze scanning the cliff line high above the island's private beach. In the distance, he spotted a lone figure standing at its edge. He couldn't tell who it was, but its sudden appearance tightened the skin along his nape. "It's getting late, you should head back."

She followed his gaze and caught sight of the figure just as it turned and moved out of sight. "Do you think—"

"Don't worry about it, just be careful, okay?" he said to her, forcing himself to ignore the niggle of apprehension that slid down his spine. It wasn't Alberto; he'd been away for weeks now and showed no signs of returning. His private helicopter was still sitting on its pad waiting to be called for a pick-up.

"Okay," she said as she stood. "Thank you for letting me see her." She thanked him, without fail, every single time they met on the beach, no matter how many times he told her that her gratitude was unnecessary.

"There's nothing to thank me for. She's your daughter, Lydia," he said.

"You're wrong, you know; you are more than good enough," she said before turning away, refusing him the chance to answer.

He watched her kneel down next to Christina and speak softly. The little girl looking up at her and nodded. She flung her shovel down and threw her arms around her mother's neck while Lydia pressed her lips to her cheeks and hair.

Finally she stood, giving him a small wave before disappearing into the trees.

TWENTY-FIVE

THE NAME *Dr. T. Patterson* was embroidered on the lapel of his white lab coat, but Sabrina would be willing to guess the real Dr. Patterson was dead in a janitor's closet somewhere. She couldn't pinpoint one exact reason she saw him for what he really was. Maybe it was the way his eyes slid around the room as if looking for potential threats. Maybe it was the way he stood, feet shoulder width apart in a defensive stance that spoke of years of combat training. Maybe. But she was pretty sure it had everything to do with the fact that the slight bulge on his hip told her he was strapped under that stolen coat.

Standing at the foot of the boy's bed, he pretended to read the chart, nodding his dark head as if he knew what he was looking at. He flipped the page and flashed her a glimpse of the back of his hand. A tattoo, some sort of gang tag. That clinched it.

The muscle in his jaw jerked and he gave her a quick glance. He knew he was made.

Shit.

The guy dropped his shoulders and reached for his waist, the chart clattering to the floor.

Sabrina stood, lunging over the bed to grab onto the tray of food, and flung it like a Frisbee. It flew the short distance, cracking him in the chin. He stumbled back, stunned. But it wouldn't last. Fisting her hand in the boy's hospital Johnny, she yanked, intent on pulling him out of bed and dragging him to safety before the bullets started flying.

The leather cuffs strapping him to the bed had other ideas.

Pulling her SIG off her hip, she took aim while her free hand flew to a set of straps and started to work. The boy was no longer pretending to sleep. His eyes were yanked wide, the blank stare replaced by one of stark terror. Twisting his wrist inside the cuff, he struggled against it. Something buzzed the back of her head, burning a path in her scalp seconds before she heard the *ssk* of the silenced round. No time.

Diving, she angled her body across the boy and returned fire. Blood burst across the white lab coat at his shoulder and side. Staggering back, the guy took aim again. *"No estoy solo, puta."*

She fired again, this time hitting center mass. His body jerked, the gun clattering to the floor. He fell back into the wall, leaving a trail of blood as he slid downward.

Wasting no time, Sabrina turned to free the boy. He'd managed to work himself loose and was jerking on the second set of restraints. As soon as the cuff was loose, she pulled him out of bed, shoving him into the space between the wall and the nightstand. "Stay," she said, hoping her tone would keep him in place.

Footsteps and shouts echoed down the hall.

No estoy solo, puta. I'm not alone, bitch.

People were coming. Among them would be someone looking to finish what his partner started. She reached across the bed and used the control panel to kill the florescent overheads. The only light now came through the window in the door. She looked down at the boy. He sat much as he had at the house after they found him. Knees pulled up to his chest, face no longer terrified. He looked blank—resigned to the violence he'd been plunged into.

Something warm and thick squirmed down her spine. She swiped at it with her free hand and brought up fingers that were sticky and dark—darker even than the gloom that surrounded them.

Blood. She'd been shot

"It's gonna be okay," she said, more to herself than him. There was a Pip in the waiting room. He'd have heard the shots, would secure the floor. Whoever was out there wouldn't get past him, but if he did…

She held her gun steady on the door and waited.

TWENTY-SIX

THE ELEVATOR OPENED ONTO chaos. Nurses and doctors running in every direction. Patients shouting. Alarms going off. Instinct pushed Michael's hand to his hip, had him lifting the Kimber .45 out of its holster. He stepped into the hall, gun held tight against his thigh. Something was wrong, but until he knew what, waving a gun around wasn't a good idea.

A nurse was cowering under the charge desk a few feet away. "What's going on?" he said, flashing her the borrowed badge on his hip to speed things along.

"Gunshots. Four of them."

Shit. Where was Sabrina? The boy—what was his name? "Alex. Alex Kotko. What room?"

The nurse pointed a shaky fingering. "Five-nineteen."

Turning in the direction she'd indicated, he brought the gun up. "Call the police." He walked swiftly, the barrel of his gun trained in front of him. The hallways had emptied and patients' doors were closed, some of them barricaded. He passed the waiting room. The flat screen on the wall showed the midday news to a deserted room.

Five-nineteen. He took a quick look through the small observation window in the door. The room was dark.

"Sabrina," he said loudly. No response.

He pulled the door open, light fell across the bed. It was empty. "Sabrina." He said it again as he stepped into the room. Finding the light switch, he flipped it on. She was standing on the other side of the bed, steady-handed, SIG aimed at his face.

She held the gun on him a second longer than necessary before dropping it to her side. "What took you so long, O'Shea?" Her voice trembled just a bit. The sound of if, the fact that she sounded glad to see him slammed his throat closed.

"Traffic," he said, letting his gaze slide to the man on the floor. The blood-soaked scrubs and lab coat said he was a doctor. The 9mm outfitted with a silencer on the floor next to him said he was something else entirely. Blank eyes, lids at half-mast, looked at the door as if he'd died while waiting for someone.

Michael nudged him roughly with the toe of his shoe before looking up at Sabrina. She was still watching the door. Before he could ask, she said, "He told me he's not alone. There's another one out there—"

"There's no one. I did a sweep."

Jamming her gun into the holster strapped to her hip, she turned and reached down to haul up the boy. "Then he's on his way." Blood matted the back of her hair.

Without thinking, he grabbed her, started running his hands over her arms and back. She tried to push him away, but he ignored her, kept probing. Lifting her hair off her neck, he revealed a thick trail of blood originating from her scalp. The deep furrow at the base of her skull wept red, the edges of it singed black by the heat of the bullet. He stalled out, felt his lungs go tight in his chest. Another half an inch would've killed her.

She pushed his hand away with a hissed, "I'm okay." She looked at the boy. "You have to take him. Get him out of here before more of them show up."

He almost laughed. "I'm not leaving you here."

"I can handle it, you have to go—we only have a couple of minutes. The Pip Ben left—"

"What? There's no one here." Alarm bells started clanging around in his head.

"Yeah, there is. Crew cut, dark suit, big as a house. I know a Pip when I see one." She angled her head to look out the window. "He was in the waiting room. I saw him when I got here."

The fact that she'd just described one of Shaw's rent-a-thugs to a T disturbed him on about a hundred different levels. "Sabrina, there's no one here," he said. Something was wrong. Very wrong. But he didn't have time to sort through what she was telling him—not right now.

Crouching, he turned toward the boy and spoke to him in Russian. The boy nodded. Michael reached for him and pulled him forward, led him over to the man slumped against the wall. He spoke again. Ben was right—his Russian was a bit rusty, but he got his point across just fine. The boy studied the dead man for a few seconds before he nodded, his answer carried on quavering tones.

"What are you saying?" Sabrina said.

"I'm asking him if he recognizes him."

"And?"

Dropping a hand on the boy's shoulder, he spoke to him quietly. The boy looked up at him and nodded again, his face a pale mask, tight with fear.

"He says this piece of shit is one of the men who sold him." He looked at her before continuing. "The only problem is that our dead friend here doesn't work for Reyes."

He expected her to ask him who Reyes was. She didn't. Further proof of just how deep she'd waded into this whole mess. "Then who does he work for?" she said, her eyes bouncing from the body on the floor between them to find him.

It was commonplace for those within cartels and other criminal organizations to brand themselves. Tattoos were used to tell others who you were: who you worked for, the rank you held. How many people you'd killed.

Michael studied the tattoo that covered the back of the man's hand. A Fleur-de-lis. He'd killed plenty of men with that same tattoo, and recently. Those alarm bells in his head got a little louder. "A man I killed thirty-six hours ago."

TWENTY-SEVEN

Within minutes, the place was swarming with cops—uniforms and suits—and Mathews had wasted no time in crawling up Sabrina's ass. Michael could hear him barking at her through her cell. Never mind that she'd defended a witness and taken out a cartel assassin. What Mathews was worried about was his own ass and how one of his inspectors turning a hospital into the O.K. Corral was going to make him look to the top brass.

He looked at the kid and wondered what the hell he was going to do with him. How he was going to keep him safe. Under normal circumstances, he'd take a witness to an FSS safe house and await instructions, but the last forty-five minutes had proved that this situation was anything but normal. Following protocol, Ben had left a Pip here to guard the Kotko boy, but Shaw's muscle was nowhere to be found once the bullets started flying. Either he'd abandoned his post … or he'd been following other orders.

He thought about the man Sabrina killed. One of Cordova's, which meant someone else was calling the shots, and the turf war that'd been brewing was far from over. And how did the Maddox boy figure in? By all accounts he'd been kidnapped on Reyes's orders. So why was it Cordova's man in a body bag and not—

"A bell. I'm putting a fucking bell around your neck, Vaughn."

Michael looked up to see Strickland standing in the doorway, a hard expression on his usually relaxed face. Sabrina mumbled something into the phone before dropping it into her pocket. "Hey, partner," she said.

Strickland ignored her, aiming a glare his way. "Surprised you're still here. Don't you usually take off after she gets shot?"

Gut clenched tight, Michael shifted his jaw around a few choice words but he kept them to himself. Strickland was right, and getting into a pissing contest with him wouldn't change that.

"Jesus Christ, it's a graze. I'm *fine*," Sabrina said in a heated rush, wrapping a hand around the back her neck. Looking up at him, she said, "We need to figure out our next move and we need to do it fast."

He nodded. Out in the open, the kid had a shelf-life of about five minutes. "I'll call Ben, have him meet me somewhere. I'll hand the kid off to him and then we'll meet up—"

"As usual, when he's around, I'm left wondering what the hell is going on," Strickland said, glaring over to his partner. "Explain."

Sabrina dropped her hand and looked down at the boy curled up on the floor next to the waiting room sofa. "I will, but not here." She reached down and held her hand out to the boy; he took it without hesitation. She helped him stand, pulled him to her, positioning her body between him and the door. "The FBI is placing our witness under protective custody and transporting him to the Russian Embassy for safe keeping. Mathews's orders," she said to her partner before finally looking at Michael. "Strickland and I are going to follow up on a lead. I'll call Ben if I find anything."

"You can't leave," Strickland said. "You just shot a guy, remember? You're gonna be stuck here for the next few hours. I'll call in surveillance on this Elm guy until we get everything sorted out. We can pick him up for questioning first thing tomorrow morning."

"No." Sabrina shook her head. "After what just happened, he needs to be picked up now."

Strickland looked confused. "Okay. Then I'll go—"

"Not without me you won't," she said and walked out the door.

———

Michael had no idea where he was going. He'd been driving around aimlessly for over an hour now, one eye on the rearview to ensure they weren't being followed.

They weren't. But that could change at any moment. Any number of people were gunning for him and the boy. Which meant he couldn't keep driving around forever, wasting time he didn't have. He was going to have to take a chance and reach out.

Using a clean prepaid cell, he dialed Ben's number.

"Is this Murphy's Pub?" he said as soon as the kid answered. It was a code they'd established a long time ago. One they'd never had to use until now.

Ben was quiet for a second. "Nope. Wrong number," he said before hanging up. Michael dropped the cell in the center console and waited. The wrong number was a signal that he was in trouble. Ben was supposed to ditch his phone and call him from a fresh one as soon as he could.

He took a look in the rearview, this time letting his gaze fall onto the kid. He sat in the back seat of the SUV, staring into middle space. He'd given no protest at being hustled out of the hospital by a total stranger. Seeing Sabrina shoot one of the men who abducted him must've done what hours of talking and persuading couldn't: he trusted them.

Which would more than likely end up getting him killed.

Michael shifted his gaze to the road behind them. Still no tail. But, then again, why bother with a tail? He was outfitted with a state-of-the-art tracking device. There was no need to put a physical tail on him when it was possible to track him via satellite. No need to send a platoon of Pips to gank his ass when all Shaw had to do was let his fingers do the walking.

He kept going over what had happened at the hospital. The disappearing Pip. Cordova's triggerman. What he'd said to Sabrina, that he wasn't alone. Something was going on. Michael's gut told him that whatever it was, Livingston Shaw was involved up to his chin.

No one at FSS could be trusted. Not even his partner.

TWENTY-EIGHT

SABRINA'S HEAD WAS KILLING her.

The dull throb of it melded perfectly with the stabbing pain she felt every time she moved—or spoke or fucking *breathed* too hard—but at least it'd stopped bleeding.

She explained everything while Strickland drove. He said nothing, didn't even seem to be listening, but she knew he heard every word she said.

Eventually she ran out of words and just sat there, waiting for her partner to come unglued on her. Silence filled the space between them for several long seconds before she finally snapped. "Say something," she said.

Strickland just laughed. "What am I supposed to say exactly? Kidnapped grandsons of US Senators. Colombian drug lords. Spanish hit men. It's all a bit above my pay grade, Vaughn."

She wished she could say the same. "Let's just focus on finding this Elm guy. Let O'Shea worry about the rest of it."

"Speaking of—we're here." Strickland squeezed his unmarked car into a compact space in front a brick building in the downtown area, not far from the station.

The small lobby was deserted, the security desk unmanned. Sabrina felt a tingle run along her arm until it settled into a faint itch in the center of her gun hand. Looking at Strickland, she could see he felt it too. Something wasn't right.

Finding the directory on the wall near the bank of elevators, they found a listing for Elm and took a car to the fifth floor. The doors slid open quietly onto a hallway just as deserted as the lobby. The stainless-steel sign across from the elevator was engraved with the words *Elm Properties & Lending.* They were in the right place.

Stepping into the hallway, the itch in her hand grew stronger. Three steps down the hall had her pulling her SIG off her hip. There was a man sprawled on the floor, half in and half out of what must've been his office. The brass plate on the door read *Cole Nielsen.*

Strickland crouched and felt for a pulse. Shaking his head, he rolled the man over to show her the clean, execution-style bullet hole drilled into the center of his forehead. The man was dead. Strickland scanned the floor and shook his head. "No brass," he said in a barely audible whisper. Sabrina swept her gaze across the room. No shell casings. This wasn't some disgruntled mail clerk who lost his marbles because he didn't get a raise. Whoever did this was a professional.

Without asking, Strickland called it in before giving her a questioning look: *Wait for backup?*

She shook her head. There was no time for that.

Together they cleared the hall. Each office they passed had another dead body, each murdered with a bullet to the head. When they reached the breakroom, things took a turn. A shattered coffee pot littered the floor, shards of glass floating in a pool of cool brown liquid. A quick sweep told her everything she needed to know. A coffee mug lay in pieces next to the door, more coffee ran down the wall to her right. Someone had caught the shooter off guard. Fought back.

"Let's move," she said quietly, sliding through the doorway, Strickland doing his best to get in front of her. Finally reaching the end of the hall, they found Elm's office. They discovered who she assumed was Elm's secretary, crammed under her desk, the damage of several bullets destroying her face. Looks like they found their fighter.

The door to the left of the desk was closed and they approached it silently, each of them pressed against opposite sides of the doorway. Strickland signaled that he would take point, and she shook her head no. He narrowed his eyes at her and before she could launch another protest, he turned the knob and flung the door open.

"SFPD! Show me your hands!" he called out. Sabrina hurled herself around the corner, SIG trained on the spot directly over Strickland's shoulder, at the man standing over who she was sure was a very dead Walter Elm. He stood facing them, face tipped down, but his sheer size was all she needed to see to recognize him. Hatred squeezed every part of her, tightening her finger around the trigger until she was sure it would fire.

"Drop the gun, Lark, or I drop you. Your choice. And please keep in mind that I'm sincerely hoping for the latter." The words were delivered in a calm cool tone at complete odds with the white-hot anger that scorched its way through her veins.

Lark looked up at her, his bald head tipping back until his eyes met hers. He smiled, his dimples popping out as the smile deepened into a grin. "Well, if it ain't the Lady Cop. Guess this means I'm livin' right."

She smirked. "Or it means it's gonna be my pleasure to punch your ticket and send you straight to hell. Put the gun down. Last time I'm gonna say it."

Lark chuckled and showed her his hands. The full-size 9mm he held looked like a child's toy, even with the benefit of the silencer-extended barrel. "This isn't what it looks like."

"Oh, that's a relief, because it looks like you systematically executed an entire building full of people," she said.

"This isn't my mess. I got here about thirty seconds before your partner stuck his gun in my face." As if to prove it, he stooped and laid the gun on the floor before straightening slowly. "I'm here with the Wonder Twins. Call O'Shea and ask him," he said, hands still raised to shoulder height. "On second thought, call Ben; O'Shea'd probably just tell you to kill me."

"Is it just my imagination, or do you know every asshole and dirtbag in existence, Vaughn?" Strickland said, his service weapon still trained on Lark's chest.

"It's not your imagination," she said under her breath, trying to figure out what to do next. Normally she'd cuff and frisk him, but that wasn't happening. Not with Lark. Getting within arm's length of him would be a huge mistake, but time was wasting. Backup was blocks away. She could hear sirens wailing in the distance, growing louder by the second. "Listen to me, Strickland. I'm lowering my weapon to make a phone call. If he so much as winks at you, start shooting and don't stop until your clip runs dry."

TWENTY-NINE

Michael hated cemeteries.

Some people saw the neat rows of headstones, heard the almost deafening silence of the dead, and felt at peace. Not him. All he saw were rows of loved ones who couldn't be saved, the silence that hung in the air heavy with questioning accusation. *Where were you when I needed you?*

"San Francisco National Cemetery. Plot eight-sixteen—thirty minutes," Ben said when he called back about an hour later. Eight-sixteen was marked with a headstone that simply read *Brother*, shaded by the widespread branches of an acacia tree. Michael made it there in fifteen and spent the rest of the time trying to piece what he knew together with what he'd learned.

Ben had followed protocol and stationed a Pip outside the Kotko boy's hospital room. Sabrina had seen him when she went in, but he'd been long gone once things got critical. If there was one thing Michael knew for sure, it was that Pips followed orders. Especially when it was Junior barking them out. They were soldiers in every sense of the word. Conditioned to carry out their mission, regardless of the cost. Nothing would've moved him from his post except one thing.

A direct order from someone with the last name Shaw.

A sudden shift in the air told him he was no longer alone. In one fluid motion, fueled by training and years of practice, Michael rounded the tree and drew his gun, pointing it without hesitation at the person approaching behind him.

"Just me," Ben said, his mouth quirked in a rueful smile.

"I know who it is," he answered back, keeping the barrel of his gun trained on his partner's forehead.

Ben took a few more steps before stopping, the smile on his face fading into an expressionless mask that gave away nothing. "What's going on, partner?" He held his hands out at his sides, palms face down in what looked like a submissive gesture.

Michael knew better.

"You tell me," Michael said. "Sabrina was just attacked at the hospital while sitting with the Kotko boy."

Ben's face changed again, this time showing something close to panic. "What? Is she okay? Where is she?" he said in a rush, his concern pushing him forward a few steps.

Michael saw the wide, angry furrow dug into her scalp, the thick trail of blood cooling against her nape. *Another half-inch and she'd be dead.* He tightened his grip on the butt of his Kimber, the hinge of his jaw so tight it almost snapped when he opened his mouth. "I've got a better question. Where were you?"

"I was at the morgue getting a DNA sample from the boy Sabrina found. We need an ID, and police channels will take time we don't have."

He'd almost forgotten about the dead boy—the real reason they were here. "The guard you put outside the Kotko boy's room was long gone when I got there. That's a bit weird, don't you think, considering he'd been ordered there by you?"

Ben started to shake his head, opened his mouth to protest, but the words died in his throat. He closed his mouth and then opened it again. "My father."

"Or you."

"You think I'm involved somehow." It wasn't a question, it sounded more like an accusation.

"Your father is in on the Maddox boy's kidnapping, that much I'm sure of. I find it highly doubtful that he'd make such a bold move without including his heir apparent," he said, his words making perfect sense, but Ben just laughed.

"Are you serious?" Ben said.

"Very."

Ben brought his hands up slowly, palms out, until they were raised shoulder high. "Do you see the scar in the middle of my left hand?"

Michael nodded. It was huge, encompassing almost his entire palm, rendering it nothing more than a thick pad of shiny white scar tissue. He'd noticed it before but never asked what'd happened. He'd assumed that it'd been about an op gone bad. They all had their fair share of battle scars.

Ben continued. "You asked me about my brother and his wife. What happened to them. Why I was so angry with my father." He stopped for a moment, chewed on his words before forcing them out. "Mason was my older brother. *He* was the heir. Our father's pride and joy. Trained from the cradle to take the reins at FSS when the time came. Me? I was the spare. Pretty much ignored my whole life, and that was just fine by me. I had no interest in my father's company. Truthfully, I didn't even know what he *did* exactly, and I didn't care. I went to college, graduated, and started a life far, far away from both of them. A few years ago, probably the same time you were slittin' throats for Reyes, Mason got married. He and his wife were kidnapped four days into their honeymoon." He stopped for a moment, took a deep breath and let it out slowly. "My father gets a call. *Do what we say and your son will live.* He told them to get fucked. Just like that. He signed his own son's death warrant and still had time for nine holes of golf."

"Your hand?" Michael said, intrigued as much by the story as he was by the unprecedented level of rage that telling it had ignited in the man in front of him.

"The people holding Mason approached me, made it clear that it was up to me to convince my father to listen to reason. I went to him, begged him to do what they wanted," Ben said. "He called me a gutless coward and refused." He smiled, but it faded quickly. "I told him if he wouldn't do what needed to be done to get them back, I would, and he laughed at me. What could I do? I had no training. I'd never even held a gun in my life." Another smile coasted across his face. "He must've seen how serious I was because he stopped laughing and forbade me to go. I called him a miserable son of a bitch and walked out. He called in his goon squad and had them stop me at the elevator. It took some doing, but they finally got me down. And then, on my father's orders, one of them blew a hole in the back of my hand. I was laid up in the infirmary for months. Nearly a dozen reconstructive surgeries so I could eventually use this hand again. All the while, they mailed my brother back to me in pieces.

"I don't doubt my father is involved in what's happened to the Maddox boy. He cares for no one beyond what they represent in terms of profit and loss—his own sons included," Ben said. "But I had nothing to do with it."

Michael hesitated for just a moment before holstering his gun. He'd seen that look before. Ben hated his father, blamed him for the death of his brother—but he blamed himself just as much, if not more, because he hadn't been able to stop what he knew had been coming.

"It wasn't Reyes's man at the hospital. It was Cordova's," he said, letting his partner in as a way of clearing the air. "I don't know what the hell is going on, but someone seized Cordova's interests and they're in it to win it."

"But she's okay. Sabrina's okay?" Ben said, dropping his hands, shoulders still a bit tense.

"For now. But that won't last long. The Russian kid recognized the guy she dropped as one of walking shit stains that snatched him." He shook his head. "This whole mess is getting twisted. We need to figure out who we've got in the game and what team they're playin' for, because—"

Ben's phone let out a chirp. "It's Sabrina," he said before putting the phone up to his ear. "Hey, are you alright?" Ben turned away from Michael, the rest of the conversation carried out in hushed tones that raised his hackles.

Michael glanced down at the marble stone stretched across the grass. Watched the gentle sway of the acacia's shadow branches dance along its surface.

Brother.

He suddenly understood. This is where Ben laid what had been left of his brother to rest. He looked up to see Ben snap his phone closed.

"We gotta go." Ben said, moving swiftly toward the Land Rover. "Sabrina found Lark standing over the dead body of the lead she was running down. She's holding him at gunpoint, but we both know that's not gonna last long."

THIRTY

THEY PARKED ACROSS THE street from the address Sabrina'd rattled off to Ben and watched the parade of navy-clad unis streaming in and out of the brick building that housed Robert Elm's offices.

They'd made plans on the drive over—what to do about Lark, how best to handle Sabrina. Neither one of them wanted her involved, but they were past that now.

She appeared across the street, marching a trussed-up Lark out the door, her SIG stowed snuggly in his ear. Strickland was a few steps behind.

"You're up. I'll take the boy; you go get our little runaway," Ben said. "Meet me back at the house."

Michael exited the car without saying a word and crossed the street, walking toward her. When Lark saw him, he smiled but stayed quiet. Sabrina had him double cuffed, two pairs strung together to accommodate his massive frame, as well as a pair of waist chains. A third set of cuffs locked his wrists to the chains wrapped around his

.

middle. There was an enormous lump just above his left temple, oozing blood. She used the gun in his ear to push him forward.

"Your prisoner, Agent Payne," she said for the benefit of anyone who might be watching the exchange.

He opened the rear door of her unmarked and shoved Lark into the back of it. "I'd appreciate help transferring him back to my field office, Inspector," he said, securing Lark's seat belt and locking it in place before sliding into the passenger seat.

She stood on the sidewalk, looking at him for a moment before turning toward her partner. She spoke in low tones he couldn't make out, but whatever she said pissed Strickland off.

"This is *bullshit.*" Strickland leaned down and pushed his face through the open car window, within inches of his, looking directly at him. "You could probably kill me with a fuckin' toothpick—I know that. But if you think for one goddamn second that I'm gonna let—"

Sabrina hauled him back. "Shut up. Shut your mouth right now, Strickland." She looked around to ensure that no one was listening. "I have to do this. Do you understand what I'm saying? I don't have a choice. I'm in this—"

"Then so am I." Strickland said it like it was the simplest thing in the world ... and for him it probably was. He had no idea what he was buying into; but Sabrina did. Michael could see fear for her partner written plainly on her face.

"Sorry, partner. Like you said, it's a bit above your pay grade," she said before rounding the front of the car and yanking the door open. She slid behind the wheel and started the engine.

"How'd you get him cuffed?"

She shrugged. "He cuffed himself. And then I knocked him out with a fifty-pound paperweight off Elm's desk."

"Pussy move," Lark said from the back seat, the laughter in his voice barely suppressed. "What's the matter, Lady Cop? Does the big black man scare you?"

Sabrina said nothing. Instead she slammed on the brakes, sending Lark's enormous body flying forward, choking him against the shoulder strap of his seat belt.

She accelerated again, relieving the pressure the belt put on Lark's throat. A thin ribbon of blood welled against his mocha-colored skin, but he just chuckled. "How 'bout you pull over, sweetheart, and cut me loose. These cuffs are starting to chafe."

"How about you shut up," Sabrina said.

Michael looked out the window, waiting for the landscape to change from busy downtown to desolate waterfront before speaking. "Pull over."

"What?" She shot him a look. "Seriously?"

"Yeah, seriously. Pull over. Now." He turned in his seat and glared at the man in the back seat. He waited for Sabrina to kill the engine before he spoke again. "Did you kill Elm?"

Lark sighed. "No. Like I told your girlfriend, I found him and the rest of them like that about thirty seconds before her numbnuts partner told me to reach for the sky."

"Then who?" The possibilities were endless. Reyes. Shaw. Whoever managed to gain control of Cordova's interests.

"Hell if I know. I forgot to pack my crystal ball," Lark shot back, but he was lying. Michael could feel it.

"How did you know about him?" he said.

"Elm?" Lark shrugged. "You and the little prince got me holed up drinking tea and eating fucking crumpets with Old Mother Hubbard. I got bored," he said.

"Yes. But that doesn't tell me *how* you knew about him, does it?" He smiled. "Where did you get your information, asshole?"

"I got a computer. Information comes to me." Lark smiled back for a moment before shifting his gaze toward Sabrina. "Like how those kids you pretend are yours started UC San Diego in August. The boy—what's his name, Jason? He's got a full ride baseball scholarship, and the girl lives off campus with a few girlfriends." He flashed her his dimples. "She's pretty."

Sabrina sat frozen in her seat for a few seconds, galvanized by the words he threw at her. Suddenly she dove at him, and Michael let her. She rammed her fist into Lark's face once, twice, three times—his head snapped back on his thick neck with each jab. She cocked back for a fourth, but Michael stopped her.

"Enough." He caught her fist and held it. Rage stained her cheeks a deep ugly red and she jerked her hand back, glaring at him. He dropped his hand to reach into his breast pocket, pulling out a small metal box. Opening it, he removed one of three stainless-steel pellets, the size and shape of a pencil eraser. "Can you hold your gun on him without shooting him?"

"Probably not." She lifted her SIG off her hip and pointed it at Lark's face. "But what the hell—let's find out."

Lark grinned through the blood that trickled from his nose. "Pull it, sweetheart. I dare you."

Michael showed him what he held in his hand. "Hey, asshole, you might want to focus. Things are about to get *real* interesting for you."

Lark's shit-eating grin disintegrated the second his gaze touched what he held in his hand. "You don't have authorization for that," he said.

"No, but my partner does." He rolled the object between his thumb and index finger. "A gift from him … and I'm giving it to you. Open your mouth."

Lark stared at him, shook his head in disbelief. "After everything I've done for you, you'd do this to me?"

"Looks like. Sabrina?" he said and was rewarded by the sound of her racking a bullet into the chamber of her SIG. "Open. Your. Mouth."

Lark hesitated, but one look at Sabrina had him following orders. Michael tossed the metal pellet into Lark's mouth, toward the back of his throat. Lunging forward, he reached across the seat to slap his hand across Lark's face, covering his mouth and nose, while using the other to anchor his head in place.

"Swallow it."

Lark thrashed against the back seat, trying to jerk his face out of his grasp, but it was no use. It was a thirty-second ride at best before Lark gave up trying to shake him loose. Instead he sat quietly, glaring at him in stubborn defiance. Nearly four minutes passed before he felt Lark's throat begin to work in an involuntary response to the lack of oxygen. He'd always been able to hold his breath. But he couldn't hold it forever.

Finally he swallowed the pellet, the hard knot of it moving down his throat. Michael unlocked his hands from around Lark's face and sat back in his seat. "Show me."

Defeated, Lark opened his mouth and lifted his tongue. His mouth was empty. "Congratulations, motherfucker. It's done. Satisfied?"

"Not by a long shot." He turned in his seat and stared out the window. "You can put the gun down now and drive."

Sabrina dropped the gun onto the seat before starting the car. She let it idle for a moment and just watched him until he could practically feel the heat of her stare burn the side of his face. Finally she spoke. "What did you just do?"

Laughter, nasty and cold, welled up in his throat, and he let it out in one harsh bark. "What I always do: what needed to be done."

THIRTY-ONE

Sabrina pulled into Miss Ettie's driveway, following it all the way to the detached garage before she killed the engine. "You gonna tell me what that thing you made him swallow is?"

That thing was a weaponized ricin capsule, rigged to detonate much like the one attached to his spine. People tended to do what you asked of them when they realized that there was a dirty bomb free-floating in their system, just waiting to kill them.

Technology was a wonderful thing.

"An insurance policy. A way to ensure he does what he's told," Michael said.

Gaining control of Lark was key, since he was Shaw's eyes and ears. He wasn't here to keep Michael in line as far as Sabrina went; he was here to stall and manipulate their investigation into Leo Maddox's abduction. To throw salt on their game if they got too close to the truth.

Time to return the favor.

"That tells me nothing, O'Shea." She removed the keys from the ignition and clenched them in her fist.

"It's a less permanent version of what Shaw had planted inside me." He glanced at Lark in the rearview. "And it's how we're going to make sure he plays by the rules. Our rules."

"Will it kill him?" she said, sounding a bit hopeful.

He shrugged. "Each pellet is charged with a low-level electromagnetic pulse that's drawn to the iron in your blood. The magnetic reaction causes it to adhere to the stomach lining, making it impossible to regurgitate. The charge should wear off in a few days and it'll pass through his system in about a week—provided he doesn't do anything stupid." *Like piss me off.* He opened his door and stepped onto the curb before yanking the back door open. He lifted his Kimber off his hip and held it casually at his side. "I'm gonna unbuckle your seat belt. If you try to go all Mike Tyson on me, I'm gonna shoot you."

"I could've killed her, you know," Lark said, his tone quiet. "Back at that office. I could've killed her and her partner both. But I didn't." Before he could respond, Lark moved his glare to Sabrina. "Do you see what you've done to him? How fucked up he is over you? If you care at all about—"

Michael unsnapped the seat belt and hauled Lark out of the car. He slammed him against the rear fender and buried the barrel of his Kimber so deep in the soft underside of Lark's chin that the tip of it disappeared.

"Shhh—stop talking." He cocked the hammer back, the *clack* of it resounded in the quiet. "Here's how it's gonna go. You're gonna shut up, because the next time you speak to her, I'm going to take this gun, jam it down your throat, and pull the trigger. Nod if you understand, asshole."

Lark jerked his head back on his neck, his jaw pulsing with pent-up anger.

Michael grinned. "Glad we had this little chat. I feel much better." He reholstered his weapon and spun Lark around to work his cuffs open. "It goes without saying that it's best for you to tread lightly. Follow directions and keep your mouth shut and this should all end reasonably well for you."

That was a lie and Lark probably knew it—he'd never been stupid. He was screwed either way. If he helped Shaw, Michael was prepared to pull the pin on the mini-grenade he'd just tossed down his gullet. But if Shaw found out that his prize pet was a turncoat, he'd kill him without even blinking.

He hadn't so much ensured Lark's cooperation as leveled the playing field. In the end it came down to who Lark was more loyal to: him or Livingston Shaw.

Michael spun Lark back around and stepped away while the other man rubbed the red welts the cuffs had raised on his wrists. His expression was flat, but his eyes told a different story.

Looking at him, Michael didn't like their odds of coming out on top. He didn't like them at all.

THIRTY-TWO

BEN GREETED THEM AT the door. "Is it done?"

Michael nodded. "Yeah," he said, tossing the kid the box containing the rest of the ricin capsules. *For all the good it's going to do.*

Ben tossed them back. "Keep 'em."

Michael caught the box and dropped it into his pocket. He thought about what he'd just done. About how it made him no better than Livingston Shaw.

Lark was equally yoked now, but he couldn't serve two masters. Michael had little advantage over Shaw. Nothing really, except the fact that he and Lark had been close once. He knew Lark better than anyone. Even so, it was going to take some doing to convince his former friend to help them.

Sabrina brushed past him before shutting the door. Her face changed when she saw Ben. Went soft, giving the kid one of those smiles of hers that felt like a sucker punch. He looked away, feeling like he was intruding on something private. Like he wanted to disrupt whatever was going on between them. He had no right to be angry. He'd left her—more than once—and if he was being completely honest with himself, up until twenty-four hours ago, he'd had no intention of ever coming back.

Ben reached out, brushed her hair off the back of her neck to assess the damage done to her head. And she let him.

"You should've had it stitched up." His hand stayed where it was, cupping her nape, his thumb sweeping down the column of her neck, from earlobe to collarbone. Michael had a sudden memory of touching her in that exact same spot. Having her pushed against the kitchen door no more than a few feet from where he stood now, his other hand working at the buttons of her cargos. Fingertips sliding beneath the elastic waistband of her panties. Fifteen months and he could still feel her skin felt against his. How good she'd tasted when she'd opened her mouth against his.

For the first time in longer than he could remember, he wanted a drink. Bad.

"Just a scratch. I barely know it's there," Sabrina said, her lips quirked in another smile.

Ben looked at her for a moment, his eyes searching her face. "Liar." He dropped his hand and took a step back, as if suddenly aware that they had an audience.

"Well, well, well …" Lark said beside him, cutting Michael a shitty grin.

Michael hands curled into fists inside the pockets of his slacks. All plans of sweet-talking Lark flew out the window. He returned the grin with one of his own. "I've got two capsules left. You still hungry?"

Lark chuckled. "You have a pretty funny way of trying to convince me to help you, O'Shea," he said before taking a seat at the kitchen table. "Making me your bitch. Threatening to kill me every five minutes." Lark shrugged. "You coulda just asked."

Michael folded his arms over his chest, nailing the man across from him with a hard look. "Last time I did that, you turned around and bit me. From now on, you get the muzzle."

"No way to treat a friend," Lark said quietly.

"We aren't friends."

The corners of Lark's mouth turned up in a semblance of a brief smile. "If that's true, then what makes you think I'm gonna help you? I'm a dead man either way."

He was aware that Ben and Sabrina were watching the exchange, knew he'd fucked things up with his mouth and not being able to control it. Whatever. It was never going to work anyway. Lark was never one for pretty words. "You're gonna help because no matter what kind of heartless bastard you might be, you pay your debts."

"Debt?" Lark laughed out loud. "Please. I don't owe you shit."

"No. But you owe her." Michael tossed his head at where Sabrina still stood next to Ben. "And you know it. That's why you didn't kill her when you had the chance. Because what you took from her, you know you'll never be able to give back."

Lark's face hardened, his eyes going flat again. "What makes you think I give a shit about some old lady?"

He was talking about Lucy—Sabrina's grandmother. The weight of the way she'd died, knowing that his trust in Lark was what got her killed, settled in Michael's gut like a rock. "I'm pretty sure you don't. What you care about is keeping your ledger clear." A smile touched his mouth, and the tingle of it almost hurt. "You never liked being in the red."

"I help you, Shaw kills me," Lark said, his face twisted into a look of disbelief. "What the fuck I care about some make-believe debt?"

"So? You *don't* help, you're gonna die anyway. At least this way, you'll die with a clean slate," Michael said. Whether he wanted to admit it or not, things like that mattered to Lark. It was his way of balancing out the shit they did, like dropping a few pennies in a charity jar helped alleviate the guilt of sin. No matter what you've done, you convince yourself those pennies make up for it.

The lies people told themselves.

Lark looked past Michael to where Sabrina stood. "I'm not gonna sit here and say I lose sleep over what happened. I did what I did—and I'd probably do it again. I take the shortest route from point A to point B and never think much about what gets destroyed between the two. But getting your grandmother killed was never the goal."

Michael could practically feel Sabrina vibrating, whether it was with rage or grief, he didn't know. Probably both. He wanted to shut Lark up. To stand and put his arms around her. Hold her. Shield her from the flood of emotion he knew was swallowing her whole.

He did neither. Had no right to.

"I don't forgive you, but if helping us makes it easier to fool yourself into believing that you're a decent person, then knock yourself out," Sabrina said.

Lark began to speak, but he was cut off by Ben's cell.

"Yeah? You got it?" Michael heard the kid say behind him. "Are you sure?" He made a few noises in the back of his throat before flipping his phone closed and moving into view.

"That was my lab rat," Ben said, looking directly at Sabrina. "The DNA off the kid you found came in. It's not Leo Maddox."

THIRTY-THREE

Cofre del Tesoro, Colombia
August 2009

CHRISTINA POKED HER BOTTOM lip out and stared at the floor outside her father's office.

"I don't want to go in there," she said quietly, her fingers twisting and burrowing themselves into the pink chiffon of her skirt. "And I don't want to wear this dress." She looked up at him, her dark eyes flooded with unshed tears. She was six and a half now and no longer wished to be her father's doll.

Michael crouched in front of her and she looked down at her feet. This went beyond a simple tantrum. Something was going on. "What's this about, Christina?" He unwound her fingers from her dress and held them. Christina just shrugged. He tucked his chin into his chest in order to catch her eye. "Are you worried we'll miss the beach?" He left the rest unsaid. It was Sunday. The one day Lydia managed to sneak away and join them for a few hours.

"No—"

"Because I promised—"

"I know ... you keep your promises. It's not about that." She looked up at him, chewing on her lip. "I don't like him," she said in a quiet rush.

That makes two of us. He let go of her hands and rocked back on his heels. "He's your father."

"I don't want him to be." She shook her head vigorously, and a curl escaped from the ruthlessly tight ponytail her maid had wrangled her hair into. It bounced and bobbed against her temple. "Not anymore."

He reached for her again, this time grabbing her by her arm, pulling her a step or two closer. "What happened? Did he hurt you?"

Christina shook her head. "No. Not me."

"What?" he said even though he knew exactly what she was talking about.

"My mama. He hit her. I saw him do it. This morning she was sitting in the garden and he found her. Yelled at her," she said in a whisper, every other word getting hitched on a shaky breath. "She started to cry, and he hit her in the face."

"Did you hear what he was saying to her?" he said as calmly as possible. Reyes always left his bruises behind closed doors. Never in the open and never in front of his daughter. Something had happened to provoke him.

Christina nodded her head, looking scared. "He called her bad names and said that if she didn't follow his rules he would ... " Her eyes flooded with tears, her tiny fingers working the chiffon of her skirt into shredded knots. "He said he would kill her."

Michael was suddenly sure Reyes knew he'd allowed Lydia to visit Christina unsupervised. Looking down at the little girl, something close to panic settled into his bones. He could leave. Just pack his shit and walk out

But he wouldn't. And Reyes knew it.

"Christina, listen to me—"

She shook her head. "I hate him. Why can't you be—"

His heart did a quick flip-flop in his chest. "Don't. Don't say it." He looked around to make sure no guards or servants were lurking. Listening. He took her by the arm and pulled her a bit closer. "I'm not the kind of guy any kid should be wishing was her father, so . . . "Michael stood, shoving the carefully wrapped box into her hand and stood. "Go give your father his gift and wish him a happy birthday so we can go to the beach." He said it roughly, took a step back, and shoved his hands into his pockets to keep from pulling her away from the door.

Tears spilled over her bottom lids and she swiped at them as if they annoyed her. Turning toward the door, she wiped her face again before giving it a soft rap with her knuckles. They waited only seconds for the door to open, finding Reyes on the other side, a young man standing beside him.

"Happy birthday, Papa," Christina said. Michael knew she was smiling, but the lift of her mouth didn't quite ease the rigid set of her shoulders. If Reyes noticed, he said nothing. He gave her a smile, placing his hand on the young man's shoulder.

"I was sure you'd be at the beach by now, Christina." Reyes looked up and over the girl's head and found Michael's gaze. "I know how much you like to build sandcastles." The last was said directly to him. The kid next to Reyes made a disgusted sound in the back of his throat and gave him a look to match.

Michael's fists balled in the front pocket of his jeans and he stared back until the kid looked away. Reyes, who'd caught the split-second exchange, laughed. "Don't be fooled into thinking he's gone soft, Estefan. He may have developed a taste for sandcastles and tea parties, but Michael is a killer. He would slit your throat in the space of a few seconds without even thinking about it—isn't that right, *Cartero*?"

Christina looked at him over her shoulder, but Michael stared straight ahead, refusing to look at the little girl in front of him.

His gaze settled on the boy again. This time he noticed the tat that stretched from his nape to his collarbone. It was new—the black ink puffy and edged in red. A scorpion, pincers raised, tail curled against his neck, poised to strike.

"Nice brand," he said, and the kid visibly stiffened at the barely veiled insult.

"I wear it proudly." Estefan tipped his chin at a defiant angle before looking at Reyes. "My father is a great man."

Father? Michael shot a look at Reyes, who just smiled without acknowledging the boy's claim. He looked to be in his early twenties—at least fifteen years older than Christina. If Reyes was his father, he'd been young when this kid had been born.

"Now that you two have met, I'd like to ask you a small favor, *Cartero*," Reyes said, his words instantly stiffening the back of Michael's neck.

"Not sure I have time for a favor—my schedule's pretty packed, what with all my sandcastles and tea parties," he replied, doing his level best to keep his voice light and casual. He had a feeling that whatever it was that Reyes wanted from him, it was something he wouldn't want to give.

Reyes smiled, trying to hide his reaction to the veiled refusal. "I'm sure you can make time for this. It's time Estefan received training, and I'd like you to be the one to teach him."

Michael cocked his head, letting his gaze travel the length of the boy beside Reyes. Teaching this kid to use a knife would be a mistake. "Combat training? Are you serious?"

"Think of it as self-defense. I was thinking a few hours in the evenings to start—after your sandcastles and tea parties," Reyes said to him before looking down at Christina. "Someday it will be Estefan's job to look after her." He looked up again; this time his gaze was as sharp as a blade. "You won't be here forever, *Cartero*."

Christina's hand found Michael's, her small fingers curled around his own, and she squeezed.

She turned to her father and thrust the package into his hands. "Happy birthday," she said again before turning to pull Michael down the hall. He could feel Reyes's eyes drilling into his back.

She was quiet for a moment, kept walking down the long stretch of hall between her father's study and the foyer. Finally she looked at him. "Mama's not coming today, is she?"

His first instinct was to lie, but in the end he simply shook his head. "I don't think so."

"Is he going to kill her?" She sounded different. He didn't want to look at her, suddenly sure it was an old woman standing next to him and not the little girl he knew.

He swallowed hard, the lump in throat making it difficult for him to breath. He shook his head again, looking down at her. "No."

She squeezed his hand, gazing up at him with eyes that seemed to have seen and understood more than could possibly fit into the tiny span of her lifetime. "Do you promise?"

He looked away. "I promise."

THIRTY-FOUR

THE DEAD BOY WASN'T Leo Maddox.

Michael wasn't surprised. Leon Maddox's only grandson was a valuable commodity, one that wouldn't be squandered or sold into the hands of a pervert—at least not until he'd served his purpose.

The Maddox boy had been granted a stay of execution, not a pardon. No one understood the concept of living on borrowed time better than he did.

He looked at Sabrina and felt the familiar knot growing in the pit of his stomach that took root whenever he was close enough to touch her. Those roots grew deep, seeming to wrap around his spine. Digging cold fingers into the capsule that hugged it, reminding him that he'd never be allowed to have what he wanted.

Miss Ettie set a fine-bone China cup in front of him. She'd come out of nowhere, Alex Kotko trailing behind her in baggy sweatpants and a T-shirt with a picture of a cat on it, and got busy pouring coffee while the boy wedged himself under the table.

Michael looked up at the old woman and forced himself to smile. "Thanks."

She didn't say anything, just patted his shoulder and gave him an odd look that was half smile, half frown. Like she could read his mind and felt sorry for him. He dropped his gaze to the boy on the floor, back slammed against the side of Sabrina's chair. On impulse, he lifted a stack of cookies from the plate Miss Ettie placed on the table and held them down at his side. The kid swiped them out of his hand and started shoving them into his mouth, two at a time. Michael smiled for a moment, but it died quickly, memories he'd thought long dead pushing in around him.

He dropped his now empty hand on the table and slouched in his chair, waiting for Miss Ettie to leave the room before speaking. "You in or out, Lark?"

Lark looked him straight in the eye. "In."

"Good. Now you can prove it by telling us what the hell kind of deal Shaw's got going with Reyes," Michael said.

Lark just laughed. "You think I know?" He flicked a glare across the table to where Ben had taken a seat. "I'm not the boss's kid; I'm his dog. I get to know precisely what I need to in order to get the job done. Not one syllable more."

"Alright. What was your assignment here?" Michael said.

"Report back to Shaw if you got close to finding the Maddox kid. Let him know if you got a bead on Reyes."

It was probably true, but it wasn't the *whole* truth. "Is that it?"

Lark cut him a humorless grin. "You know how it is."

Michael nodded, understanding perfectly—Lark was here to kill him. Nothing he didn't know already, but having it confirmed wiped out any residual guilt he might've been feeling about throwing that capsule down Lark's throat. Ironically, the capsule and the help from Lark it ensured were the only things stopping him from reaching across the table and snapping Lark's neck. For now, trying to kill each other would have to wait.

"What were you doing at Elm's office this afternoon?" Sabrina said.

Lark hesitated, seeming to be choosing his words carefully. "Shit went down—and not like it was supposed to."

So things had gotten messy and he'd been called in to clean up. Too bad for him that Sabrina and her partner had gotten in the way.

"Who ordered the hit on Elm?" Michael said, but he already knew the answer, even if Lark didn't.

Lark shrugged. "Either Reyes or Shaw. Take your pick."

His money was on Reyes. Shaw had nothing to gain by Elm's death.

"So who'd the shooter belong to?" Ben said.

Lark shook his head. "I never saw 'em, but I'd put my money on Team Reyes. Pips don't usually get down like that."

Michael leaned forward. "Like what?"

Lark didn't answer him. Instead, he looked at Sabrina. "You saw Elm's secretary. That shit wasn't necessary."

Sabrina nodded. "Every kill in the building was totally methodical. One bullet, head shot at close range. We found a mess in the breakroom, like someone put up a fight—my guess is Elm's secretary. I'll have the ME scrape her nails for trace. Maybe she got a chunk of him. We might get lucky with an ID," she said.

"Whoever it is will come back as a known associate of Alberto Reyes. The hit on Elm was a mop-job. The rest of them were just collateral damage." Michael looked down at the boy again. He was practically catatonic. The Reyes he knew wouldn't waste the price of a bullet, let alone the manpower it took to track down and kill one

150

small boy. But it'd been Cordova's men at the hospital, not Reyes's. Which meant whatever Alex Kotko knew, whoever he was, he was valuable—not only to Reyes, but also to his enemies.

Michael took a few seconds, weighing the boy's importance against that of Leo Maddox. He calculated the odds of getting them both out alive and measured them against his need to complete the mission. He glanced up and found Sabrina watching him. She knew what he was doing—considering a trade—and she'd shoot him before letting him apply the most logical solution.

He looked away from her, told himself that he averted his eyes because he found her almost obsessive need to save everyone annoying—not because the wary expression on her face was one she'd give an untrustworthy stranger.

"*Shooters,*" Lark said out of nowhere. "Plural. As in there were two of them."

"What?" Ben said in a bored tone that was at total odds with the interest that sharpened his gaze.

"Robert Elm wasn't shot at close range." He shot a glance at Sabrina and cracked a smile. "Don't sweat it, sweetheart, it was an easy miss. You had your hands full with trying to figure out a way to bash my skull in with an ashtray—no way you or your partner'd notice something like that," he said to her before turning his attention back to Ben. "It was a long-distant, lateral shot." Lark reached out and jabbed a finger at Ben's forehead, drilling him in the center of it. "There was no stippling around the entrance wound. Clean, high-powered round. Only place to make a shot like that is damn near a mile from the crime scene." Lark shifted around in his seat and spoke to Michael directly. "I clocked it on the way here, while you and Lady Cop were busy getting reacquainted."

Michael studied his former friend. Every twitch and tic. He'd always been able to tell when he was lying, and Brian Lark was telling the truth.

"You're the only person I know that's ever been on Reyes's payroll with those kinds of skills." Lark said to him. "Shit, only a handful of you in Shaw's stable, for that matter."

So who made the shot?

He had a sudden flash. The scarf girl, Eliza—the bright red stain on her forehead. The spray of blood across the cool white tablecloth. All she'd wanted was her little brother back. She'd been desperate and stupid. And about to tell him something he wasn't supposed to know.

"Who is it?" he said quietly, his words a blanketing weight, suppressing every other sound. "Who'd Shaw send to clean up Reyes's mess?" But he already knew.

Lark was right—there weren't many of his kind running around.

"I don't know for sure, but I'm pretty sure it was Church," Lark said, confirming his suspicions.

Things had just gone from insanely bad to downright unsurvivable.

THIRTY-FIVE

CHURCH.

The name formed a rock in his gut. Church was in San Francisco. It suddenly became a very real possibility that none of them would survive the next forty-eight hours.

"Church? Here?" Ben gave a low whistle, slouching back in his seat. "And you're just deciding to tell us this *now*? Did your mom drop you on your fuckin' head or something?"

From the look on his face, Lark had reached his limit. He stood, the force of the move sending his chair skittering across the hardwood floor. "*Look*, I got Lady Cop tryin' to beat my brains out, him"—he jabbed a finger in Michael's direction—"throwing ricin down my throat and threatening to shoot me every time I blink, and *you* running your goddamn mouth nonstop. Sorry I've been a little too preoccupied to sweat the small stuff."

"Church is hardly small stuff," Ben said.

What Church was, was a game changer.

Lark had the good sense to look a bit worried. "I'm sorry. You're right. I wasn't tryin' to keep it from you guys, I just…" He ended it on a shrug, his excuses running out of steam.

"What is a church?" Sabrina said out of nowhere.

"Church isn't a what. It's a *who*," Ben said.

"Another FSS operative?" she said, bouncing a look around the table.

Ben shrugged. "We're not really sure. All we know is the name."

"So no one's ever actually seen this Church?" Sabrina sounded dubious, like Ben had just told her he'd had a Bigfoot encounter.

Ben caught the tone and smiled. "I'm sure plenty of people have seen Church. I'm also fairly certain that the vast majority of those people are dead."

"And how do you know that?" From the look on her face, Sabrina still wasn't buying it.

"Because my Daddy told me so," Ben said, his smile growing wider. "He's a lying jerkwad, but not about shit like this. I've seen firsthand what this asshole can do."

Sabrina shook her head, about to speak, but Michael was done listening to them. "Enough," he said, cutting a look at Ben that matched his tone. "Church is just one in a long line of problems. Right now, figuring out a way to buy Leo Maddox some time is our first priority."

They all looked at him, counting on him to know what to do. To do the right thing when he didn't have a fucking clue what the right thing was.

Finally he spoke. "You're gonna call Shaw and tell him that the Maddox boy is dead," he said to Lark. "You're gonna tell him that Ben is in the process of falsifying the DNA report to make it look like he's still alive to buy me some time in the States."

"What good is that gonna do?" Lark said, sounding nervous at the prospect at telling Livingston Shaw anything but the absolute truth. He lifted his cup to his lips. The frail china looked ridiculous in his massive hand.

"A lot, actually," Michael said, a smirk playing at the corner of his mouth. "It might cause a rift between him and Reyes. Play them against each other. Shaw might've had a hand in Leo's kidnapping, but I have a feeling that keeping him alive is essential to whatever plan he's working. If he thinks Reyes killed his golden goose, he'll demand proof of life. We might have a shot at intercepting the information. It's our best bet on figuring out where Reyes is keeping Leo. He's running out of time. As soon as Reyes gets what he wants from Shaw, the Maddox kid is as good as dead." *Or worse.*

"That's all well and good, but if Shaw thinks you're lying to him in order to keep yourself here, the first thing he'll do is call you back to Spain," Lark said.

"Exactly."

"You want to go, but Shaw can't know that," Sabrina said, understanding instantly.

"Despite appearances, San Francisco is not where the action is at for this. If I want to figure out what Shaw's up to and how Cordova fits into all this, I have to go back," he said.

"What are we gonna do with him?" Lark said, aiming his coffee cup at Alex.

"He can stay here with Miss Ettie," Ben said. "She won't mind."

Michael looked doubtful. "She won't be able to protect him if shit goes south. Not with Church running around."

"She won't have to," Sabrina said. "The lab is running Elm's DNA against what was found on Alex and the trace Mandy found on Johnny Doe. Based on the financial records that Strick found, we'll have a warrant to search Elm's residence by morning. My case is as good as wrapped. I've got some vacation time. I'll take it."

He had that feeling again. The one he'd had at the hospital, looking at that deep, ugly furrow dug into her scalp. That feeling that told him he was going to lose her.

"None of this matters without proof—documented proof—that the dead kid is Leo Maddox," Lark said, his words cutting through Michael's thoughts. "Cause you know Shaw's not taking my word for it."

Sabrina flashed them a tight smile and stood. "Leave that to me."

THIRTY-SIX

SABRINA LEFT THEM SITTING around Miss Ettie's kitchen table, drinking coffee out of ridiculous cups and plotting on how best to destroy Livingston Shaw. Though he'd agreed to help, Lark was a liability until proven otherwise. She seriously doubted that either Ben or Michael would trust him with every aspect of whatever plan they worked up, but right now that wasn't her concern.

Stepping out onto the front porch, she took a seat on the swing, sinking into its deep red cushions with a barely audible sigh. Taking her phone out, she dialed Mandy and let it ring.

"This is Black," Mandy said.

"Hey, it's me. Got a minute?"

"For you, I've got about five, maybe ten." She could hear the concern in Mandy's voice, knew what was coming next. "I got a look at your friend from the hospital. You plugged him pretty good. One of the bullets destroyed his liver. Another blew out his left ventricle." Mandy always talked shop when she was stressed. "I heard you were shot and refused treatment." It wasn't a question.

Sabrina had a thing about refusing treatment, and for a moment she was glad that she hadn't been at Elm's office when the bullets started flying. She'd probably be strapped to a gurney somewhere while Mandy stitched her up. Without a painkiller.

"It's just a graze. I'm fine, promise."

"We have very different ideas on what *fine* is, Sabrina." Mandy also got snippy when she was worried.

There was no arguing that, so she let it go. "I need a favor," she said quietly. Even though she was on the porch, she didn't want to take a chance that someone might overhear her. She was choosing to involve Mandy; that didn't mean she couldn't minimize her exposure as much as possible.

The other end of the line was quiet for a moment, and then, "Okay. Hold on." There was noise on the other end of the phone, the swinging scrape of a door across linoleum, a loud *clack*, followed by another. "I'm in cold storage, so please hurry."

Sabrina took a deep breath. And another. Looked around to ensure she was truly alone.

"Hello? Freezing my ass off here."

"Yeah, I'm here. It's about the boy—Johnny Doe," she said, waiting for her words to sink in before continuing. "I need you to work up a DNA report and a death certificate for him."

"But I have no idea who he is. I just sent prints and samples to the lab this morning, but even with a rush order, I won't have results for a few days," Mandy said.

"I know. That's why I'm asking." The longer it took for Mandy to get the results back, the longer Michael and Ben had to work with. "I need documentation stating that the body belongs to Leon Jonathan Maddox the third."

Complete and utter silence. Shit.

"I'm not asking you to put them in the system, I just need hard copies of the reports," Sabrina said, explaining as much as she could. She waited a few seconds before speaking again. "Mandy—"

"I'm sorry, did you just ask me to falsify DNA and a certificate of death for a Senator's grandson?" Mandy said in a whispered rush.

"Yes."

More silence. "Are you in trouble?" Now Mandy sounded worried.

"Yes." *Please don't ask, please don't ask, please don't—*

"I'll have to wait until after hours. Forging official documents is generally frowned upon around here," Mandy said.

Had she just agreed? "So you'll—"

"You'd never ask me to do something like this unless it was extremely important, right?"

"Right."

"And we're friends, right?"

She thought of Strickland. The way they'd left things. "Right."

"So, yes. I'll do it," Mandy said. "You can pick them up tomorrow morning. I have a nine o'clock, so, say around eight?"

"Okay," she said. "Thanks. I owe you."

"You don't *owe* me anything. You're not very good at this whole *friend* thing, are you?" Mandy said before hanging up.

No, she really wasn't.

Before Sabrina could change her mind, she dialed another number from memory. The call was answered on the fourth ring.

"Inspector, I was wondering when you'd finally call." Phillip Song's voice, smooth and confident, chided her gently. "You have an unhealthy habit of cutting it close. A form of self-punishment, I'm sure. Completely unnecessary, by the way."

"Have you been talking to my therapist again, Phillip?" She smiled in spite of herself when he laughed. The two had formed an unlikely friendship, despite—or maybe because of—the fact that she'd killed his brother.

"I would never pry into your private matters, Sabrina," he said. This time it was her turn to laugh.

"*Lies.* Prying is what you do best." She kept her tone light, playful, as she usually did with him. It was what worked best between them.

"I do it for your own good, *yeon-in*," he told her, and she was sure he believed it to be true.

The first time he'd pried had been a few months after his brother's funeral. She and Strickland had decided to meet for lunch in the Tenderloin. He'd chosen the restaurant and surprisingly, it had belonged to Phillip Song. It was the first time she's seen him since that day in the stockroom behind David's store. The day he'd told her that his older brother had always been sick, and that the death of their father had likely driven him over the edge.

She'd expected him to have them escorted out of the restaurant. Even if the fact that she killed his brother hadn't been an issue, the Song family had strong ties to the city's *Geondal*—Korean organized crime. Phillip Song was the head of Seven Dragons. Cops weren't exactly appreciated by him.

Instead of being asked to leave, or shot, Sabrina was surprised to find herself face to face with Phillip himself. He'd welcomed her warmly, insisting that their meal was on the house, that anything he could do for her, he would do.

As if to prove himself, he'd called her later that night and asked that she meet him. Even though she knew it wasn't exactly smart, Sabrina went. There was one thing she knew for sure—if Phillip Song wanted her dead, she would have been dead months before. Going to see him at his restaurant was no more dangerous than stepping outside her house every day. When she arrived, she was ushered into a private dining room to find Phillip waiting for her.

"You are being haunted by a *Gae Dokkaebi*—an evil spirit," he'd said, shooting her a lopsided grin. "At least that's what Eun says." He raised his eyes to the woman hovering in the doorway of the restaurant's private dining room he used to conduct his business. "My cousin," he said, motioning the young woman in. With her came the warm delicate scent of tea.

"Before coming to America, she was in training to become *sana mudang*—a shaman." He smiled up at his cousin, inclining his head slightly while she slid the tea tray onto the table between them. "She senses a darkness inside you. She's afraid of you. And for you."

Smart girl. The words hovered on Sabrina's tongue, but she managed to keep them to herself. "And she's going to exorcise my demons with a cup of tea?" she said as small fine-boned hands poured a translucent brew into a teacup.

"Not a demon—a ghost."

His words crawled along her nape to slither down her spine. She had to fight to keep herself in her chair. Before she could question him further, Phillip continued.

"Unfortunately, according to Eun, there is no getting rid of what's inside you." He sat back, elbows braced on the arms of his chair, tugging the French cuffs of his hand-tailored shirt over his heavily inked wrists. "The tea will give you relief, not peace. She warns, it will not hold the *Gae Dokkaebi* at bay forever."

"Eun sure says a lot for someone who never speaks." She shot a wary look at the cup in front of her. It unnerved her to know that she'd been the topic of conversation between them. "Why is she helping me?"

"Because I asked her to," he said, as if that answered everything.

"Why would *you* want to help me?" she said, fighting the urge to look away from his intense gaze.

"It is simple: my family owes you a debt that can never be repaid. If my father were here, he would feel the same."

Sabrina didn't see it that way at all—she had killed his brother; that didn't constitute a debt—but she didn't argue. She drank the tea, more out of politeness rather than an actual belief that it would work against the voice she couldn't silence inside her head.

When she left, Phillip pressed a red silk pouch into her hand, his long, cool fingers wrapping around her own. "I wish there was more I could do." He frowned. "If it works, come back."

Incredibly, it *had* worked. That night she'd slept without interruption and the next morning, there was nothing but blessed silence. Every few weeks she went to visit Phillip at his restaurant and when she left, it was with tea.

"But I think you called me for more than tea this time," he said now, pulling her away from the memory.

"Is it okay if I come by tonight?" she said without answering his question.

"Of course, *yeon-in*," he said. "I'll see you then."

The line went dead and she stood, dropping her cell in her pocket.

"You shouldn't be out here."

She looked over to see Michael standing in the doorway. She had no idea how long he'd been there. Looking at him, her stomach tripped over itself on its way to her throat. "I needed the privacy." She glanced away, unable to take the pressure that seeing his face built up in her chest.

"Who were you talking to?" he said, his eyes roving the yard. The street. Neighboring houses. Assessing threats. Looking for targets.

This was a very different Michael than the one she knew. Harder. Distant. More controlled. She remembered the way his arms felt around her, his face buried in her hair, his breath skating across her collarbone. Holding her so tight she could scarcely breathe. Where was *he*? The man who'd watched over her while she slept? The man who walked through hell to save her? Suddenly she wasn't sure he even really existed.

Irritated by his terse behavior, she leaned back against the railing and crossed her arms over her chest. "A friend."

Michael sighed, mirrored her stance, propping himself against the doorjamb, arms folded. "One that's going to help, I hope," he said, a smirk on his face, his eyes constantly roving the yard and street behind her.

She shrugged. She wasn't telling him about Mandy's involvement. Not because she didn't trust him, but because she didn't want to think about what she'd just done. Roping Mandy into this mess was probably a huge mistake. And mentioning Phillip ... that would just be asking for trouble.

"Come inside. It's not safe out here."

"Because of Church?" she said.

"Yes. Because of Church. And everyone else who's looking to serve our heads up on a platter," he said, that half smile fading in favor of the hardened expression he seemed to always wear now.

She shook her head, refusing to move. "How is it possible that no one has ever seen this person?"

He scanned the street again. "Because that's the way Shaw wants it. Chances are plenty of people have seen Church, we just don't know who he is or what he really does. Shaw keeps sleepers—operatives with classified identities. Rumor has it he recommissions burned and disavowed agents from intelligence agencies worldwide. CIA, NSA,

MI-6, KGB, Mossad... FSS is the last stop in a long line of acronym agencies. The freakin' Island of Misfit Toys for rogue spies. "

"What for?" she said, but she could imagine that such tools would have their uses.

"For shit like this. Intelligence operatives aren't renowned for their strict moral code." He looked uncomfortable, like he was telling her things he shouldn't. Things that could get her killed.

"Are you afraid of Church?"

His expression changed again into something unreadable. "No. And no more questions—come inside."

It was only a matter of time before whoever was controlling Cordova's men found out that the attempt at the hospital had failed. That the Kotko boy was still alive. There was no doubt they'd be looking for him or that they'd eventually find him. Maybe they already had. "Please," he said softly.

It wasn't the word, it was the look he was giving her that finally moved her. Like he was seconds away from manhandling her into the house if needed. Either way, she was coming inside.

He didn't say anything else. Just stood there, staring at her with the same calm expression he always wore. Finally she walked toward him, but he didn't move from the doorway, forcing her to squeeze past him on her way through the door. Chest and thighs brushed against one another...

And then she was caught, his fingers closing around her wrist. He held her, the gentle pressure of his hand on her as unrelenting as the weight of his gaze, those gray eyes of his locking onto her face like he was starved for the sight of her.

"I have something for you," he said quietly, the lazy pattern his thumb was drawing against her wrist was making her dizzy.

She felt the corner of her mouth lift in a crooked grin. "Should I be scared?"

He smiled back. "Yes, but you've never been that smart," he teased while reaching into his suit pocket to pull out another case. This one was long and flat, roughly the length of a pen. He opened it and showed it to her. A silver bracelet made of thin, elongated links as wide as her finger. He lifted it from the case before snapping it closed. A bracelet that wasn't really a bracelet at all. It remained straight and stiff in his hands, the links locked together to form something that resembled a hiltless blade, its end tapering off into a sharp point.

"It's titanium, so it's light but strong," he told her, showing her the small button on the underside. He pushed it and the links unlocked, pooling into his hands. He looped it around her wrist, tucking the pointed clasp into its hollow end, securing it in place.

"Does this mean we're going steady?" she said, hoping the joke would alleviate some of the pressure that had built up between them.

He looked up at her, his gray eyes nearly black as he stared into her eyes. "It means if something happened to you, I think it would kill me." As suddenly as he caught her, he let her go, releasing her wrist before looking away. "Don't take it off."

"Okay," she said, nodding. She continued through the door and into the house. She kept walking. Didn't stop, didn't turn around. Because if she did, she was certain that the man she fell in love with would disappear.

THIRTY-SEVEN

MICHAEL WATCHED SABRINA WALK away, waiting before following her into the kitchen. He used the time to remind himself there were reasons he stayed away from her. Reasons he should've *kept* staying away.

Ben … it was his fault he was here. The kid was worse than a twelve-year-old girl with his schoolyard bullshit.

But it hadn't been Ben who forced him to follow her out here. It hadn't been Ben who'd opened his mouth and said things to her he'd had no intention of saying. And it hadn't been Ben who'd touched her. No, as usual, he hadn't needed any help fucking things up. Just point him in the right direction and things got destroyed. That's the way it had always been.

Story of his life.

He shed his jacket, tossing it over the back of the nearest chair. Reaching up, he pulled the knot loose on his necktie, yanking it wide to stave off the trapped feeling that suddenly gripped him. He kept pulling until the thing came loose in his hand and then popped open the first few buttons on his shirt. Nothing he did made it any better.

He remembered this feeling. Hated it. It was like a slow-moving train wreck only he could stop, but no matter how hard he pulled the brake, the wheels just kept rolling. People dumb enough to love him had a habit of getting killed. His parents. Frankie. Lucy. How many times could Sabrina dodge a bullet before one finally caught her? How many times could she die before it finally took?

He shut the front door and locked it, impressed with the heavy brass fixtures that secured it. Those were new. For the first time, he noticed the discreet security panel set flush into the wall, rows of lights offset by a pad used to read thumbprints. This was no commercial-grade system. He'd seen this kind of system plenty of times.

In FSS safe houses.

Apprehension tingled along his scalp. Taking a trip around the room, he noted things he'd been too preoccupied to see before. The way the front parlor window refracted the setting sun, bending the light with its thickness? Bulletproof glass. The blinking red lights in every corner of the room? Motion detectors. The almost springy feel of the floorboards beneath his feet? Pressure plates that almost surely triggered an off-site alarm. He rapped a couple of knuckles against one of the exterior walls. Solid. He'd bet his account in the Caymans that every inch was outfitted with Kevlar panels.

What. The. Fuck.

But he knew. Ben. It always came back to him, didn't it? He spent time here. A lot of time. Miss Ettie treated him like he was one of her grandkids. Probably baked him fucking cookies and tucked him in at night. It made perfect sense that Ben would make sure the place was secure, so why did it piss him off so bad?

Because it hadn't been him who thought of it, that's why.

Get your head in the fuckin' game, O'Shea—none of this matters. Not if you don't let it.

Michael shoved his hands into the pockets of his slacks and finally headed for the kitchen.

He entered quietly, leaning against the doorframe without a sound. Sabrina looked at him over her shoulder, stopping mid-sentence before continuing with what she was saying. "Like I said, all you need to know is that I'll have a DNA report and death certificate by tomorrow morning."

Lark, standing across the room, hips resting against the kitchen counter, looked like he was suddenly having second thoughts. "And like *I* said, I deserve to know where you're getting your documents because it's my ass doing the lying here. Shaw won't fall for no Mickey Mouse shit," he said.

"Oh, well, in that case, I'll tell my contact to lay off the crayons," Sabrina said, straightening her legs under the table. "And if you think that concern for *your* safety is going to entice me to give up my source, then Shaw *should* kill you, because you're too stupid to live."

Lark shifted again and rubbed a hand across his jaw before cutting him a look. "You wanna reel your girl in, O'Shea, before that mouth of hers gets her in trouble?"

Michael slid his gaze across the kitchen until it rested on the back of her head. "She's not my girl."

The words stiffened her spine, as if he'd punched her between the shoulder blades. She swung a look at him, hurt and anger flitting across her features. He held her gaze, forcing every shred of emotion he held from his face until it was nothing but a mask. He counted to five, letting her see the void before he looked at Ben. "Take her home."

Ben hesitated. "Maybe you should be the one—"

"I've got more important things to do. Besides, I'm sure you walked her home plenty of times." He kept his gaze locked on Ben's face. He didn't want to look at her. Couldn't. Not when he was seconds away from coming completely unhinged.

"I'll walk myself home," she said in a hard tone, drilling him with a glare to match. The heat of it was like a hot poker in his chest. She left without a backward glance.

Good. The angrier she was at him, the easier it would be. He angled his head at the door, signaling Ben to follow her. "Stay with her."

Ben paused for a moment, looking almost as pissed as Sabrina before he hit the door, slamming it closed behind him.

"You've always been way too good at that," Lark said in the quiet, his booming voice held just above a whisper.

"Good at what?" He looked down at the boy curled into a ball on the floor next to Sabrina's empty chair, sleeping what Michael would be willing to bet was the first real sleep he'd had in months.

"Pretending shit doesn't matter."

He looked up at Lark and laughed. "Are you fuckin' serious? An hour ago you were running your mouth about what a number she's done on me, now you're pullin' a Dear Abby because I won't walk her home?"

Lark shrugged. "What can I say? I'm a complicated kinda guy."

Michael leaned forward a bit, dropping his voice so it wouldn't carry beyond Lark's ears. "How's this for complicated—that capsule I made you swallow is the least of your worries. If you fuck us over …" He shook his head, the corner of his mouth lifting slightly. "The things I'll do to you. By the time I'm done, you'll be begging me to make the call."

Lark smiled. "Yeah. You've always been good at that too." He turned to leave, but Michael's words stopped him cold.

"You think you're up to the task?" Michael said. There was no need to elaborate, and Lark proved it by throwing him a look over his shoulder before turning to face him.

"To killing you? Probably not," Lark said. "But I got a better shot than most."

"What I don't get is *why*. Shaw can kill me anytime he wants. So why get you to do it?" he said, pulling his shoulder away from the doorjamb to stand up straight.

Lark just laughed. "One thing I learned in my twenty-three months and eighteen days as his personal guard—Livingston Shaw gets off on making people do things they don't want to do." Lark picked his cup up off the counter and rinsed it out before placing it carefully in the sink. "Good night, partner," he said before heading upstairs.

THIRTY-EIGHT

"Go home."

Sabrina had said it about a hundred times in the past hour, but he wasn't listening.

Instead, Ben shuffled the deck of cards and dealt in stubborn silence. Sometimes she wanted to strangle him. He picked up his cards and fanned them out, studying them intently. "It's your turn to go first," he said.

She walked around the bed from one window to the next. "I don't want to play cards," she said a bit too harshly. She hadn't felt like this in years. Scared. Angry. Paranoid. The back of her head throbbed in a reminder that she was smart to feel all three.

Ben hardly seemed to notice. "I've already told you, I'm not having sex with you, Sabrina." He smirked at the cards in his hand, moving a few here and there. "Begging only makes you sound desperate."

She laughed in spite of herself. "The only thing I'm desperate to do is get you out of my house."

"Not gonna happen. You heard O'Shea; I'm supposed to stay here," he said, glancing up at her.

"Oh, and you always do what you're told?" Stepping away from the window, she approached the bed, giving him the once-over.

Ben shrugged. "When it suits me."

"You mean when it bugs *me*?" she said dryly and picked up her cards. He wasn't leaving anytime soon; might as well pass the time. "Do you have any fives?"

Ben scowled and tossed her a card. She paired it with the card she already held and laid them on the bed, next to her SIG.

"Got any jacks?" he said.

"Go fish."

Ben picked up a card and stuck it in the middle of his hand.

She'd meant to ask him if he had any threes—what came out of her mouth was a different question entirely. "Why did you bring him here?"

He shot her a look and shrugged. "You called. We came."

"Bullshit. You've been here a dozen times over the past year and never once have you even mentioned him. You could've just as easily split up and come here while sending him on to question the Maddoxes. Instead you plopped him in front of me like a cat would a dead bird. Why?"

Now he wouldn't look at her. "I told him."

She stared at him for a full ten-count, but he didn't elaborate. Didn't explain. The realization of what he meant detonated in her belly, knocking her slightly off-kilter. "You told him *what*?" she said, just to make sure they were on the same page.

"You know what." Ben glared at the cards in his hand, not even having to look at her to gauge how angry she was. "Don't look at me like that. It's not like I had a choice."

172

"You're Ben Shaw—if there's one thing I've learned about you, it's that *you* always have a choice." She continued to watch him, looking for a sign that would tell her what angle his confession had helped him play. As far as she could tell, there wasn't one.

"Look, Lark started running his mouth about you. In front of my father." He shrugged. "When Michael realized that your existence wasn't exactly a revelation, he damn near shot Daddy Dearest in the face."

"And that's a problem for you *how*?" She was well aware of how Ben felt about his father. That he would intervene was surprising.

"A problem for me? Hardly. But for you? Michael..." He sighed. "My father's realized that my tenuous loyalties have shifted. I'm no longer his failsafe when it comes to our boy, which means if something were to happen to good ol' Dad..."

"Michael would be killed." Someone else, besides Shaw and Ben, had their finger on Michael's kill switch. The thought about how close he'd come wiped her anger clean.

"Bingo. So, back to your original question. Why did I bring Michael here." Ben looked up at her. "Because there is a very real, very frightening part of him that works very hard at getting himself killed, and it's getting stronger by the day. I brought him here because he needs to remember that he still has things in this world worth fighting for. He loves you. He wouldn't be fighting it so hard if he didn't."

He loved her. Yes, at least that's what he told her a year ago. But things change. "You think he's suicidal?" she said, barely able to get the words out.

His eyes slid away from her face, resting on a spot just above her shoulder. "No. I think he no longer cares if he lives or dies. There's a difference."

She had more questions, but she knew Ben well enough to know that when he wouldn't look at you, it was because there was something going on in his head that he didn't want you to see. She also knew that pushing him was counterproductive. "Got any threes?" she said, closing the subject.

He fished a card from his hand and tossed it at her. "No one likes a cheater, Sabrina."

"I don't cheat." She smiled as she matched up the card with her own and set it to the side. "I lie a lot, but I never cheat."

He smiled back for a moment, but it faltered. "You're still bleeding."

She swiped at her neck, her hand coming away wet and red. "It's nothing," she said, tossing her card on the pile before she stood.

"You've been bleeding off and on for the past six hours. That's not *nothing*. Let me stitch it up," Ben said to her back as she headed for the bathroom.

She sighed. "Alright. There's a suture kit in my—" Her cell rattled against her hip. She pulled it off and glanced at the screen. It was a text, alerting her that one of the motion detectors she'd set around the property had been triggered.

There was someone on the front porch.

She looked up, ready to explain, but Ben must've been able to tell by the look on her face that something wasn't right. He stood, the offer of first aid forgotten, and twitched the curtain away from the window just a touch. "I can't see who it is."

She wiped her hands on a towel before leaving the bathroom. "Avasa, come," she said, swiping her SIG off the bed and tucking it into the waistband of her jeans.

"Where do you think you're going?" Ben said, stepping in front of her.

174

"Move."

"I'll go. You stay here. It's probably just a cat or something," he said, but they both knew it wasn't a cat. The sensors set around the house and surrounding property didn't register anything under seventy-five pounds. Despite the doubt she'd been tossing around earlier, she felt a certainty settle into her bones. One word chased itself around her head.

Church.

From the look on Ben's face, he was thinking the same thing. She looked down at the .40 Desert Eagle he held in his hand and shook her head. "Yeah? That's a pretty big cat, Shaw." Sidestepping him, she managed to make it to the door before he dropped a hand on her shoulder.

"At least let me go first. If you get shot again, O'Shea will kill me."

She highly doubted that, but she moved aside, letting Ben ease the door open on silent hinges. They both stepped onto the landing, letting their eyes adjust to the dark before making their way down the stairs.

THIRTY-NINE

SABRINA FOLLOWED BEN DOWN the dark stairs, Avasa at her side. She was a good dog, trained to follow commands without hesitation. She took the stairs as silently and vigilantly as her master. Catching a scent on the early autumn breeze, she lifted her head to take it in. She stopped for a moment, as still as stone, ears laid flat against her skull. She didn't bark, but the pause in her step told Sabrina everything she needed to know.

Whoever or whatever was on the porch didn't belong there.

Sabrina kept the muzzle of her SIG trained to the right, over the railing, watching the shadows for any sign of movement. She imagined the faceless Church lurking in the dark. Suddenly Ben's stories seemed less like a ploy to scare her into toeing the line and more like a warning. One she should've heeded.

Reaching out, she grabbed his shoulder, stopping him just before he rounded the corner of the house. Ben turned a bit, shooting her a questioning look. He must've read her face because he tipped his head to the side: *go back upstairs.*

Instinct told her that was the smartest thing to do, but she fought it tooth and nail. She'd never left a partner behind, and she sure as the hell wasn't going to start now. She shook her head and resettled her grip on her SIG, tipping her chin at the shadow cast across the front yard by the porch light. What kind of assassin announced their presence like that?

Ben held up a finger. One shadow. Whoever was on the porch was alone—or wanted them to *think* they were. He held up three fingers and counted down. *Three … two … one …*

The two of them took the corner together, leading with their guns, muzzles trained on the source of the shadow.

"*Holy shit.*" The woman on the porch squeaked out, shooting her hands toward the sky, eyes yanked wide with fear. She was wearing a pair of loose jeans and a logo T, her dark hair pulled back into a ponytail away from her pretty face.

Ben immediately tipped his gun toward the ground, shooting Sabrina a questioning look. "You know her?"

"Nope." She shifted her SIG a few inches to the left, farther on down the porch. "It's a little late at night to be selling magazine subscriptions, isn't it?" she said to the woman on the porch, watching her face carefully. "Turn. Slowly." She twirled her finger in the air to demonstrate what she meant.

"Okay …" The woman turned slowly.

"She's not carrying," Ben said, roaming his eyes over the woman's form, looking for the bulge of a holster against her hip or tucked into the small of her back.

"Carrying what? Oh God … Look, I'm just here to see Val—Valerie Nickels," the woman stammered out, hands still held high.

"I've never seen you before in my life." What the hell was this? Some sort of decoy meant to distract them? Or was she what she looked like—a poor woman, scared shitless by a pair of guns shoved in her face? "Where's your purse?" Sabrina said, still driven by the instinct that whispered to her that something was wrong.

"My … I left it in the car. I just came by to drop off some pictures I took of Valerie and her baby today at the park."

Ben shot her a look. Would Val be dumb enough to give their address to a total stranger she met in the park? The answer slumped her shoulders and ticked the muzzle of her gun a few more inches to the left. "Where are they? The pictures?"

Now the woman started to lower her hands. Sabrina swung the muzzle back in her direction, centering it on her chest. The woman froze in terror, her eyes zeroed in on the gun in her hand. "On a disc in my pocket."

Just then the front door flew open. "What's going on?" Val stepped out onto the porch, a sleeping Lucy nestled against her chest. She looked down at the baby to make sure she was still sleeping. "Have the two of you *lost your minds*?"

Sabrina lowered her gun but didn't tuck it away. "Do you know her?" she said, ignoring Val's question completely.

"Yes, I do," Val said. "Her name is Courtney. I met her this morning at that coffee shop on Berry. She's a photographer, we started talking…" She shot a look at Ben. "What did you do to her?"

Ben held up his hands. "Don't look at me, she was crazy when I found her." He tucked his .40 into the waistband of his cargo shorts, a sly smile creeping over his face. "But, better safe than sorry, right?"

Valerie gave him a withering look. "Good. Great. Just what I need, *two* of you running around." She turned to the woman standing next to her. "Sorry about that. My roommate, Sabrina." She flung a hand in the direction of the yard. "Sabrina, this is Courtney."

"Nice to meet you," Courtney said, her hands still in the air. She looked at the gun in Sabrina's hand. "Can I put my hands down now?"

No. "Yes." Sabrina tucked her SIG into the small of her back and dropped her arms to her sides, her hand falling onto Avasa's head. The dog was still quivering. She gave her a few long strokes, urging the tension from her neck and shoulders.

"Come in." Valerie stepped back, opening the front door a bit wider. "Now that my friends have waved a gun at you, the least I can do is offer you a glass of wine."

Courtney smiled. "That'd be great, I—" She was cut off by the chime of her cell. Reaching into her pocket, she gave the screen a quick scroll before shooting a look at Sabrina across the porch. "But, actually, I can't stay." She reached into her back pocket and produced a paper sleeve with a cellophane window. "I just wanted to drop these by. If you like what you see, give me a call and we'll set up a shoot. I'd love to use this little cutie in my portfolio," she said, running her hand along Lucy's soft black curls with a smile. She handed Val the disc and turned to leave. "It was … life-affirming to meet you, Sabrina," she said, taking the steps in a rush and following the length of the driveway to the ancient Ford Bronco that sat curbside.

She jumped in and started it up, the rattle and chug of it was deafening. How in the hell had they not heard that thing when it pulled up? Pulling away, Courtney gave the horn a couple of beeps and waved, disappearing from sight. Sabrina watched her go, not wanting to turn around and face her friend.

"I thought we'd finally pulled clear of this, Sabrina," Val said quietly, pulling her gaze to the porch. It was late August, so the anniversary of her kidnapping was right around the corner. How many times had she lost it in the past, let herself be consumed by memories? Let paranoia and anger take root? She couldn't blame Val for seeing her behavior and believing that this was just one of her annual freakouts. But that wasn't what happened here.

She sighed. "It's not about that, Val—"

"You always say that," she said before looking at Ben. "I can't do this right now. You deal with her." Val went back inside and shut the door with a firm *click*.

She turned away from the porch and fixed Ben with a cold look. "*She was crazy when I found her*? Seriously?"

Ben just shrugged. "What was I supposed to say? *We're out here hunting wabbits?* So she thinks you're losing it, what's new?"

"Asshole." She turned away and made her way toward the stairs that led to her third-floor studio. Ben took a few steps in her direction, and she looked at him over her shoulder. "If you take one more step, I'll shoot you were you stand." She turned away and continued around the side of the house and up the stairs, Avasa at her heels.

FORTY

HE WAITED UNTIL HE heard the muffled thud of Lark shutting the door to his room before he moved. Standing, he bent and picked up the boy.

Michael carried him up stairs to the room across from his own. He pulled back the covers on the bed and deposited him in it. He was thin. Too thin. Dark shaggy hair lay flat against the skeletal angles of his face. The baggy shirt and sweats practically swallowed him whole. He saw himself as a child, shell-shocked and broken—a half-feral boy no one wanted.

He'd been eight when his smack-addicted mother finally managed to kill herself. He sat, locked in the closet in a puddle of his own urine for three days, waiting to die. Hoping to, really. But the smell of his mother rotting away in the bathroom finally won out over the warm garbage stench that permeated the shitty tenement they lived in.

He'd been pulled out of that closet. Cleaned up and fed. Put in an endless parade of cars and taken from placement to placement. Eight of them in less than a year before he landed on Sophia and Sean's doorstep. His life with them stuck. Not because he'd finally settled, but because they refused to give up on him. Because they loved him.

Because, finally, someone wanted him.

He looked at the boy. *Who are you? Why do both Reyes and Cordova want you dead? What do you know that's so important?* Instead of asking questions he was sure there were no answers for, Michael tugged the covers up to Alex's chin, over his frail shoulders. "Good night," he mumbled in Russian before heading for the door. He could've sworn he'd heard the kid whisper, "*Spasibo,*" just before he shut the door behind him.

Spasibo. Thank you.

———

Michael stopped in his room long enough to change his clothes, exchanging the rumpled suit for a pair of track pants and a faded T-shirt before pulling on a shoulder holster to house his Kimber .45. A lightweight jacket completed his newest disguise.

In his track pants and cross trainers, he looked like a regular guy out for a late-night run.

Nothing could've been further from the truth.

He circled the block, his head on a swivel. Scanning the street, the surrounding yards. Cars parked along the curb. All was quiet—for now. It was only a matter of time before the place was crawling with Spanish thugs and Colombian henchmen. This was the calm before the storm. Time to batten down the hatches.

Reapproaching the street that held Miss Ettie's B&B, he continued on toward Sabrina's. She wasn't asleep. She'd be up, pacing and worrying. Figuring out a way to keep the Kotko boy safe. Waiting for the same thing he was—for it all to come crashing down on them.

He stopped as soon as he reached her fence line, allowing the hydrangeas to hide him from view. He stood there for a moment, fighting the urge to climb her stairs and knock. To apologize and smooth things over.

Suddenly the door at the top of her third-floor landing opened and she appeared, a large rust-colored dog at her side. She took the steps quietly and cut across the yard to the street where she'd parked her car. He watched her unlock the door, letting the dog in first before she slid behind the wheel.

He crossed the street at a quick clip, reaching the car seconds before she turned the engine over. Raising his hand, he rapped his knuckles against the passenger side window. The dog in the seat next to her let out a sharp bark, floppy ears flattened against a sleek skull, quivering lips peeled back from large teeth.

Sabrina jumped in her seat, turning to place a hand on the dog's flank. She looked through the window before she said something he couldn't hear. The dog's demeanor changed instantly; it no longer looked poised to attack but rather like it was waiting.

She said something else to the dog just before the window a few inches from his face was powered down. "Do you ever sleep?"

"About as much as you do," he said with a shrug. "You finally got your own dog."

"She was a gift," Sabrina said as if she needed an excuse. "What are you doing here?"

"Funny, I was about to ask you the same thing."

"I'm hungry. Thought I'd go grab a bite," she said, the lie flowing smoothly. He could always tell when she was lying because she looked you right in the eye when she did it.

He chuckled and made a point to look at his watch before answering. "Yeah? Me too. Mind if I tag along?" He wasn't hungry, but it was nearly eleven o'clock at night. She wasn't going anywhere without him.

Her eyes narrowed slightly. "Yes."

"Excellent," he said, reaching through the open window to open the locked door from the inside. The dog shifted in the seat in front of him, letting out a low-level growl. He looked at the woman behind the dog. "You want to tell your bodyguard to relax?"

For a moment it looked like she would do no such thing but then she relented. "*Stil en rustig,* Avasa," she said firmly and the dog's demeanor changed again. Craning her neck around, she gave her mistress a few wipes with her tongue. Sabrina smiled and ran a hand over the dog's head, ruffling her ears. "Okay, okay—*achterbank*," she said, and the dog immediately did as she was told, moving to the back seat.

"Your dog responds to Dutch," he said, opening the door and easing himself into the seat that had been vacated.

Sabrina started the car and shifted into drive. "Just a few key commands," she said, pulling away from the curb.

The canines used by FSS were trained to follow Dutch commands. He knew without asking who had given her the dog.

Ben.

It bothered him more than it should. Here was more proof that while he had been busy trying to do the right thing and stay away, his partner had made himself at home in Sabrina's life. Dwelling on Ben's motives would prove dangerous, so he pushed the thought from his mind. They traveled in awkward silence for a while before he spoke again. "I'm sorry about earlier—"

She held up a hand, stopping him cold. "Don't. There's no need to apologize. I understand perfectly."

"I don't think you do," he said. "Lark is Shaw's lapdog. Sent here to keep tabs on me—on us. It's safer if I ..." He let his gaze drift out the window. Gone were the affluent homes and wide manicured lawns. In the space of twenty minutes they'd traded St. Francis Wood for the Tenderloin, one of San Francisco's toughest neighborhoods.

She made a left onto Eddy and parallel parked in front of a Korean restaurant. "Safer if you what?" she said, killing the engine.

He didn't answer, couldn't really. Not without tearing down the wall he'd worked so hard to build between them.

Thankfully she let it go. "If you're coming with me, you're going to want to leave your gun in the car," she said before looking over her shoulder. "*Blijven en beschermen.*"

Stay and protect.

As soon as the words were spoken, she was out of the car and around its front, heading for the Korean restaurant and leaving him little choice but to follow.

FORTY-ONE

THE RESTAURANT WAS NEARLY deserted, nothing more than a group of straggling tourists and a couple of hookers on their lunch break. Seeing them, Michael was reminded of how late it was. Too late for short ribs ... Whatever Sabrina was after, it wasn't food.

The woman manning the front was dressed in the traditional *hanbok*—a high-wasted skirt over a fitted long-sleeve top, her dark hair secured at her nape in a low bun. When she saw Sabrina, she inclined her head slightly. "Please wait," she said to Sabrina before disappearing.

"I was serious about the gun," she said without looking at him. "I hope you left it in the car."

"I did," he said, taking in the interior. Low ceilings, booths separated by mahogany partitions. For some reason, his thoughts turned to David Song, the man who'd nearly killed him. "What are we doing here?"

"Getting answers," she said softly.

Before he could press her, the woman returned. "Come, please," she said before turning and leading them through the restaurant, heading for what looked like a private dining room. The paper partition slid open to reveal a couple of thugs dressed in dark suits, tattoos peeking out from the cuffs of their dress shirts. Korean Pips.

Sabrina entered the room uninhibited, taking a chair at the table. Without being asked, he held his arms up and submitted to a patdown, his eyes scanning the room until he found who he was looking for.

The man sat with his back in the corner, facing the door, watching him with a mixture of curiosity and amusement. "You've brought a guest this time," he said to Sabrina. "And I thought you were ashamed to be seen with me."

"Michael O'Shea," she said, and the man's face changed instantly.

He stood before speaking to the young woman behind him in Korean. She bowed in response and scurried off to do the man's bidding. "Let him in," he said, the thugs nearly tripping over themselves to do as they were told.

As soon as the partition was closed, the man offered him a deep bow, the collar of his expensive silk shirt pulling away from his chest and neck to reveal extensive ink work. Michael inclined his head to show respect before taking a seat next to Sabrina.

"This is Phillip Song," she said, placing her hands carefully on the table in front of her. "He's the head of Seven Dragons."

Song settled into his chair and gave her an easy smile. "I am no such thing, Inspector. I am as my father was before me—a simple immigrant who is deeply entrenched in his community." His dark eyes glittered, the corner of his mouth lifting in the slightest of smirks. This was obviously a game they'd played before.

"Regardless of what you are, she killed your brother. Why would you help her?" Michael asked, intentionally attempting to get a rise from their host.

Song's eyes flashed a warning, but it was fleeting. He turned his gaze on Sabrina. "What is it that brings you here, *yeon-in*? Not just tea, I think."

Michael's teeth were instantly set on edge. *Yeon-in* meant sweetheart.

If she understood the intimacy involved in his words, she didn't show it. "People. Specifically, children." Sabrina sat back in her chair and crossed her arms over her chest. "I want to know who's selling them in the city and from where."

Song's face folded up tight, his solicitous demeanor instantly gone. "I have nothing to do with such filth."

"I know you don't, but you're the only gangster I'm on a first-name basis with, so my options on who to ask are limited." She dropped her arms and leaned in, fixing him with a long look. "This is important, Phillip."

Song hesitated for a moment before sighing. "There are a few. The Russians and Albanians corner the trade around here. They generally keep it quiet—use Hunter's Point to import their … cargo." The paper partition slid open and the hostess reappeared with a tray laden heavy with an assortment of steaming dishes.

She poured tea and lifted the lids off dishes, revealing enough food to feed a small army. As soon as she was finished, she took the tray and held it behind her back, offering Song a bow.

"*Gamsahabnida*," Michael said, drawing her attention.

She blushed slightly and offered him a bow. "*Cheonman-e*."

"You speak Korean." Song inclined his head a bit.

He shrugged, evading the question. "Who is she? She hasn't been here long."

"My cousin Eun," Song said as soon as the partition slid closed. "Our family is very traditional. She's been in the States for a year and is still having trouble adjusting to the brashness of America ..." He cocked an eyebrow, shooting a crooked grin in Sabrina's direction. "Especially its women."

"So I've been told," Sabrina said wryly, reaching for a platter of *bulgogi*. "About the Russians. What does their *cargo* consist of?" She was thinking the same thing he was: Alex.

Song turned his teacup slowly in its saucer, the steam winding between his long tapered fingers. "Women mostly. Those who come here for a better life but get something else entirely. Some children, but ... I'm not involved in such matters, so it is hard for me to say."

"You tellin' me that Seven Dragons doesn't trade in skin?" Michael piped up before lifting his cup to his mouth, taking a careful sip.

"What I'm telling you is that Seven Dragons does not kidnap and sell humans into slavery." Phillip's mouth drew in tight around the words, making it obvious that he was trying very hard to remain calm. "This is all speculation, of course. I have no real knowledge of what kind of business Seven Dragons participates in."

"Of course," Sabrina said, shooting Michael that *stop talking* look of hers before turning back to their host. "You said *some children*. That means you *have* heard of the Russian trading in kids, right?"

"The Russians are little better than animals. Brutal. No real sense of honor." Phillip picked up his tea and took a long swallow, watching him over the rim, his expression telling him that Song's opinion of him was in line with what he thought of the Russians.

Michael clamped his jaw shut, his teeth grinding together so hard they nearly fused together from the pressure.

Phillip lowered his cup to reveal a brief smile. "They've been known to kidnap the children of rivals and traitors, sometimes for ransom, sometimes as a punishment. I can only imagine what is done with these children when they are not returned home."

"What about the Colombians? Have you heard any noise about the Reyes cartel setting up shop around here?"

At the mention of Reyes's name, Song looked away. He was either working with him or afraid. If Michael had to guess, he'd say the former rather than the latter. "They are a more recent arrival. The Russians are less than pleased with the competition they offer."

He stood, reaching into the dark recesses of his suit jacket. Michael tensed. He'd left his gun in the car as Sabrina instructed, but that didn't mean he wasn't armed. Song must've read his thoughts because he laughed, pulling a red silk pouch from his breast pocket. The smell of its contents drifted through the thin fabric, light and delicate. Like one of those sachets women kept in their underwear drawer.

"How are you sleeping, Sabrina?" That solicitous tone again. One that said he had every right to expect an answer to such a personal question.

Sabrina looked up at him and shrugged, which Michael guessed was as close as she would ever come to telling the truth.

Song nodded and pressed the pouch into her hand. "Next time, don't wait so long to come see me," he said before moving toward the door. Michael stood, putting himself between Song and the way out. He was getting an answer to his question, one way or another.

"My brother dishonored my family when he killed those women and very nearly you." Song looked him in the eye, his head tilted just a bit. "A debt is owed ... and I always pay my debts. There is a warehouse at the corner of Bayshore and Loomis. The Colombians and their ilk use it as a marketplace. Perhaps you might find what you're looking for there," he said, giving Michael a slight bow before stepping around him. The paper partition slid open to reveal the same pair of thugs who'd frisked him. "Sweet dreams, *yeon-in*," he said, and then he was gone.

FORTY-TWO

Sabrina kept staring at him, that blue-eyed glare of hers cutting him to the quick. He recognized an interrogation tactic when he saw one, and she used it beautifully—letting the silence between them grow into something so big and heavy that he shifted uncomfortably beneath its weight. "I forgot how good you were at this," he said, shooting her a glance.

She smiled. "I'm good at a lot of things, O'Shea. You'll have to be more specific."

He arched an eyebrow, a slight smirk coasting across his mouth. "Now, *that* I remember."

Incredibly, she blushed, a red stain rushing across her cheeks. "You're trying to distract me."

He shrugged. "Is it working?"

"No." She broke eye contact, looking out the window. "You're going to find that warehouse alone," she said.

"Yes." There was no use lying. There never had been where she was concerned.

"Why can't I go?"

"It's too dangerous," he said automatically, giving her the first answer that popped into his head.

"Bullshit," she said, not buying a word of it. "Why can't I go?"

He felt something inside him shift, the truth he fought to keep buried, bubbling to the surface. He clenched his jaw shut and shook his head, eyes glued to the road.

"I'll just follow you—"

"I don't want you there," he practically yelled, causing the dog behind him to let out a low-level growl. "*Rustig*," he said firmly and was rewarded with a split-second look of confusion before the dog did as he commanded and quieted. He shot Sabrina a glance, struggling with what came next. "I won't be able to do what I have to if you're there."

"You can't go in alone, O'Shea."

"Sure I can," he said with a shrug. "I do it all the time."

The blush on her cheeks had faded, but now what color remained drained from her face. "I don't care what you're used to doing. I don't want you going by yourself."

"And I don't want you with me." He looked away, directing his gaze out the windshield, focusing on the road so he wouldn't have to see her face when she finally understood. "I don't use silence to get answers. My interrogation tactics are a little more *physical*."

"You think I don't know that?"

Her blasé tone pulled his attention for a moment, reminding him that she worked for Shaw now and there was nothing he could do about it. "No ... but that doesn't mean I want you to watch while I use a pair of gardening shears to play This Little Piggy with one of Reyes's underlings," he said bluntly. "Look"—he raked a hand over his face and shook his head—"I'm not going to apologize for—"

"Good, because I'm not looking for an apology."

He risked a glance at her. She sat turned toward him in her seat, shadows splashed across her face, rushing and retreating through the windshield, making her expression hard to read. He felt it again, that nearly desperate need to put space between them. To push her away. Keep her safe. "How you liking the new job?" He hadn't meant to say it—hell, he hadn't even meant to admit that he knew she was working for Shaw, but there it was, a ticking time bomb between them that had suddenly detonated.

"Oh, am *I* supposed to apologize now?" she said, shaking her head. "There's a lot of shit I'm sorry for, a lot of shit I regret, but calling Shaw isn't one of them."

"Give it some time," he said as he angled the car against the curb outside her house and cut the engine. "He won't play nice forever."

She stared straight ahead for a few moments, her attention focused on something other than him. "That day, when David told me I couldn't save you both, I was confused. I didn't understand—I didn't know you were there," she said, turning toward him, meeting his gaze head-on. "Then I realized what he was saying. You came to rescue me. Again. And I'd have to choose between you and Val. I couldn't. Don't ask me to be sorry about that."

"I'm not worth saving," he said quietly.

She popped her door open and dropped a foot onto the curb before looking at him again. He could read her expression plainly now; it was a mixture of sadness and the kind of resolve he knew he'd never be able to break, no matter how hard and far he pushed her away.

"That's not something you get to decide." She stepped out of the car and levered the seat, motioning for Avasa to follow her. She stopped on the sidewalk, looking down at him through the open window. "I love you." She said it plainly, and he could see just how much it cost her to lay herself bare like that.

He looked away, unable to take the full weight of her gaze. "You shouldn't."

"You don't get to decide that either," she said before she turned and led the dog across the yard and into the house.

FORTY-THREE

Cofre del Tesoro, Colombia
April 2010

MICHAEL DREW HEAVY VELVET drapes the color of Pepto-Bismol across windows, careful to sidestep the Victorian dollhouse that hugged the wall. Looking down, he had to laugh at the ridiculous picture his black lace-ups made next to the delicate structure. Like a giant, ready to conquer and destroy.

"Michael."

He turned to see Christina in a nest of pink satin and lace. "No talking. It's late." He resettled the drapes and stepped away from the window, heading for the door.

As usual, the little girl ignored his brusque tone and curt words. "Can I see her?"

He looked at his watch. It was nearly ten o'clock. Way past her bedtime. He shook his head, started to deny her, even though he knew he'd give in in the end.

"Please." She looked at him, her dark hair plaited into a braid, the thick rope of it hung over her shoulder, her eyes too desperate to belong to a child. She was her father's princess, locked away in a tower. In the two years he'd been her guard, Christina had never so much as spoken to another child. Her best friend lived on a scrap of paper he carried around in his pocket.

Caving, he pulled the picture out of his pocket and handed it to her. She took it, held it with both hands, smoothing her small fingers over the wrinkled paper. She smiled and looked up at him, expectantly. He sank into the pink brocade chair next to the bed and returned her smile. "Which one?"

She wanted him to tell her a story about Frankie when she was a little girl. Her smile deepened, her eyes drifting down to the picture in her hands. "The one about the bicycle."

He should've known—it was her favorite. Settling in to the chair, he told the story about how when Frankie was eight, she'd ridden her bike off the roof of their house on a dare. He could still see her, black hair a wild tangle around her tanned face, sailing through the air. She'd landed horribly, banged up beneath her BMX racer, the neighbor boy who'd done the daring left standing on the porch, mouth hanging wide open.

"She was brave," Christina said, her eyes eating up the sight of his baby sister trapped on paper.

"She was hard-headed. Never could walk away from a dare." He felt the familiar tightening in his chest whenever he talked about his sister. He hadn't seen her face to face in five years. Not since she was twelve. She was about to graduate high school, would be starting college in the fall. Starting a life he would never be a part of.

"Do you think she would've liked me?" Christina said, reluctantly handing the picture over.

He took it and stood, slipping it into his pocket. "I think the two of you would've been inseparable."

She looked away from him, down at the hands resting quietly in her lap, chewing on her bottom lip for a moment before she spoke. "I wish—"

"Good night, Christina." He wouldn't let her finish the sentence. Never did. He knew what she wished; he wished the same thing.

Christina snuggled down into her nest of satin and smiled again but despite the lift of her mouth, she looked sad. "Good night, Michael."

"Night," he said, clicking off her lamp and closing the door.

———

He retrieved his satellite phone from his room and slipped outside, carrying it across the courtyard to an open field of grass surrounded by high walls. He dialed the number and listened to it ring, praying she had it set to vibrate like he'd instructed. There was only an hour difference between Colombia and Texas so it wasn't so late that he'd wake her, but that meant that his aunt and uncle could still be awake. The official story—that he was presumed dead, rotting away in the Colombian jungle after his entire team, along with a small cadre of local police, had been ambushed by the Moreno cartel— was what they'd told what little family he had left. Frankie, grief stricken and unwilling to believe that he was dead, called the emergency number he'd given her before being deployed. Unable to let her go, he'd answered.

"Hold on," she said by way of greeting. He heard her doing as he'd told her. Going into the bathroom, turning on the shower as cover noise to muffle their conversation. A few moments later, the soft hiss of running water droned out of the earpiece, then she was back. "Hi."

She knew it was him. The number he'd called belonged to a prepaid cell only he had the number to. As soon as they finished talking, Frankie would destroy the phone and he'd use an anonymous courier to send her another via a PO box. She thought he was still in the military. That his death was faked for the sake of national security and these cloak-and-dagger maneuvers were to keep his location a secret from insurgents. She had no idea what he really was. That he killed people for money. That his likeness was splashed across wanted posters hung in countless agencies in over a half a dozen countries, or that there were entire task forces dedicated to hunting him down. She'd never even heard the words *El Cartero*. To her he was just Michael, her big brother.

"Hey, how's my baby sister?" he said, hearing the smile in his voice as they settled into a familiar rhythm.

"Good. I got a job," she said.

"A job?" For some reason the idea bothered him.

"I've been waitressing at the Wander Inn after school and on weekends. If I'm lucky, Mr. Onewolf will hire me full-time for the summer and keep me on for weekend shifts once I start MU in the fall."

She was moving on. Growing up. He couldn't help but feel like he was being left behind.

Michael frowned. "You don't need a job."

"Yes, I do. College isn't cheap."

"I told you I wanted to pay—"

"I'm not taking your money, Mikey," she said, that hardheaded streak of hers coming out in full force. "No way is my brother risking life and limb to keep me in nail polish and fashion magazines."

Michael thought of the thick bricks of cash he'd traded for bullets over the years. Millions. He had millions tucked away in offshore accounts, and the only person he had to spend it on refused to take it. "You don't read fashion magazines."

She laughed; the sound of it so much like their mother's that it cut him to the bone. "Maybe I do. I'm all grown up now—last time you saw me, I had scabby knees and braces."

"You were beautiful."

"And you were so obviously blind," she said, the laughter dying in her voice. "You're not coming to my graduation, are you? I'd really hoped you'd be there."

"I can't…" It was an old conversation, one that never changed.

"I know, but I thought maybe… Stupid, huh?" She sounded hurt.

"Frankie—"

"I love them, you know? Aunt Gina and Uncle Tony. I'll always be grateful for the way they took me in and raised me after mom and dad…" She let her words trail off, unable to say it, like saying the word *died* was the same as killing them all over again. "But they aren't my family—not the way you are. I miss my brother."

He closed his eyes, picturing his petrified fourteen-year-old self holding baby Frankie when Sophia and Sean, his adoptive parents, first brought her home from the hospital so many years ago. He'd been so angry, so scared. But she just looked at him with complete trust in her dark-blue eyes. And now she was going to college. Jesus.

"I miss you too."

"So come home."

He wished things were that simple. Instead of saying what he always said—*I can't*—he looked up. "Go to your window," he said and listened to her comply.

"Okay," she said.

"Do you see the moon?"

"Yes," she said.

"So do I," he said. "I see the same moon. We aren't so far apart. I'm always with you."

Her voice was wistful and sad. "I wish that were true."

So did he. "Good night, Frankie. I love you."

"I love you too," she said, and then she was gone.

FORTY-FOUR

LET HER GO.

That was what Michael's brain was telling him to do. Just let Sabrina go. It was better this way. Easier. Every time he managed to put some distance between them, he caved. Ended up pulling her closer. Let her sink in just a little bit deeper.

He got out of the car, allowing himself the satisfaction of slamming the door behind him. She didn't look back, just kept walking, her dog hugging her left flank, watchful of the shadows.

Let her go.

He made sure to lock her car before pocketing her keys. He wasn't dumb enough to think that keeping her car keys would stop her from following him if she wanted to; he was just hoping her impulsive nature didn't get the better of her. He dropped the wad of metal into his jacket pocket and headed back to Miss Ettie's.

She knew what he really was, what he was capable of. But despite her false bravado, he knew the truth: Sabrina had no desire to see him go to work.

That made two of them.

He rounded the corner quietly, giving the exterior of the house a sweeping glance from the shadows, letting his instincts take over. No cartel thugs or sleeper agents lurking in the shadows. All was quiet … which made him very nervous.

He let himself in through the back, pressing his thumb against the small blinking touchpad mounted next to the door. Like he knew it would, the pad read his thumbprint and stopped blinking a few seconds before the auto-locks engaged.

"To tell the truth, I miss my keys."

Michael turned toward the kitchen table to find Miss Ettie sitting, a cup of tea in front of her. He leaned across the counter to take a look in the Blue Willow bowl she kept on its surface. It was empty.

His shoulders slumped a bit as the weight of one more regret settled in place. "I'm sorry."

Miss Ettie gave him a smile before raising her cup to her curved mouth. "For what?"

"For this. All of it." He waved a hand around. "Bio-scanners and bulletproof glass. For not staying away when I should have."

She lowered her cup, a slight frown multiplying the soft winkles on her face. "Then you're sorry for the wrong thing, Michael," she said as she stood, her chair making a faint scraping noise across the hardwood floor. "What you should be apologizing for is staying away as long as you did."

She traveled the short length of space between the table and the sink with her empty cup before she spoke again. "I heard you leave a while ago and had hoped I wouldn't see you until morning," she said, running water into her cup before setting it in the dish drainer.

"Sabrina's better off without me," he said, not even bothering to pretend he didn't know what or who she was talking about.

"Says who? You?" She chuckled softly on her way to her room, the sound telling him what a fool she thought he was. "One thing I know for sure, Michael, is that happiness in this world is a fleeting thing," she said, reaching out to pat his cheek. "It's selfish and cruel to deny it. To yourself or to others." She stood on tiptoes and planted a kiss on his jaw. "Good night," she whispered against his lowered cheek before continuing down the hall to her room.

He stood there for a moment, trying to digest her words. Trying to deny the sense they made. The Felix the Cat clock above the sink, with its swishing tail and ping-pong ball eyes, let out a single meow. Eleven p.m.—time to go to work.

Michael took himself upstairs, quietly checking on Alex before letting himself into his room. There he shed his track pants and running shoes, trading them for cargo pants and heavy boots before pulling out his case and setting it on the bed. Thirty seconds later there was a soft-knuckled rap against his closed bedroom door, moments before it swung open.

"Going somewhere?" Ben said, watching him slip knives and guns into various compartments and holsters.

"Got a lead on where Reyes might've set up shop," he said, mulling over the merits of a few concussion grenades.

"Am I invited?"

Deciding against the grenades, he tossed them back into the case before shutting the lid to look up at his partner. "Nope."

Ben sighed, shouldering himself off the frame to stand up straight. "Maybe you should wait. I got a couple of local guys I trust—I can send them in to gather some intel before you go all Lone Ranger." Ben knew better than to try and push his way in. The kid was a lot of things, but stupid wasn't one of them.

Michael smirked in spite of himself but shook his head. "As soon as it gets back to your father that the body Sabrina found isn't Leo Maddox, he's going to yank my ass back to Spain. Waiting isn't an option."

Ben shook his head. "At least let me send a couple of—"

"What's going on between Sabrina and Phillip Song?" The question came out of nowhere, etching a frown onto Ben's face. But as much as he wanted to take it back, Michael wanted answers more.

Ben shrugged, seemed a little reluctant to answer. "I don't know. She goes and sees him at his restaurant every couple of weeks—usually late, after everyone's gone to bed. She hangs out for an hour or so and she comes home," he said. "Why? Is that where the two of you went tonight?"

He nodded. "He gave her something before we left—a red silk pouch. Asked her how she'd been sleeping." *Called her sweetheart.*

"Like shit," Ben muttered, seemingly unaware that his knowing that revealed just how close he'd become to Sabrina over the past year. "Wait, is he where you got your intel? I hate to say it, but I'm not sure Song has your best interests at heart. Now I *really* think you should wait."

Michael reopened the case and pulled out a pair of binocs before he stooped to shove it back under the bed. "Like I said—not an option."

"Nothing."

Michael looked up. Ben was watching him carefully, shoulder leaned against the mantle. "Nothing what?"

"That's the answer to the question you're kicking around that thick skull of yours. Nothing." Ben quirked his mouth into a smile that looked almost wistful. "Nothing is going on between Sabrina and me. She's my friend—just like you're my friend. I don't have many."

Michael didn't know what to say, so he didn't say anything, just kept heading for the door. He stopped in front of his partner, slapping the field glasses into his open palm. "Keep an eye on her. If she leaves, text me."

FORTY-FIVE

THE WAREHOUSE WAS EXACTLY were Phillip Song said it would be, crammed into to the middle of an industrial park on Bayshore, just south of Loomis. Michael drove past the deserted-looking building before circling back and parking a few blocks away. The place may have looked abandoned, but he knew a front when he saw one. Discreet security cameras, wire mesh embedded in high-set windows, a single door set off the street and partially hidden by a Dumpster, what looked like a bay door big enough for a box truck around back.

With its lack of entry points and hidden security cameras, a stealth approach was going to be nearly impossible. Good thing he came prepared.

Without the soft rumble of the car engine, Michael could hear the distant thump of music coming from the nightclub across the street, the line to get in wrapped around the building. It made him think of the night he'd spent with Pia Cordova. What he'd done to her father. What he'd done to her.

He could still see her standing at the top of the stairs, open blouse clutched against her exposed breasts, staring down at him with a mixture of fear and confusion that quickly bled into something else ...

Recognition.

He'd lied to Ben when he'd said that Pia hadn't recognized him from that night at the club. She'd known exactly who he was and as soon as the bullets started flying, she'd known exactly what he'd done. He swiped a rough hand over his face, trying desperately to scrub away the memory, but it wouldn't budge.

Guilt ate at him. Pushing him to do something he hadn't done in years. Not since he found out Frankie was dead.

He wanted to drink.

If he was completely honest with himself—which was a rarity these days—he'd admit that the urge had very little to do with Pia Cordova or the shit storm he'd unleashed on her over the past few days. She was just another job, just another casualty. No. This was about Sabrina and what being so close to her did to him. What it made him want and wish. What it made him remember and regret.

Leaning into the dash, Michael popped the trunk before stepping out of the car to circle around back. He shrugged out of his jacket, tossing it into the trunk before reaching for what Ben liked to call the prop box. Inside it was a variety of umbrellas, a few baseball caps, sunglasses, a couple of maps, a fake arm cast ... and a bottle of booze.

He stared at it for a few seconds, contemplating what he wanted, measuring it against what he should do instead.

Before he allowed himself to think it through, Michael snatched the bottle out of the box and cracked the lid. Lifting it to his lips, he pulled the liquor through clenched teeth and into his mouth. He held it there for a moment, eyes closed, letting the taste and sting of it settle against his tongue. He could feel the urge to swallow working at the back of his throat. A reflex he'd never been able to fight. Had never even wanted to.

It had been a promise he'd made to Lucy, nothing more, that forced him to dry out—and Lucy was dead. There was nothing and no one who cared anymore. No promises left to break.

Sabrina's face flashed in front of him and that was enough.

Michael swished the liquor around his mouth a few times before he turned his head to the side and spit it into the street. Next he poured a bit into his hands and rubbed them together before applying it to his skin like aftershave, coating himself liberally until he smelled as drunk as he wished he actually was.

Recapping the bottle, he tossed it back into the box before fitting the fake cast onto his arm and grabbing a pair of mirrored aviators. Easing the trunk lid down, he heard the muted *click* of the latch as he pocketed the keys.

He staggered away from his car and covered the couple of blocks between where he parked and the warehouse in a drunken gait, weaving slightly, like a guy who was tore up but still trying to keep his cool. He passed a few groups, tight clutches of people on their way to the nightclub he'd seen, hoping tonight was the night they'd get past the velvet ropes.

He kept walking, straight for the building, the drunken lurch he'd affected announcing his approach as he purposely slammed into the side of the Dumpster, the cast on his arm ringing against the sheet metal like a gong.

For the benefit of the security camera mounted to the side of door, he spun around in a quick circle as if looking for the source of the sound. "Oh, shit," he said, tipping into the door, knocking his aviators askew. To whoever was manning the feed, he'd look like nothing more than another harmless Saturday-night douche bag looking for a party. He knew the old adage, People only see what they want to see, was a lie. People saw what you showed them. Most were too lazy and arrogant to look past what was shoved in front of their face. No one wanted to see the truth. To believe they were vulnerable. That they were about to die.

"Lemme in," he slurred loudly, banging the cast against the heavy metal door, the clang of it much deeper than the Dumpster. Solid core—no way he was kicking that bitch in. A couple of those concussion grenades were looking pretty good right now. He kept up with the banging, drawing as much unwanted attention as he could. People passing on the street were looking in his direction, wondering what the hell was going on. Good. The more people looked, the more likely they were to open the door, just to shut him up. "Hey, come on … open up, I got friends in the VIP—"

There was a scraping noise, metal on metal, a few seconds before the door opened. "Get the fuck out of here, man. The club's down the street," the guy at the door said as he tossed his head, flashing his scorpion neck tat. This was Reyes's place alright.

"Naw, man—this is the place." Michael shouldered his way in, leading with his cast, using it to distract the guy from the fact that his other hand was reaching into the folds of his jacket to draw his Kimber. A few yards away, three men sat at a folding card table, topped with a pair of dice and a scattered stack of crumpled bills. "Hey, whaddya playin'?"

The guy grabbed his casted arm, yanking him back. "This ain't no fuckin' club, white boy—"

That was as far as he got, the suppressed bullet that slammed into his chest throwing him back against the wall. The trio stood in unison, each reaching for their weapons with varying degrees of speed, but it didn't matter—two of them were dead before they even pulled their guns clear, leaving the third with his hand hovering above the grip that protruded from the waistband of his pants, eyes glued to the gun in Michael's hand. He was one of Reyes's lieutenants—older, more seasoned than the dead guys that bracketed him.

Michael kicked the door shut behind him before speaking. "Hey, Hector." He removed the aviators so the last guy standing could get a good look at his face. "Remember me?"

"Yeah. The nanny." The guy cracked a smile that didn't quite reach his eyes.

"That's right, I *am* the nanny. But you can call me *Cartero*." He smiled back a split second before he pulled the trigger, blowing out Hector's knee. The guy dropped like a rock, any thought he'd had of pulling his gun and trying to shoot his way out gone, leaving him a writhing bloody mess.

Michael holstered his gun long enough to pull the fake cast off his arm and drop it on the ground. Now Hector was screaming, clutching at the ragged jumble of meat and bone where his knee had been only a few seconds before.

Michael waited, gun leveled at the hallway leading to a bank of offices to the right. No one came running. No one else was here. "Anyone else in the building?" he said, just to be sure.

Hector's head shook back and forth, his voice too strangled with screams and tears to answer him properly.

"Is that a no?" he said, watching Hector dispassionately. This man sold children. He deserved no sympathy.

"Alone…we…" Hector managed to choke out between screams.

"Perfect." He pulled off his belt and hunkered down next to the wailing man. He used it as a tourniquet to control the blood flow. "We can't have you bleeding out just yet, can we now?" Michael said, giving Hector a heavy-handed pat on his injured leg. "Not before you give me what I'm looking for."

FORTY-SIX

Hector lasted twenty minutes before folding. After that, he'd been so eager to share information that it was almost embarrassing.

Reyes's operation was now global. He had two-man teams all over the world, with the sole objective of abducting children. Some were specified targets—children of wealth, held for ransom; others were targeted for their vulnerability—homeless, runaways, neglected. Easy prey.

Those were the children Reyes sold. Auctions were held online, money delivered via wire transfer. The warehouse was a way station for West Coast shipments. Reyes had identical setups in Florida and Texas.

Michael jammed his shears into the mangled mess of Hector's knee and twisted, staring into his bulged eyes, hand clamped over his gaping mouth to hold in his screams. "We talked about this, Hector. They aren't *product*; they're children. Understand?"

Hector's head bobbed, fast and jerky, sweat and tears mingling with the smears of blood and snot that covered his face. Michael pulled the shears from the wound and wiped them on the guy's gore-splattered shirt. He lifted his hand from the man's mouth. "Now for the million-dollar question, Hector: where is Leo Maddox?" he said.

The man's head changed direction, shaking from side to side. "Who?"

Michael sighed. "Leo Maddox. Grandson of Senator Leon Maddox. One of your teams snatched him in Barcelona a few weeks ago."

"I don't know—*I swear,*" he said, shrinking away from the look Michael gave him. "I don't know! I just handle West Coast operations. I never see the prod—*children* that are held for ransom."

"Who does? Who handles that arm of the operation?" he said. Looking around the warehouse he saw several computers, a few cages, and web cams—everything needed to pull off the kind of operation Hector had outlined for him. He felt an overwhelming urge to burn it all to the ground.

Hector hesitated and Michael smiled. The lift of his mouth shifted the cold visage around but did nothing to warm it. He shot a look at Hector's bare feet, the gaping space between his big and little toe where three other toes should have been. "Really, Hector?" he said, turning back to face the man. "I thought we understood each other."

Hector swallowed hard, his gaze skittering away from the look Michael gave him. "Estefan. Estefan is in charge of that stuff."

He remembered what Estefan had said to him only a few days ago. That he was Alberto's second-in-command these days. "Where is he?"

"Here. He was … showed up out of nowhere …" Hector said, his voice thin and thready.

The news clenched tight around his spine, squeezing it straight. "How long ago?"

"Hour."

Shit. He'd just missed him. Sixty minutes sooner and he would've had the bargaining chip needed to get the Maddox boy back. "Where'd he go?"

Now Hector smiled, thin white lips peeled back against blood-stained teeth, words softly slurred. " ... across the street."

FORTY-SEVEN

HE STOPPED AT THE car long enough to ditch his Kimber. Michael thought about calling Ben for backup, but in the end, he just tossed his phone in the trunk. Estefan belonged to him, and he didn't feel like sharing.

Crossing the street, he left the drunk-guy routine behind, heading straight for the pair of heavily muscled security guards who manned the front of the club. Ignoring the long line of hopefuls, Michael pushed his way to the front. "*Cartero.* I'm on the list."

The bouncer's eyes, pale blue and glassy from steroids, scraped along his frame, taking it all in. He was a mess: hands bloody, dark stains splattered across his shirt, reeking of another man's sweat and fear. It wasn't hard to guess what he'd been doing thirty minutes ago.

Aiming his skeptical gaze at the clipboard in his hand, the security guard scanned the list in front of him before coming to an abrupt halt. He looked at him again, his 'roid-swollen face taking on a wary cast.

"Hold 'em up," he said, motioning with his clipboard for Michael to lift his arms. As soon as he did, he was frisked. This guy wasn't nearly as thorough as Song's men, though. A few pats here and there and he was done. "Zip up your jacket," the man mumbled, eyeing the bloodstained shirt. Michael obliged while the bouncer unclipped the braided gold rope to let him pass.

Behind him he heard the grumble of club kids who'd been waiting all night, but they faded fast behind the pulse and bump of the house DJ. A sea of bodies was in front of him, grinding and writhing against each other. Mindlessly undulating under a dizzying throb of light and sound.

"This way, please."

He turned toward the voice to find a scantily clad woman next to him, the silver mesh that barely covered her catching and throwing the sweep of light that was timed perfectly to the music. She started to move and he followed—up the stairs, leaving the lights and the heavy crush of bodies behind. She stopped and moved to the side, ushering him into the VIP area.

As soon as Estefan saw him, his face split in to a grin, the facial movement wrinkling and bunching the scar tissue on his face.

"I'm so glad you found me, *Cartero*," Estefan said as if they were friends. "Hector?"

"Dead."

Estefan's smile deepened. "You must be thirsty. A drink, yes?" He snapped his fingers, and the woman who escorted him appeared next to him.

"I don't want a drink." His throat burned, calling him a liar.

Estefan shrugged. "Some things never change, eh?"

"When it comes to me and you, no, nothing ever will." He shot a quick glance at the pair of guards that flanked the leather sofa their boss lounged on. The same ones who'd been with him at the club in Spain.

"We don't have to be enemies, *Cartero*. Not anymore." Estefan lifted a glass to his lips and drank—watching him the entire time—until it was drained dry. "You and I, we want the same thing."

"Oh, yeah? What's that?" His hands were shaking—rage and adrenaline washed through his blood in a wave so fast and deep his whole body throbbed.

"To put an end to my father's reign." Estefan held out the glass in his hand and the woman nearly tripped over herself at the opportunity to refill it. "It's long overdue, don't you think?"

Michael laughed. He tipped his head back and cut loose until tears streamed down his face and his stomach ached. The entire room went still. Watching him. Looking at him like he'd lost his mind. He finally ran out of steam, wiping his hands across his face. Trading tears for blood. "Junior … it's not your father's retirement I want." He shook his head. "It's his head in a box I'm after. Yours too."

He could do it. He could be over the table in a heartbeat, shattered glass jammed into his carotid. Estefan would be dead before his guards had time to react.

As usual, Estefan seemed to read his mind. "*Tsk, tsk, tsk* … Now is not the time or place for such things, *Cartero*." He wagged a finger at him, settling into the sofa with a fresh drink.

"Any time would be the perfect time to watch you bleed." His hands cranked into fists. His weight redistributed, shifting toward the balls of his feet, readying him for launch.

"What of your woman? Have you considered what happens to her if you kill me? There are people—my people—watching her as we speak. Waiting…"

"Sabrina can take care of herself." Even as he said it, he forced himself to relax. Push back against the rage that crowded around him.

"So I've heard. But we both know how much you enjoy playing the hero, don't we?" Estefan said with a grin. "What it must do to you to love a woman who doesn't need one."

"Fuck. You."

Estefan took a genteel sip and sniffed as if the use of foul language offended him. "If not a partnership, then I propose a truce. I won't lift a finger against you or your Sabrina."

"In exchange for what?"

"You let me finish my business here and leave. With my head intact."

Accepting would be his smartest course of action. He had bigger things to worry about right now. "Where is Leo Maddox? As a sign of good faith."

Estefan sighed, inclining his head slightly. "Quite safe."

"*Where*?"

"The same place my father keeps all of his prized possessions. I'm sure you remember." Estefan offered him another smile. "Do we have a deal?"

If their plan worked, he'd be gone within the next twenty-four hours. Until then, he had to do what he could to keep her safe. "Forty-eight hours. After that, if you're still here, all bets are off."

Before he could get his answer, the guard to his left cocked his head slightly, listening to the comm in his ear before bending down to whisper something to his boss. Estefan's face slammed shut, his pleasant expression morphing into something much closer to the truth. He brushed the guard off and stood moments before the house lights snapped on and the music came to an abrupt end. Downstairs the

219

collective groaned in unison but were cut off by a voice over the PA, telling everyone to evacuate the building immediately.

"You've been busy, *Cartero*," Estefan said as one of his guards helped him into his jacket. Without the mask of music to hide behind, he could hear them: sirens wailing in the distance, getting closer by the second.

"I've reconsidered my offer. I think I should like to meet your Sabrina after all. What is it you Americans say? Game on."

He didn't answer, and Estefan didn't wait. He turned, letting his security team lead him to an elevator and safely away.

Michael waited until he was gone before leaving, taking the service corridor that led down a narrow set of stairs, feeding him into the alley. The smell of smoke greeted him. At the mouth of the alley the partiers stood in the street, murmuring and gasping as they watched Reyes's warehouse burn, the flames dancing high in the distance.

FORTY-EIGHT

HE DROVE, HIS BLOODSTAINED hands wrapped about the steering wheel so tight the skin that covered his hands was as pale as the bone underneath. He tried to pretend he didn't know where he was going. Like it hadn't been the plan all along.

Michael let himself in quietly, pressing his thumb against the small square screen outside the door. The lock popped, just like Miss Ettie's, and he pushed his way inside. He'd expected to find her dog guarding the door, all teeth and snarl, waiting to rip his throat out. Instead he found her alone, sitting in the ladder back chair next to the window. The one he'd sat in that first night, watching over her while she slept. The night he'd realized that he was lost when it came to her and no matter how hard he tried, there was no hope of ever finding his way back.

She knew he was there but didn't turn. She just kept staring out the window, bare feet pulled up, heels tucked snugly against her ass, chin propped on top of her knees. She wore nothing but a tank and boy shorts, a heavy ceramic mug in her hand. A police scanner sitting next to a baby monitor on her nightstand.

She lifted it to her mouth, the faint smell of it drifting over to him. Something light, delicate ... almost floral. Tea.

He stood stock still for a moment, staring at her. Waiting for her to turn. To look at him, say something. The sounds of SFPD dispatch and soft even breathing filled the space between them, and he was suddenly sure she knew what he'd done.

He waited a few more seconds, her refusal to acknowledge him feeding his anger, somehow making it easier to do what he came to do. "Okay," he said, his tone low and even. "That's how you want to play it ..." He hooked his thumb into the hem of his blood-splattered shirt and pulled it up over his head, tossing it on the floor.

She looked at him then, tipping her face toward him to rest her cheek against her knee. Her eyes on him, roving over the scars and wounds that chronicled his life, felt like a confession. He let her look, let her see what he really was a moment longer before he circled around to the far side of the bed and sat down, giving her his back while he unlaced his boots.

He could hear her behind him. The creak of the chair as she stood. The quiet *click* of her cup when she set it down on the crowded nightstand. The silencing of one monitor and then another—plunging them into silence. From the corner of his eye, he could see her move around the bed, disappearing into the bathroom.

He didn't look at her. That ugly thing he carried around with him, that tangled knot of selfish need, wound tight against his gut. He shouldn't be here. He knew that, and if he were better—*cleaner*—he wouldn't be. If he really loved her he would leave her alone, but he didn't. Couldn't. He just concentrated on his boots until they were undone and on the floor beside him.

Now came the soft rush of water and another *click* followed by a wash of dark as she shut off the bathroom light. Then she was kneeling in front of him, reaching for his hands. He pulled away from her. Didn't want her to touch what covered them. She leveled a look at him, one that said more than words ever could. This time when she reached for him, he let her.

He watched her clean the blood off his hands, her head bent— the dim glow of the bedside lamp setting a burnished glimmer to her dark auburn hair. He was hit with the sudden memory of doing almost the exact same thing for her, not so long ago.

"Have you been drinking?" she said quietly, drawing the wash-cloth down the length of his arm, the sickly sweet smell of booze rising off his skin.

He almost lied to her, told her that he had. That he was drunk and that it was the only reason he was here, but in the end he shook his head. "No. I gave myself a Jack Daniels sponge bath. Men like the ones belonging to Reyes don't feel threatened by drunk white guys with broken arms." He waited for her to ask what he meant by that, but she didn't, and he could feel his anger flare again. "Don't you want to know what I did?" he said quietly, while she scrubbed at his hands, taking great care to run the cloth over each separate finger, the callused pad of his palms. His bruised knuckles. "Who I did it to?"

She finished cleaning off one hand and reached for the other. "You did what you always do." She looked him in the eye. "What needed to be done," she said, handing his earlier words back to him. She rocked back on her heels, dropping the washcloth. "Beyond that, I don't care." He looked down at the hand she still held. The blood was gone. Or maybe it had just seeped beneath his skin to a place he could never reach.

He barked out a hollow-sounding laugh, pulling his hand out of her grasp, lunging forward to clamp both around her arms, tight enough to cast shadows in her eyes. "I liked it. Enjoyed every *fucking* second of it. That's the kind of man I am, Sabrina—do you care about *that*?" That dirty knot suddenly pulled straight and wound itself around his throat, tighter and tighter, until he couldn't breathe. He swallowed hard against the strangling length of it but forced himself to keep talking. To make her see him. Not the heroic version she stubbornly clung to, but the real him. "I keep trying to tell you. Keep trying to show you, but you're either too stupid or too fucked in the head to get it." He glared down at her. He could feel his rough fingers digging into the tense muscles of her biceps and fought against the urge to soften his grip. "This isn't going to work, you and me," he said, forcing as much scorn and anger into his tone as he could find. "Not ever. I need you to tell me you understand that."

She glared back at him, her eyes dark blue shards of glass that cut him to the bone. "If that's true, then why are you here?" She leaned in— or maybe he pulled her to him, he wasn't sure. All he knew was that she suddenly surrounded him, so close it made him dizzy. "Tell me …" She craned her neck, bring her mouth as close to his ear as his hold on her would allow. "Why did you come here?" she whispered, her words skating along his collarbone, the warmth of them spreading around his ribs to run a trail of sensation along his spine that murdered every lie he had lined up, leaving him nothing more to offer but the truth.

"Because I'm selfish," he said quietly. "Because when it comes to you, I can't make myself do the right thing. I can't make myself walk away. I just … can't. I never could."

"Then stop trying." Her face softened, her gaze losing its sharp edges. "It doesn't matter. All I care about is that you're here with me *now*."

"Say it again. What you said before, in the street…" He let his gaze drift down so he could watch her mouth form the words. "Say it…" he whispered, suddenly desperate to hear it, even if it was a lie. Even if she had no idea who or what she was really saying it to.

"You're a good man, Michael." Her hand slipped between them, lifting to cup his face. Her fingers brushed along his brow, and he realized he was frowning, instantly rejecting the words she spoke. "Even if you can't see it. Even if you can't believe it—I *can*…because I love you."

He raised his gaze to hers and found something that rattled the very foundation he'd built his life on.

Truth.

I love you. That was all it took, three simple words, to snap the last of his self-control. He relaxed his hold on her arms, allowing her to press herself against him, her mouth rushing up to meet his, soft and wet, opening to invite him inside.

She kept moving, pushing against him until he was reclining on the bed. She followed, keeping their mouths locked together, fisting her hands in the sheets, pulling herself onto the bed as he fell, drawing her knees up, straddling him, grinding her hips into the erection that suddenly pushed into the junction of her thighs. He gripped her thighs, pressing himself against her, doing his damnedest to control the frenzy of need that broke out beneath his skin.

"Sabrina…" The voice that said her name was little more than a strangled croak, and it took him a second to realize that desperate sound had come from him.

She broke away, rearing up to look down at him. Her hips went still beneath his hands, her gaze and fingers trailing the loops and whorls of the tattoo that splayed across his chest, and for an instant he was sure she could see them—the names of his dead, trapped under the surface of his skin, hidden beneath dark ribbons of ink. Her fingers continued across his stomach until they found the button of his cargos, lifting herself onto her knees in order to give herself room to free it from its loop and work his pants down until they hit the floor.

Cool fingers wrapped around his cock, pulling another sound from him, this one more guttural, ending on a harsh breath as her hand slid down the hard length of him. She leaned into him again until they were face to face, her long hair forming a curtain between them and the outside world, her hand and hips working him in perfect rhythm with her mouth on his.

Naked. He wanted her naked. That was all he could think about. All that mattered. Without thinking, he reached up and caught the bottom of her tank, moving to pull it off. Her hands followed his, covering them, her gaze instantly wild and unsure. She never took her shirt off. He knew that, and he was suddenly sure he'd pushed her too far, asked for too much. But it was too late to take it back, and he was too far beyond caring. He tightened his grip on the hem of her tank, his gaze nailed to hers and continued dragging it upward, following the lean lines of her arms, and she let him until it was nothing more than a wad of fabric in his hands. She stayed where she was for a moment, parted mouth hovering above his, exposed breasts pressed against his bare chest. She sat back, her long dark hair catching fire as it tumbled across her shoulders, the strands of it shifting from brown to red with each breath she took.

She had nearly as many scars as he did. Slashes and burns. Bumps and cuts. Each one a memory of what had been done to her. A tangible badge announcing her strength. Declaring her survival. Jaw set, chin held at an almost defiant angle, she let him look, her eyes hot and dry as she accepted his gaze on her, and in that moment he'd never seen anything more fiercely beautiful.

He gathered up her hair, moving it to the side so he could see all of her. The hard knot of scar tissue at the top of her thigh. Another at the inside of her arm. The ropy scatter of them across her belly. He could still see her face the night she'd brought his hand against her stomach, the way she pressed his fingers into them while she looked at him, telling him what they were.

They spell out the word mine...

Michael pushed the memory away. He used the self-control he was so proud of to lock it down. To concentrate on the only thing that mattered. *Now.* "You're beautiful..." He trailed a hand down the length of her, mesmerized by the feel of her skin, the way it slid and shifted beneath his. He cupped her breasts, brushed his thumbs across her nipples, the blood rushing from his brain as they instantly tightened beneath his touch. She arched back slightly, eyes closed. Offering him more—anything he wanted.

Settling a hand on the top of her leg, gripping her hip, he let his thumb cruise along the snug hem of her underwear, following it around to the junction of her thighs, running it lightly over the small swatch of fabric that covered her. She caught her breath as he slipped beneath it, running the pad of his thumb along her silky wet cleft.

She moaned, the sound getting caught in her throat as her hips pushed against his hand, his thumb sinking in deeper and deeper until it settled on her core and she rode it, grinding herself against him, her breath coming in short soft pants, setting him on fire, pulling him apart until he couldn't think straight. Lost, he reared up and turned, covering her with his body, settling his hips into the cradle of her thighs, his erection pushed against her, nothing between them but the thin cotton barrier of her panties.

She went still again, her chest pumping against his with an unsteady rhythm, her wide-eyed gaze telling him she was fighting for control, and he realized too late what he'd done. What kind of memories his weight on top of her would incite. He raised himself instantly, started to pull back, but she shifted her hips again, fitting her knees against his rib cage, locking her ankles around his hips.

"It's okay … it's okay …" She said it softly, over and over, glazed eyes locked on his mouth, and he wasn't sure who she was talking to—herself or to him. "It's okay … don't stop," she said, focusing on his face. "Just … don't stop."

He took her at her word, kept his eyes locked on her face as he dipped his head to run his tongue along the swell of her breast, the slight salty taste of her like a fist in the gut, leaving him breathless and dizzy. He drew her nipple into his mouth, relishing the way it went taut against his tongue when he sucked, softly at first but then grazing it with his teeth, causing her breath to catch in the back of her throat. Her arms came up and for a split second he was sure she'd push him away or maybe break his neck … but then her fingers delved into his hair, gripping it tightly. Pulling him closer. Offering him more.

He shifted to the side, ignoring the pounding pulse of his erection as he worked his hand between them again, cupping his hand against her to work the heel of his palm against the top of her cleft. Raising himself up, he looked down at her, skimming his fingertips along the thin stretch of cotton between them. "Is this okay?" he whispered between delivering feather-light kisses to her jaw line, running the tip of his tongue along the taunt column of her neck.

His mouth on her breast again, his tongue skimming along the swell of it before he pressed a kiss to her sternum. "Are you okay?"

She gave him a jerky nod. "Yes…it's okay," she said, pushing her hips against his hand, her breath catching, coming short and soft as he traced his tongue down her stomach, right to the center of her. "Take them off…" Her hands left his hair and began pushing at the last barrier between them, trying to pull her boy shorts down her hips. "Please, Michael…take them off…"

He jacked up off the bed, her pleas instantly whipping that frenzy of need that crawled beneath his skin into a raging hornet's nest of mindless desperation. He got them off, though he wasn't sure how, and he lunged at her again just as she pushed her hips forward, unaware of what was happening until it was done. Until he was buried inside her so deep that stars exploded in front of his eyes and the breath he'd been holding came out in a sharp exhale, like he'd been kicked in the gut.

He buried his face in her neck, fists caught up in the sheets beneath her head, eyes squeezed tight as he tried to remember how to breathe. He tried not to move, but she wasn't having any of it. She pulled her knees even higher, widening the cradle of her hips.

"I can't—I can't—" He had no idea what he was saying, only knew that every time she rocked herself against him, felt the soft, wet slide of her around his cock, he fell a little deeper. Was pulled under with each and every roll of her hips until he was drowning.

Her tongue licked its way to his ear, her fingers trailing down his spine to grip his ass. "Then stop trying, Michael," she whispered, her teeth nipping the side of his jaw. "Stop trying and just…let go."

He did as she said. He let go of it all. Focused all of his senses on this single point in time until there was only *now*. The way she felt, stretched and wrapped around him, the way her breath caught every time he flexed his hips against hers. The taste of her against his tongue, the way it slid down his throat, salty and sweet. He loved her until everything else faded away. Until nothing else mattered.

Until he was able to convince himself, at least for a while, that nothing else ever would.

FORTY-NINE

She was sleeping when the phone rang, its muted beeps originating from one of the pockets on his discarded pants. Michael reached down and found it, swiping his finger across its screen to silence it.

"Hello, Alberto," he said, affecting a lazy tone.

"*Cartero*, it's been a long time." The voice on the other end of the line delivered the words smoothly. "I trust you're well."

"Better than Hector," he said, standing carefully so he didn't wake Sabrina.

"Ah, yes, Hector. Estefan told me," Reyes said as if Michael had broken a wineglass instead of tortured and killed a man who'd served him for the better part of a decade.

"Sorry about your warehouse."

"You are only sorry that I was not inside it when you struck the match." He could hear amusement in Reyes's voice when he spoke.

He moved to stand at the window. "When I kill you, it's going to be a little more hands-on than arson," he said quietly, watching the darkness beyond the glass. "Hector told me everything."

Reyes chuckled. "And what is *everything*?"

"That you kidnapped the grandson of a US Senator ... and that you did it for Livingston Shaw." It was a lie, but the silence that greeted him from the other end of the phone line told him he was right.

"Hector has always been weak," Reyes said, his tone hard and even. "I supposed I should pay you for killing him."

Michael smiled, the flash of white reflected back to him by the smooth black glass he stood in front of. "Or you could just tell me what Estefan is doing here and we can call it square."

"His job. My little squabble with Jorge Cordova has finally come to an end. My West Coast foothold has been precarious of late, but now that he's dead, Estefan is securing my interests there," Reyes said, his tone heavy with satisfaction. "Thank you for that, by the way."

It was the way he said it that told him the truth: Michael may have killed Cordova on Livingston Shaw's orders, but he'd pulled the trigger for Reyes all the same. He clamped his jaw shut and took more than a few calming breaths so that he didn't scream loud enough to wake the dead.

"Are you still there, *Cartero*?" Reyes laughed. "You seem to have lost your tongue."

"Leo Maddox. I know Estefan's crew snatched him and I'm pretty sure it was done under your orders, so ..."

"You haven't even asked about Christina. Have you forgotten her so quickly?" Reyes countered quietly, the threat so vague that no one but him would even know it was there.

"She's your daughter, not mine," he said, the words tightening around his throat.

Reyes kept talking as though Michael hadn't said a word. "For so long, she actually believed you would keep your promise. She's always thought you were some great hero, but Lydia … Well, in the end, she knew better, didn't she?"

For the space of a breath, he could see Lydia, eyes wide and terrified, her mouth working silently, her words both prayer and plea.

Remember your promise …

"Your daughter was a job, Alberto, nothing more," he said. And for just a moment, he actually believed it.

"And what of my wife, *Cartero*?" Reyes voice whipped out, edged in ice. "Was she just a *job* as well?"

Lydia, sitting beside him on the beach, dark hair lifted away from her face by the light coastal breeze. Bare toes dug into the sand. Brown eyes alive and happy as she watched her daughter build a sandcastle. "I barely remember her."

"I think she would be hurt to hear you say that," Reyes chided gently. "She cared deeply for you, right until the very end."

"The Maddox boy. He's the job now. That's all I care about." The lie came out smoother than he thought it would.

"That's not exactly true, is it, *Cartero*?" Reyes said, his words barely above a whisper. "She's not beautiful in the traditional sense, but there is something about her I find intriguing, your Sabrina. She's a warrior. A fighter. Is that what drew you to her? Her will to live?" Now his voice hardened, truth ringing in every word. "You kill everything you touch, everything you love, but she's different, isn't she? She's strong— seemingly invincible. She has survived so much. Maybe she *can* survive you … but do you really think she can survive us both?"

Sabrina.

"Don't." The word was spoke calmly, even pleasantly. A warning more deadly than any he had ever delivered.

"Amazing. After all these years, it looks as if an attachment has finally been made. I'll hurt her and her family in ways even you can't imagine," Reyes said. "You took my Lydia from me. It's only fair that I return the favor, don't you think?"

He looked at Sabrina. She was still sleeping. Had turned onto her stomach, hands tucked beneath her chin. Her lips slightly parted, long lashes casting dark shadows across her cheeks. She looked soft and warm. Like every good thing he'd ever wished for but had never deserved.

"I'm coming for you. Do you hear me?" He felt something cold and heavy wrap around his chest, squeezing the air from his lungs. "I'm coming, and there isn't a damn thing you can do to stop me."

Reyes chuckled. "Stop you? Now why would I want to do that? In fact, I'm counting on it, *Cartero*. Hurry. Little Leo and I will be waiting."

FIFTY

MICHAEL MOVED QUICKLY AND quietly, straight for the room at the end of the hall. He passed an open door and looked inside to find the baby's nursery, with Avasa stretched out on the rug beside the crib. She lifted her head, ears pricked forward, just as he pulled the door closed, shutting her inside the room with the baby ... Lucy. They'd named her Lucy. Somehow, knowing that bolstered his resolve.

He reached the end of the hall, the door to the master bedroom open just a crack. He pushed it wider and stepped inside, pulling it closed behind him. Standing at the foot of the bed, he could see them sleeping comfortably.

The cop slept on the side closest to the door, instinctively placing himself between his wife and whatever might come through it to harm her. That's the kind of thing a husband would do. Protect. Love. Provide. Michael felt another stab of guilt, made heavy and bitter by regret.

He clapped a hand over the cop's mouth, and he jerked awake in an instant—eyes wide and alert, but he didn't make a sound. Didn't want to alarm his wife.

Michael waited for his vision to adjust, for Nickels to see him clearly before he backed away from the bed and cocked his head toward the door, giving the other man room to stand and follow him out into the hall. He checked his watch while Nickels pulled the door to his bedroom shut with a quiet *click*, shooting him a guarded look.

"That's an excellent way to get yourself shot, asshole," Nickels said, his tone low and even. Michael ignored the obvious—while the cop was no doubt able to handle himself, if he'd been so inclined, he could have murdered him with ease.

The cop seemed to realize this too because he let the fact that Michael had just snuck into his bedroom slide. "What the fuck are you doing…?" His question trailed off as he took in Michael's bare feet and chest. "Oh." Nickels rubbed a rough hand over the back of his neck, averting his gaze to the spot just over his shoulder. "Okay… What do you want?"

"I want you to leave." He reached into his pocket and pulled out a small manila envelope. "This is a key to a storage unit in Oakland. The address and unit number are on the keychain. Inside you'll find everything you need to get your family as far away from here as possible."

Nickels looked down at the envelope in his hand before bouncing that disbelieving look back to his face. "Are you kidding?"

"No, I'm not." Michael ran a hand over his hair, blowing out a frustrated breath. "You'll have to get Riley and Jason. Strickland too. Don't call them—just show up. Pick a place none of you have ever been. A place as far away from friends and family as you can get. There'll be a car; use it. Stay away from airports and train stations. Ditch your cells and identification—"

Nickels laughed out loud. "If you think I'm gonna be able to get Strickland to leave her, you're friggin' delusional."

Like he didn't know that. He'd considered the old duct tape/ trunk routine, but Sabrina's partner hated him enough already. "You're going to have to try."

"Where are we supposed to go?" Nickels said, his tone edged with distrust.

"I don't know and I don't *want* to know."

The cop narrowed his eyes. "I'll send Val and Lucy. She'll get the twins, but I'm not leaving." His tone said he thought he was closing the subject.

Michael shook his head. "They won't make it a day without you. Val's tough, but she'll get scared. She'll reach out to someone she trusts, maybe her mother or a cousin, and it'll be over. They'll all be dead—or worse. Much, *much* worse."

Every word he spoke drained more and more color from the cop's face until he was a bloodless ghost. Nickels glanced down at the small space they shared, as if he wondered if his touch would infect him with some disease. "What the fuck did you do? What the *fuck* did you bring to my doorstep?"

He could deny it. Pass the blame on to Ben or even Sabrina herself. Hadn't Ben been the one to recruit her? Hadn't Sabrina been the one to lead herself to Livingston Shaw like some sort of suicidal lamb to slaughter? He hadn't caused this. He wasn't at fault.

Like most lies, it sounded good. It even sounded true.

"I think it's best you don't stick around to find out." Michael blew out another hard breath, scrubbed a rough hand over his face. "Look...I know you care about her, but this isn't your fight." He reached behind him and opened the door to the nursery; let the door swing open so Nickels could see the crib where his daughter was sleeping peacefully. "*This* is your fight—a wife and child who depend on you. So take the key and leave. Sooner rather than later," Michael said, playing the one card he knew the cop wouldn't be able to deny.

Nickels blew out a disgusted breath as he shook his head. "You dirty, cheating son of a bitch," he growled, swiping the envelope from his hand. "You want to explain to me how I'm supposed to get my very opinionated, very uncooperative wife on board with your little escape plan? Especially without letting her say goodbye to Sabrina?"

"That's your problem, not mine." Michael cracked a cold smile as he backed himself down the hall. "But however you do it, I suggest you do it quickly. You don't have much time."

FIFTY-ONE

Cofre del Tesoro, Colombia
March 2011

MICHAEL TOOK A QUICK look around, glancing down the hall, both left and right, before rapping light knuckles against Lydia's bedroom door. In his fist he held a key, but he decided to respect her privacy instead of using it—unlike her husband. Reyes hadn't been on the island for weeks, his visits becoming even less frequent, more sporadic—but that didn't mean he didn't know everything that went on here.

Between the household staff and the recent unwelcomed addition of his son, Estefan, Michael had no doubt that Reyes knew everything that happened on Cofre del Tesoro. Standing here, in front of Reyes's wife's bedroom, waiting for her to open the door was dangerous and stupid—for both of them.

But this was worth the risk.

He lifted his hand again, but the door opened before it made contact. Lydia stood on the other side, hand on the knob, managing to look both excited and apprehensive at the same time. "I don't think this is a good idea," she said, her hand falling off the knob to lace fingers with its partner. "Maybe you should just go without me. I can watch from one of the upstairs—"

"No. You get to have this, and so does she." He reached for her hand, pulling her across the threshold and into the deserted hallway. He pressed a key into her hand and closed her fingers around it. Her eyes went wide when she realized what he was giving her. "It's Sunday—everyone is off island for the day. It's just us," he said. She nodded and slipped the key into her pocket to be hidden later.

He'd been trying to coax her out of her room for months now, to see Christina, but whatever threats Reyes had levied against her had kept her firmly in place. Until today.

"What about … him?" Lydia said, pulling her hand from him. "Is he gone?"

She was talking about Estefan, and he shrugged. "I haven't seen him in days." It was the truth, but saying it did little to calm the niggle of doubt that worried at him. He hadn't *seen* Estefan, but that meant nothing. He could be anywhere, watching and waiting for his opportunity to glean a bit of juicy information to feed to his father. It wasn't a question of *if* Estefan found them out; it was a question of what Michael was willing to do to keep him quiet when he did.

"Do you trust me?" he said. A memory, fast and bright, of asking Christina the exact same thing three years ago. The same day he'd met her mother and went tumbling, headlong, down the slippery slope he'd been treading since he first laid eyes on her daughter.

Lydia nodded and pulled her bedroom door shut. "Yes," she said, giving him a smile.

The worry nested in the back of his brain no longer niggled. Now it poked and pushed, but he ignored it. Christina deserved this, and he was going to make sure she got it.

"Then let's get this show on the road." He cocked his head toward the stairs. "Meet you outside in ten minutes."

He took the stairs to the second floor, winding this way and that until he stood in front of a door as familiar to him as his own. Knocking again, this time he opened the door without waiting for an invitation. Christina sat in the pink chair by the window, only it wasn't pink anymore. She'd found a sheet somewhere, probably in one of the half dozen laundry rooms, and spread its sunny yellow expanse across the chair, covering the color she'd come to hate over the last year. She could do little about the drapes and walls, but the chair she made her own.

"Hey, you want to go for a walk or something?" he said, fighting to keep his tone flat. It was her eighth birthday and she was sure he'd forgotten.

Christina looked up from the book in her lap. "On the beach?"

He pulled a face. "I was thinking maybe the garden."

She sighed, moving her bookmark so it could keep her place before standing. "Okay," she said, stopping to slip her shoes on before stepping into the hall. "I'm tired of the beach anyway."

They walked in silence toward the back of the house. He had to curb the urge to hurry her plodding pace. When they reached the bank of French doors, covered with heavy drapes, that lined the rear wall of the huge formal living room, he rushed ahead and stood in front of one of them. "Knock, knock," he said, and she rolled her eyes at him.

"Who's there?" she mumbled.

"Happy birthday."

She looked up at him, a smile teasing the corners of her tiny mouth at last. "You remembered." Tears sparkled, caught in her lashes, and she blinked them away. She was only eight—barely more than a baby. She had no idea what waited for her on the other side of the door, but he could see she didn't care. Someone remembered her birthday. That was all that mattered. He'd never celebrated his own birthday. Not until he was twelve. The first birthday after he'd been placed with Sean and Sophia. He remembered the cake and candles. The two of them singing to him as if they were actually happy he'd been born.

He cleared his throat. "Seriously? Like I could forget. You've been jabbering about it for weeks now."

Her smile widened into a grin. "I didn't think you cared."

For a moment he grappled with his emotions, dangerous and slippery, before he was able to force them back into the vise grip he usually kept them in. "Maybe I *don't* care. Maybe I'm just tired of the moping," he said with a shrug, pretending to himself that he'd managed to fool her. "Now, close your eyes."

She obeyed instantly, bouncing on her tiptoes, her dark cork-screw curls buoyant around a face that was suddenly lit with joy.

He reached for her hand. "Keep 'em closed."

Christina nodded, giggling as her fingers closed around his, gripping him tight. "Thank you."

Those emotions slipped loose again, and he tried to pull his hand from hers. "You don't even know what it is."

Her hand flexed in his, holding him where he was, surprisingly strong for a young girl. "It doesn't matter."

He pushed the drapes aside to get at the doorknob. He unlocked the door and pulled her onto the veranda. "You can look now," he said quietly.

She didn't move, she simply stood there for a moment with her eyes closed, face turned up to the sun, enjoying the anticipation of what waited for her. He was about to prod her when she finally opened her eyes, a soft fluttering sigh escaping her.

Lydia stood on the flagstone path at the foot of the stairs that led to the garden, a bright-blue BMX racer leaning on its kickstand beside her. "I feel the need to point out that this house is a four-story building the size of a Holiday Inn," he said looking down at her. "You may not, under any circumstance, ride it off the roof."

She launched herself at him, arms and legs scrambling to hug him and for once, he didn't fight her. "Thank you, thank you, thank you…" She said it over and over through the tears before pressing softly pursed lips to his cheek. "I love you too." She whispered it a split second before she was down the stairs, streaking past the bike and into her mother's arms. That was the real gift. They lived in the same house, yet they hadn't seen each other in ten months.

"You live dangerously for a nanny."

His shoulders instantly stiffened, but he turned to give Estefan an indifferent shrug. "She'd been crying for months, whining about seeing her mother," he said fighting to keep his tone even. "I got tired of listening to it."

The younger man pushed himself away from the doorway he slouched against. "Yes… I'm sure that was it," Estefan said, his words dripping with sarcasm. "Where did you get the bike?"

Michael could hear amusement is his voice, as if the thought that he'd bother with such a thing for a child was a ridiculous notion.

And he supposed it was.

"Amazon." Michael cut the young man next to him a caustic smile. "Feel free to leave anytime," he said quietly, not wanting to alarm Lydia.

Estefan ignored him, watching the scene between mother and daughter play out in front of him, barely disguised lust plastered across his face. "She is beautiful, isn't she?"

For a second Michael was unsure which girl he was referring to, and that uncertainty clenched at his gut. "She's a child." He turned to face Estefan head on. "They both are," he said, his tone heavy with warning.

"Mmm…" Estefan shrugged. "Who are you reminding, *Cartero*? Me or yourself?"

He took a quick glance at the two girls behind him. They were lost in each other, paying no attention to what was going on between him and Reyes's son, but he took a few steps forward to close the gap between them just in case. "So there's absolutely no confusion—I'm not warning you. I'm telling you very plainly. If you touch either one of them, I will lay you open and watch you bleed."

Estefan laughed, retreating into the shadows of the house. "So protective of things that don't belong to you, *Cartero*. What would my father say?" he said before he walked away.

It was a threat, veiled and vague. But then again, the most deadly of threats usually were.

FIFTY-TWO

HE KNEW THE SECOND she woke up. Could almost feel her breath catch in her chest as her hand skated along the cold stretch of bed beside her to find him gone. She thought he'd left, and for a moment he wished he had.

"I'm here." He spoke from the window, where he stood, fully clothed, watching a lone hummingbird bump along the fence line, its wings tipped in gold from the rising sun. Nickels had left shortly after their conversation without any indication of where he was going or when he would be back. He'd tried—he couldn't be blamed for what happened to them now.

Sabrina relaxed and turned toward his voice. The rustle of sheets behind him was a whispered invitation to come back to bed. *Forget what's right. Take what you want.* He had to ground his boots into the hard planks of the floor to keep from falling apart.

"Is everything okay?" she asked, her sleepy tone edged with worry.

"Why didn't you read the file on me that Croft gave you?" he said quietly.

"What?" He heard confusion but also something else. Something wary, like even half asleep, she knew she'd been dropped into a minefield. "That was a year ago. What does it matter now?"

"It matters. It's all that matters." He pushed forward, ignoring the part of him that wanted to protect her. The part that loved her. "Was it because you wanted to keep lying to yourself about the kind of man I am?"

She sighed. "I thought we were past this."

He shot her a cold smile over his shoulder without turning fully to face her. "Why? Because I finally broke down and fucked you?"

She went rigid, breath caught in her lungs for a moment before she released it slowly on a shaky laugh. "Is that all you've got, O'Shea? Slut shaming? *Lame*."

Not the response he'd expected. "You *should* be ashamed," he ground out, his jaw trying to lock itself around words his mouth didn't want to form.

"You seem to forget I wrote the playbook on emotional withdrawal." She sat up, sheet clutched to her chest. "If you want to get rid of me, you're going to have to do better than that."

He forced his hands to relax, opened them against his thighs in an effort to at least appear in control. "Answer the question. The file?"

"Okay. I didn't read the file because I didn't need to," she told him, dragging the sheets with her as she moved to sit on the side of the bed and look up at him.

Again, not what he expected. "What does that mean?" he said, even though he had a pretty good idea.

"That means I already knew … *Cartero*." She looked him in the eye. "I know everything, and I knew it long before Croft threw that file at me, so you can spare me the dramatics."

He stared at her for a moment before shaking his head. "I don't know what's more pathetic: the fact that you just spread your legs for a monster," he said, turning toward her fully, pushing a disgusted look onto his face, "or the fact that you spread them knowing I was a monster all along."

She went pale seconds before red flooded her cheeks. "Is that it? Is that what this is all about? You think you're some kind of monster?" she said with a small shake of her head. "You think that somehow, if you push me hard enough—if you're a big enough prick—you'll save me?"

"I'm not a prick." He leaned into her, practically roared the words in her face. "I'm a *murderer*, Sabrina."

She went still, eyes filled with a terrible sort of understanding that he'd have given his life to take from her. "I know what monsters look like, Michael, and I know how they behave. They pull you in; they don't push you away."

"How?" he said, even though *how* didn't matter. "Who told you I was *El Cartero*?" The name got stuck in his throat, latched on, and for a second refused to leave his mouth. He hated it. Hated who it made him. Most of all, he hated that it was *El Cartero*—not him—who had the guts to do what needed to be done now.

"Ben." Sabrina must've accurately read the expression on his face because she sighed again, raking trembling fingers through her long dark hair. She was afraid of him.

Good.

She shook her head. "It's not his fault. None of this has played out the way he planned," she said. "You want to blame someone, blame me."

"Oh, I do. I blame you." As soon as he said it, he knew. These were the words that were sharp enough to cut her. These were the words that would make her bleed and in that moment, he hated himself more that he'd ever thought possible. "For Frankie. For Lucy … for *everything*."

She went still, her eyes bright with the sudden rush of angry tears, seconds before she launched herself at him. He took her head on, let her hit him more than once—sharp, heavy blows that brought pain and blood—before he spun her into the wall, corralling her arms to pin them high above her head, his wide palm and long fingers circling her wrists, squeezing them together.

The sheet was gone, tangled around their feet, leaving her naked. Exposed. He fought the urge to let her go. Every instinct he had was screaming, telling him this was wrong. So terribly, horribly wrong.

He pressed his full length against her, shoved his knee between her legs, forcing them apart, pushing himself into the juncture of her thighs. He smiled down at her, used his free hand to mop up the blood that trickled from his nose and mouth. "You done yet?"

She swiveled her wrists against his hand, trying to pop the lock he had on her. "Why don't you let me go and find out?"

"I don't think so." He tightened his grip, felt the bend in her bones as he twisted the smile into a grin, made himself laugh at her. "You wanted *Cartero*, Sabrina." He trailed a finger along the swell of her breast to tease its tip. "Well, now you've got him."

"Fuck you," she snarled at him, chest pumping, breath ragged against his neck. "And if you think you're scaring me, think again. This isn't scared. This is *pissed*."

"Well, that's an easy fix." He pushed his hand between them, started to work the fly of his cargos open, even though he knew he'd rather die than hurt her.

"You're not going to hurt me, Michael," she said, nailing him with a gaze that saw right through him. "You can't."

"Oh, yeah?" He leaned into her as he slipped the last button from its loop, his mouth hovering above hers. "Why is that?"

"Because you love me."

He let go of her, so fast and abrupt that she staggered under the sudden pull of her own weight. He turned away from her, rubbing his hands on his thighs before giving in, allowing them to crank themselves into fists even as he resisted the urge to punch himself in the face.

"You *love* me, and all this?" She threw her hands in the air, he knew because he heard them slap against her thighs a second later. "All this is just your wacked-out idea of a rescue." She sighed, a shaky breath that told him she wasn't going to give up so easily. "Please tell me. Just tell me what happened. We'll figure it out together."

Do you really think she can survive us both?

Michael stared out the window, watching the sun break over the horizon, wanting nothing more than to turn to her. To ignore everything he knew to be true and just be with her. Tell her the truth. He almost did it. He almost gave in.

Instead, he forced himself to finish it.

"*Love you?* I don't love you," he lied. "I'm *infected* by you." He turned on her then and spat a mouthful of blood on the floor between them. "Lark was right, you're a goddamned disease. You've ruined me—" He slammed a fist against his skull, hard enough to scatter stars across his field of vision. "Mind-fucked me six ways to Sunday." He dropped his hands to the front of his pants to close his fly, button by button, concentrating his attention on his working fingers so he wouldn't have to look at her. Could she see them shaking? Did she know how much he regretted the things he'd just done and said? "This is over, you and me—you understand? Done."

"Lark might've been right about me, but Lucy was wrong about you." Her tone pulled his gaze up to her face. She glared at him, spine straight, arms at her sides, chin tilted in a challenge that made him feel small. Like she was looking down on him. "You're nothing but a coward after all."

He held her glare and shrugged. He pretended her words and the look she was giving him didn't slice him clean to the bone. "Yeah? Glad you're finally getting the picture," he said before he turned and walked out, leaving the door standing wide open when he left.

FIFTY-THREE

MICHAEL LET HIMSELF IN through the front door in an effort to avoid Miss Ettie and her all-knowing eye. He could hear her moving around in the kitchen, opening drawers and shutting them again. The low rumble of Lark's voice was answered by her soft, lilting tone. Through the doorway connecting the kitchen to the dining room, he could see the Kotko boy sitting at the table, skinny legs dangling from the seat he perched on. At least he was sitting in an actual chair today.

The kid must've sensed him because he turned, pinning Michael with that dark vacant gaze of his. It lasted for less than a second, but he'd felt it. Connection. Recognition.

Michael looked away. Unwanted memories pushed at him from all sides. Things he'd tried his whole life to hide from.

You're nothing but a coward after all.

No one knew just how true that really was.

"Miss Ettie is looking for her gardening shears."

He looked toward the stairs to see Ben standing at the foot of them. He thought of the shears, of what he'd done with them. "I'll buy her a new pair."

Ben laughed, but the sound died as he cocked his head at a curious angle. "You okay?"

"What? Yeah. Fine." He moved, squeezing past his partner to mount the steps to his room.

"I want to know what happened," Ben said, catching his arm as he passed. For a second he thought he was pressing him for details about his night with Sabrina. Then he remembered what he'd been doing before that.

"Let me get cleaned up," he said, forcing himself to look his partner full in the face. Ben did a quick appraisal before letting him go. As he'd hope, the kid had attributed the cut lip and swollen cheek he was sporting to his trip to Reyes's warehouse last night.

"Make it quick," Ben called over his shoulder on his way to the kitchen, leaving Michael alone.

He made his way to his room and let himself in, shedding his clothes immediately. Lifting his shirt above his head, he caught the smell of her on his skin. Felt the dizzying flash of heat as blood rushed from his head. For a moment he saw her. Felt the way she'd moved under his hands. Under his mouth.

The way she'd looked at him when he'd told her that he blamed her for his sister's death.

He tossed the bloodstained shirt on the floor and worked the front of his pants open, kicking his boots off as he did. It was over. Done. He'd made the right choice. For once in his miserable life, he did the right thing. So why did he feel like shit?

He glanced at the window that faced her house, spotting the binocs that he'd handed to Ben before he'd left the night before, propped on the sill.

No wonder Ben hadn't given him shit about his walk of shame or asked where he'd been all night. He knew because he'd probably watched the whole fucking thing. He took an angry swipe at the binocs, meaning to knock them off the ledge, but they somehow ended up in his hand. He raised them to his face and suddenly Sabrina was there in front of him, so close he felt like he could reach out and touch her.

She was sitting on the side of the bed, wearing a dark blue robe, hands in her lap. He could see the ugly red rings his fingers had left on her wrists. They were beginning to fade, but he could still see them, plain as day. He'd hurt her, in more ways than one.

None of it mattered. Not if he didn't let it.

He yanked his pants off and headed for the bathroom. Starting the shower, he stepped under the rush of hot water, scrubbing furiously with the bar of soap until his skin felt like it was ready to peel off. He waited until the water started to cool before turning it off. He was wasting time he didn't have, attempting to delay the inevitable.

He toweled off before dressing, pulling on a pair of cargos and the first shirt he found. Dialing his phone, he listened to it ring, ignoring the feeling that each tone built in the pit of his stomach. Under normal circumstances, calling Livingston Shaw was not something most people in his position would do. His circumstances were far from normal.

"Michael, is everything okay?" Shaw's voice, alert and rested, was more curious than concerned.

"It depends on your definition of *okay*, Livingston," he drawled. "If you ask me, the situation you've gotten yourself into is pretty fucking far from okay."

"I'm sure I don't know what you mean." The curiosity smoothed out, filling cracks. Hiding holes. But Michael could hear it; Shaw was worried.

"It's over. Reyes called me last night. He told me everything. That you hired him to kidnap Leo Maddox. That the Cordova hit was ordered by him."

He took Shaw's silence as confirmation.

"He told me something else … " He dropped his voice in to a mock whisper. "A secret."

"Do tell."

"Leo Maddox is dead." He blended truth and lie perfectly until even he couldn't distinguish one from the other. "And your perfect plan—whatever it was—has gone to hell."

FIFTY-FOUR

"Here? Shaw is coming *here*?" Lark's voice pealed off the walls, a baritone bell filled with trepidation. "This is bad. Fucking *bad*."

Michael couldn't blame him. The last time they'd faced Livingston Shaw together hadn't ended well for either of them.

"Would it've killed you to stick with the plan?" Ben said, leaning back in his chair to glare up at him.

"It's the same plan, I just hit fast forward." He shot a glance over Ben's head, his gaze landing on Sabrina. She'd been here when he came downstairs, standing as far away from him as she could get, hips leaned against the counter, watchful dog at her feet. She'd performed some sort of emotional triage—tying off her feelings about everything that had happened between them over the past eight hours, letting them atrophy. The look she gave him was relaxed. No anger. No hurt. It was as if the last night never happened.

He envied her.

"How long?"

He looked down to find Ben watching him and gave him a tired shrug. "Who knows? Ten, twelve hours at the most."

"You know too much," Ben said, his tone ringing with certainty. "He's going to kill you."

"Not before I kill Reyes. Your father is smart enough to want that tie good and cut, and he knows I'm the only one who can do it." He shrugged. "Who knows, maybe if I manage to bring the Maddox boy back, he'll change his mind." He took a look around the room and knew he hadn't managed to fool any of them. They all knew the truth. No matter what kind of miracle he managed to perform, as soon as it was over, Michael was as good as dead. "Reyes is keeping the kid on his private island. That's where I'm headed."

"How do you know?" Lark said.

"A little birdie told me," he said before filling them in on the what had happened the night before. His infiltration of Reyes's operation. His confrontation with Estefan. His late-night conversation with Reyes himself. He left out the parts that really mattered: that Reyes had threatened Sabrina and that Estefan was looking to overthrow his father. Ricin capsule or not, Lark was still a liability.

"This whole thing has been a setup, from start to finish." He looked at Sabrina. "The fact that *you* found Leo Maddox's doppelganger. That he was dumped in a house tied to Alberto's operation. Reyes wanted us here; he wanted you involved." He left the rest unsaid. That she was in danger—always would be in danger as long as he was around.

Ben looked at his watch and stood. "If I know my father, he's already halfway here. That ten- or twelve-hour window he gave you? Cut it in half," he said, taking charge of the situation. "Sabrina and I are going to go meet her contact for the death certificate on

256

the Maddox kid." He shot a look at Lark. "You ready to make the Internet your bitch?"

Lark grinned, flexing his fingers. "It's what I do best."

"Good. I want to know why my father targeted the Senator's grandson. He didn't have him kidnapped for shits and giggles. You have three hours to find out why," Ben said.

Lark nodded and stood, ready to work.

"Before you go," Michael said, tossing him a flash drive.

Lark snatched it out of the air and gave it a glance. "What is it?"

"A list of every scumbag Reyes sold a kid to. I want every single one of them burned," he said.

Lark gave him a lopsided grin. "I'll put it on my to-do list," he said, heading for the sunroom where he'd set up shop.

As soon as Lark was gone, he looked at Ben. "What about me?" he said. "I'll be damned if I'm just gonna sit here and play fattened calf."

Ben smirked. "I have a video conference set up with the Senator at nine o'clock. You can take it. Fill him in on what's happening."

Michael shook his head. Leon Maddox wasn't going to listen to a word he had to say. He'd been branded a traitor to his country and had worked as a hitman and personal guard for the drug lord responsible for kidnapping his grandson—neither of which exactly inspired trust. "You really think that's a good idea? No way is Maddox going to talk to me."

"You'd rather go with her?" Ben cocked his head in Sabrina's direction. "Right. Like I was saying, I'm gonna go grab my jacket." With that he was gone, leaving the two of them alone.

He looked out the window, watching Miss Ettie lead Alex around her garden. The boy shuffled after her, head cocked to the side like he was listening while she jabbered on about her flowers in a language he didn't even speak.

"Do you know why I went to see Phillip last night?"

Caught off-guard, he redirected his gaze. Looking at her, he shook his head slowly. He wasn't sure he wanted to know. She reached into the pocket of her jeans and pulled something out. The red silk pouch.

"After I killed Wade, I thought it was over. I thought I'd won, gotten my life back. And then he started talking to me," she said in a low voice, like she was afraid to wake someone who was sleeping in the next room. "Every day, he got louder and louder, closer and closer until he was *here*." She touched the side of her head. "Living inside me. I couldn't get rid of him." She dropped her hand. "You don't have to tell me how crazy I sound, trust me . . . but Phillip's cousin, the one you met last night, she saw it. She saw *him*," she said, her fingers tightening around the pouch. "She called him a *Gae Dokkaebi*—a ghost."

"What's in the pouch?" he said, even though he didn't want to ask. Didn't want to care.

"Tea." She looked down at the bundle of red silk in her hand. "When she gave it to me I thought she was crazy, but it worked. When I drink it, Wade's quiet. It's like there's a wall between us . . . one I can't hear him through." She frowned for a moment before looking up at him. "But he's still there. I can feel his . . . weight inside my head. Scratching at that wall between us. Trying to push his way through." She grinned. "Crazy, right?"

He thought of them—all of them. The friends he'd lost. The family he'd failed. All of them dead because he'd been too selfish or too stupid to save them. "Not even a little bit."

She shook her head, her mouth twisted in an expression that said she didn't believe him. "When he gave me the tea, Phillip warned me it was a temporary fix. That once a *Gae Dokkaebi* finds his way inside you, you'll never be rid of them. You'll be haunted forever. Or until they destroy you . . ." She offered him a smile that held an odd mixture of humor and sadness, and he could see that her front was crumbling. "You want to hear something funny?"

He shrugged.

"Last night, when you and I were together? Wade wasn't there. Not just quiet; he was *gone*. I was truly and completely free of him for the first time in what feels like forever." She dropped her hands to her sides, fists banging against her thighs, one of them strangling the pouch of tea she held onto. "So now I need you to tell me something, Michael, because I'm having a hard time figuring it out on my own."

He looked away from her, forced as much contempt into his tone as he could scratch together to hide the ache in his throat. "And what's that?"

"How am I supposed to give that up? How am I supposed to walk away from the only person who's ever given me peace? The only person who's ever made me forget?" She jammed the pouch back into her pocket. "Because, I've gotta tell you, whatever Reyes said to you last night, whatever he threatened to do—it's worth the risk to me. *You're* worth the risk."

He shook his head, opened his mouth even though he wasn't completely sure what was going to come out, but before he could say a word, Ben walked into the room.

"Ready?" he said, adjusting the way his black leather jacket sat on his shoulders. He bounced a look between the two of them. "I'll just go wait in the—"

"No. I'm ready. Let's go," Sabrina said, shooting Michael one last look before she walked out the door.

FIFTY-FIVE

"HE'S AFRAID."

It was Ben's tone more than his words that made her look at him. They'd been driving in silence for a while. Ben behind the wheel, her staring out the window. She cast a sidelong glance in his direction and frowned. "He's an idiot."

He laughed, the sound at total odds with the pensive expression that etched his usually neutral features. "He's created quite the cluster fuck, I'll give you that, but he's right to worry." He shot her a quick look. "Reyes's wife was pregnant when he killed her. Shot her right in front of our boy."

She felt sick, her fingers closing around the links of the bracelet Michael had given her. "Why? What did he used to do for Reyes?"

"On the surface?" Ben cut her a look. "He was hired to protect Reyes's daughter, Christina. She was four when he started—a little older than Frankie was when their parents died."

Sabrina remembered her. Rosy cheeks and dark, bouncing curls. Kerry blue eyes and olive skin. The perfect mixture of her parents,

Sophia and Sean. She could imagine Michael looking at another little girl and seeing a way to start over. To get it right. "He loved her."

Ben shrugged. "I think if not for what happened with Lydia, he'd still be there with her."

Lydia. Christina's mother. The wife Reyes killed. What would drive a husband and father to do such a thing? "Was the baby his?"

"Michael's?" Ben shook his head. "He's surprising moral for an assassin. Lydia was only twelve when Reyes bought her from her father and married her. She was young—too young for anyone with a conscience. She was like a sister to him. Between Christina and Lydia, Michael had Frankie back—the little sister he walked out on and the young woman she'd become."

She didn't ask how he knew all this. She'd learned a long time ago that when Ben was involved there was no such thing as secrets. "I don't understand. Why would Reyes kill his own child? Everything I've heard about this guy tells me he's a classic narcissist. Killing his child would be like killing himself."

Ben's jaw went tight. "Just because the baby wasn't Michael's doesn't mean it belonged to Reyes."

She stared straight ahead, fingers worrying the links of titanium beneath them. A man like Reyes chose his underlings carefully. He'd find the perfect balance between cruelty and cowardice. No way one of his men would be stupid enough to have an affair with his wife … but someone who saw himself as his equal would.

"His son, Estefan," she said. It wasn't a question.

Ben nodded. "Reyes kept the wife and kid on his island and installed Michael there as his personal watchdog, but he didn't spend much time there. Not enough people to worship him for his tastes," he said, blowing out a disgusted breath. "When she got pregnant, Estefan knew Reyes would never believe the baby was his, so he very carefully and quietly pointed the finger at Michael."

She imagined Reyes's reaction to the news. Rage … but also humiliation. In a man like him, the latter would be a far more dangerous emotion. Bringing a man like Michael into the fold had been a power play. To own *Cartero* had been the ultimate show of supremacy and it had ended in his own betrayal—something that Reyes's ego wouldn't allow him to accept.

Ben spoke. "As luck would have it, the confrontation happened the same night he found out about his sister's disappearance. He was leaving anyway, but it meant he couldn't go back for Christina."

Christina. She could imagine he'd grieved her loss almost as much as he grieved Frankie's. "Reyes just let him leave?"

Ben gave a snort. "Let him? No, but there isn't much that can stop Michael when he decides he's going to do something—another slap in the face for Reyes. By the time he tracked him down, Michael was already under my father's protection. Untouchable."

"Until your father asked him to kidnap Leo Maddox."

Ben smiled, but it looked more like an angry show of teeth. "Bingo." He parked the car and turned to look at her. "My father can't be trusted. Sooner or later, he's going to figure out that Michael lied to him about Leo being dead. If recovering the kid proves too costly or if it suddenly no longer serves him, he'll abandon him and anyone else he's sent in to retrieve him."

"Even you?" she said, surprised to see what looked like pain flit across his face. He looked down at his hand for a moment, the one that was heavily scarred, curling his fingers around the knot of hard flesh in the center of his palm until he clenched it in his fist.

"Especially me."

FIFTY-SIX

Sabrina led the way through a heavy metal door and down a brightly lit corridor to a swinging door at the end of the hall.

She pushed her way through it and into a small room with a call button. Ben followed. She leaned on the button, a faint buzzing erupting from the other side of the door. "That look always scares me," she said, and a few seconds later they were buzzed in.

"What look?"

"The look that says you're planning something that no one else knows about."

"Who? Me? Plan something?" He grinned at her. "I would never."

"Liar, liar …" She pushed the door open and stepped into another small windowless room dominated by a big desk and a bank of black metal filing cabinets. "Hey, Dean. New piercing?" Sabrina said jerking her chin at the skinny kid behind the desk.

He nodded, tossing a mop of crow-black hair out of eyes rimmed with enough black eyeliner to give Ozzy Osbourne pause.

"Oh, yeah," he said, flipping the bullring jammed through his septum up into his nasal cavity, hiding it completely. "Got it last month."

"Nice," Sabrina said with a half-smile, scribbling a tethered ballpoint across the sign-in sheet. She handed the clipboard to Ben and he took it, following suit.

"I heard you were back with Homicide. New partner?" Dean said, dropping a clear plastic box on the desk while giving Ben the once over.

"No—transfer. I'm just showing him around," she said, pulling her SIG off her hip and ejecting the magazine before depositing it into the box. "Dr. Black here? I have an appointment."

Dean nodded. "She's in her office. You too," he said, nudging the box at Ben, eyes widening to the size of softballs as he pulled his pair of Desert Eagle .40s from his double shoulder holster. He popped the magazines and placed them in the box, giving the lab tech a slight smirk.

"Holy Dirty Harry, Batman," Dean muttered, hitting a button mounted to the wall next to his desk. A few seconds later the lock on a second door popped. This one led to another interior corridor.

"Mandy is a … friend, so please—play nice," Sabrina said to him as she led the way down the hall.

"She hot?"

She stopped in front of the half open door and turned on him. "I'm being serious, Ben. I don't want her involved."

"Then you shouldn't have called her," he said, shouldering his way past her to rap his knuckles against the door jamb.

Over Ben's shoulder she could see Mandy's sunny blond head bent over a stack of paperwork. As soon as he knocked, the head popped up to reveal a freckled nose and a pair of sharp green eyes. "Hotness has been established," he said loud and clear, forcing Sabrina to dig an elbow into his ribs as she pushed her way to the front.

"Hey, Mandy. Don't mind him," she said, planting herself in between Ben and the woman behind the desk. "He was raised by wolves."

"Hey," Mandy said, her eyes settling on Ben immediately. There was no doubt she'd heard what he said. "I didn't know you were bringing company."

"Me either," Sabrina said, sweeping a hand through the doorway to usher him inside. "This is—"

"Ben. Ben Shaw," he said, holding his hand out. She took it, looking him straight in the eye. "And I wasn't raised by wolves." He shot her the grin over their joined hands. "I was raised by a cold emotionally unavailable mother and a father whose plot to take over the world kept him too busy for a game of catch."

"Dr. Black," she said, her tone a touch too cool to be considered polite. "Nice to meet you," she said, sitting back in her chair, effectively removing her hand from his. As soon as the door clicked shut, the smile fell away. She produced a set of keys and used one of them to open the bottom drawer on her desk. She pulled out a manila envelope and tossed it on the desk.

"Thanks," Ben said, picking up the envelope.

Mandy shot a look at Sabrina before narrowing her eyes at Ben, her cool professionalism wiped away to reveal something a bit more challenging. "Who are you again?"

"I'm the guy in the top hat with the bullwhip, organizing this circus," he said.

She laughed at him.

Ben bounced a look between her and Mandy, utterly confused. "Did I say something funny?"

Ben never knew when to quit—especially when he was ahead. "Thank you," she said, dropping a hand on his shoulder to pull him out the door.

"I thought maybe you'd like to know who he is before you go." Mandy cocked her head at the pair of chairs across from her desk.

"You know who he is?" Ben said, sounding skeptical.

Mandy arched a brow at him. "I know enough about him to tell you that his abduction was anything but random."

After exchanging a look, Ben and Sabrina sat.

She sat back in her chair. "The boy was approximately seven years old, and I estimate that he was abducted no more than a week or two ago."

"What makes you think that?" he asked.

"X-rays show several fractures—hairline and spiral—on his arms and legs. Probably from struggling against being repeatedly grabbed and forcibly moved. All of these fractures were made at roughly the same time, and remodeling suggested that the injuries were sustained no more than two weeks ago. Whoever he is, he was abducted *after* Leo Maddox."

"Sexual assault?"

Mandy shook her head. "My initial examination was negative for sexual assault."

The same couldn't be said for Alex Kotko. Experience, both professional and personal, told her exactly how much the boy had suffered. She knew better than anyone that even though he was dead, the boy in Mandy's autopsy room had been the lucky one.

"So far, I'm not interested," Ben said, baiting her shamelessly.

"I also found this," Mandy said, pulling a photo from the envelope. It was a picture of a tattoo, magnified to show the detail.

Ф

"It's Cyrillic. The letter F—on the back of his neck, hidden under his hairline. It's small, no bigger than the head of an eraser, and it's been there for a while. The ink has had time to settle into the skin, so a lot longer than a few weeks. Even without running DNA or prints, I could have told you that the boy you found isn't Leo Maddox." Black tucked the picture back into the envelope. "I can't tell you much more about it without running the tattoo through our database."

"You ran him through your database?" There was something strange about his voice. It took Sabrina a moment to realize what she was hearing. It sounded like urgency, bordering on panic.

Mandy shot her a puzzled look before shaking her head. "Well, no. Not yet."

"Don't," Ben said as he stood, giving Sabrina a look that was undeniable. He knew something and he wasn't going to share in front of Mandy.

Sabrina shot him a questioning look before following suit, rising slowly from her seat. "Thanks, Mandy," she said.

"He has a family somewhere, looking for him," Mandy said, her troubled gaze bouncing between her and Ben before landing on the packet of papers on her desk. "I can't just leave him in cold storage. It wouldn't be right."

"Twenty-four hours," Ben blurted out. "That's all we need." He swiped the documents and pictures off the desk, along with a business card from its holder. "Mind if I take one? I might have some questions later."

Mandy cocked an eyebrow at him. "Be my guest."

"Thank you," he said, latching onto Sabrina's arm and pulling her along on his way out the door.

————

She didn't speak again until they were in the car.

"Are you going to tell me what's going on or are you going to make me guess?" she said, fastening her seat belt with a quiet *click*.

Ben said nothing, just worked the gearshift into reverse and backed out of the parking space slowly, giving himself time to think. Obviously seeing that tattoo on the back of that kid's neck changed everything.

"Ben?" She sounded impatient but also a little apprehensive. "Tell me what's going on."

He blew out a long breath, eyes focused on the road ahead. "That tattoo on the kid's neck. Dr. Hotness is right—it *is* a Cyrillic F. It also happens to be the mark of Sergey Filatov."

She let out a low whistle. "Sergey Filatov? *The* Sergey Filatov?" she said, leaving little doubt that she knew exactly who he was. Between being Livingston Shaw's pawn and the dinner companion of a Korean mobster, her new life had given Sabrina the education of a lifetime.

"Yup. That's him," he said evenly, gripping the wheel so tight she was sure he was about five seconds away from ripping it off the steering column.

Sergey Filatov.

"So maybe Michael had it wrong. Maybe the kid *wasn't* abducted by Reyes's crew. Maybe he had nothing to do with—"

"No, you don't get it." He cut her a hard look. "Michael was right—that kid has everything to do with what's going on here."

She gave him a confused frown. "Okay…"

"Filatov doesn't mark the people he buys and sells. He's too smart for that." Ben shook his head. "That mark is reserved for immediate members of the Filatov family. It labels them as untouchable." Tension gathered in his shoulders and neck as the implications of what he was about to say came crashing down on them both. "If that kid is sporting it, then he's important."

"Is he that crazy?" Sabrina said. "Is Reyes crazy enough to kidnap a close relative of a Russian mob boss?"

Not *a* Russian mob boss. *The* Russian mob boss. As *Pakhan,* Sergey Filatov ran it all. Unlike most organized crime syndicates, the Russians operated as a single entity. There were no factions, no competition within the family. As far as the Russians were concerned, Sergey Filatov was God.

Ben shook his head. "I doubt it. Reyes is a barely functioning sociopath, but he's not stupid."

"Then the question is, who hates Reyes enough to abduct a close family member of Sergey Filatov and drop him in the middle of his operation?" Sabrina said, her tone telling him she understood just how dangerous the situation was.

"I don't know," he said, cutting her a quick glance. "But I bet Michael has a pretty good idea."

FIFTY-SEVEN

MICHAEL POWERED UP BEN's laptop and logged on to the secure conferencing site that FSS used to conduct long-distance meetings. Using his partner's laptop would make it less likely that the meeting would be monitored, but it wouldn't make a difference in whether or not Leon Maddox would agree to speak to him.

"Hey," Lark said from the doorway, a file folder in his hand. "I got that stuff Ben asked for." He walked in and tossed the folder on the table next to the laptop. "Some pretty heavy shit in there. Shaw finds out we're poking around in his business, ain't none of us gonna make it outta this one. Junior included."

He waited for Lark to make his exit before flipping the file open, but it didn't take him long to realize he was right. If Shaw knew what they were up to—what they knew—he'd kill them all.

The laptop let out a chime a second before an image of who he was sure was the Senator's aide filled the monitor, her flirty smile fading when she saw who was on the other side of the screen. "Oh, you're not—"

"No, I'm not. Mr. Shaw is attending to other matters, so I'm keeping his appointment with the Senator," he said, carefully avoiding the use of his name. Maddox might know who Michael was, but that didn't mean his staff did.

"Let me see if the Senator is available." She placed him on hold, the display going dark.

Michael sat back, swiping a hand over his face. Knowing Shaw, he was already halfway here. He didn't have time to sit around while some politician decided to grace him with his presence or not.

"Fuck this," he muttered, scrolling the mouse pad over the disconnect icon.

"I agree, Mr. O'Shea."

He winced, looking up to see Leon Maddox staring at him from Ben's computer screen. "Sir. I was just—"

"Going to hang up on me, so let's cut the crap, shall we?" Maddox barked, his tone brusque. "I was expecting you and Mr. Shaw to arrive yesterday afternoon. I take it from the San Francisco area code that you were waylaid by what I can only imagine to be a break in my grandson's disappearance."

"Yes, sir. Ben received a report from a contact of his that a young boy matching Leo's description was found in an abandoned house." He didn't know how to say the rest. He'd never had to do this before.

"Is he dead?" Maddox said plainly, his gruff words at complete odds with the stark grief in his eyes.

"No, sir. The boy that was found isn't your grandson. But I've managed to identify Leo's abductor. Alberto Reyes." He nearly choked on the words and the look Maddox gave him when he said them.

"Alberto Reyes. The head of the Moreno cartel. Your former boss." Maddox's expression went from wary to downright hostile. "And how did you come upon that information?"

271

He sighed. "I happened to get a lead on where he's basing his operations here in San Francisco, and I paid them a visit. I'm sure you're aware of how persuasive I can be when I'm properly motivated."

Maddox narrowed his eyes and leaned in to the camera just a bit. "Just what are your motivations, Mr. O'Shea? A man like you—my grandson's welfare is hardly of any importance."

"A man like me, sir?" He nearly bit the words in half.

"I know what you've done. Who you've done it for," Maddox said. "Why Livingston put you in charge of Leo's recovery is a mystery."

"That would be the question, wouldn't it?" Michael glanced at the file folder spread out next to the computer and decided to go for broke. "When did you get word about your appointment to head Appropriations Committee B1217, sir? This morning? Maybe late last night?"

The Senator visibly stiffened, his eyes narrowing on the screen. "That information is classified. How did you—"

"You're right. It is classified. So classified that the committee itself doesn't even officially exist and only three people are involved in choosing its chair," Michael said. "And yet, Livingston Shaw has known about your pending appointment for weeks now."

Appropriations Committee B1217. The committee that would be charged with reviewing and approving how and where the government's black budget was spent. An estimated eighty-five billion dollars, used to fund military research programs and covert operations that Uncle Sam didn't want his citizens to know about. It also funded the country's growing dependence on privatized military companies. According to the dirt Lark dug up, Livingston Shaw and FSS were attached to well over half of the programs and operations that would be up for approval, to the tune of fifty billion dollars.

"What are you saying? That Livingston had my grandson kidnapped in order to force me into giving his company government contracts?" Maddox said, practically spitting the words out of his mouth. "If that's so, then where are his demands? The committee meets in three days; surely he'd have made his move by now."

"Demands?" he laughed, causing the Senator to bristle even more. "This is Livingston Shaw we're talking about—he'll simply return Leo to you, unharmed, in the nick of time and let your conscience be your guide."

"He's got the largest privatized military operation in the world at his disposal. Why hire a two-bit drug lord to do his dirty work?" Leon said, still trying to punch holes in a theory that was quickly becoming fact.

"If you were going to kidnap the grandson of a US Senator, would you do it yourself or would you hire someone to do it for you?" Michael sighed, running a rough hand over his head before settling it on the back of his neck. "There was no money exchanged. No payment. It was a handshake deal as far as I can tell—no way to tie it back to Shaw if things went sideways."

"Then why? If not for money, then what? What could Livingston give Reyes that would be worth the risk of kidnapping my Leo?"

"Me. Reyes has been looking for a way to kill me for a very long time," Michael said quietly. "You wanted to know why Livingston would put me in charge of finding your grandson; there's your answer. Revenge."

Michael told him everything. He started at the beginning, with him and his unit getting sent to Colombia to help Marisol Ramos and her team disable Mateo Moreno's fleet of drug subs and the ambush that followed and ending with his agreeing to work for Livingston Shaw.

Through it all, Maddox listened. When Michael was done, Maddox sat back in his chair, a look of betrayed defeat on his weathered face. "The appointment system was put in place to keep things like this from happening."

"If I've learned anything over the last several years, it's that anyone can be bought. Money. Secrets. Silence. Everyone has a price, and people like Alberto Reyes and Livingston Shaw have a knack for sniffing them out and exploiting them."

"What about you, Mr. O'Shea? What's your price these days?"

He thought of Sabrina. What he'd be willing to do to be allowed to stay with her. How far he'd go to earn the privilege to lay down next to her every night. "What I want, no one can give me—not even you," he said, scrolling the mouse over to the disconnect icon.

"So where does that leave me? Where does that leave Leo?"

Michael looked up to find Maddox watching him. "I'm going to go get him and bring him home, sir," he said. "I made a promise to you and I intend to keep it, whatever the cost."

FIFTY-EIGHT

Cofre del Tesoro, Colombia
June 2011

Reyes was back.

He'd flown in just days after Christina's birthday, his helicopter touching down only yards away while she practiced riding the bike Michael had given her. He stepped down from the Black Hawk, barely sparing them a glance before disappearing into the house. Wedged between two guards was a slouching figure with a black bag over its head.

"Is that man in trouble?"

He'd looked down to see Christina standing next to him, feet flat on the ground, bike balanced between her knobby knees. She looked worried. Like she wanted him to do something about it.

"Probably." He frowned. "I think it's time to go inside."

For once she hadn't argued. Wheeling her bike over to the set of stone steps that led to the veranda, she leaned it onto its kickstand while he watched and waited. When she was finished, they went inside.

That had been months ago. Reyes was still on the island and he'd shown no signs of leaving. Michael and Christina went on with their daily routine of trips to the beach and bike rides, both doing their best to ignore the fact that the longer her father stayed, the more eggshells they seemed to walk upon.

It was late. The small wind-up clock on the bookshelf that served as his nightstand told him it was past midnight. He'd put Christina to bed hours ago before retreating to his own room.

His sleeping quarters had originally been a three-room suite on the opposite side of the house. Not long after he'd accepted the job, he'd relocated himself to the closest room outside of Christina's apartments. He suspected that it'd been a closet before he moved in. It was barely big enough to hold the twin bed, shelf, and dresser he'd hauled in, but that didn't matter. There was a two-by-two window set high into the exterior wall that offered him a view of the grounds and ocean. That was good enough for him.

He stood there now, studying the thick, hulking lines of the Black Hawk squatting on its pad, willing it to come to life. To take Reyes away so that he could go back to pretending he wasn't hiding from the things he'd done. That he wasn't ashamed of what he was.

The loud knock on his door moved him away from the window and he pulled it open to see Hector, Reyes's second-in-command standing on the other side.

"*Hefe* sent me. He wants to see you," Hector said, craning his neck a bit to see into the room behind him. No doubt the man was wondering the same thing everyone else did: Why would a man like *Cartero* choose to sleep in a glorified closet?

276

Michael made a show of looking at his watch, forcing his face into a mask of irritation. "I'm off the clock. If the kid needs something, get her mother to—"

"This isn't about Christina." Hector moved to the side, making it obvious that Michael was to follow him whether he wanted to or not. "Oh, and *Hefe* says for you to bring your knife."

———

Hector led him to Reyes's office before stationing himself beside the door, hands clasped in front of him, leaving him to enter the room alone.

In the pair of chairs in front of the desk were two men he'd never seen before. One was dark complected, with eyes and hair to match, while the other had sandy blond hair and pale eyes, his skin tone several shades lighter than his friend. Their differing looks didn't matter. Both sported fleur de lis tattoos on the back of their hands. That made them brothers in the Cordova cadre.

Stretched across the floor between him and the men was a wide square of plastic sheeting. It crinkled beneath his boots every time he shifted. Michael had little doubt what he'd been called here to do.

"Thank you for joining us, *Cartero*," Reyes said from behind his desk, as if he'd been given a choice. Estefan stood behind his father's desk, literally at his right hand, glaring at him with a mixture of disdain and self-importance that he'd come to recognize as the kid's natural state of being.

"Of course, Mr. Reyes," he said, careful to keep his tone respectful while choosing his words wisely. "Hector said you wanted to see me."

Reyes smiled. "I'd like you to meet Javier and Enrique—they work for an overseas competitor to whom I'd like to deliver a message."

He felt the length of his spine stiffen as he watched the two men seated in front of him shift uncomfortably in their seats, each wondering who would be chosen to be message and who would be messenger. With barely a nod, Michael reached behind him, into the small of his back, and found his blade. Pulling it from its sheath, he stood with it held casually, the flat of it tucked against his thigh...and waited.

Without warning, an interior door tucked into the corner of the room opened. Two of Reyes's men entered, dragging a third behind them. They dumped him onto the plastic before situating themselves on either side. His captive audience.

Michael recognized him instantly as the man who'd been pulled from the helicopter the day Reyes arrived. The black sack was still in place, soured with the stench of sweat and fear that wafted around him as he was forced to his knees in the middle of the plastic sheet but it was him, Michael was sure of it.

Is that man in trouble?

He gazed down at the hand that held his knife. The same hand that'd held Frankie as a baby. Had soothed her through nightmares after their parents died, before he'd given up completely. The same hand that'd held onto the back of Christina's bike seat and guided her down the garden path while she pedaled, struggling to find her balance. The same hand that'd tucked her in no more than a few hours ago.

Michael looked up from the hooded man kneeling in front of him to find Reyes watching him closely, like he was an animal being examined for disease or defect. One that would be culled from the pack if he didn't prove to be as vicious as he'd once been.

He was being tested and failure meant death.

He cocked his head, forcing the corners of his mouth into the semblance of a smile before stepping forward to yank the hood off the figure in front of him. His shirt was expensive beneath the grime, his dark eyes wide and sharp, words fumbling against his lips as soon as he saw him. Beyond him, the blond one—Enrique, let out an outraged bark, trying to lunge from his seat, across the plastic. He was corralled by Reyes's goon, cuffed viciously with the butt of a gun before the barrel of it was jammed into his ear. His rebellion was quelled before it even really began.

The young man in front of him started to beg. "Please, I'll give you anything you want. I'll do whatever—"

Michael didn't let him finish. He fisted his hand in hair, jamming his knife into the side of the young man's neck, following the curve of his jaw until a river of red poured from its underside. The man in front of him gurgled, spewing and spitting as he choked on his own blood. Michael shifted his hold, reaching his fingers into the gaping wound he'd just carved into the man's throat. Finding and gripping the tongue, he pulled it though the wound, yanking and tearing until it hung, flapping, against the underside of his chin.

As soon as it was done, he let the young man drop onto the plastic, where cooling blood continued to weep from the gash in his throat. He looked at the two men seated no more than four feet away. Close enough to touch, Michael reached out and wiped the flat of his blade against the shirt of the man sitting closest to him. Enrique. His name was Enrique.

"You make sure your boss gets Mr. Reyes's message," he said, flipping his knife over to drag the other side across the man's shirt. Now he looked up at Reyes. "Will that be all?"

Reyes shot his son a smug look and stood. "Yes, *Cartero*. I think that's everything," he said, and Michael had the insane urge to dirty up his newly cleaned knife by jamming it into his boss's eye socket. If Reyes read the impulse as it ghosted through him, he said nothing.

He turned and left the room, walking past Hector without a backward glance. What happened *after* was never his concern.

Ducking into the first bathroom he found, he dropped his knife in the sink and turned it on, running the water as hot as he could stand before slushing the bar of soap over his hands and forearms, doing his best to wash off the red stain that covered them.

Michael scrubbed until his hands were clean, letting the water run ice cold before he was finally satisfied. Relieved, he looked up into the mirror above the sink to see that it wasn't just his hands.

The blood was everywhere. He was covered in it, and he had a feeling that no matter how long or how hard he scrubbed, he always would be.

FIFTY-NINE

Sabrina had Ben drop her off at home. It was just before ten. The second day of SWAT recertification was shooting qualifiers, which meant that Nickels didn't have to be to the range until noon. With any luck she could catch him before he left for the day.

"I have to talk to Nick—get him to take Val and Lucy somewhere until this is all over," she said while Ben pulled curbside to let her out.

"Michael already took care of that," Ben said.

She paused as she was getting out of the car and looked back at him. "What do you mean?"

"Last night," Ben said with a shrug. "Michael arranged to get them out of town; they should be gone by the end of the day. He didn't tell you about it?"

She shook her head, trying to reconcile the man she woke up to this morning with someone who made arrangements to keep her family safe. "He didn't say anything to me about it." She gave Ben a quick smile. "I'll just do a quick walk-through, make sure everything's okay, and then I'll be over," she said to him, shutting the car door before rounding the hood and heading up the driveway. Nick's truck was gone but Val's car was in the driveway, so she headed for the back door and let herself in. From the kitchen she could hear the murmur of voices in the living room. Val was talking to someone.

"Hey, it's me," she called out as she locked the door and reset the alarm.

"Hey, we're in here," Val answered. "Grab a glass if you want mimosas."

Mimosas? Sabrina looked at her watch as she came through the dining room. "You know, adding orange juice doesn't negate the fact that you're drinking champagne on a Wednesday morning," she said, looking up to see Val sitting in the living room with the woman she'd seen on the porch yesterday. Obviously Nick hadn't shared their imminent travel plans with his wife.

"One won't kill you, right Courtney?" Val smiled. "Besides, we're celebrating. You remember Courtney?" she said with a *be nice* warning look.

"I'm on duty." She *so* did not have time for this. "And yes, I remember." She jerked her mouth into a quick smile. "Nice to see you again. What are you celebrating?"

"Only that she has the cutest baby in the whole wide world," Courtney said, tipping a bit more champagne into her flute. "Our photo shoot this morning was fantastic. I don't think I've ever shot a more photogenic little girl."

Something about the way she said *shot* stiffened Sabrina's spine. "Where is Lucy?"

"Sleeping," Val said, taking a sip of her drink, sloshing a little over the side of her flute.

She looked around the room. Nothing seemed out of place but, Val's day drinking aside, there was definitely something off about this whole scenario. "Where's Nick? He doesn't have qualifiers for another couple of hours."

"Devon?" Val said, taking another drink, looking at the woman sitting across from her. "She calls my husband Nick—he used to be in love with her." Val looked up at her then with a look that might have been jealousy, but it passed too quickly to cause anything more than a momentary clench in her gut. "*Devon* was gone when we got here—just us girls."

"He was never in love with me, he was just too stubborn to admit it," Sabrina said.

Before Val could answer Courtney leaned in, taking the glass from her friend's hand. "Why don't you go get the proofs from our shoot and show them to Sabrina?"

Val nodded and stood, the tension that had suddenly sprung up between them set aside. "Good idea! You're gonna love these, wait here…" she said, her voice trailing down the stairs.

As soon as she was out of earshot, Sabrina cut Courtney a scathing glare. "What the hell did you do to her?"

The woman sitting in front of her gave her a wide-eyed look. "Me? I didn't do anything. You, on the other hand…" She wagged her finger back and forth. "I think the two of you have some deep-seated issues to work out."

"Val and I are fine," she said, the insistence in her voice sounded like a lie, even to her.

"Everything can't be fine all the time, Sabrina," Courtney said, lifting Val's flute in a mock toast. "Honesty—one of alcohol's finer side effects. You should try it sometime."

"How many has she had?"

"Just this." Courtney set the half-empty glass on the table between them and sat back in her chair.

"Really? Because she looks like she's half in the bag."

"She's a bit of a lightweight—and *totally* starved for fun," Courtney said, slouching back in her chair, taking the champagne bottle with her, leg draped over the low-slung arm. She looked to be around thirty, her long brown hair pulled away from her face in a simple ponytail. Her jeans were faded, frayed at the cuffs. Her T-shirt had a picture of Einstein with the words *keepin' it relative* across the bottom. She lifted the bottle to her mouth and took a drink before continuing. "But I like her. She's…uncomplicated. What you see is what you get." She tipped the bottle in her direction. "Not like us."

Apprehension tingled along Sabrina's scalp. She stood. "I think you've caused enough trouble for one day."

Now Courtney laughed, swinging the leg that was hooked around the chair's arm in a lazy circle. "I haven't even gotten started."

"I'm sorry; let me be clear." Sabrina leaned over the coffee table, putting her very much in the other woman's personal space. "Get the fuck out of my house. Now."

"We'll leave in a minute…" Courtney said, looking up at her and smiling as if she hadn't just been asked to leave. "You know, she barely knows me. Didn't even ask me my last name. That's another thing I like about our Val; despite her harrowing, near-death experience at the hands of a serial killer—a harrowing, near-death experience that was completely your fault, by the way—she's still trusting. Another thing you and I lack."

"What *is* your last name?" Sabrina heard herself ask. Somewhere upstairs she heard a muted thump, like something heavy had fallen onto the carpeted floor.

Val.

She reached for her SIG, had it cleared and aimed at Courtney's chest in the time it took to draw a breath. "What the fuck did you do to her?"

"Please, one question at a time."

Sabrina answered by thumbing the hammer back on her SIG.

"I'm chipped, the same as Michael," Courtney said, that playful tone of hers suddenly gone. "I die, my chip goes dark; my chip goes dark, your boyfriend's an oozing pile of muck that'll have to be cleaned up by a hazmat team."

Sabrina reset the hammer but kept hold of the gun.

"Good. We're beginning to understand each other." Courtney smiled, setting the bottle on the table. "Now, don't get mad, but ... I drugged your friend," she said, holding up her hands in a *stay calm* gesture. "She's fine; it's nothing life-threatening. She'll wake up in about an hour with a pounding headache, swearing to never drink champagne again. And Lucy is fine too, scout's honor." To prove it, she picked up the baby monitor on the end table and turned up the volume. Behind the soft crackle of static, Sabrina could hear the baby's even breaths.

"I know who you are," she whispered, unable to understand how she'd been so dumb ... so blind. "What do you want?"

"It's simple. I want you to disarm yourself and follow me out that door," she said, finally standing. "There's a car waiting that will take us to the airport."

"And then?"

"And then we're going to get on a plane and fly away," Courtney said, as if she were asking her to go to the movies.

Sabrina shook her head. "I don't have to kill you. I could shoot you in the arm. Or maybe just kick the shit out of you."

"You and I will have our day in the sun, Sabrina...someday. But not today. Today we're on a bit of a schedule." She looked at her watch, quirking her mouth into a sheepish grin. "We have less than a thirty minutes to get to Moffett Field. If we're not there, my boss is going to rain holy hell on this place. A lot of people will get hurt—including your BFF and that pretty little girl of hers. Tick tock."

Sabrina ejected the magazine from the grip of the gun and set both of them on the coffee table before doing the same to the LCP strapped to her ankle.

"Your pockets too."

She hesitated a moment too long before digging into her jeans and pulling out the red silk pouch Phillip had given her the night before. Panic flexed its muscles, spreading inside her chest like wings unfurled. "It's nothing, just—"

"I don't care what it is. Drop it on the table."

She gripped the pouch tighter for a moment, as if hoping to be able to absorb whatever it was that managed to keep Wade at bay through the fabric and into her fingers. But then she let it go.

"Good girl," Courtney said an encouraging smile on her face. "Circling back to your original question, my last name is Tserkov'. It's Russian for Church."

SIXTY

Movement flickered in the corner of his eye. Michael turned away from the laptop, expecting to find Lark. Instead, it was Alex standing in the doorway, Sabrina's dog by his side. "*Vse v pory-adke?*" Is everything alright?

He couldn't be sure, but he thought the boy nodded before entering the room, shuffling across the floor to curl up on the floor next to his chair, leaning his temple against Michael's knee. He felt it again: connection, recognition.

The back door banged open seconds before Ben called out, "You here?"

He looked down at the boy. "Yeah, in the dining room," he said without standing. Ben appeared in the doorway a few seconds later, his eyes zeroing in on the boy.

"Looks like you made a friend," Ben said.

"You know me," he said, shooting his partner a wry smile, "I'm Mr. Personality. Where's Sabrina?" he said, looking at the laptop's display. It was 10:15 a.m. Ben's time estimate of when his father would arrive was just that—an estimate. He had no real way of knowing where his father was or when he'd show up. They had to assume that Shaw could waltz through that door at any moment.

"I dropped her at home. What'd you find out?"

"Alone?" He looked past his partner, out the window at the fence that separated Sabrina's yard from Miss Ettie's.

Ben rolled his eyes. "We're less than thirty seconds away, Nervous Nelly—she'll be fine. You want to tell me what you found?"

"For starters, the reason your father targeted Leon Maddox," he said, launching into the full explanation.

Ben listened, his face growing grimmer by the second. "I *knew* it. Everything goes back to money with him. Did you tell Maddox about my dad's involvement?"

He nodded. "Not sure if it was a good idea, but he needed to know who he was dealing with."

Something he said jerked Ben's spine a bit straighter. "Speaking of … I need you to do something," he said, his gaze dropping to the kid on the floor. "And don't ask questions."

Michael's gaze followed his partner's. "Okay … "

"Look at the back of his neck, just above the hairline. See anything weird?"

Michael placed a gentle hand on Alex's head. The boy went stiff, but he didn't move. "*Eto normal'no. Ya vam ne povredit.*" It's okay. I won't hurt you.

He feathered the hair along the boy's hairline, looking close. "What am I supposed to see?"

Ben let out a relieved breath. "The Cyrillic letter F tattooed on his scalp."

Oh shit. Michael looked up from the boy's head. "Does that mean what I think it means?"

"If you think it's the personal stamp of ownership, used by a certain Russian mob boss to mark his immediate family … then yes, it means what you think it means."

He looked even closer. "There's nothing."

"Good." He took a step away from the doorway. "Can I talk to you in the kitchen for a minute?"

"Yeah, hold on," he said. "*Smotri*," he said, and the boy looked up at him. "*Vy khotite igrat' v videoigru*?" You want to play a video game?

The boy nodded, and Michael motioned for him to stand before searching the laptop for the zombie-killing game his partner was currently addicted to. When the kid was settled, he cocked his head toward the kitchen and Ben followed.

"Sergey Filatov?" he said, looking around to make sure they were alone. "This *cannot* be happening."

"Oh, it's fucking happening, partner—it's happening. I just can't figure out the how and the why." Ben passed a hand over his face, the look on it telling him that there was something else. Something he wasn't saying.

"What's with the look? Tell me—"

There was a knock at the front door, a firm pounding that advertised exactly who it was. Ben looked at his watch. "No way. It's too soon," he said, charging through the doorway into the foyer. The sharp expletive that followed told Michael everything he needed to know.

Time had just run out.

SIXTY-ONE

"GET ALEX, TAKE HIM upstairs," Michael said, pulling Ben away from the window in order to look for himself. Two men were standing on the front porch. Their dark suits and even darker shades made them look like Secret Service, but he knew what they were: Pips sent by Livingston Shaw to collect him.

He threw a look over his shoulder to see Ben speaking quietly to the boy while he closed up the laptop. Alex looked at him, his usual blank expression laced with fear. Michael nodded and tried to give him what he hoped was an encouraging smile. As soon as Ben and the boy disappeared up the stairs, Michael opened the door.

"Let me guess—out spreading the good news?" he said, leaning himself against the doorframe.

The man on the left slapped a meaty paw against the door and gave it a push. "News is never good when you're involved," he said in a conversational tone. He looked like a white version of Lark—hulking frame and clean-shaven head, hands the size of baseball gloves.

Michael stopped the door's progress with his boot. "And don't you forget it," he said, somehow managing to match the Pip's easy tone. "You can also forget about stepping so much as one polished wingtip over the threshold of this house."

The Hulk smiled and took a half-step forward.

"It's time to go," the Hulk's partner said to Michael, wrapping a restraining hand around the other man's bicep. "Mr. Shaw is waiting."

"Hold up." Ben came down the stairs, his jacket and case in hand. Both Pips took a step back and folded their hands in front of them, eyes averted. They always reacted like that when they saw Ben—almost like they were scared of him. Ben threw them a wink that sent them shuffling while he handed Michael his stuff. "Have a good day at the office, dear," he said, tapping a finger against Michael's jacket before throwing it over his shoulder. Whatever it was that he'd managed to slip into it was something he didn't want his dad to know about.

Michael gave a discreet nod, indicating that he understood before turning toward the pair of thugs on the porch. "Let's go, boys, I ain't got all day," he said, muscling his way between them to make his way down the stairs.

He set his case on the sidewalk in front of the sleek black limo and pulled his jacket on while waiting at the curb. The Hulk popped the trunk and tossed his bags inside while the other Pip frisked him, pulling his Kimber and his knife from their holsters before handing them to the Hulk to be put in the trunk. He also pulled out Michael's cell phone and dropped it on the sidewalk, where it shattered. "Oops," he said while grinding it beneath his heel. "What's this?" he said, pulling a small sliver case from his inside jacket pocket.

"Breath mints," he said, his tone bland, expression bored. "Help yourself. Please."

The suit gave the box a shake, listening carefully to the rattle inside before stuffing it back inside his pocket. "Fuck you," he growled, giving him a shoulder check and leaving him curbside to circle around the front of the limo to climb into the driver's seat while the Hulk opened the back door for him. As promised, Livingston Shaw was waiting inside.

Michael slid across black leather, settling back against the seat. He remembered the last time he and Shaw had taken a ride together; it had ended with him being told that he'd been carting a dirty bomb around in his back. He wondered what Shaw had in store for him this time.

The Hulk closed the door and climbed into the front passenger seat. Looking out the window Michael could see Ben standing on the porch, doing his best to conceal the worry on his face.

"How is it that you always manage to find your way back here, Michael?" Shaw said in a bewildered tone that said he didn't understand the attraction.

He thought of Sabrina. "It's my home."

"Yes, well... your perpetual return has become tiresome," Shaw said, following his gaze out the window. As soon as Ben caught his father's attention, he flipped him the bird. Shaw sighed and settled back into his seat. "Almost as tiresome as my son's incessant lack of respect or discipline."

Michael turned his face away from the window as the limo began moving and met Shaw's glare head-on. "On his worst day, your son is ten times the man you'll ever be," he said quietly, the corner of his mouth lifting in a half-smile at the look that passed over his boss's face. "Save your threats, Shaw. We both know you can't kill me."

"And why is that, Michael?" Shaw said, disinterested, while he watched the scenery whip past the window. "Considering that you lied to me this morning about Leo Maddox's death, I'm hard-pressed to find a reason not to kill you at this point."

Shaw had spoken to Reyes and gained proof of life, then, so he must know that Michael's earlier call had been a ploy. The fact that Shaw came for him anyway spoke volumes.

"I *am* the fattened calf, aren't I? If you kill me, you'll lose the only thing keeping Reyes in check." He shook his head, disgusted. "Are you really that stupid? Did you really think you were going to be able to control him?"

For a split second, he was sure Shaw would deny everything. Instead, he flicked a finger over the switch that raised the privacy partition between the front seat and the back. As soon as it was fully raised, he spoke. "I'll admit that my partnership with Reyes has proved to be problematic, but I have every confidence that things will right themselves."

"And how will things *right themselves*, Shaw?" Michael said, his tone low and even. "You want me to kill him for you? Rescue the Maddox boy? That *is* why I'm here, isn't it? To clean up your mess?"

"You're here to do exactly as I say, Michael." The limo slowed as it turned into the parking lot at Moffett Field, stopping only long enough for the Pip behind the wheel to flash their credentials before being let through the security gate.

They rounded the hangar. Next to Ben's older Lear was a jet. Both looked ready for takeoff. Next to the Lear, a Range Rover sat on the tarmac. Shaw reached into his pocket and pulled out his cell phone to dial a number. "You may board the plane now," he said before ending the call.

Michael watched as the driver's side door to the Rover popped open and a Pip climbed out to open the rear passenger door. A familiar brunette in jeans and T-shirt stepped out and turned, motioning for someone else to follow her.

It was Mary, the nurse who always conducted his exams after coming off assignment. "What's she doing here?" Michael said, confused.

"Regardless of your momentary indispensability, you'll do well to remember that there are others—less important others—relying on you to complete your mission." Shaw tapped a manicured finger against the glass. "Pay attention, please."

In the moment before she appeared, Michael had the insane thought that if he closed his eyes, he could actually stop it from happening. He could keep her safe, as long as he didn't see her. "You rotten bastard," he said, leaning his forehead against the glass, completely defeated as he watched Sabrina climb out of the Rover.

Mary said something to her and she turned toward the limo where he sat, actually took a step in his direction before the Pip who'd opened her door grabbed her by the arm. He watched as she whipped her arm around in his grasp, reversing the hold he had on her so fast the Pip didn't know what hit him until she popped him in the mouth with a rabbit punch.

Michael took a deep breath. Schooled his face into an emotionless mask. "Okay, I get it. You can let her go now."

"I'm afraid that's not possible," Shaw said. "Ms. Tserkov' has very specific instructions, and Ms. Vaughn, well . . . she has her part to play in all this, just as you do."

Tserkov'. The Russian word for *church*. He looked out the window at the woman who'd been pretending to be nothing more than his nurse for nearly three years. "What is she—*really*?"

"I think you know what she is, Michael, but I'll indulge your curiosity a bit. Her parents were Russian counterintelligence, embedded in the US in the early eighties." While Shaw spoke, he watched the woman he knew as Mary step between Sabrina and the Pip. She continued to speak, jerking her chin in his direction. "When the Cold War ended, they were abandoned here by their government, eventually rooted out and killed by the CIA. Korkiva—or Courtney, as she likes to be called—is more than a bit disgruntled over the desertion."

He could literally see the fight drain out of Sabrina and she nodded, casting another look at the limo over her shoulder. Even though he knew she couldn't see him behind the tinted glass, she seemed to look right at him, her mouth moving soundlessly.

It's okay.

She turned and allowed herself to be led toward Ben's plane, mounting the steps before disappearing inside. He didn't need to ask where Shaw was taking her.

"He'll kill her," he said as he watched the Lear's hatch close and its stairs fold up. "He's been planning this from the moment he learned about her."

As soon as the plane started to taxi down the runway, Shaw popped the locks on the limo door. "You're correct. Reyes will kill her ... but not right away. You have time, though not much. Ms. Vaughn's fate very much depends on the choices you make within the next twenty-four hours."

"You're not calling the shots anymore, are you, Shaw?" Michael said, remembering his conversation with Reyes the night before. How he'd thanked him for killing Cordova, like he'd done it for him and him alone. "Sucks to be someone's bitch, doesn't it?"

Shaw smoothed a palm down the crease of his five-thousand-dollar hand-tailored pants, his expression telling Michael he was fighting for control. "I have every intention of sending you after her *and* the Maddox boy; but before that, there's something I need you to do."

"*You* need me to do?" he said, even though he knew exactly what Shaw was talking about. "Cut the shit and just tell me what Reyes wants."

Shaw stepped a foot onto the tarmac as soon as the Pip opened the car door. "It's very simple, Michael: you need to finish the job you started," he said, still unwilling to admit that he'd lost control of the situation he now found himself in. "If you want to save your Sabrina, you're going to have to kill Pia Cordova."

SIXTY-TWO

BEN KNOCKED AGAIN, RAPPING his knuckles against the thick glass set into the back door that led into Sabrina's kitchen. He looked at the kid standing next to him, Sabrina's dog at his side, and smiled. "*Kruto, malen'kiy chelovek,*" he said. Be cool, little man—even though cool was the last thing he felt. He should have known his father was already stateside. The asshole prided himself on being ten steps ahead of everyone around him.

Why the hell wasn't Sabrina answering?

The kid mumbled something, so soft he wasn't even sure he was speaking so much as breathing.

"*Ty chto-to skazal?*" Did you say something?

The boy looked up at him, concern ghosting across his face. "*Rebenok plachet.*" The baby is crying.

Ben went still for a moment, head cocked toward the door. The modifications made to Sabrina's house made it nearly impossible to hear anything going on inside. A small bomb could be detonated within its walls and no one on the outside would even know, but…

"*Vy uvereny*?" You sure?

The boy just nodded, tilting his head toward the door.

"You better be sure," he muttered to himself as he pressed his thumb to the small scanner mounted next to the doorframe. Val hated it when he just barged in.

The scanner let out a small beep a few seconds before the door lock clicked and he pushed it open. Lucy *was* crying; her screams were shrill and laced with panic.

He closed the door and re-engaged the lock as quietly as possible. Sabrina's car keys were hanging on the hook next to the back door and her backpack was dumped onto the table.

Reaching into his coat, Ben wrapped his hand around the grip of his Desert Eagle. He looked at the boy standing next to him and pulled it out, the weight of it cool and heavy in his hand. "*Podozhdite zdes'*," he said. Wait here.

He started across the kitchen, pushing his way through the swinging door that separated the kitchen from the dining room. The room was empty and he walked through it slowly, gun tilted at an angle that would ensure an easy fire if needed, and into the living room. Things took a jump from mildly alarming to *what the fuck* in an instant.

Next to a puzzling collection of flutes and a half-empty magnum of Cordon Rouge, Ben saw Sabrina's service weapon, along with her backup piece. Both were lying on the coffee table, their magazines removed. Propped against one of them was a business card. He picked it up.

Chapel Photography
Courtney Tserkov'
415-555-9321
You'll love the way I shoot

"Sabrina," he shouted, darting into the foyer and pounding up the stairs. As soon as he made the landing, he started up the set of stairs that led to her room, but he stopped short when he saw what was in the second-floor hallway.

It was Val, face down at the end of the hall, halfway between her bedroom and Lucy's.

Shit.

Ben quickly altered his route, charging down the hallway, clearing rooms as he went. "Val? Val, what happened?" he said, even though he knew she wouldn't answer. Holstering his gun, he hunkered down next to her. No blood. No obvious signs of trauma. He rolled her over gently, careful to stabilize her neck as he checked her pulse. Her heartbeat was strong and steady. Her chest moved, her breath deep and even, as if she were sleeping. Hearing him, Lucy started screaming even louder, her confusion and distress obvious. He stood and entered the room.

"Hey, Lucy-goose," he said softly. As soon as she saw a face looming over her crib, the baby's screams broke off into a round of hiccupping sobs. Ben reached for her, picking her up gently. The moment she made contact with his chest, her sobs tapered off into a series of shuddering breaths, her face buried in his neck, tiny hands holding on to his shirt. "That's right—it's okay. You know me. It's gonna be okay. I'm here." He was talking nonsense. Nothing was okay. Not even close.

Val let out a faint groan, her hand fluttering on the carpet as she tried to sit up. "*Aleks, mne nuzhna vasha pomoshch',*" he shouted, with no real hope that the boy would come. Lucy still in his arms, Ben crouched next to Val again, smoothing his free hand over her face. It was red and welted, like she'd been laying with her face mashed into the carpet for hours. "Val, I need you to wake up. Tell me what happened. Where's Sabrina?"

Val tried to open her eyes but screwed them shut against the bright light of the hallway. "Lucy... where's Lucy?"

"She's here. She's fine. I need you to tell me what happened." He did his best to keep the panic from his voice. Movement swayed in his peripheral and he looked up to see the kid standing at the top of the back stairs, less than a yard away, his face completely void of anything resembling emotion. Ben plastered an encouraging smile on his face. "*Eto normal'no. Oni v poryadke. Mne nuzhno, chtoby vzyat' rebenka, chtoby ya mog pomoch' yey. Khorosho?*" It's okay. They're okay. I need you to take the baby so I can help her. Okay?

In answer, Alex reached for Lucy, lifting her out of his arms carefully, hands planted firmly on her neck and back as he brought her to his small chest, and Lucy settled in without protest. Alex turned and stepped over Val's splayed-out legs and into the nursery, where he settled into the rocking chair beside the crib. Lucy firmly anchored in his arms, he began to pilot the chair back and forth, humming an unfamiliar tune. For the first time since they'd found him, the kid looked at total peace.

Just when Ben thought it wasn't possible for this situation to get any stranger...

Val let out another groan. "The light is really bright, Ben. Kill the switch, willya?" she said, her speech slightly slurred.

Ben thought about the champagne bottle on the table downstairs. "Are you drunk?" It sounded crazy, but it wasn't any crazier than any of the other scenarios racing through his head. He stood and bent over, picking her up to carry her into her room. Looking over his shoulder, he could see the boy, still rocking the baby, still humming like he'd been possessed by a *babushka*.

"*Ostavaytes' zdes'*," he said—stay here—without waiting for an answer before carrying Val into her room and placing her on the bed.

The room was dark and cool, and she visibly relaxed. "Where's Sabrina?" he said, his tone harsh enough to have her looking up at him, puzzled.

"What? Sab—" Her expression clouded with confusion. "I don't know."

"What the hell does that mean?" He didn't need answers as much as he needed confirmation. He'd already guessed what'd happened.

"It means *I don't know.*" She looked up at him, panic rapidly replacing confusion. "Is she in trouble?"

"Shit," he said under his breath, looking up at the ceiling for a moment to give himself a moment gather his thoughts. "What day is it, Val?"

"Uhhh…" Her voice trailed off, helpless for a moment, and he looked down at her to see that panic had settled in deep. "Sunday?"

It was Wednesday, but he nodded. "Was your friend here? Courtney? Did she come by this morning?"

Nausea rippled across her face. "My—" She lunged up and turned, vomiting over the side of the bed. Directly onto his boots. "Sorry." She wiped her mouth with the back of her hand, shaky and pale, even in the darkened room. "What the hell is wrong with me?"

She looked like she'd downed a fifth of tequila. He thought of the champagne flutes on the table downstairs. One had been empty, the other half full. "You've been drugged. The photographer, was she here?"

"Wait, stop for a minute." She laid back on the pillows, a hand pressed to her eyes.

"I can't wait, Val. Sabrina is gone and so is your new friend." He sat down on the edge of the bed and showed her the business card he found. "Who poured the drinks?" he said, starting with the most important questions first.

"Drinks? Friend?" Val's hand fell away from her face and she looked at the card, comprehension finally taking root. "What happened, Ben? Where is she? Where's Sabrina?"

The questions pressed down on him, and his shoulders slumped beneath their weight. But only for a moment. He dug his phone out of his pocket and dialed. "If I had to guess? Halfway to Colombia by now."

SIXTY-THREE

Sabrina looked out the window of the plane and continued to do the same thing she'd been doing for past six hours. Figure a way out of this mess. No one said where they were taking her or what they planned to do with her when they got there, but judging from the length of the flight and the terrain below, she knew exactly where she was headed: Colombia. Home to Alberto Reyes. As for what they planned to do to her … the scenarios running through her head were less than pleasant.

Courtney's phone chirped and she answered, shooting Sabrina a quick glance as she angled her body away from her so she could talk without being observed.

She spoke quietly into the phone for a few minutes before moving down the aisle toward Sabrina. "For you," she said, holding her cell out in front of her.

Sabrina took the phone. "Please tell me they're okay."

"They're both fine," Ben said. "You wearing the boots I gave you?"

"Of course," she said, looking up at Courtney, wondering if she heard his question.

Ben sighed into the phone. "Good. Look, I'm sorry. I should have known—"

"Stop," she said, unwilling to let him take the blame. "This isn't your fault. Just take care of them, okay?"

"Yeah, okay," Ben said, but he wasn't very convincing.

"I'm serious, Ben. They're the priority here. If something happens to them—"

Courtney reached out and took the phone from Sabrina's hand, and she had to press herself into the seat to keep from launching herself at her.

"There. Satisfied?" she said a few moments before she smiled. "Why, Mr. Shaw, do you kiss your mother with that mouth?" Courtney hung up and pocketed the phone before taking a seat in the plush leather chair across from her. "We need to have a little talk, you and me," Courtney said, leaning into the space between their seats, elbows braced on her knees.

Sabrina cut her a short look before turning back toward the window. "I've got nothing to say to you."

"Just listen, then," Courtney said. "Those one million and one escape plans you've got running through your head? Forget every single one of them. There're men—men with guns—who are going to meet us. They'll use zip-ties to restrain you, put you onto a helicopter, and take you directly to Alberto Reyes. I need you to let them."

"Why?" she said, a humorless smile touching at the corners of her mouth. "Do you get a bonus if I'm delivered alive?"

Courtney sat back, absorbing the bumps and jolts of the Lear's obvious descent. "You think I work for Reyes?"

She shrugged. She wasn't entirely comfortable with the chiding tone that the other woman used on her. "Is it so far-fetched?"

"Well, yeah, considering we're sitting in Benjamin Shaw's private plane."

Now Sabrina looked her full in the face. "If you expect me to believe that Ben had anything to do with this, you're crazier than I thought."

They landed, bumping along a strip of dirt running down the middle of a clearing, surrounded by dense jungle. As soon as the plane rolled to a stop, Courtney stood, forcing Sabrina to look up at her. "Huh. I wouldn't have figured you for a blind loyalist."

"And I wouldn't have figured you for a murdering bitch," she said, cocking her head to the side. "I guess we were both wrong."

The door to the cockpit opened, the pilot poking his head out. "The helo is five minutes out," he said, casting his gaze past the woman he was talking to. Something passed over his face and for a second, Sabrina could have sworn it was regret. "They want her waiting on the tarmac."

"Okay. Give me a minute will you?" Courtney said over her shoulder, and the guy behind her nodded before retreating into the cockpit. "Hate me or love me, Sabrina—I really couldn't give a shit which—but if you're smart, you'll trust me and listen to what I'm telling you," she said once the door was shut.

Sabrina stood slowly. "And why would I want to do that?"

"Because you aren't being handed over to Reyes so much as you're being activated," Courtney said, tossing her a tank top.

"Activated?" The word rocked her back on her heels and she stared down at the wad of fabric she suddenly found in her hand. "What are you talking about, *activated*?"

"Mr. Shaw feels like it's time you started earning your keep," Courtney said. "You need to put that on."

Sabrina rubbed the fabric between her fingers for a moment. It was made of lightweight neoprene. Some sort of mesh between the layers. "I've already got clothes on, but thanks," she said, her tone laced with sarcasm.

"Do yours stop bullets?" Courtney lifted her shirt to reveal a garment identical to the one she was holding. "Put it on."

For once in her life, Sabrina did as she was told, turning and stripping off her button-down and undershirt to pull the tank on. It lay thick and cool against her skin as she wrestled back into her shirt. She turned back to find Courtney looking her up and down like she was trying to find something.

"Where is it?"

The back of her neck went hot. "Where's what?"

"The weapon you've got stashed."

Her gaze zeroed in on the Glock 33 Courtney had strapped to her hip. "Maybe I planned on taking yours."

"We really don't have time for this. Tell me where it is because they're gonna look—*hard*—and if they find it, we're both dead." Courtney rolled her eyes at her reluctance to fess up.

She could hear the faint *whoomp* of helicopter blades cut through the air, getting closer by the second. "I have a six-shot LCP hidden in the sole of my left boot. Two extra magazines in the right."

Courtney smiled. "How very James Bond of you. Only use it if you absolutely have to. Once you start shooting, the gloves will come off, and Reyes isn't one to dick around."

The cockpit door opened again. "They're less than a minute out and asking why she's not waiting."

"Alright. Tell them we're headed out now." Courtney took her by her arm and gave her a tug. "Let's go."

The woman guided Sabrina down the center aisle of the plane to the hatch, letting go of her to pop the door lock. They stood there, side by side, while the hydraulic motor dropped the stairs onto the dirt runway. As soon as they were deployed, Courtney drew her gun and jerked her head. "After you."

Sabrina did at she was told, taking the stairs slowly. About five hundred yards out, she could see a helo, coming in fast. "You haven't told me what I'm supposed to be doing. If I'm not being marched to my death, then why am I here?" she said as she walked toward the concrete pad about fifty yards from the plane.

They came to a stop just as the helicopter touched down. Two men climbed out, each wearing dark fatigues, AR-15s strapped to their chests. The one at the head of the helo held the door open while another man stepped out. He was no taller than her own five-ten, but even beneath the Armani suit, she could see a wiry strength that would prove formidable in a close-contact fight. His dark hair was threaded with just enough silver to be considered distinguished. The emeralds in his cufflinks winked in the late afternoon sun and he flashed them; whether it was intentional or habit, she couldn't tell. The designer sunglasses he wore hid his eyes, but she didn't have to see them to know they would be small and cruel. As soon as he saw Sabrina, his face split into a broad grin.

Courtney leaned over her shoulder, bringing her mouth close to her ear so she could speak without being heard by the men in front of them. "You're plan B."

SIXTY-FOUR

ONE OF THE ARMED men swung his AR-15 to his back and came forward, barking at her in Spanish. Sabrina lifted her arms, holding them out while he ran his hands over her body so he could check her for weapons. He reached her breasts, his hands molding along her curves as he squeezed before running them down the length of her torso and between her legs, a leering grin on his face as he ran rough fingers along the center seam of her jeans.

"You can't save Leo if you're shot dead before you get there," Courtney said into her ear, reading her perfectly. The roar of the rotor blade ensured that what she said was kept between them.

Sabrina looked past the man in front of her to his partner, who was standing next to the still-grinning Alberto Reyes, his AR-15 aimed directly at her face.

"If we come for you, it'll be at night. Give it twenty-four hours. If we don't show, you'll have to get the Maddox boy out alone."

Sabrina didn't acknowledge what Courtney said, just brought her hands together and held them out to the guard, who slipped zip-cuffs onto her wrists and pulled them so tight they cut into her skin. He grabbed her by the arm and hauled her toward the waiting helo. She waited for Reyes and the remaining guard to board before allowing herself to be shoved through the open door.

As soon as the door slid closed, the helicopter lifted off, and she looked down. Courtney stood at the edge of the pad, looking up at her. She looked worried, like she wasn't sure she was up to saving Leo Maddox on her own.

That made two of them.

"I hope you'll forgive the precautions, Sabrina. I've heard many wonderfully dangerous things about you."

Sabrina turned away from the window and looked at the man sitting across from her. He'd removed his sunglasses to reveal eyes that were just as she imagined: small and cruel, the intensity behind them almost crippling. She'd seen that look before; Wade and David both had it—right before she killed them.

She looked down at the thick plastic cuffs that bound her wrists before lifting her gaze to the two armed men who sat on either side of her. "I'm flattered."

Reyes chuckled. "Yes, yes. This is what I've looked forward to the most. Your biting wit." He leaned across the small space between them. "Tell me, what did she say to you? The woman who brought you, she was whispering in your ear."

"She was warning me not to break your man's neck for putting his dirty hands on me," she said evenly.

Reyes's chuckle deepened into a full-fledged laugh. "We are going to have great fun, you and I," he said, giving her a friendly smile that was an absolute lie. "I hope *Cartero* takes his time in coming for you."

She looked away from him. "Michael won't come."

"You're right—*Michael* will not come for you," Reyes said the intensity in his eyes sharpening into something close to fanaticism. "What will come for you is a completely different animal, one I'm quite certain you've never met. But he *will* come for you, and when he does, the fun truly begins."

She didn't answer, thinking of where she'd been just a few hours ago—pinned naked against her bedroom wall, Michael's hands, suddenly rough and careless, his knee shoved into the juncture of her thighs as he worked the fly of his pants open between them.

You wanted Cartero, *Sabrina—well, now you've got him.*

She shrugged, aiming her gaze out the window. Below them, green and brown had given way to glittering blue. "You. Shaw. You both sorely overestimate my worth to him. He doesn't care what you do to me."

"We will see just how much you are worth, won't we?" he said to her, his easy words smoothed over a solicitous tone. "We go to my private island, Cofre del Tesoro. Do you know what that means, Sabrina?"

"Treasure chest." She spoke to the window. In the rapidly approaching distance she saw a dot of green, fat and wide, surrounded by blue.

"You speak Spanish?" he said as if the thought delighted him.

"A little. Not much," she said with a shrug.

"This is where I keep my most prized possessions." He gave her a smug look. "The things I treasure above all others."

"Is this where you kept Lydia?" she said.

It took him a moment to answer her. "*Cartero* told you of my Lydia? This surprises me."

She flicked him a dismissive look and lied: "He told me everything."

310

"Everything? This I doubt." That smug look gave way to something that resembled a snarl. "Did he tell you that while he was supposed to be watching over my daughter, he was also fucking my wife?"

The helicopter touched down gently, jostling her in her seat. "He told me she was a child when you bought her from her family and that you killed her because you're a raging dickbag."

Reyes's right hand shot out, his palm connecting with her face, so fast and hard that her head rocked back on her neck. Blood, warm and salty, burst in her mouth and Sabrina had to grind her boot heels into the floor beneath her to keep from launching herself at him. Courtney's words echoed in her ears: *You can't save Leo if you're shot dead before you get there.*

"I killed her because she defied me." He jerked his chin at the door, and the guard closest to it nearly fell over himself to open it onto a manicured lawn and garden.

Reyes exited the helo, and Sabrina was yanked out next. He stood staring at her for a moment before reaching into his pocket to pull out a large folding knife. He flicked it open and she tensed, thoughts and memories flooding her system.

"Yes, this is where I kept Lydia; this is also where I keep Leo Maddox. But I think you already know that." He slipped the knife between her wrists and the plastic cuff, giving it an upward twist. The blade slid through the sturdy plastic like it was slicing nothing but air. "If I hear even a whisper of trouble from you, the very first thing I will do is kill him, and believe me when I tell you that he will suffer for your insolence while I make you watch. After that, I will give you to my guards." He smiled at her while he refolded the knife and dropped it into his pocket. "You'll surely manage to kill more than a few, but not all of them. They'll eventually subdue you, and then they will rape you to death. I'll videotape it of course, so that *Cartero* will see how much you suffered before you died. That isn't the end I have planned for you, but it will work just as well. Hopefully you understand how much is depending on your choice to behave."

"I understand," she said, nearly choking on the words. The humiliation of submission tingled along her jawline, mingling with the sting of the slap.

"Very good. Take her to her room," he said to the guard next to him. "And make sure no one touches her . . . for now."

SIXTY-FIVE

FSS HAD A FLEET of planes and as soon as Ben's Lear took off with Sabrina inside, Michael was hustled onto one of them. Within minutes they were airborne, flying in another direction.

He was alone, but that didn't mean he was unobserved. A quick scan of the jet's interior revealed several security cameras. Mapping out their trajectories, he took a seat to the right of the main entrance. There was a camera aimed directly at him, but the visual would be obstructed by the high-backed leather seats in front of him. Taking the window seat, he slumped into it, casually reaching into the breast pocket of the suit jacket Ben had insisted that he take with him.

His fingers closed around the same small metal case the Pip had been shaking only an hour before. He pulled it out. Nothing inside it would help him now unless he was interested in killing the pilot and crashing into the ocean.

Keeping his movements as small as possible, he pulled off his boot. Reaching inside, he lifted the insert that covered the heel. Hidden inside the molded compartment was a satellite phone. When

Ben had given him the boots for his birthday a few months ago, he'd thought they were a gag gift. Now he was convinced of their practical applications.

Powering it on, the cell's screen came to life. There was only one number programmed into the phone. Rather than place a call he knew would be overheard, he used the keypad to punch out a text message.

Your father took Sabrina.

He hit send and waited. After a few minutes, he tried again.

He's taking her to Reyes.

No response. *Fuck.*

Ben. Answer me.

He dropped the cell into his lap and stared out the window. It had been Ben's plane that Shaw used to take her. Maybe Ben knew everything.

Maybe he was in on it.

Ben, I swear if you had anything to do with this, I'll kill you.

Calm down, Mikey. WTF are you talking about?

Only one person called him Mikey. Lark. He swiped a hand over his face. Just what he needed.

Go get him, Lark. Now.

Hold up…Shaw took her? To Reyes?

Quit talking and do what you're told.

You quit being a bitch and let me help.

He focused on the words—what they meant. Once upon a time, Lark had been the only person he trusted. That trust had nearly cost him everything and here he was, being forced to trust him again.

Come on, man. Let me help.

Shit.

Find me everything you can about Pia Cordova. Known contacts. Where's she's been in the past six months. Financial activity. Surveillance photos. Everything.

If he was going to have any sort of chance at saving Sabrina, he'd need all the help he could get. There was a reason Reyes wanted Pia Cordova dead so bad. On the surface she was nothing but an over-indulged party girl who spent her days working out her Black AmEx Card so hard you'd think shopping was an Olympic sport and her nights dropping ecstasy and doing lines of coke off the glass tables in the VIP lounge of whatever club she was at. Why she mattered was a mystery, but Pia Cordova posed some sort of threat that he couldn't quite see. Not yet anyway.

The phone buzzed in his hand and he took a look at the screen.

Give me thirty minutes.

SIXTY-SIX

Cofre del Tesoro, Colombia
August 2012

CHRISTINA COVERED HER EYES, tiny fingers splayed across a face that was pressed into the wall. "It's your turn to hide, Michael. One, two, three..." She kept counting slowly while he moved down one of the upstairs hall, trying doors as he went. Some opened onto empty guest quarters while some opened onto bathrooms or closets. A few seconds before she landed on ten, he stepped into a random room and waited for her to find him.

Colombia's wet season was in full swing, so their daily trips to the beach had been replaced by games of hide-and-seek and Disney movie marathons. They hadn't seen Lydia in over a year. Not since Christina's eighth birthday.

As soon as Reyes left the island last June, he knocked on her door, tried to coax her out, but she wouldn't answer. When he finally broke down and picked the lock, he understood why.

She'd been gone.

From somewhere down the hall he heard Christina yell "Ten!" She was nine and a half now and as fearless as her mother. He listened while she threw open doors, talking to him as if she knew exactly where he was.

The sound of a doorknob jiggling came from directly across the hall from the closet where he hid. "Locked doors are against the rules, Michael," she said, rapping her fist against the hardwood. "I found you, fair and—"

Her protest stopped abruptly when he opened the door behind her, her hand falling to her side. "There you are. I tried the knob, but it's locked. That's weird, right?"

He looked down at the crack between the door and the floor and caught the split-second shift—a shadow sliding across the floor, that told him that someone was behind it, listening. He jerked his shoulder into a haphazard shrug. "Weird? Not really. One of the maids probably locked it on accident and can't find a key is all." He shut the closet door behind him, cocking his head toward the stairs. "Ice cream sundae break?"

Christina's mouth quirked into a rueful smile and for a second, he was sure he'd been caught. "Promise not to spray the whipped cream *directly* into your mouth this time?"

He grinned at her, holding out his hand to cover up the relief that coursed through him. "I promise no such thing. That's the best part."

"It's gross," she sniffed at him as she slipped her hand into his with a barely suppressed smile. "That's why I asked Rosa to buy you your own can."

"You love me." The words slipped out before he could reel them back in. They hung there for a moment, exposed and untried, sending

317

him scrambling for cover. But before he could pull back, she squeezed her fingers around his palm.

"I do, even though you don't have a mustache," she said. "And don't even get me started on your knock-knock jokes."

"They're not that bad," he said, letting go of the panic, letting is slide right through him.

"They really are," she said, laughing while she pulled him down the stairs toward the kitchen. "But I don't mind, as long as you're here to keep telling them."

———

Two sundaes and four Disney movies later, Christina was tucked safely into her bed. Michael waited for the slow, even draw of breath to move her chest before he made his way back to the upstairs hall they'd been playing in earlier.

There were so many doors, so many hallways, he wasn't even sure he had the right one until he reached the third-floor landing and saw light leaking from beneath the door Christina had found.

He didn't knock. Didn't want to alert anyone who might be inside that he was there. Not yet anyway. Instead he pressed his ear against the door and listened. No talking. No murmur of voices. He listened harder for the smaller sounds within the room. The pad of bare feet across a carpeted floor. The faint rustle of a page being turned in a book. It was Lydia. It had to be.

And she was alone.

Before he could talk himself out of it, Michael pulled his picks from his pocket, fitting them into the lock and giving them a few twists. The metal clicked and gave way. She must've heard him because the book hit a hard surface seconds before he pushed the door open to find her standing behind a high-back chair, fists bunched and raised. When she saw him, her hands relaxed, dropping to her sides. Her expression was lost, swept away in an uncountable number of emotions—confusion, relief, hope—before settling on fear.

"I've been looking everywhere for you," he said, taking a look around the room. "How did you get in here?"

"He moves me a lot," she said. "Every week or so. He knows you're looking for me."

She wasn't making any sense. Reyes hadn't been on the island for months now.

"I'd hoped when you led Christina away today, that meant you understood … you can't be here. He will kill you both if he finds you here." She was shaking, her fingers knotted together against the chair's upholstery.

Michael took a step forward, shaking his head. "Alberto? He's not here. He's been gone for months. It's safe. You're safe—"

Lydia lifted a hand, stopping him in his tracks. "No." Her voice broke, the hand she'd used to ward him off trembling against her mouth. "I'm sorry. I'm so sorry, Michael. I just wanted … You need to leave." She sounded terrified. Desperate to make him understand. "Not this room—this *place*. Tonight. Right now. You need to leave and never come back."

Her fear reached out and slapped him, cold and bracing. Something was happening. Something he didn't understand. Something she was trying to protect him from. "Okay. We'll all leave. Right now. We'll take one of the boats to El Valle and—"

"No, Michael. Just you. You need to go alone. If we go with you, he'll never stop looking for us." She unknotted her hands, smoothing them across the back of the chair she stood behind. "You can't protect us from him. You have to leave us. Let us go."

She was right. He knew that. He was a fugitive, a deserter, and worse, a traitor to his own country. He had nowhere to take Lydia and Christina. No way to keep them safe, but in that moment, none of that mattered. "I'm not leaving you," he said through gritted teeth. He could still feel the weight of Christina's hand in his. Feel her fingers squeezing around his palm, a rare smile lifting the corners of a mouth that had grown too serious over the years. "I'm not leaving *her*. You don't understand. I did that once before and ... I can't. I *can't* do it again."

Lydia sighed, dropping her head as she stepped from behind the chair to reveal a belly that was large and swollen. She was pregnant. How far along he couldn't tell, but it didn't matter. She was right. There was no way Alberto would let her just *go*. Not with his unborn child.

"Then you're going to die," she said quietly, as she looked up at him, tears welling in her eyes to spill down her cheeks. "We both are."

He stared at her. "I don't understand. Why—"

She laughed, a slightly crazed sound that worried him. "I know you don't. You don't understand because you're a good man, Michael." She rubbed a soothing hand over her stomach and shook her head as if to clear it. She looked up at him. "I need you to promise me something."

He nodded. "Anything."

She sighed, her hands going still on her unborn child. "When Alberto kills me ... promise me you'll let him."

SIXTY-SEVEN

BEN HUNG UP THE phone and stood, making the trip to the bath-room doorway to watch Val, knelt over the toilet, puking up the last of whatever Church had given her.

Church was a woman. Ain't that a kick in the ass.

Val rocked back on her heels, face white and clammy. "Did you talk to her? Is she okay?"

"Yeah, everything's unicorns and lollipops," he said, doing his best to squelch his impatience.

"You don't have to be such a—" She turned toward the bowl to make another deposit.

"You're right. I'm an asshole. Sorry," he said, cutting her off. She was an idiot but then again, so was he for not catching on sooner. He waited for her to finish puking before he started peppering her with questions again. "What's the last thing you remember?"

Val shook her head, swiping the back of her hand across her mouth. "I don't know." She shook her head, looking up at him.

"Standing in line, waiting for coffee. I was taking Lucy to the park after her four-month checkup but..." Tears flooded her eyes.

"You don't actually remember being at the park," he finished for her. Whatever Church had used on her had planted a big black fucking hole smack dab in the middle of her memory.

Clever girl.

"Try not to worry about it right now," he said, turning on his heel. Once he was in the hallway, he checked on the kid. He was still in the rocker, humming quietly to the baby.

"*Ona goloden.*" She's hungry. He said it quietly, his small pale hand patting a comforting rhythm on Lucy's back.

"*Khorosho. Ya seychas vernus'.*" Okay. I'll be right back

He turned and took the back stairs fast, the soles of his boots gripping to the floor firmly on the landing. He pulled his cell and dialed the number, listening to it ring while he opened upper cabinets to grab a bottle.

"Hello, Benjamin."

"I want my plane back." He filled the bottle with purified water from the gallon jug that sat next to the can of formula on the counter. "FSS has a whole goddamned fleet of planes and you decide to use mine to commit a kidnapping?"

"Kidnapping? Hardly. Ms. Vaughn has been in my employ for over a year now, Benjamin," his father said in a distracted tone. "It's time for her to earn her keep."

"And by *earn her keep* you mean die violently." Ben measured three scoops of powder into the bottle before fitting the collared nipple in place. Screwing it shut, he could feel the ache in his hand, the stiffness in his fingers. He studied the scar that covered the back of it. "Why does this all feel so familiar to me, Dad?"

"Because you can't let the past go, Benjamin."

It was a low blow, and he felt every bit of it. "I'll let it go when you're dead."

His father sighed. "Don't be ridiculous," he said as if he'd just revealed that he still believed in Santa Claus. "As soon as Michael completes the task I've set him, he'll be moving on to deal with the Reyes situation. I assure you, she's completely safe until then."

Task. What the hell had his father forced Michael into? Instead of asking, he let it go. If his father wanted him to know, he would. Asking wouldn't change a thing. "Let me help her," he said, plugging the hole in the nipple with his pointer before giving the bottle a good shake. "Put me on a plane. I can be there within—"

"Stop trying to save everyone. The role of hero is one you are ill-equipped for," his father said before hanging up on him.

Ben chewed on that and what it might mean while he climbed the stairs to the nursery. As soon as he stepped through the doorway, Alex repositioned Lucy in his arms before reaching for the bottle. He could hear Val retching and imagined her bent over the toilet, trying to get rid of whatever Courtney hit her with.

"*Yavlyayetsya li ona budet v poryadke?*" Is she going to be okay?

Ben nodded while he handed the bottle over. "*Da, s ney vse budet prosto otlichno.*" Yeah, she's gonna be just fine.

He could lie in eight different languages. His father would be so proud.

SIXTY-EIGHT

THE ROOM REYES'S GUARDS led her to was hardly a dungeon. With its huge four-poster canopy bed and coffered ceilings, it looked like the executive suite at a five-star hotel.

But Sabrina recognized a prison when she saw one.

Standing in the middle of the room, she counted eight surveillance cameras that were activated by motion sensors. Every move she made was being monitored ... which would make retrieving her weapons nearly impossible.

What was she going to do? How in the hell was she supposed to save the Senator's grandson when she was just as much a prisoner as he was?

The answer was simple: she couldn't.

What did Shaw expect her to do? She was a cop, not some highly-trained operative. Stealth was hardly one of her strong suits.

Sabrina sat down on the edge of the bed and carefully took in her surroundings as she wondered if Leo Maddox was being kept in a similar fashion. Was he locked away in some posh room somewhere close by, or was he being held captive in a cage like Alex Kotko had been?

A knock sounded at the door and she stood seconds before the door was opened. A young girl of about twelve or thirteen stood in the doorway, her hair pulled back into a tight tail at the nape her neck, the wild, dark curling mass of it falling nearly to her waist. She was slender, bordering on scrawny, all limbs and big eyes.

"The cameras are visual only. No audio," the girl said without preamble, cruising the room with an air of familiarity. "And the man assigned to watch them is lazy. As long as you appear to behave, my father will never know otherwise."

My father …

"Christina." Hope jittered inside her chest, too stupid to know better. "Christina Reyes?"

The girl went still, a wary expression on her face. "Yes. How do you know me?"

"Michael speaks very highly of you."

No response.

"Christina?"

"He talks about me?" the girl said. "I'd begun to think … I thought my father killed him."

Sabrina shook her head. "No. Michael's alive."

An understanding she was too young to harbor settled into Christina's face. "That's why my father brought you … to lure him back to the island."

She looked up and over, eyes trained instantly on the security camera perched in the corner above the girl's shoulder. "I don't think you should be here. You father made it clear that there would be consequences if I broke the rules." What would happen now that Alberto Reyes's daughter had introduced herself to her father's kidnapping victim? It wasn't something she was eager to find out.

Christina took a slow turn around the room, ignoring her protests. "This was my mother's room for a while," she said softly, as if any loud voice would disturb the ghost that lived with in these walls. She wandered over to the vanity to trail a finger along the gleaming line of a silver-plated brush, turning it over. Something rattled softly inside the handle. "Her things are still here. Sometimes I think she is too."

The mention of her mother snapped Sabrina out of whatever insane plan she'd been harboring. She couldn't get this girl involved. Not after what Reyes had done to her mother. "Christina, please, there's no time. You need to leave."

"I was sent by my father to invite you to dinner," the girl said calmly, turning to look at her. "I would—*we* would—very much like your company."

Sabrina looked at the porcelain clock perched on the mantel. It was eight o'clock. Food was the last thing she wanted, but this was a chance to get out. To get a look at the layout of the house. To see if she could figure out where Reyes was holding the Maddox boy.

"Okay," Sabrina said, heading toward the bathroom. "Just give me a moment to freshen up."

In the bathroom, a cursory glance revealed a camera mounted in the corner, facing the toilet. She'd be willing to bet money there was one in the shower as well. No possible way she'd be able to retrieve her weapons in here either.

Sabrina used the restroom while staring into the camera before washing her hands. She splashed cold water onto her face and dried them both on a thick white towel. Her jaw was tender from where it'd connected with Reyes's hand. The corner of her mouth was cut, and the blood leaking from it stained the towel she used.

Sabrina dropped the towel on the floor and exited the bathroom without giving the camera another glance.

Christina was sitting on the rose-colored settee, hands folded into her lap. She looked up, a faint smile on her lips. She looked nothing like her father—her eyes were wide and expressive, so dark her iris and pupil blended almost seamlessly.

"I'm ready," she said, and Christina stood, nodding.

The young woman crossed the room to the door and, producing a key, she unlocked it. "Follow me," Christina said quietly as she pulled the door shut.

"Thank you," Sabrina said, unsure of what else to say. Unsure if she was reading the girl correctly.

"Many things changed after my mother's death. My father has become very paranoid."

Christina led her down a wide, dimly lit hallway, turning here and there, leading her deeper and deeper into the house. "He trusts no one. All guards and household staff are shuttled off the island after dinner and living quarters are equipped with timed locks. They are engaged at nine p.m. and released at six a.m. If you're caught outside your room between those times, you'll be shot."

"What about you? If you're caught sneaking around, will you be shot too?"

The girl looked up at her, her expression carefully drawn blank. "There's no exceptions."

"If there are no guards at night, then who's going to stop me?" she said, unable to curb the insolent tone that crept into her voice.

The girl didn't look at her, instead choosing to stare straight ahead as she walked. "There are cameras everywhere except for my father's study and his living quarters. No matter where you are, you are always watched. If you're caught wandering, someone *will* kill you."

Sabrina followed along quietly, so many questions begging to be answered that, for a moment, she found herself unable to ask any at all. Finally, she spoke. "Your father blames Michael for your mother's death. Do you? Blame him?" The question seemed ridiculous when there were a million other, more relevant ones she could be asking, but she had to know if this girl could be trusted if and when the time came to defy her father.

"The person I blame is beyond my reach," Christina said, casting her a glance. "No matter what face he shows you, my father is very dangerous. Do not forget and do not defy him." She stopped in front of a set of heavy double doors and pushed them open.

Sitting at a long dining room table, laden with china and crystal, was Alberto Reyes. He'd changed into a pair of creamy white linen pants and a silk button-down, casually open at the throat. "Sabrina," he said warmly, standing as she came into the room. "I am so glad you agreed to join us." He beamed at her, but it, like his tone, was nothing more than pretend. The smile, the solicitous cadence of his voice—it was all a lie.

Before she could say a word, he continued, holding his hand out to someone behind a large centerpiece in the center of the table. "Come, say hello to our guest."

A small blond head peeked around the polished silver urn that held the flowers. Leo Maddox looked at her, his green eyes flat and hollow. "Hello," he said quietly. "Are you here to take me home?"

SIXTY-NINE

Sabrina took a seat at the table across from Leo, pushing the centerpiece to the right so she could see his face. He looked dull, like he'd been drugged or like maybe he'd given up hope of ever seeing his family again after nearly a month.

She could relate.

"Leo," she said, well aware that Reyes still stood over her, watching and listening to everything she did and said. "Leo, I need you to listen to me, okay?"

The little boy looked up from his empty plate, his flat gaze trained on her face. Before she could speak, Reyes cut in.

"Choose your words wisely, Sabrina," he murmured, taking his seat at the head of the table. "The wrong ones will cost you both."

"You're not alone," she said, struggling to keep a balance between giving him hope and saying something that would set Reyes off. On impulse she reached out and gripped the hand of the girl sitting beside her, squeezing it beneath the table before letting it go. "Not anymore."

"And what will you do now that you're here, Sabrina?" Reyes said, baiting her. "How will you save the day?"

Kill you, for starters.

"If you know me as well as you think you do, *Alberto*, then you know that I've been here before," she said, fighting to keep her tone light. "As for saving the day … I'm sure I'll think of something."

The look he gave her told her that there would be a price to pay for her insolence. "No more talking," Reyes said, ringing a silver bell that waited next to an empty wine glass. Instantly, a small army of servants pushed through a door, each carrying trays and dishes of food.

Sabrina watched silently as these dishes and trays were passed around. Reyes was served first, servants eager to please him.

Each time they came her way, she shook her head no. They would look to him for direction, and he'd nod. They scooped and piled food onto the plate in front of her before depositing dishes onto the sideboard behind her.

Sabrina kept her hands in her lap.

"Don't be stubborn, *querida*," Reyes said, raising his fork to his mouth to take a bite. "You'll need your strength if you're going to play the hero, yes?"

Sabrina looked down at her plate. Beef Wellington. Asparagus. Herbed potatoes. Leo was watching her from across the table, his eyes once again flat and vacant. She picked up her fork, using its tines to spear a potato. She winked at him and shoved it into her mouth, eliciting no more than a ghost of a smile from him.

But it was enough.

"Our newest guest is a friend of *El Cartero*—you remember him, don't you, Christina?" Reyes said, choosing to ignore her small rebellion.

The potato in her mouth turned to glue as she watched the girl beside her. Christina took a small sip of water before nodding. "Yes, father," she said without looking at him.

"He'll be coming soon. You'd like that wouldn't you, Christina?" Reyes said, his voice dangerously soft. "To see your old friend again?"

She looked at him then, her eyes finding her father's face and Sabrina felt her heart seize in her chest with the insane urge to slap a hand over the girl's mouth to stop her from speaking.

"Yes, father," she said—the same words as before but in a tone that narrowed Reyes's eyes. Christina wasn't just paying her father lip service; she was defying him.

Small rebellions, it seemed, were going to be their undoing.

SEVENTY

BEN DIALED REESE'S CELL number and listened to it ring. He'd been calling him every fifteen minutes ever since he'd hung up with Sabrina's sexy doctor friend, and he was going to keep calling until that son of a bitch answered.

He wanted his goddamned plane back.

Again, the pilot's voicemail took over and he disconnected the call without leaving a message, dropping his phone on the counter. Beside him, Avasa whined, pressing her head into his knee, and he dropped his hand to give her head an absentminded pat. "Don't worry, girl. Sabrina's gonna be okay. They both will."

"You talk to dogs. Is that a perk of being raised by wolves?"

He turned toward the doorway connecting the dining room and kitchen to see Mandy Black.

"One of many," he said, picking up his phone and slipping it into his pocket. "Thanks for coming."

She shrugged. "I didn't do it for you," she said, entering the room. "Besides, I'm not sure what I can do to help."

"My team consists of a three-and-a-half-foot-tall Russian kidnapping victim, a worried dog, a woman who's probably been roofied, and a baby," he said. "Right now, you're my star player."

Mandy sank into one of the kitchen chairs, gnawing on her bottom lip. "Where's Strickland? Or Nickels? Since it was his wife who was roofied, he should be here, don't you think?"

Ben leaned against the counter, rubbing a thumb across his forehead in an attempt to chase away the headache that was threatening to settle in. "I don't know."

"Then that's what I can do," she said, pulling out her phone.

"What's that?"

She gave him a halfhearted smile while dialing her phone. "Recruit better players."

―――――

Within twenty minutes, the kitchen door banged open, Nickels rushing through it, followed by Sabrina's partner. "Where is she? Where's my wife? Lucy?" Nickels demanded, eyes wheeling from face to face.

Mandy stood. "She's upstairs and she's fine. They both are. They're sleeping."

"Vaughn?" Strickland bounced a look between Ben and Mandy. "Where is she?"

Ben took a moment to quiet the emotion that the cop's question brought to the surface. "I'm not a hundred percent sure, but if I had to take a guess—Colombia."

"Colombia?" Strickland's glare zeroed in on him. "Reyes took her?" He looked at Mandy. "Is that what happened?"

Took her? No, my father delivered her like a fucking pizza ... "Pretty much," he said. "I'm working to get a bead on her location. We should know within the hour." Another lie, but he just threw it onto the pile along with the other ones he'd told.

"Where's O'Shea?" Nickels said, jaw locked at a dangerous angle.

"Gone."

"*Gone...*" Nickels turned toward Strickland, a harsh bark of laughter ripped out of his throat. "What did I tell you?" He swung his glare back around to settle it on Ben. "I guess his work here was done, huh?"

"Careful, cop." Ben stood up from the table, leaning across it. "This is your fault, not his."

Nickels's jaw slammed shut, and it took him a second to recover. "What did you just say?"

"Oh, I think you heard me—he told you to get them out of here pronto, and yet here you all are." Ben skirted his way around the table until he was nearly nose to nose with cop. "If you'd done what he'd told you to do, your wife and child wouldn't have been available to be used as leverage against Sabrina to get her to leave," he said, thumping Nickels in the chest with his pointer finger. "This isn't on Michael. This is on you."

For just a second, it looked like the cop was going to take a swing at him but in the end his shoulders slumped, the fight suddenly gone. "What can I do now?"

Ben took a step back. "Nothing. The damage is already done. Go be with your wife and stay the fuck outta my way." His phone rang, letting out the first few notes of "Fly Me to the Moon" by Sinatra. He moved into the dining room without excusing himself so he could answer it.

"That kooky bitch better have a gun to your head, Harrison," he all but growled into the phone. "Because that's the only acceptable excuse for bouncing my calls into voicemail for nearly two hours straight."

"Look, I'm sorry—"

"You allowed my father's minion to hijack my plane. We passed *sorry* a long time ago."

Harrison sighed. "It was a direct order from your father, Ben. What did you want me to do?"

He was right. Ben took a deep breath and let it out slowly. "Just tell me she's okay," he said. They both knew he wasn't talking about his plane.

"Last I saw her, she was fine."

"Okay. Great. Fuel up and come get me," Ben said but his order was met with silence. "*Reese.*"

"Yeah. Still here."

"I want my plane back," he said through clenched teeth.

A shifting. An uncomfortable, almost restless sound. "I can't."

Not the words he wanted to hear. "What do you mean, you can't?"

"I mean, I can't. You know how you said earlier that the only acceptable excuse for ignoring your calls was if that kooky bitch had a gun to my head?"

Ben sighed. "Yes."

"Well, it's not pointed at my head. It's pointed at my johnson. You're going to have to find your own ride here, because she says we're not going anywhere."

"Where is *here*?"

"An airfield just east of El Valle, Colombia," Reese said, rambling off coordinates.

"Have you seen Michael? Is he there yet?"

Another round of silence, like he was waiting for permission to answer. Church was listening in. "He's not here yet. There were other things he needed to do before your father would clear him to go after Reyes."

He drew a blank for a few seconds before it hit him. "Pia Cordova."

Reese didn't answer. "The kooky bitch says to hurry. We don't have much time."

And then the line went dead.

Ben tightened his fist around his cell for a moment before dialing a different number. His father wasn't the only one who had sleepers.

"I need you to find out where they're holding Pia Cordova, and then I need you to put a bullet in her skull," he said, waiting only long enough to get confirmation before hanging up again. He turned, intent on leaving. He had to find a plane to take him to—

Mandy stood in the doorway. The look on her face said she'd heard the order he'd given and for a moment, he was sorry for it.

So naturally, he snapped at her. "No one likes a snoop, Doc."

She didn't even try to deny it. "You weren't raised by wolves. You were raised by sociopaths," she said, shrinking away from him as he approached. For some reason, he was sorry for that too. And it made him angry.

"Truer words, Doc. Truer words," he said as he pushed his way past her and out the door.

SEVENTY-ONE

Barcelona, Spain

THE LIMO PULLED UP in front of an industrial rust-colored building, too modern to belong in a city that was well over a thousand years old. It also looked too small to perform the functions of a police station and municipal jail, but Michael knew that its looks were deceiving. The structure extended three stories underground and housed nearly two hundred and fifty inmates awaiting trial and transfer.

The rear door popped open, the driver standing aside so he could climb out. Taking a few moments to straighten his tie, Michael studied the building's exterior, looking for points of entry and escape. While getting in would pose little challenge, he doubted they would allow him to waltz out the front door after killing their most high-profile inmate.

He smoothed the lapels of his suit jacket and took the briefcase the driver held out to him with a wink. "Don't wait up," he said before he turned and made his way up the concrete steps leading to the building.

Despite his outward behavior, Michael had serious reservations about what he was about to do. Even after everything he'd found out about Pia Cordova over that last few hours, the idea of killing a woman, any woman, was distasteful.

He pushed his way through the heavy glass doors into the lobby, informing the desk sergeant that he was Ms. Cordova's attorney and that he was here for an appointment. Uniformed officers ushered him into an antechamber so that they could search him, and he submitted without protest while they rifled through his pockets and his briefcase.

Their search bore little fruit—nothing more than case files and a Montblanc pen. He extracted the pen from the officer's grasp, tucking it into his breast pocket with a smile. "I'd like to see my client now, if you don't mind."

Despite the fact that it was nearly three a.m., he was led into a private visitation room as if he'd been expected and left to wait.

As soon as he'd placed his briefcase on the room's only table, the door opened and Pia swept in like she was wearing Versace instead of jeans and a plain white T-shirt. Another sign that he'd been expected.

She'd only been arrested a few days ago, but she looked worn, older without her usual armor of makeup and hair extensions. Trailing a manicured finger across his shoulder and down the length of his arm, she rounded the table to take a seat across from him. "Hello, *Cartero*," she all but purred, holding her manacled wrists at chest level so that the guard who escorted her could cuff her to the table. The length of chain was generous enough to allow movement, and she folded her hands on the flat surface between them. As soon as she was secure, the guard circled back around to stand behind him, next to the door. Michael tracked his progress from the corner of his eye.

Pia rattled her chains, drawing his attention. "I'm glad you decided to come. I was worried we wouldn't have the chance to see each other again."

He wasn't surprised that she knew who he really was. If he'd learned anything over the last few hours, it was that Pia had spent her life being underestimated by everyone around her, which was exactly how she wanted it. While the world saw a rich, flighty party-girl, she'd been busy building an empire in her father's shadow.

He smiled at her. "The man you sent to the hospital—the one Sabrina killed. He wasn't there for the Kotko boy, was he? He was there for her."

"Who is Sabrina?" she said, her eyes wide and innocent.

"You want her dead, and I want to know why," he said, his tone more desperate than he'd intended.

"You seem quite fixated on this woman, *Cartero*." Her mouth curved in a smile he'd seen before. One that was meant to seduce and tease. "Should I be jealous?"

The desperation flattened out, hardening into a resolve as thick as stone between them. "No. You should be afraid."

She drew an invisible doodle on the flat of the table with the tip of her finger, laughing like he'd made a joke. "Do you love her?" She looked up at him. "I hope so."

"No more games, Pia." He opened his briefcase and pulled out the files inside. They weren't the ones Lark had sent him; to tell the truth, he had no idea what was even on them. But she didn't know that. "I see you. The *real* you." He flipped open one of the files before drawing the Montblanc from his breast pocket and setting it on the table. "Graduated with honors from Harvard's Law and Business Schools simultaneously and yet turned down multiple lucrative job offers to return to your life of opulent squandering here in Spain, happy to play the part of daddy's little princess. But in the three years since you graduated, your father's holdings have increased by nearly six hundred percent. Gun running doesn't generate that kind of jump. When did he find out you'd started trafficking children behind his back?"

Pia spread her fingers out on the table, clicking her nails a few times before she sat back, glancing at the guard who'd accompanied her into the room. The smile fell from her lips like discarded trash. "My father ... he had no vision. No drive." She shrugged. "He was a traditionalist. *No drugs. No children.* Boring. When I returned from the United States I had the tools to build the kind of operation *I* wanted. And that's what I did.

"By the way, I had those two guards thoroughly distracted before you caused such a racket." Pia tsked. "So unprofessional, *Cartero.* Are you slipping?" Now the smile returned, but it no longer flirted. This one was hard, turning her entire face into a mask of hatred and ice. "Ask me again about your precious Sabrina."

"Why did you try to kill her?"

Pia lifted her hand to examine her nails before looking at him. "It's simple. I tried to kill her because you love her. And I won't stop. Not until she's dead."

SEVENTY-TWO

AFTER DINNER, SABRINA WAS escorted back to her room by one of Reyes's men. She walked as slowly as she possibly could without arousing suspicion, desperate to gain an advantage in this game he was playing with her.

She and Christina had been ordered to eat the rest of their meals in silence and even though it'd killed her, she'd complied without protest. As soon as his plate was cleared, Leo was led away by a guard. His little arm stretched up, legs working double time to keep up with the long-legged stride of the man who'd been charged with returning him to wherever he was being kept. Even as he was being taken, Leo watched her, his neck craned so he could keep her in his sights, waiting for her to object. To do something to help him.

To rescue him.

She looked at the guard walking next to her. The gun housed in the sole of her boot seemed to burn a hole in her foot. So close and yet unreachable. She was going to have to do something to change that.

"I need to use the bathroom," she said, stopping in her tracks.

The guard turned and reached for her arm. "You have a bathroom in your suite. You can wait."

"I wouldn't touch me if I were you," she said, pulling her arm from his grip.

"Oh, yeah? Why's that?" he said, snatching at her bicep again, this time clamping down on it with more than a little strength, giving her a shake that slammed her head into the wall.

Reaching through the stars that danced in front of her, Sabrina grabbed his sleeve, dropping her hip and pivoting to pull the guard off balance while bringing her hand up, cupping it so that she could drive the L formed between her pointer and thumb into the soft flesh of his throat, directly into his windpipe. His shoulders snapped forward, free hand grabbing at his throat while he visibly sucked wind. "Because I don't like it," she said, letting go of the arm she held while taking a step away from him, waiting for the hornet's nest she'd just kicked to erupt on her.

Laughter sounded from farther down the hall. For a moment she thought it was Reyes, but no ... it belonged to a man about twenty years his junior. Same small features. Same cruel mouth. Same vacant eyes.

"To be fair, Eduardo, she did try to warn you," he said, his laughter tapering off into a disgusted chuckle. He glanced at his watch. "Go." He looked up at her and smirked. "I think I can handle our guest from here."

They watched Eduardo stagger down the hall for a moment before she turned to the man standing beside her. "I'm Estefan Reyes," he said, holding his hand out to her.

She looked at it. Didn't take it. "I know who you are. I still need to use the bathroom."

Estefan dropped his hand and looked at his watch. "Of course," He gave her a small bow, sweeping his arm toward a set of double doors. "This way."

Opening the doors onto a darkened room, he clicked on a table lamp that revealed a well-appointed study. Lifting a crystal carafe from a table near the door, he poured a small glass of something clear, drinking its contents in a single shot. "Would you like one?" he said, refilling the glass before holding it out to her, half invitation, half dare.

Sabrina glanced quickly at the desk clock to her left. It was 8:47. She had thirteen minutes to get back to her room before the door locked her out. Was he purposely stalling her so she'd be punished or was he just playing a game of chicken, trying to see how far she'd go before she flinched?

"Thanks," she said, taking the glass from him. Tipping it back, she poured the liquid down her throat, barely feeling the burn before her belly caught fire. She handed the glass back, careful to keep their fingers from touching.

He flicked a glance at her to gauge her reaction while pouring himself another shot. This one he sipped. "Absinthe. My father has it imported from Prague. Nearly a hundred and eighty proof. He has a collection of them—high-proof spirits. The more dangerous, the better." He took a sip. "Care for another?"

Another shot of that would knock her on her ass. She shook her head. "No, thank you."

He grinned at her "*Cartero* never drank. Never quite fit in here, despite the things he did for my father."

"That's because he's a good man," she said, her veiled insult pulling another smile from her host.

"*Good man* ... Should I tell you of the last time I saw *Cartero* kill for my father? It was right here." He gestured toward the carpet they were both standing on. "His name was Garrett—an American college student. Your lover—" He cocked his head at her, running his eyes up the length of her before settling them on her mouth. "He *has* fucked you, hasn't he?"

The urge to flinch, to simply leave and find her own way back was almost too strong to resist, but she had a feeling that's exactly what he wanted. Before she had the chance to tell him to go to hell, he continued.

"Your *lover* gave him a Colombian necktie." He stepped into her, lifting his hand to her throat. "That's where we take a knife and slice you from ear to ear," he said, trailing a finger along the underside of her jaw, the slide of his skin against hers making her feel as if she were crawling with insects. "Then"—he reached up and gripped her chin, pulling her mouth open—"we tear your tongue out and pull it through the gash in your neck." She jerked her chin away from his hand and he smirked, eyes locked on hers. "*Cartero* cut his throat right here, where we're standing, while poor Garrett begged for his life. We put down a plastic sheet so the blood wouldn't ruin my father's favorite rug. Would a good man do that?"

Sabrina resisted the urge to look away, refusing to let him see how much his story had affected her. "I think a good man would do anything he had to do to protect the people he cared for," she said, fighting to keep her tone even. "And I still need to use the bathroom."

He laughed, and just like that, whatever dark spell he'd been able to spin around them was broken. "My apologies," he said. "It's just through there." He took a seat on the plush leather couch across from her.

As soon as she was in the bathroom she locked the door, leaning her forehead against it for just a moment, trying to breathe her way through the doubt and fear that heaped around her.

Get your shit together, darlin'.

Wade's voice came through loud and clear, and for once, it wasn't the most frightening thing going on inside her head.

She lowered the toilet lid and sat down to work her boots off. They'd been a Christmas gift from Ben, of course, and he'd been beyond proud to show her the molded compartments built into their soles. Pulling up the inserts, she retrieved the LCP and magazines, setting them down quietly so she could relace her boots.

Standing, she flushed the toilet just as someone knocked on the door. Quickly, she tucked the compact gun and extra magazines into the top of her boot, her pant leg covering them completely. "I'm almost finished," she said, washing her hands and drying them before she opened the door.

Alberto Reyes stood on the other side.

SEVENTY-THREE

MICHAEL LOOKED AT THE woman in front of him and thought about what he'd come here to do. Whether she knew it or not, she'd just made his job a hell of a lot easier.

Pia's gaze flicked upward, connecting with the guard again, before she resettled her attention on him. "I'd like to tell you a story," she said, leaning forward, arms folded on the table between them, an almost wistful smile on her face. "It's a sort of fairy tale. About a princess who goes to a faraway land and meets a boy and falls in love. This boy, knowing how much the princess loved her father, decides to travel to her kingdom to ask the king for her hand in marriage." The smile soured and she sat back, letting her arms fall apart. "The king had no intentions of allowing this boy to marry his daughter, but instead of telling him no, he decides to send him on a dangerous journey to prove his worth. The boy agrees, willing to do anything if it meant a chance at winning the hand of the princess."

She paused for a moment. "The journey the king sent the boy on was to another kingdom, this one ruled by an evil tyrant. This tyrant saw what the princess's father had built and wanted it for himself, and he was willing to start a war to get it. It was the boy's job to persuade him otherwise." She shook her head. "But the evil tyrant would not be persuaded. He took the boy and did terrible things to him until the princess was certain she'd never see him again. The princess begged her father to rescue the boy, and so he in turn begged for the boy's return. The evil king agreed. The father sent two of his knights into the wicked kingdom to bring the boy home ... but while the evil king had agreed to return the boy, he never said he would return him alive."

Michael could still hear the thick plastic beneath his boots, the way it crinkled when he shifted. Could feel the wet weight of the knife in his hand, blood dripping off his wrist while he worked it through the thick meat of the boy's neck—hating himself for what he was doing but unable to stop. Unable to change the path he'd set himself upon.

"The evil tyrant kept a pet—a fierce dragon whose taste for blood was only rivaled by its love for his master's wife and child ... " Pia tilted her head, a beatific smile, tinged black, playing across her lips. "Can you guess what happens next, *Cartero*?"

"I killed your boyfriend." Michael leaned forward, closing his hands around the pen he'd placed on the table. "*Me*. Not Sabrina and sure as hell not the hundreds of kids you've kidnapped and sold to pedophiles over the past three years. Where's your fucked-up fairy tale excuse for that one?"

"If the princess doesn't get her happily ever after, then neither does the dragon." She flicked her gaze upward, casting it past him. "I'm finished here."

Without warning, something thick and unyielding was dropped in front of him and tightened quickly around his neck. Michael's counter-moves, born from instinct and muscle memory, were fast. His right hand shot up, grabbing the belt before it tightened around his throat even as his left hand swept across his chest, twisting in his seat to drive the Montblanc into the meat of the guard's outer thigh. Michael rocketed out of the chair before the guard had a chance to scream. He shot straight up, crashing the top of his skull into the underside of the man's jaw, breaking teeth and cutting off his only chance to cry for help.

The blow loosened the guard's grip on the belt, allowing him to pull it free. Stepping behind him, Michael slipped the belt around the guard's throat, drawing it taut as he fell to the ground. Planting his polished dress shoe in the center of the guard's chest, he gave the belt a vicious yank, snapping his neck in two.

The entire episode took less than ten seconds.

Pia sat staring at him, her smug look cooling into one of defiance and disbelief. She watched as he rolled the guard over to retrieve what he knew had to be there. A .22 with an attached suppressor was tucked into the small of his back, hidden by his gun belt. "Should have just had him shoot me." He pulled the gun and held it up.

She glared at him. "But then I wouldn't have been able to look you in the eyes while you died."

"Best laid plans, right?" He shook his head, pulling the guard's keys off his belt. "What *was* the plan—kill me, plant the gun? Make it look like I was hired to kill you?"

She licked her lips, a nervous gesture that told him that this was it. The entire sum of her botched revenge fantasy lay crumpled at his feet. "People know you're here. If you kill me—"

"Let me guess ... Estefan Reyes?" He smiled. "Trust me when I tell you he doesn't care about you." He stood slowly, the extended

348

barrel of the .22 pointed at her chest. "Matter of fact, I'd be willing to bet he's hoping I kill you."

She must've heard the truth in his words because she held up her hands, the cuffs that secured her to the table sliding along her slender wrists. "I'm a defenseless woman, Michael. You couldn't kill me three days ago, and you won't kill me now."

"You forget, I'm not the knight in shining armor in your story," he said, thumbing the safety off. "I'm the dragon, and there isn't anything I wouldn't do—no one I wouldn't kill—to keep what I love safe."

SEVENTY-FOUR

Cofre del Tesoro, Colombia
September 2012

MICHAEL LOOKED AT HIS watch and swore under his breath. Estefan was late.

Again.

"You shouldn't curse," Christina chirped at him from the high stool she perched on, legs swinging in haphazard circles. They'd been waiting in the ballroom that Reyes had turned into an indoor training facility for nearly an hour now, and he was seconds away from walking out.

Without warning, one of the floor-to-ceiling doors swung open and Estefan sauntered in.

Michael watched him stroll across the parquet floor to the center of the room where he stood. "And your brother should be more respectful of other people's time," he said, barely able to hide his contempt.

Estefan smirked, making a point of reaching down to close his zipper before wiping at the corner of his mouth. "Sorry. I was busy."

Like father, like son. There were nearly two dozen household staff members on the island—all of them women and none of them over the age of twenty. They wore uniforms and performed the basic functions of housekeepers, laundresses, and cooks, but to live and work for Alberto Reyes meant you were his for the taking or giving as he saw fit. In the years since Estefan had become a permanent fixture on the island, he'd followed in his father's footsteps in more ways than one.

Late-afternoon rain slashed against the wide windows, the sound of it a ceaseless drumming. "Go to your room and wait for me there, Christina," he said quietly.

The little girl jumped down from her stool. "But—"

He shot her a look over his shoulder that killed her budding protest. "No *buts*, just do what I say," he told her before turning around to look at her brother. "This isn't gonna take long."

Christina nodded, moving toward the door at a snail's pace, casting looks over her shoulder at him as she went. As soon as she was gone and the door was closed behind her, Michael pulled his tactical knife from the sheath strapped to his thigh. He looked at his watch. It was ten minutes to five. "Your hour's almost up," he said, cocking his chin at the knife Estefan kept in a holster at his hip. "But I think I can still squeeze in a lesson."

"Three years we've been doing this, *Cartero*," Estefan said, pulling his knife while he circled slowly to the left. "I think I've learned just about all I can from you."

Michael followed suit, the hilt of his blade held casually. "Oh, I can think of a few things I can still teach you. Common decency, for starters."

Estefan laughed. "*El Cartero* wants to teach me decency?" His blade whipped out, slicing an arc through the space between them. He was fast, but Michael was faster; the kid caught nothing but air.

"Someone should." He sidestepped another attack, countering with a downward strike with the tip of his knife, a shallow cut at Estefan's wrist.

The kid hissed, yanking his wrist back, face twisted with hatred. "And that someone is you? When did you become a hero, *Cartero*?" He lunged again, and Michael stepped into it, taking the wound—a deep slice across his shoulder—as if he'd asked for it. The pain cleared his mind and allowed him to focus.

"Refraining from strong-arming the help into giving me a blowjob in the laundry room doesn't make me a hero," he said, sidestepping another attack. "It makes me a man who doesn't have to force women to have sex with me." Using Estefan's own momentum against him, Michael jerked his knee upward, crashing it into the kid's face with enough force to drop him like a sack of dirt.

Estefan rolled onto his back, his face painted with blood, contorted by rage and humiliation. "Whoever said it was the maid I've been fucking?" He looked at him, sitting up to mop the back of his hand across his face.

The implication of his words rang clear. There was only one woman on the island who was not a part of the household staff.

Lydia.

He thought of her face the last time he'd seen her. It had been less than a month ago, but it seemed longer than that. How scared she was, hopeless, her hands pressed against her protruding belly. He understood now. It wasn't Alberto she was afraid of. Not entirely.

"What did you do?" he said quietly, staring down at the young man on the floor beneath him, a sick feeling slithering around in his belly, so cold he was surprised he couldn't see his breath.

Estefan looked up at him. "It's not what I did, *Cartero*. It's what I've *been* doing. With her."

Something shifted inside him. That cold slithering thing wrapping itself tight. Heating up. Settling in. "Get up." Michael circled him slowly, shifting his grip on the blade from defensive to an offensive position. "Your lesson's not over."

"Sometimes she cries." Estefan stood, tracking his movements with small flat eyes. "She thinks I don't notice, but I do," he said, his tone edged in something ugly. "I know it's not my father she cries for, so it must be you." He grinned, blood smeared across his bright-white teeth. "I've had her many times, *Cartero*. I wonder … how many times has my stepmother spread her legs for you?"

A strange sound came out of him, a strangled growl that propelled him forward, directly into the path of Estefan's attack. The blade slipped into the meat of his left shoulder, scraping bone, slicing muscle.

He didn't even feel it. He just kept coming.

Michael dropped his shoulder before twisting it away, forcing Estefan to relinquish his hold on the knife still embedded in his flesh. His right hand rocketed past Estefan's defenses, latching around his throat, thumb pressed into the pocket of nerves nestled behind his ear so hard his eyelids began to flutter.

Dropping his own knife into its sheath, Michael reached over and pulled Estefan's knife from his shoulder and showed it to him before pressing its tip into the corner of his eye. "I believe," he said, drawing the razor-sharp edge down the length of his face, the thick, heavy blade exposing the muscle beneath the river of blood that coursed down his cheek, "I made you a promise. Something about laying you open and watching you bleed."

It took everything Michael had not to angle the blade across his throat. Instead he dropped Estefan onto the hard floor, taking a step back to watch him wail and writhe.

"Class dismissed," he said, stepping over him on his way out the door.

SEVENTY-FIVE

SABRINA CAST A GLANCE over Reyes's shoulder at his son, trying to decide if this had been his plan all along. Trying to formulate a plan of her own if shit went south.

"Why is she bleeding?" Reyes said, casting his glance along with hers. Looking to his son for an explanation.

For a moment she thought he was referring to the bruise and busted lip he'd given her earlier, but then she felt the wet trickle against her neck and she swiped at it. The bullet graze from the hospital. It must've reopened when she and the guard had gone a round in the hallway.

Estefan stood, his insolent manner instantly replaced by one of respect that bordered on reverence. "When I happened upon her, she was in the hallway with Eduardo. They were … fighting."

"And you thought to bring her into my office?" Reyes spoke to his son while continuing to scrutinize her, looking for cracks he could dig his fingers into.

"She was visibly upset. I thought a quick drink would calm her," Estefan said, the lie so smooth she almost believed it herself.

Reyes reached out, cupping her neck to angle her jaw so that he could get a better look. She had to fight to stop herself from jerking out from under his grasp. "Was it Eduardo who injured you, Sabrina?"

He was close—too close. She wasn't ready. She still had no idea where they were holding Leo. Even if she managed, by some miracle, to kill both Reyes and his son, she'd never find the boy. Not before she was killed.

Now ain't the time, darlin'. Be cool.

She wiped at her neck again, angling herself away from Reyes. The blood had gone thick, tacky under her fingers. "It's just a wound that's reopened. No big deal."

"But he touched you, yes?" He smiled at her reluctance to point fingers. "It's okay. The truth is all that's required."

Looking past him, she found the clock perched on his desk. It was 8:55. "I'd like to go back to my room now."

Reyes chuckled, letting go of her chin to take a step back. "Of course. It's getting late." He looked at his son. "You know what to do."

Estefan nodded. "Yes, father," he said, his gaze passing over her before he left.

Reyes swept his arm in a grand gesture. "Please, allow me to escort you," he said, playing the part of perfect gentleman instead of sadistic murderer.

Swallowing the shitty remark that bubbled in her throat, Sabrina forced her mouth into a cool smile. "Thank you."

They walked side by side, quiet, while she fought the urge to look at him.

"I spoke with *Cartero* last evening," he told her. "It won't be long until he comes for you."

"You mean it won't be long before you kill me, don't you?" she said, careful to keep her tone conversational.

"That doesn't mean we can't behave in a civilized manner until then, does it?" He smiled at her, glancing at his watch. "We have a few minutes left. Come to the window, there is something I wish you to see," he said, turning the knob beneath his hand to usher her inside.

The room was as she'd left it save for the fact that the heavy velvet drapes were drawn away from the windows, the carefully manicured lawn brightly lit beyond it.

Eduardo knelt in the grass facing the window, no more than ten yards away. He was close enough that the terror written on his face was stark and visible through the glass between them. When he saw her, his mouth began to move rapidly, but the windowpane was too thick to allow the passing of sound.

Estefan stood behind him, the 9mm in his hand pressed into the base of the man's skull.

"Let's play a game," Reyes said beside her, and for just a moment, it was Wade who stood beside her. Wade who wanted to play.

Don't go there, darlin'. Stay sharp now.

"I don't like games," she said quietly. "They usually prove too complicated for my tastes."

"Yes ... you are a simple creature, aren't you?" He brushed his fingertips along her collarbone, smearing her own blood across her skin. "This game is as simple as they come. It has only one rule: when I ask you a question, you tell the truth," he said, settling his gaze on her face. "My son said that when he happened upon you and Eduardo in the hall, you were fighting. Is that true?"

357

She looked up at Estefan. He was watching her.

"Yes."

"Why?"

She flicked her gaze toward the man kneeling on the lawn. "I wanted to use the bathroom before returning to my room. He wanted me to wait."

"And so you fought?" He all but purred the words into her ear. *Don't look at him, darlin'.*

"Yes."

"Was it he who put his hands on you first, Sabrina?"

"No," she said, turning to look him in the eye, despite Wade's warning echoing inside her head. "You were when you bitch-slapped me earlier. Technically, he's the second."

He smiled widely as if the memory of it bonded them together. "Let me rephrase. During your altercation with Eduardo, was it he who decided to use his hands first?"

She remembered how he'd grabbed her arm to try to move her along. "Yes."

"And you warned him not to touch you, but he didn't listen." There was an excited edge to his voice. One that unsettled her.

"Yes." She looked away from him then, unable to stomach another second of eye contact between them.

"And you struck back." He touched her again, trailed his fingers along the length of her arm until he found her hand, caressing the back of it. "You hit him. Injured him."

She fought the urge to yank her hand away from his. "Yes."

"If I were to put my hands on you ... if I were to hurt you, would you try to kill me?"

A howling wind took up inside her head, one that rattled her bones and clouded her vision. She curled her free hand into a fist but kept her head turned straight ahead, staring into the middle space between her and the man who knelt before her on the lawn. "Yes."

"Even if it meant the death of both you and little Leo?"

God help her ... "Yes."

Reyes laughed, the sound of it obscene as it slithered into her ear. "I believe you."

Some unseen signal passed through the window between father and son, and the trigger was pulled. The 9mm round rocketed through Eduardo's skull to burst through his eye socket, spraying blood and brain across the bright green of the grass.

"The only thing I tolerate less than disobedience is lies." He tightened his grip on her hand until it almost hurt. "What were you doing in my office, Sabrina?"

She kept her eyes trained on some fixed point beyond the window. The LCP tucked into her boot bit hard into her ankle. Reyes's thumb brushed against the inside of her wrist, the bracelet Michael had given her shifting against her skin, and for a moment she was sure he knew what it really was.

"Your son took me into your office and offered me a drink like he said. I accepted and after I used the toilet, I flushed and then washed my hands." She forced herself to look at him again, allowing herself to be caught in the flat, emotionless dark of his eyes. "I was just finishing up when you knocked."

He smiled. "See, that wasn't so bad, was it?" Reyes leaned into her, pressing his mouth against hers. His tongue snaked out to run itself along the cut his earlier blow had drawn across her lip, the pressure of it igniting a hissing sting against her mouth. Before she had time to react, Reyes had pulled away and was moving toward the door. "Good night, Sabrina," he said as he pulled it closed.

Seconds later, the auto-lock engaged on her bedroom door, trapping her inside.

SEVENTY-SIX

Ben found a ride.

It'd taken some negotiating and more finesse than he had time for, but the outcome had been worth it. He was leaving for Colombia within the hour.

Leaving Nickels and Mandy in charge of Val, Lucy, and Alex, he'd headed to Miss Ettie's to pack up his gear. No matter the outcome with the Maddox situation, Ben doubted he'd be coming back here for quite some time.

He had other matters to attend to.

His phone rang just as he hit the front walkway, and he answered. "Is she dead?" It was his man in Spain, the one he'd ordered to kill the Cordova woman.

"Your boy beat me to it. Worked my way in and found the guard with his neck snapped and the chick with a cluster of bullets in her sternum."

He stopped walking for a second, squeezed his eyes shut. "Damn it…" No matter what Michael said, no matter how good he was at his job or how emotionally void he liked to pretend to be, he wasn't built for this shit. Neither of them were. "Did he get out?"

"When I got there, the whole station was in an uproar looking for him, but yeah, he was gone." The man on the other end cleared his throat. "Anything else?"

Ben started walking again, up the porch steps to press his thumb against the print scanner. The lock disengaged. "No. If you hear anything, let me know."

"You got it." And then the line was dead.

He found Lark in the sunroom, fingers clicking across the keyboard attached to several monitors, endless streams of data flowing his way.

"What are you doing?" he said, not entirely sure that leaving Lark alone for so long was a good idea.

"Where you been? Mikey called your SAT phone right after you left. He asked me for a full jacket on that Cordova woman. Found some pretty interesting shit," Lark said without even looking at him. "She and Estefan Reyes have been—"

"Did you know my father was going to have Church take Sabrina?"

The clicking stopped, Lark's massive head turning slowly to look at him. "Shit . . . I admit that she ain't my favorite white girl but, I swear, I didn't know that was going to happen," he said calmly, recognizing that he was suddenly fighting for his life. "You believe me, right?"

Ben stared at Lark hard. At the beads of sweat that popped up along his upper lip, the way he flexed his fingers around empty air—probably wishing for a gun—waiting for him to answer.

"Why did you really do it, Lark?" Ben said quietly, asking the only question that mattered to him right now. "Were you jealous? It was obvious, even then, that Michael had feelings for her. Was

362

she interrupting your little bromance? Changing him into some-one you didn't like? Did you get Lucy killed to punish him for wanting something more than a lifetime of killing?"

Lark sat back in his seat, looking away for a second before re-settling his gaze on the man in front of him. "Getting Lucy Walker killed was *never* my intention." He shook his head. "Sabrina is dangerous. She does more than make him want; she makes him *forget*. When he was here looking for his sister's killer, he was six weeks gone and he had no intention of coming back. He was going to stay here—and *die*—for her," Lark said, holding up his thumb and forefinger. "Your father was *this* close to letting his finger do the walking ... I did what I had to do to keep him alive." He shrugged. "You gotta kill me, kill me. Tell the truth, it'd be a relief. I'm sick and fucking tired of living under your daddy's thumb."

Ben believed him. He even understood him. How far he was willing to go in order to protect his friend, what he was willing to throw away. It was what he'd been hoping for. Counting on. Why he'd asked his father to send Lark with them when they left Spain.

He was going to need Lark for what came next.

"I'm not gonna kill you. Not today, anyway." He smiled. "Pack your shit. We're outta here in twenty," he said, leaving Lark to stare after him.

Upstairs, he dragged his duffle from the closet and tossed it on the bed before he started pulling drawers open to collect his stuff.

"I'm going with you."

Ben looked up to find Sabrina's partner standing in the doorway of his room. He arched an eyebrow and kept packing. "How'd you get in here?"

Strickland held up his thumb and wiggled it before repeating himself. "I'm going with you."

Ben gave him an absentminded scowl. "Yeah…no."

"I don't think you understand," Strickland said, walking into the room, forcing him to stop packing and focus. "She's my partner. I have to go with you. I'm *supposed* to be there."

Ben clipped the carabiner through the eyelet of his duffle. "I'm pretty sure you're the one who doesn't understand," he said, tossing his bag toward the door where it landed, leaning to the side in a disheveled slump. "If I take you within a hundred miles of this shit storm, Sabrina will harvest my testicles, and you know what? I like my balls. I'm attached to them. I want to keep them, so again…no."

Strickland glared at him, that Average Joe disguise he'd perfected slipping a bit to give Ben a glimpse of what was going on below the surface. "You're not listening and I'm not asking. I *am* going after her. Either with you or on my own."

Ben didn't answer or argue. Instead, he reached under his bed to pull out his case and dialed in the combination before turning it forward so Strickland could get a good look at what was inside. Guns. Knives. Compact explosives. Weapons and equipment that would take more time and explanation than he had patience for. "Take a good look, cop. Tell me what you *don't* see."

Strickland dropped his gaze, his face paling a bit at the contents of the case, but his jaw maintained its stubborn jut. "A point to all your rambling bullshit."

He laughed in spite of himself. "*A point*…that's funny. I'll tell you what you don't see. Handcuffs. A badge. A warrant. You want to know why you don't see those things?" Ben slammed the case shut and lifted it off the bed. "Because I'm not a cop. I'm not a good guy, and I'm not going after Reyes with the intention of arresting him. I'm not going to read him his rights and make sure he stands trial for his crimes. I'm going after my friends, and if I'm very lucky, I'll be the one who gets to put a bullet in the back of that sick fuck's head," he said, skirting the bed to make his way toward the door. He stopped, his shoulders slumping a bit. Pissing on this guy's parade wasn't nearly as fun as it should've been. He turned around to see him standing where he'd left him, eyes narrowed, staring at him. "Look," he sighed. "You're a good guy, Strickland. You believe in the law. Right from wrong, cops and robbers. But there is absolutely no place in this fight for morality or decency, because that's the kind of shit that will get you—and more importantly, *me*—killed." He turned back around, heading for the hall.

"Fuck you, you smug little prick." Something shiny whizzed past his head before smacking into the wall. A badge.

Ben turned to look at the man standing behind him. "Excuse me?"

Strickland lifted his service weapon from his holster, ejecting the magazine and checking the chamber before dropping both on the ground. "You heard me. You don't know me or what I believe. You don't know where my moral compass points or anything about my *delicate sensibilities*." Next, he pulled his handcuffs from his belt and tossed them next to his gun. "And you sure as fuck don't know what I'm willing to do or how far I'm willing to go to get my partner back. You want a shot at putting down that son of a bitch? Well, you're gonna have to get in line because I'm goddamned sick and tired of riding the bench."

Ben felt a slow smile stretch across his face while he gave the cop in front of him the up-down—not so much sizing him up as he was recalculating what he'd thought he knew about Sabrina's partner. "Okay. You're in. We leave in an hour."

SEVENTY-SEVEN

MICHAEL BOARDED SHAW'S JET immediately after leaving the Barcelona police station, heading straight for the back to stretch out on the long leather bench seat at the back of the plane. As soon as he was horizontal, he closed his eyes, unable to take a relaxed breath until he felt the gentle rock of the jet taxiing down the runway.

Killing Pia came down to simple math. When she told him she wasn't going to stop pursuing Sabrina until she was dead, he believed her. He knew that kind of conviction. That kind of rage had a way of justifying any choice and destroying everything in its path. He'd do whatever he had to in order to protect Sabrina from that, to shield her from the aftermath of the mistakes he'd made. Yeah, it'd been easy.

At least that's what he kept telling himself.

He kept his eyes closed, concentrating on the subtle roll in his gut when the plane lifted off the ground. It didn't matter. Pia. Her father. The ever-growing list of shit he'd done and kept on doing. None of it mattered.

What mattered now was that he was on his way to Colombia.

The SAT phone in his jacket pocket rang and he answered it. "Hey."

"You weren't supposed to be there," Ben said without greeting. "Standard protocol has you checking in at the nearest FSS field office for operational debrief *before* you're released on an assignment."

He could hear the frustration in his partner's voice and oddly enough, it soothed him. "I'm fine, Ben," he said quietly. "Pia is dead."

"I know." Ben let out a frustrated sigh. Caring was obviously costing him a lot of effort. "I also know that being the one to put her down was hard on you."

"Walk in the park," he said. "I was in and out in under twenty minutes."

"That's not what I mean and you fucking well know it," Ben shot back. "Your sister's murder. Watching Reyes kill his wife … what happened to Sabrina."

What keeps happening to her.

One of these days, he was going to find out who Ben's information source was and he was going to have a stern talk with them about privacy. "Is it your turn to play Dr. Phil?"

"You know what? Fuck you. I'm trying—"

He rubbed a hand over his face, a few days' worth of stubble rasping against his palm. Ben Shaw never tried, not with anyone. Busting his balls for being human was a dick move. "You're right. It was hard. For a second, I didn't think I could do it. I almost didn't, but it had to be done."

"I sent someone in to do it for you. You weren't supposed to be there yet," Ben said, sounding almost helpless for a moment. "You didn't give me enough time."

"I knew you'd try to figure out a way to get me off the hook, that's why I went to the precinct straight from the airport. It had to me

367

done by *me*. Reyes's orders. If anyone else had pulled the trigger, he would've killed Sabrina."

Ben was quiet for a moment, digesting what he'd just said before letting out a disgusted chuckle. "This asshole *really* needs to die."

"One of the few things we agree on, partner," he said.

"We're going to get her back," Ben said, taking charge again. "I'm on my way now and I'll have wheels down in less than six hours. I can—"

"You're going to wait until I get there." He opened his eyes, stared hard at the domed roof of the jet. "Do you hear me, Ben? Reyes is *mine*."

A second or two of silence and then a sigh. "I hear you."

"Good." He closed his eyes again. "I'll see you in Colombia."

SEVENTY-EIGHT

Rise and shine, darlin'.

Sabrina's eyes popped open, the sound of Wade's voice fading behind the heartbeat that pounded against her eardrums. She sat up, swinging her legs over the side of the bed, eyes instantly drawn to the large picture window. She'd tried to draw the curtains last night after Reyes left, but they wouldn't budge. Must've been on some sort of automated system that allowed them to be open and closed by remote. Her gaze was pulled past them, to the stretch of grass beyond the glass. After Estefan shot Eduardo, he'd simply walked away, leaving the guard where he fell.

He was still there.

While she slept, someone had covered the body with a sheet. It was a soft, sunny yellow, tucked under his feet and cheek so as not to be carried away by the breeze floating in off the ocean. The sheet stuck to the back of his head, the blood and gore seeping through to darken the yellow fabric to the brownish orange color of dried mustard.

Game time, darlin'.

Someone knocked on the door and she turned just in time to see it open. It was Christina. She had a black eye, the swollen bruise creeping out toward her temple.

The girl smiled even though the facial movement must've caused her pain. "Good morning. I thought maybe you'd like to have breakfast with me." Christina's gaze drifted past her for a moment to rest on the fluttering sheet framed by the picture window she stood in front of. The girl's invitation was casual enough, but her meaning was clear: *Do you want to get out of here?*

Sabrina smiled and nodded, calling on the manners her grandmother had instilled in her when she was no older than her hostess. "That sounds lovely, thank you," she said, stepping into the hallway ahead of Christina, standing to the side so she could pull the door shut.

They walked down hallways and under arches, through lavishly furnished rooms that were probably never used, past formally uniformed maids who kept their eyes downcast and their hands busy.

One such maid stood on a beautifully tiled veranda next to a large round table laid heavy with fruit and pastries. More savory fare was also offered, and a man in a white jacket and pants was waiting to make omelets and waffles.

Leo Maddox sat at the table with a large stack of waffles covered in strawberry syrup and whipped cream. "Hi," he chirped around a mouth full of food. He almost looked happy. Almost normal.

"Hi," Sabrina said, sliding into the seat next to him. She looked around before letting out a low whistle. She draped her napkin across her lap while leaning into him with a conspiratorial whisper. "Holy cow. Is breakfast always like this?"

Leo's gaze strayed to the breakfast chef. "Yeah, it's my favorite part, so far."

She smiled in spite of herself. "Favorite part of what?"

Leo looked at her, a bite of red-soaked waffle hanging off his fork. "Getting kidnapped."

The smile on her face wobbled, threatening to crumble, but she held onto it. "I bet. Strawberry waffles would be my favorite part too."

Christina joined them, speaking softly in Spanish to the maid who stood watch over the table. The maid, who looked barely old enough to drive a car, nodded and went to talk to the chef. "Good morning, Leo," Christina said, lifting the silver pot from the center of the table to pour a cup for her guest and then herself. It was coffee.

"Morning," Leo said, smiling around another mouthful of waffle. His gaze lingered on the bruise on Christina's face, but he didn't ask what happened.

"Did you eat fruit first?" the girl said, lifting a sugar cube from the bowl beside the pot, plopping it into her cup.

"Pineapple and mango with blueberries," he said, holding up his fingers to show her they were stained purple. "Can we go?"

Christina flicked a glance at Sabrina, hiding a barely suppressed smile behind her cup. "I'm not sure."

The boy's shoulders sagged a bit. "Pleeeease."

"We'll see," Christina teased gently, and for a moment Sabrina could hear Michael in her words. Had Michael been playful with her like this when he'd been her protector? Had they eaten decadent breakfasts and played in the sun? She hoped so. She hoped that he'd been able to give this girl a small measure of happiness inside the bleak life she led.

The rest of breakfast was spent in similar fashion. The children spoke to each other, both shooting her looks every now and then. She ate despite the fact that her gut churned and roiled against the thought of food. Reyes was a sadistic bastard, but he was right; food was fuel, and she'd need it if she was going to get through whatever came next.

"Sabrina?"

She looked up from her nearly empty plate to find both of the children staring at her like they'd been talking to her for a while. "Yes?"

"Leo and I were going to take a walk. Would you like to come with us?" Christina said, laying her napkin beside her plate before she stood. Leo jumped up, the corners of his mouth caked with red syrup, and he swiped at them with sticky fingers. "But first, Leo is going to go with Magdalena to wash his hands and face."

The maid took the boy by the hand and led him away. "Wait for me," he called back to them as he disappeared into the house.

As soon as they were alone, Sabrina turned to look at the girl standing beside her. "I'm having a hard time with this, Christina." She looked around to make sure they were alone. "What kind of game is your father playing? Why is he allowed to just run around? And me? I don't get why I'm being allowed to just roam free."

Christina laughed, but the soft sound had a sharp edge that pricked at the back of Sabrina's neck. "Come with me," she said, leading her down the tiled steps to the garden below. They walked a short way before they stopped, Christina taking her by the shoulders, turning her toward the house. "We're allowed to roam, but we are hardly free," she said, looking up. Sabrina followed her line of sight, her gaze landing on the roofline and the long barrel of a sniper rifle aimed in her general direction. "They're everywhere, and they have orders to kill Leo if you stray within twenty feet of the retaining wall."

Before Sabrina could answer, the boy came flying down the steps, face and hands freshly scrubbed, "I wanna go first," he yelled, blowing past them, his short little legs carrying him down the cobblestone path.

Christina smiled after him, as if she hadn't just told her that his death warrant was all but signed. "Come on, I'd like to show you something," she said, snagging her sleeve to turn her to the path Leo had just rocketed down.

They walked for a while, passing by elaborate flowerbeds and under shade trees until they came to an enormous oak that had no business growing on an island off the coast of Colombia. There was a tire swing hanging from a low-slung branch, and for a moment she thought of her grandmother's house. Not the one she had grown up in, but the house Lucy had shared with Michael—the one she'd died in.

"He built this for me when I was five," Christina said, watching as Leo threaded himself through the hole in the tire and begin to swing back and forth. Sabrina didn't have to ask who she was talking about. She knew.

"See, I knew what he did. I knew he killed people—a lot of people—for my father." Christina looked at her, her eyes glittering in the early morning sun. "I knew that people were afraid of him. The other guards whispered about him. The maids. They all told stories of the horrible things *El Cartero* did for money. How merciless and brutal he was." She shook her head. "But I never knew *El Cartero*. I knew Michael. He taught me how to ride a bike and built me a tire swing," she said. "He would push me on that swing and take me to the beach. I loved him, and even if he never said it, I know he loved me."

Sabrina could hear a million questions trembling behind those words. She didn't have answers for any of them except one. "He still does."

"He'll come for you, won't he?" Christina said, sounding both hopeful and sad.

Sabrina shook her head. Looking at the swing, she was suddenly sure. "No; he'll come for *us*. All of us."

SEVENTY-NINE

Cofre del Tesoro, Colombia
October 2012

LYDIA WAS RIGHT. HE needed to get out of here.

It'd been nearly three weeks since his altercation with Estefan, and he still couldn't stop thinking about it. What he'd said. What he'd done.

His only regret is that he hadn't sliced that little bastard ear to ear and dropped him into the ocean. Estefan hadn't given him the chance; he'd left that night—taking one of the boats docked on the beach—and hadn't returned.

As soon as he'd heard the boat pull away from the dock, Michael made his way to the room where he'd last seen Lydia to find her gone. He'd searched the house from top to bottom—every room behind every locked door—with the same results.

Wherever Estefan had gone, he'd taken Lydia with him.

Michael dropped the book he'd taken from the library onto the floor and stood, making his way to his little window, looking out across the walled compound to the sea beyond it. It was late—in the small hours just before sunrise—and he couldn't sleep. He found the satellite phone he kept hidden and dialed the only number he knew by heart, not caring that it was too late to call her. He needed to hear her voice. To tell her he was finally coming home.

He stared out the window, listening to the long distance hiss between rings. He wasn't really worried that Frankie wasn't answering—it was barely three a.m. her time, and a Monday, so that meant she'd worked a dinner shift at the diner the night before. She'd probably gotten home late and stayed up until God knew when, studying or doing homework. He hung up without leaving a voicemail, tossing the phone on the bed.

Lydia was gone, but Christina was still here.

He'd made her a promise, one that until now, had been easy enough to keep. He'd promised to stay. To take care of her. She wouldn't understand and she'd be hurt, but there was nothing he could do, was there? He wasn't her father. He wasn't anyone. Just some merc her father hired to watch over her.

The phone rang quietly, its volume turned down, and he snatched it up, instantly recognizing the number on the display screen.

"Hey, kiddo. I didn't mean to wake you up—"

"Who is this?"

The voice on the other end didn't belong to Frankie, but he recognized it. His Aunt Gina. He almost hung up, silently cursing his sister's carelessness at leaving the phone where their aunt could find it.

"Please … who is this? Do you know where she is?" his aunt sobbed into the phone, not so much desperate as hysterical. "I'll give you anything you want, just—please let her come home."

The level ground beneath his feet shifted, tilting him forward, banging his forehead against the glass he stared through. "Gina. What are you saying? Where's Frankie? What's happening?"

His aunt's sobbing quietly into something that sounded like humming, the line between them crackling. "Mikey." The moment she said it, he knew. She never called him that—not ever.

"Oh no. No, Gina. Don't say it. Don't you fucking—"

"Mikey, you've got to come home. Frankie is missing," she said.

Frankie is missing.

"How long?" She was crying again so he yelled, determined to be heard over the keening sobs that vibrated against his ear. "Damn it, Gina, *how long*?"

"A week. She didn't come home from work last Friday night and I thought maybe…" Her words dissolved into another round of sobs. "I thought—"

"I'm coming. Do you hear me? I'm coming."

A soft breath, like a relieved sigh. "Hurry."

And then she was gone.

He held the phone, staring at it for what felt like hours. It took him a few minutes to figure out what he hadn't been able to place before. His aunt hadn't sounded surprised to hear the voice of her supposedly dead nephew. She knew he was alive. For a moment he allowed himself to believe that it was a trap. That DHS or the CIA or whoever the fuck was looking for him these days had figured out that he'd been in contact with Frankie, and they were using her to lure him home.

It was possible. His Aunt Gina had never been his biggest fan. She'd do just about anything if she thought it meant keeping Frankie safe. He allowed himself to believe it. Let relief wash over him … but only for a moment.

She'd been frantic, teetering on the edge of hysteria. There was no faking that kind of emotion.

Questions like *how* and *how long* didn't matter. Not now.

Michael dropped the phone in his pocket and reached under the bed to pull out his duffle. Yanking drawers open, he threw his clothes inside, wadding and stuffing as fast as he could. Rifling through the books he kept on his shelf, he pulled out a small fortune in cash and a clean passport, tucking both into his boot. Buying his way onto a container ship or smuggling outfit would take time he didn't have. He'd have to fly direct. That meant international airports. Customs. Almost certain capture. But it didn't matter; he still had to try.

Home. He needed to get home. To Frankie. He needed—

The little window he'd been staring out of only minutes before started to rattle softly in its frame. He didn't have to look to understand what it meant. He imagined the modified Black Hawk lowering itself onto the pad, signaling the last thing he needed right now.

Alberto Reyes had returned.

EIGHTY

MICHAEL STEPPED OFF THE plane, his boots sinking into the thick, damp Colombian soil, his gaze going directly to the sturdy-looking outbuilding about twenty-five yards south of the runway. Next to it was Ben's Lear and another plane he'd never seen before. As soon as he was clear of the jet, it turned itself around on the runway and taxied down the strip of dirt, flying back to Spain or wherever it was supposed to go next.

The bay door on the shed rolled up, its sharp metal clang loud enough to scatter a flock of sunbitterns, their large wings lifting them in the air to carry them away.

"You catch any sleep?" Ben said, meeting him halfway between the shed and the airstrip.

"Some," he said, looking at his watch, doing a quick calculation in his head. It was seven a.m. local time, which meant they had about twelve hours to plan out and execute a full-scale assault on an island fortress fifty miles away. "We should probably get started."

"We already have," Ben said, falling into step beside him. Michael was about to ask who *we* was, but a few steps closer meant he didn't have to. The kid must've read his expression because he started talking—fast. "Look, I know it's not ideal, but—"

Michael looked at the small group of people clustered around a map they had spread out on a worktable. Lark and Strickland he recognized right away, and the woman too, but the other man he could only vaguely recall. "*Ideal?* Is that code for *we're all gonna die*?"

"Speak for yourself," the woman he knew as Mary said, straightening her bent posture to give him the once-over. "I happen to enjoy living and have no intention of dying for some broody cop and a snot-nose kid."

"Yeah, let's start with you." He turned to Ben, who was rubbing the back of his neck like it hurt. "Why is she here?"

"I never left," she said, leaning her hip up against the table. "Someone had to keep an eye on the situation while you were busy cleaning up the mess you made in Spain."

"Being Livingston Shaw's personal pet doesn't make you bulletproof, Church," he all but growled at her. "Yeah. I know who you are."

She laughed, her hand settling on the Glock strapped to her hip. "You kill *one* chick and suddenly—"

"Both of you need to shut the fuck up," Strickland said, still bent over the map they'd been studying. "Because neither one of you are helping. Now"—he looked up, aiming his narrowed glare directly at Michael—"why don't you get your ass over here and tell us the best place to do a night drop on the island."

Michael approached the table to see that they were studying a map of the island. "Where'd you get this?" he said, recognizing the layout and shape of the beach, the dense jungle between there and the house.

"It was here," Lark said. "This is Reyes's private airfield. There's all kinds of shit here."

"And he just left it unguarded?" Michael looked around before letting his gaze land on Ben. "That doesn't sound like Reyes at all."

"There were six of them when we landed yesterday, but they started getting antsy when we didn't take off right away," Church said, distracted by the map.

"So…"

She looked up at him. "So I killed them," she said, dropping her finger on the map near the coastline. "What about here? I think it's a good drop zone, but Officer Friendly here thinks it's too open."

Michael looked where she was pointing. "He's right," he said, trailing his fingers up the line where water met sand. "Reyes's compound is less than a mile from here." He tapped his finger on the spot on the map that marked the house. "I'll have to drop on the other side of the island and pack it in."

"We."

He looked up from the map to see Strickland watching him. "Look. I get that you care about her and I get that—"

"Save it. Your sidekick over there already gave me the *we're gonna kill 'em, not arrest 'em* speech and you know what?" Strickland gave him a cool smile. "I'm down with that."

He studied Sabrina's partner for a few seconds, trying to find out if this facet of his personality was a new development or if it'd been there all along, buried beneath the rumpled suits and ketchup-stained ties before deciding it really didn't matter. He was here and he knew what he was asking for. Michael decided to give it to him.

"Then *we'll* drop in here," he said. "It's about a two-mile jungle hike to the base of the mountain the compound sits on." He bounced a look between Lark and Church, not liking his choices. Not one fucking bit. Finally he settled on Lark. "You can set up comms—"

"Sorry, partner. Green Mile's already spoken for," Ben said, a look passing between him and his former partner. "There's some shit he's got to straighten out for me. I'm running comms, so you'll have to take Super Spy."

Church must've read the *fuck that* all over his face because she smiled. "I realize I'm not Miss Popularity, but I *am* on your side."

"Today," he said, the word flexing against the hard set of his jaw. "What about yesterday when you handed her over to Reyes? Were you on my side then?"

"Believe it or not, yes." She stopped smiling, the glint in her eyes dimming just a bit. "But unlike the rest of you fuckwits, I follow orders. I did what I could for her within the parameters I was given. She's armed and has an approximate mission window; if she's as bad-ass as everyone thinks she is, that's plenty."

With Ben running comms and Lark working on whatever it was Ben had him doing, his choices were slim. As in, he didn't have one. "Fine."

"I have a question …"

They all turned to look at the man who'd so far remained quiet. A quick flash of recognition brought Michael a memory. It was the pilot. The same one who'd medevaced Sabrina out of those woods the day she'd killed Wade. Harrison. His name was Reese Harrison, and he was apparently not rotting away in a hole or enjoying a fat pile of hush money like Michael had envisioned. He was Ben's pilot. He looked at his partner for confirmation.

Ben shrugged. "I told you I'd take care of it, didn't I?" he said before looking at Harrison. "What's your question?"

"How are you going to get in the house?" the pilot said. "We did a flyover on the way here. It looked like security is pretty tight."

"That's the easiest part of this whole thing." Michael rocked back on his heels and smiled. "I'm gonna walk right in."

EIGHTY-ONE

THE GUARD WHO ESCORTED Sabrina back to her room after dinner kept a wide berth. He wouldn't even look at her—just kept his slightly panicked gaze aimed down the hall as they walked. She couldn't blame him.

She'd spent her day with Christina and Leo. Watching them take turns on the tire swing and play tag in the wide stretch of grass that surrounded the trees they played under. It would have been a good day if not for the armed guards on the roof and the turrets that dotted the retaining wall overlooking the ocean below. Everywhere she looked there were guards and guns—security woven together so tight that she was beginning to have serious doubts that even Michael could find his way in. She began to worry that she was on her own here. That it was up to her to save Leo. And Christina.

Somewhere between breakfast and walking down that long stretch of hallway after dinner, she'd decided that if she got out of this mess, she'd be taking the girl with her.

The guard stopped in front of her door and took a step back so she could open it. Shutting it in the man's face, she leaned against it for a moment, just as relieved as he was that his assignment had not ended with his brains splattered across the lawn in front of her bedroom window. Twenty-four hours had come and gone, and no one had come for her. She was on her own.

We ain't alone, darlin'.

The warning came seconds before the voice spoke in the dark. "I take it Pablo kept his hands to himself."

Somewhere a light clicked on, and she turned to find Estefan lounging on the settee, shoulders relaxed, knees parted as if he'd made himself comfortable while waiting for her. As if he'd done this exact thing before.

Careful, now—this one's got teeth and he's itchin' to use 'em.

She listened to the voice inside her head. A predator always recognized their own kind. The gun in her boot was useless; no way she'd be able to get to it in time. She thought of her bracelet, the one Michael had given her. "What are you doing here?" she said, walking into the room, careful to make sure he didn't see the apprehension his sudden appearance caused her. A casual glance cast to the corners of the room told her that the security cameras were still active. As long as they were recording, she was relatively safe ... and so was he.

"I wanted to make sure that you have everything you needed, Sabrina." He smiled at her, his eyes flat and dark, tracking her movements across the room. "We are not savages, my father and I. We wish you to be comfortable."

She stopped in front of the ornate dressing table tucked into the corner near the bathroom door. On its glossy surface lay the heavy silver brush and mirror that had once belonged to Lydia, Christina's mother.

"Pretty sure my *comfort* isn't very high on his list of things he gives a shit about. Your father plans on killing me in front of Michael…" She reached out and rocked the brush on its rounded back like Christina had the night before. Like the night before, something rattled inside its handle. "Just like he killed his wife."

Estefan draped his arm across the back of the settee and smiled. "Lydia was a fickle whore who got what she deserved."

"Lydia was twelve when your father married her. How old was she when you started raping her?" She did her best to strain the anger from her voice before she spoke, but it seeped through anyway, and his smile turned into laughter.

"She was nineteen… and I would hardly call it rape." He shook his head, the picture of exasperated amusement. "Is that what *Cartero* told you? That I forced myself on his beloved Lydia?" he said with a shrug. "I supposed believing that would make her manner of death easier for him to swallow…"

"You loved her." She watched him closely, the traces of bitterness and envy that surfaced in the flat pools of his eyes before being pulled under again. "But she hated your guts, didn't she? You disgusted her."

"When I realized she was pregnant, I offered to kill my father so that we could be together. Do you know what she said to me?" he said, leaning into her just a bit like they were sharing a juicy secret. "She said, 'Michael will take care of us.'" For a moment, he looked toxic— like a simple touch from him could kill.

Sabrina imagined them standing face to face like they were now. Lydia, outwardly defiant even while facing down her own rapist. Estefan, so sick he couldn't even recognize that what he was doing to her was wrong.

"Michael." He spat the word at her, his lips twisted into an ugly smile. "I realized then that he was the reason she would never love me."

"From a female perspective, I gotta tell you," she said quietly, "it was all the *raping* that made it impossible for her to love you."

If they'd been closer, she was certain he would have hit her—and not an open-palmed slap like his father had given her, either. He would have hit her with a closed fist and more than once.

He stood, and she took a step back, dropping in a defensive stance that told him the violence he had in mind would not go as smoothly as he was used to. Her hip bumped into the vanity, her sudden movement answered by that faint rattling again.

"Lydia believed he was her savior. That he could protect her from my father." Estefan smirked, reading her posture perfectly, and changed courses. "From me." He reached up to finger the scar that ran down the length of his face, and for a moment she could see just how much he hated both Michael and his father. How twisted he had grown living in their shadows.

You're runnin' out of time here, darlin'… tick tock.

As if on cue, a metallic click filled the silence between them and her eyes automatically darted to the clock perched on the mantel just over his shoulder. It was nine o'clock, and the sound she'd just heard was the auto-lock engaging on her bedroom door.

EIGHTY-TWO

THE RECEIVER HE'D PUT in his ear hissed and crackled seconds before Ben's voice came online. "You ready for this?"

Michael adjusted the straps on his parachute while watching
Church do a pre-jump check on Strickland's rig. He was about to
jump out of an airplane with a hapless cop and Livingston Shaw's
pet spy. "I was ready an hour ago."

"So you keep saying." Ben chuckled. "If you had your way, you'd
have swum to the island hours ago with a KA-bar clenched in your
teeth and a live grenade in each fist."

His partner was right. It was what his instincts were telling him
to do. What they always told him to do: *Save her. Protect her.* He'd
been ready to go the second he stepped foot off the plane, and he
would have gone if Ben hadn't been there to stop him.

"There's no way to tap into the compound's security feed; I'm
going to have to cut the cameras completely, so once you're in, I can't
be your eyes," Ben said, going over the plan for what seemed like the

fiftieth time. "Give me a check-in when you hit the island and another when you make the mountain. I'll kill comms and cameras then."

"Got it," he said. "What I don't *got* is an explanation on why you're running interference while Lark rides the pine." When they'd left, Lark had been nothing more than a pair of hulking shoulders hunched over a bank of computer screens, so intent on what he was doing that he hadn't even looked up when they left.

"I told you, he's got more important things to do," Ben said. "Trust me."

"Not even as far as I could throw you."

Ben laughed again. "Then trust that I hate my father and take great pleasure in ruining his day."

Michael felt a smirk coast across his mouth. That was as close to an answer as he was going to get from his partner. "That I *do* trust," he said, cutting the mic as soon as Church turned toward him. She'd traded her jeans and Einstein T-shirt for standard-issue FSS garb—dark fatigues and long-sleeved shirt—and her honey-colored hair was pulled away from her exotic-looking face. He remembered what Shaw had said about her. Born in America but raised to hate everything it stood for and then abandoned there by the country that was supposed to be her family's home. The term *issues* had to be an understatement.

She approached him, stepping around so she could stand behind him. He moved to turn, not comfortable having her at his back. She grabbed him by the shoulders and stopped him mid-turn. "I need to check your rig," she said, her tone slightly exasperated, like she was talking to an unreasonable child who was trying her patience.

"I'll let you do me," he said, turning against her hands until they were standing face to face, "if you let me do you."

She pushed a smile onto her face and batted her eyelashes at him, fluttering them around the dark hazel of her eyes. "What would Sabrina think?"

"That I'm right not to trust you," he deadpanned.

She dropped the act completely and suddenly she was the no-nonsense woman he knew, the medical tech who examined him after each mission. "Just in case you missed it, the enemy is down there," she said, nodding her head to the side. "*He's* got your girl, not me. I'm here to help you get her back."

He stared at her, could feel Strickland behind him, watching the exchange. "Why?"

She rolled her eyes and sighed. "Let's take it from the top, shall we? Shaw wants the Maddox boy back. He also wants you *and* the little incentive program she represents to you intact. That means Sabrina lives."

Shaw had been content to keep him ignorant of the fact that he not only knew about Sabrina, but that he'd been controlling her for over a year—she'd been his ace in the hole. Now that Michael was aware, Shaw knew that there would be no pulling his strings without her dangling over his head. It was either lose him or save her.

And Livingston Shaw hated to lose.

Church was still talking. "There are too many objectives in this mission for you to hit all your marks alone." No longer antagonistic, she was now the voice of reason. "You need me."

"Like a fucking hole in my head," he muttered, but she was right and they both knew it.

"I'll make you a deal, O'Shea. I give you my absolute word that you can trust me completely for the next four hours."

"What if Shaw changes his mind? What if he decides he wants us dead?" Shaw could kill him anytime he wanted, but his death wasn't the issue. It was always looming, inevitable. But Shaw would need more than a phone code and password to kill Sabrina.

He'd need someone on the ground. Loyal. Capable.

Someone like Church.

He could see that she was conflicted; the stress of it played across her face, but only for an instant. She reached into the long pocket of her fatigues and pulled out her cell, offering it to him. "I can give you four hours—take it or leave it."

Michael hesitated for only a moment before he took it.

EIGHTY-THREE

BEN LISTENED TO THE exchange between Michael and Church, a slight frown resting on his face. Church couldn't be trusted, and his partner knew it—but he was also desperate. Desperation often turned smart people stupid. For Michael's sake, he hoped his father's minion was on the level.

"We've reached jump altitude," Reese Harrison's voice came through with minimal interference. So clear that Ben could hear the unease in his tone.

"Got something on your mind?" Ben said, keeping the question casual, but the pilot's instincts were usually spot on. If there was a reason he was feeling anxious, he wanted to hear it.

"No ... yes." A short sigh that might have been a snort. "I don't fucking know—maybe."

"Getting dizzy. And bored ... " He used his smartass remark to cover up the fact that Harrison's trepidation bothered him.

"Okay. Church spent a lot of time on her phone while we were here waiting for you guys, mostly getting chewed out by your dad.

392

Apparently, she was supposed to make a clean sweep of Sabrina's friend and anyone else who was in the house when she went in for the extraction."

Ben didn't have to ask what that meant. Church had been ordered to kill Val, or anyone who'd been there when she had been sent in to bring Sabrina out. Harsh? Yes, but you didn't maintain a covert cover by allowing people who've seen your face to live to tell about it.

"Is he sending in a scrub team?"

"Yeah…" Harrison hadn't been on the FSS payroll long, but before flying medevac he'd been a Nightstalker—a Special Forces helicopter pilot charged with flying elite military in and out of their most dangerous missions. He was no stranger to high-pressure situations, and he never balked at following orders. It was what made him so valuable. Too valuable to kill when he'd recognized Michael in the field and made himself a liability.

"You could have told me this sooner, numb nuts," he said evenly.

"That crazy bitch had a gun pointed, literally, at my dick the entire time you and I were on the phone. I was afraid to *breath*, much less talk." Harrison sighed. "There's something else."

"Fuck it all…of *course* there is." He ground the heel of his hand into one of his closed lids and felt the gritty rub of adrenaline and not enough sleep scrape across his eye. "Well, you gonna make me guess?"

"He's on his way here. He told Church he'd be landing around three a.m. He's coming for Michael. Doesn't trust you to bring him in. And…I think she wanted me to know that. She held the phone away from her ear so I could pick up parts of the conversation."

There was no *around* with his father. He knew exactly when he'd be here, down to the minute. If he'd said three a.m., Ben gathered he'd be here no later than midnight. That meant they had less than four hours to get in, get the Maddox boy, and get out.

"Can you stop him?" Harrison's voice was thick with worry.

Him was his dad, and stopping him had never been easy. "Yeah, I can stop him," he said, ending the call. He pressed his thumb, hard and heavy into the keypad for a moment before he dialed his father.

"Call them off."

His father sighed. "Benjamin—"

"Goddamned it, Dad—call them off!" he bellowed it into the phone, his thick shell of *who gives a fuck* cracking wide open.

"They pose a risk. A risk Courtney should have eliminated immediately." He sounded annoyed. "She understood the parameters: no witnesses. Why is that such a hard concept to grasp?" he said, like taking a life was as easy a task as taking out the trash or re-capping the toothpaste after brushing your teeth.

A smartass remarked bubbled on Ben's lips but he held it, his brain circling around something Church had said to them not more than a few hours before.

Unlike the rest of you fuckwits, I follow orders. I did what I could for her within those parameters.

Clever girl.

"There are no witnesses."

His father made a sound he'd heard more than once, one reserved for proven liars and people who generally pissed him off.

"Whatever Church used to incapacitate Valerie Nickels punched a huge hole in her memory," he said, relief washing over him. "She can't remember anything past Sunday night. She and her baby were the only ones who had contact with her besides Sabrina and me. No one else knows who she is." He chose to ignore the fact that Sabrina's partner not only knew who she was, he was now on a first-name basis with her.

His father was quiet for a moment, mulling over what he'd been told, pretending to discount the truth he must've heard in his son's voice. "That's hardly a guarantee, is it, son?" he said, his cadence smoothing out, wrapping silk around each word.

He knew instantly that his father had no intention of calling off anything. Oddly enough, it was Mandy, Sabrina's doctor friend who popped into his head. She wasn't there when Church had taken Sabrina, but that mattered little. His father would wipe out everyone involved in this mess. If his father had his way, none of them would live.

"Fine. I'll do it."

"Do what?" his father said. No longer smooth, he seized onto the words almost immediately, not wanting to give Ben time to change his mind.

"You know *what*. I'll do it. Just call them off." He sighed. Nearly choked on the words that came next. "Please, Dad."

His father was quiet for a few moments before answering. "Why do these people matter to you so much, Benjamin?"

It was the one thing he didn't know. The one question he couldn't answer, so he didn't. Just sat quietly, waiting for his father to either agree to his terms or not.

"Very well," his father finally said. "I'll call them off . . . and I expect you to keep your promise."

"Keeping promises has never been my problem, Dad—that's yours," Ben said before hanging up the phone.

EIGHTY-FOUR

THEY TOOK THE JUMP at eighteen thousand feet. It was high enough so that Reyes's guards wouldn't notice the plane circling the island but not so high that they'd need the equipment for a high-altitude jump.

Falling through the dark, Michael could see the lights of the compound winking in the distance. Sabrina was in there somewhere, locked away like Lydia had been. Held against her will.

The thought of it had him moving into a free fall, head pointed toward the earth, arms straight and tight against his sides as he rocketed through the sky. He pulled his chute at the last possible second, less than two thousand feet above the ground. The landing was hard, his boots barely touching down before he hit the emergency release on his rig. He stumbled a bit but found his feet quickly, running for the cover of the trees that surrounded the small clearing he'd chosen as their drop zone.

Turning, he fell into a crouch to watch the others fall. Like him, Church waited until the last possible second to pull her chute, and she tumbled, shoulder first, as she tucked herself into the fall, cutting her chute as soon as she sprang to her feet. She was beside him a few seconds later, hunkered down, expression hidden by the deep shadows of the trees they squatted beneath.

Strickland was last, having pulled his chute at a more prudent altitude. Michael watched as he landed, boots first, taking a few running hops before he managed to find the ripcord that would release the chute. He was rusty, but beneath the rust was a confidence that surprised him.

This wasn't Strickland's first rodeo.

Michael watched Strickland jog across the clearing to join them. "Something you feel like sharing with the rest of the class, Christopher?" Church said before he had a chance to say anything. Her voice was quiet, carrying no farther than the tight circle they formed in the dark.

He could see the bright flash of teeth in the gloom as Sabrina's partner shot Church a smile. "Not really," Strickland said, looking at him. "What's the plan?"

Michael hadn't told them anything before they'd boarded the plane beyond assuring them that he had a way inside. He hadn't wanted to risk tipping his hand with Lark around and even now, he was having a hard time coming clean with Church so close. Stalling, he pressed a finger into his ear. "All boots on the ground," he said into his comm, and it crackled in response. "Moving toward our next rally point."

"Roger that," Ben said. "Once I kill comms you'll have to move fast. It won't take the guards very long to realize they can't communicate."

Michael knew better. It was after nine o'clock. According to Hector, Reyes evacuated the island every night. There was no one left to call. Reyes was alone on the island, waiting for him.

"I'll let you know when we've reached the mountain," he said before clicking off his comm.

Reaching into the pocket of his fatigues, he pulled out his compass. The soft greenish glow of its arrow pointed northwest. He turned his body until it rotated by a few degrees.

"Two clicks northeast from here we'll run into the base of the mountain the compound sits on. There's a secret entrance that leads through the mountain and into the house. Once we gain entrance into the compound, we'll split up." He pulled a piece of paper out of the same pocket that'd housed the compass and pressed it into Strickland's hand. "I need you two to find someone for me. Reyes's daughter, Christina. She's—"

Church grabbed his arm and spun him, her face held tight in a scowl. "That's not the mission. Sabrina and the Maddox kid— that's why we're here."

"She'll know where they're holding him," he said. "Enlisting her help will make things go a lot smoother."

Church glared at him. "She takes us to the boy, but we leave her here."

Michael could still see Christina standing at her bedroom window, staring down at him. She hadn't known what was happening. She hadn't understood that her father was about to kill her mother. But she'd known he was going to leave her.

"I'm not leaving here without her." *Not again.*

She shook her head. "We're not kidnapping Reyes's daughter."

"Think of it more as a rescue. Besides, you told me you were mine for four hours—whatever I needed." He smirked at her when she swore under her breath. "Is that a yes?"

She let go of him and snatched the map out of Strickland's hand. "I never liked you," she muttered while studying it.

"Same goes, sweetheart," he said before turning toward Strickland again. "She won't go easily. She's been trained to resist abductions and since she doesn't know you, she'll think that's what this is. We had a code word: pink pony. Say it as soon as you have eyes on her and she'll cooperate." Even as he said it, he wasn't sure. He'd let her mother die, left her alone when he'd promised otherwise. What if she hated him? He wouldn't blame her if she did.

Strickland looked at him for a moment. "I've got to go with Church on this one—I didn't tag along to rescue some drug cartel princess."

"Think about your partner for a moment. Now you tell me how'd she respond to leaving a child on this island. *Any* child."

Strickland closed his eyes for a moment before he sighed. "Pink pony. That's cute," he said, his tone thick with sarcasm. "Okay, I'll do it, but you better save her. Do you hear me, asshole? You better save her."

Michael nodded. "Trust me, saving Sabrina is all that matters."

EIGHTY-FIVE

She was trapped.

Sabrina offered Estefan a cool smile, even as her brain scrambled around looking for a way out. The windows were out; even if they weren't locked, they were bulletproof. The door was just as solid. Oak veneer over something that felt as heavy as a bank vault. No way was she shooting her way out of here.

Keep 'em talking, darlin'. This one likes the sound of his own voice even better than I do.

"I get it. Lydia rejects you, Michael outpaces you at every turn...they had to be punished." She shrugged a bit, turning to the side so she faced the vanity she'd backed herself up against. "What I don't get is your dad." She cast a quick glance in the mirror to catch his refection. What looked back at her from the mirror hardly looked human, it was so twisted with rage. She kept talking as though she didn't notice, distracting him while she worked her fingers into the space between her wrist and the bracelet Michael had given her.

"What do you mean?" he said, his tone innocent even as the corner of his mouth lifted in a humorless grin.

"Sergey Filatov." She found the button on the underside of the bracelet and pushed it, releasing the clasp. "You kidnapped someone very important to him and had him murdered and then left him in that house for me to find."

"Involving you was Pia's idea." He gave a dismissive shrug. "She insisted we dump him on your doorstep so that when you died, Michael would blame himself. She's very angry with him."

Pia Cordova. The daughter of the man Michael had killed in Spain. "The two of you are partners?"

Now he smiled at her. "We have similar goals—kill our fathers and make Michael suffer."

"Who was the boy?" She took another look in the mirror to find him watching her. Something behind him caught her notice; the motion sensor attached to the camera mounted in the corner was dark. The camera itself was still—the blinking red light that announced its presence was off.

Someone had killed the cameras.

Estefan was still talking, and she looked at his reflection. "…nephew. The son of Viktor, Filatov's little brother. My father had Viktor killed last year when their negotiations over territories turned sour. When I saw the boy, I knew he would be a stone that would kill many birds."

She found the release button on the underside of the bracelet and pushed it, its titanium links dropping into her palm. She held it for a moment, heart hammering against her sternum. She would only have one shot. She had to make it count. "Filatov was your plan B. If Michael failed, Filatov would come after your father as soon as he found out that his nephew was found dead in your father's drop house."

"The plan was flawless..." Estefan's gaze flickered downward, trying to catch a glimpse of what she was doing with her hands. "Until I realized that you somehow managed to stop the boy's identity from being released."

She turned toward him, facing him instead of his reflection, the end of the bracelet held in her fist while the rest of it lay across the outside, secured by her thumb. She hadn't noticed him move but he must have. He was standing closer now. Close enough to touch her. "What can I say? I'm a ruiner."

He gave her another shrug, this one saying that her inference was of little consequence. "What have you got there, Sabrina?" He glanced down at her hand, caught the flash of silver and he reached for it, causing her to flinch away. He smiled. "You fear me," he said as if the thought pleased him.

"Fear you?" She shook her head, casting a casual glance down at her titanium-wrapped fist. "An hour from now, your father will be dead. As will you," she said, sounding much more confident than she felt.

"Can I tell you a secret, Sabrina?" He leaned in even closer, his breath hot against her face. "*Cartero* isn't your savior any more than he was Lydia's. *Cartero* is dead... Did I happen to mention how angry Pia was with him?"

The words hit her hard. Not because she believed them, but because *he* did. Estefan believed with every fiber of his being that Michael was dead. Panic rose, all sharp teeth and blinding speed, and for a moment she was frozen.

You don't need him, darlin'. Not when you got me...

She hardened herself, shut off the part that wanted to scream. Instead she smiled, dropping the sharp end of the bracelet, the links clicking together as gravity did its job, forming a short metal pike gripped in her fist. A fast glance over Estefan's shoulder told her that the cameras were still off. Either he had them turned off to hide what he'd come here to do to her, or Church had kept her promise to bring the cavalry.

Either way, it was time to go.

"It hardly matters, Estefan," she said, matching his tone perfectly. "Because Michael was never going to be the one to kill you." She whispered the words, soft and quiet, leaning into him like a lover. "That's my job."

EIGHTY-SIX

TWENTY MINUTES AFTER LANDING, they came to the base of the mountain and stopped, Church and Strickland both looking at him expectantly. He clicked his comm. "We're here." He didn't want to say where *here* was because he wasn't sure who was listening.

"Killing comms and cameras now. Watch your six," Ben told him, and he knew that Ben had the same reservations about trusting Church as he did. At the end of the day, she belonged to Livingston Shaw, and he'd do well to remember it.

"Roger that," Michael said before clicking off the comm. He checked the compass again to make sure he had the right coordinates. "It's there," he said, pointing the same way as the arrow. "Behind the brush."

Church drew a wicked-looking machete from the sheath strapped to her thigh and started to hack away the dense overgrown foliage. It was obvious the entrance hadn't been used in years. Not since Lydia had used it to sneak down to the beach to see her daughter.

"Where does it lead?" Strickland said, standing next to him while they watched Church swing her blade.

"Second-floor laundry room. Reyes had it added into the plans when he built the compound. My guess is it's his escape route if he's ever raided." Michael looked at him. The bumbling detective was gone, leaving the single-minded pit bull in its place. "I'm glad you're here," he said impulsively and was instantly sorry he said it when Strickland turned on him, eyebrow arched over his cool brown gaze.

"I love her, you know," he said, staring him right in the eye. "She's a pain in my ass. She causes me trouble—the real kind—and she can't seem to go six months without someone trying to kill her, but she's my partner ... so there's nowhere else for me to be."

There was no surge of jealousy at his admission like there had been with Nickels. No grinding need to defend what was his, and he knew it was because Strickland's love was born from something pure. Strickland loved Sabrina like Michael had loved Lydia and Frankie. There was nothing romantic between them, and there never would be.

"We're getting her back. And I promise, neither of you will ever see me again." It was the best he could offer.

Strickland laughed in his face.

"Dude, you really don't know her at all, do you?" he said, shaking his head. "It doesn't matter if you love her or not. She loves *you* and the best and worst thing about her is that once she decides you're hers, she hangs on to the bitter end. Leaving her won't change that and it won't keep her safe—trust me on that one."

"You don't happen to know the combination, do you?" Church said. Both of them looked up to see her standing beside a heavy metal door that had been buried beneath the green. One he'd never seen before. The kind used to seal a bomb shelter or a walk-in safe.

"Well, shit," Strickland breathed besides him, shoulders slumping when he got a load of the large combination lock that all but promised to keep them out.

"Try 03-16-03." Christina's birthday. He said it without looking in Strickland's direction, unwilling to admit defeat so soon. He watched the dial spin beneath Church's competent fingers right, then left and back again. She pulled the lever.

Nothing.

He rattled off another number, the date he'd agreed to work for Reyes, and watched her go through the same process as before. Again, it didn't work.

"I'm not sure how many more times I can try without tripping some sort of alarm, O'Shea," Church warned him. "The next one better work."

He was drawing a blank … it had to be something he'd remember. Reyes *wanted* him here. He wouldn't make it impossible for him to gain entry into the compound.

"Think … it has to be a date that would mean as much to him as it does to you," Strickland said, prodding at him quietly. "One he wants you to remember."

And suddenly he knew. "10-09-12."

Church worked the dial this way and that, taking a deep breath before levering the handle downward. The door swung open, revealing a small room that was little more than a wide mouth for the steep, narrow staircase beyond it.

He started to move toward it, ready to go. Ready to finally put an end to the misery Reyes had been dealing all these years. Before he took two steps, Strickland reached out an arm, clamping a hand around his shoulder to stop his progress.

"What was it? The date?"

Michael looked at him over his shoulder, jaw set. "October 9th, 2012. The day Alberto Reyes murdered his wife in front of me."

He shrugged out from under Strickland's grip and ventured into the dark.

EIGHTY-SEVEN

Cofre del Tesoro, Colombia
October 9, 2012

HE MADE IT AS far as the front lawn before he was stopped.

"Going somewhere, *Cartero*?" Hector called to him from across the grass, sun creeping up out of the ocean to cast soft gray light between them. Estefan was with him, along with a few of Reyes's more experienced guards.

Michael—headed for the steep, winding switchback that led down the cliff wall and onto the boat dock—stopped in his tracks. "Yeah. Home."

Hector nodded, smiling. "Home will have to wait. There's a matter *Hefe* would like to discuss with you."

So far Estefan hadn't said a word. The stitches that must've held his face together had been removed to reveal a thick, ugly scar that ran the length of his face, from the corner of his eye to his mouth. Now he smiled, pushing the scar upward until it crinkled and bunched against his skin. "I told you, didn't I, *Cartero*? I told you that you'd pay."

He shifted his duffle, rolling it from one hand to the other so that he could have quick access to his gun. The switchback was a good fifty yards away. He wouldn't make it. Not without killing these two fucks first. "Is that what you were saying?" He chuckled to mask the mounting desperation he could feel heaping on his chest. "To tell the truth, I couldn't really understand you, what with all that blubbering and crying you were doing."

Estefan flushed, a deep red wash that paled his scar in comparison. He took a step forward, but Hector held a restraining arm across his chest. "You will want to look up, *Cartero*," Hector said.

Something about his tone turned his neck, had him scaling the walls with his eyes until they settled on a window with pink drapes. They were parted, Christina standing in the bare wedge between them, staring down at him, her face pale with confusion and fear.

A man he didn't recognize stood behind her. He had a gun in his hand.

"*Hefe* would like to see you," Hector repeated his earlier request. "It won't take long, and then you will be free to go."

It was a lie and they both knew it, but he nodded anyway, dropping the duffle at his feet. He was going to have to move fast when the time came, and it would only slow him down.

"The gun too," Estefan said, jerking his chin at the .40 holstered on his hip.

"Sure thing," he said, lifting it slowly. "But can we hurry this along? I've got more pressing matters." He dropped it in the grass before going palms up.

Hector nodded, lifting his own gun from his hip and using the barrel of it to motion him along. "Let's go."

They didn't take him into the house. Instead they guided him across the lawn, around the corner of the house until Reyes came into view, standing behind a heavily pregnant Lydia. Michael barely spared her a glance, focusing all his attention on the man behind her.

"*Cartero*, were you going somewhere?" Reyes said in a cheerful cadence that dismissed the gun he had pressed into the space where his wife's belly rounded away from her hips.

"Yeah," he said, keeping his tone casual, just tinged with boredom even as the thought of his Aunt Gina's voice shook him with its broken desperation. "I've got some shit to deal with back home. Shouldn't take more than a week or so …" He flicked a glance at Lydia. Her face was as pale as Christina's, but there was no confusion. She knew exactly what was happening.

"And then you will return?" Reyes cocked his head.

He could see Christina's face turned up to look at him, her tiny fingers splayed wide to weave between his own. *Are you going to leave too?*

He promised her he wouldn't leave her alone, but Frankie's disappearance changed everything. Still … "Well, yeah. That was the plan," he said carefully.

Reyes chuckled, shaking his head. "Why? Why would you return after what you've done? Surely you don't love her."

The back of his neck went hot and tight—a surefire sign that shit was about to get critical. "What the fuck are you talking about, Reyes?" he said, letting his eyes wonder down to the gun in the other man's hand. "I really don't have time for whatever kind of domestic squabble you've got—"

"How long?"

He kicked his eyes up to Reyes's face. "What?"

"*How long!*" he roared, his face contorted with rage and something else. Something more disturbing than anger. Something fanatical. Almost gleeful. Whatever happened next, there would be no stopping it. No talking Reyes out of whatever choice he'd already made.

"How long *what*?" He looked at Lydia for help. She knew the answer but all she could do was stare at him, eyes wide and dark, lips moving silently, fumbling over the same words over and over. *Let us go, let us go, let us go ...*

Reyes took a deep breath, letting it out on a soft chuckle as he shook his head. "*How long* have you been fucking my wife?"

Michael looked at Estefan, who'd moved to flank his father. "I never touched her."

"My wife is the Virgin Mary, then?" he spat, digging the barrel of his gun into her swollen belly deep enough to cause Lydia to cry out in pain. "The proof is right in front of us both, *Cartero*. Do you think me a fool?"

There was no reasoning with Reyes. Estefan had been hard at work, tending the lies he'd planted. Even if he did tell him the truth—that it was his son who'd raped his wife, that it was his grandchild and not some bastard that grew in Lydia's belly—Reyes would never listen. His own conceit would never let him believe that he had been so thoroughly deceived.

"What do you want me to do?" he said, speaking directly to Lydia, eyes trained on her face. "Tell me what to do."

"*What you promised,*" she breathed, seconds before her husband pulled the trigger.

Everything stopped. The world ground to a halt as he watched her fall, the bright splash of blood across her belly growing even as

411

she fell to the ground. He screamed, the feel of it, raw and clawing at his throat, was real even though there was no sound.

Reyes leveled the gun at her, pulling the trigger again and again, and Michael lunged forward. There was too much space between them for him to stop what was happening, but he had to try.

Bullets smacked into the ground all around him, hitting him in the shoulder, grazing his rib cage.

Let us go.

He changed direction, heavy boots tearing into the grass as he ran, bullets swarming him like wasps. The retaining wall was low here, so as not to obstruct the view of the ocean from Reyes's study, and he leapt at it, hands gripping the top to pull himself over.

The ledge between the face of the cliff and the wall was negligible, mere inches, but it didn't matter. His feet barely touched it as he flung himself over and into the sea.

EIGHTY-EIGHT

SABRINA LUNGED FORWARD, FAKING with her left hand in order to draw his attention. Estefan turned his head and lifted his hands to block the attack, leaving the left side of his face vulnerable.

She jabbed fast with her right hand, burying the pike in his eye, its trajectory cut short by the side of her fist as it punched into his socket. She let go even as he screamed. It was the kind of scream that told her she'd only managed to wound a rabid animal instead of put it down. There was a sickening popping sound, followed by a gush of something warm and thick against her hand. Leaving the pike, she planted her hands on his chest and shoved, sending him tumbling over the back of the settee he'd been sitting on when she arrived.

He reached for her as he fell and she stumbled back, hips slamming into the vanity at her back. Her hands skittered along its surface until she found what she was looking for. The hairbrush.

Estefan lay on the floor between her and the door, hands clutching at the pike she'd driven into his eye, moaning as blood,

413

turned a yellowish orange by the viscous fluid it was mixed with, ran down his face.

She finally managed to unscrew the handle from the paddle of the brush. It was hollow and something was inside. *Please… please… please…*

Shake a tail feather, darlin'—that ain't gonna hold him off for long…

Dumping it out with shaking fingers, she closed her fist around what was inside. A key. Lydia's key.

Run.

She dropped the dismantled brush and moved, skirting around the settee, sights zeroed in on the door. She wasn't sure if the key would even work, but she had to try. Staying here was suicide.

Estefan was stretched out between her and the door. There was no going around him, and even as she took the leap she knew what would happen. His hand shot out and snagged her pant leg, and she went down hard, chin clipping the coffee table as she fell. She clamped her teeth together to keep them from breaking but even so, she felt them crack, blood filling her mouth so suddenly that she gagged. The key bounced out her hand, spinning across the hardwood floor.

She flipped over, drawing her knee to her chest to hammer him in the face with the heavy sole of her boot, but he was still lying flat on his back, his hand an iron clamp around her ankle. The gun she had hidden there bit into it, metal grinding against bone. The moment his hand tightened around her ankle, she knew he'd felt it for what it was.

"Naughty, naughty…" he said, rolling onto his side so that he could grab her with two hands. She could see that he'd pulled the pike from his eye. He was grappling with her boot, trying to pull it off to get to her gun. He was too far away for her to deliver a kick

414

that would do any real damage, so she changed course, bringing her heel down on his hands, breaking his grip on her.

It all happened in a matter of seconds and she scrambled back, the LCP falling from her pant leg onto the floor between them, but he was closer, and the bloody grin he gave her said he knew it.

Time to get dirty, darlin'.

Wade's voice sounded strangely composed, a spot of calm in the panic that swirled inside her head and she listened, popping forward to deliver a superman punch to his damaged eye just as his fingers closed around the grip of the gun.

The momentum of the blow stunned him, landing her on top of him and she straddled his chest, raining blows down on each and every part of him that she could reach.

He flipped her and she was suddenly on her back, staring up at him no more than a moment before she was seeing stars again, delivered by the fist she caught against her temple. Another blow glanced across her cheekbone, but it was enough to stun her. Slow her down.

He was between her legs, saying something, taunting her, and she blinked stupidly, trying to clear the buzzing that muddled her brain. He hit her again—a vicious open-handed slap meant to stun and shame her before he wrapped his hands around her neck to squeeze.

She brought her fists down on his forearms, trying to break the hold he had on her throat, and it worked for a moment, loosening his grip enough to allow her to take a hurried breath before he re-applied pressure.

She used the breath to clear her mind, allowing her to push panic away just enough to remember her training. Kicking her leg straight up, she popped her hip off the ground, angling it enough to hook an ankle around his neck. Using her own body weight as a fulcrum, Sabrina levered herself up and over him until she straddled his chest.

Using the momentum of the switch, she barreled down on him, breaking the hold he had on her throat. She swung hard with heavy fists, feeling things break and bleed beneath her hands, her training and technique giving way to blind rage. She beat him until he stopped moving, stopped trying to protect himself. And then she took the chance to roll off of him, fitting the LCP in her hand as she did, coming up with it pointed squarely at his face.

Do it, Melissa.

Wade's tone had gone dark—no longer playful, no longer serene. It was a command, and she felt the momentary tension of her finger as it tightened around the trigger, ready to do as he said.

Kill him. Do it now.

Church had warned her that the gun was a last resort. A gunshot would alert Alberto Reyes that something was wrong, and she'd lose the element of surprise.

There was a pillow a few feet away on the bed. She could see herself dropping down to her knees to press it into his face, the barrel of the gun deep in its folds. She could pull the trigger then, couldn't she? She could kill him and no one would hear a thing.

That's the way, darlin... put him out of your misery.

Blood dribbled down her chin and her teeth ached almost as bad as her hands. She looked down at them, her fingers shaking, knuckles split open and weeping, more than one of them broken. As bad as she felt, he looked worse.

Estefan's nose, smashed into his face, was nearly as swollen as his eye, both oozing blood and other bodily fluids. His face was lumpy bruised knots sprouting up under broken skin, mouth open in an effort to keep breathing, and she could see how much it cost him just to take a breath. She could hear the gurgle of blood in his throat.

Dropping the pillow, she took her finger off the trigger.

You can't let him live, darlin'. You know that.

Tucking the LCP into the small of her back, she focused on finding the key, blocking out the truth she heard in her head. Estefan was attempting to roll over onto his side, probably so he wouldn't drown in his own blood. His mouth was moving, broken and mangled—the words sliding from it sounding as wet and fat as slugs. She couldn't understand them, but she knew he was talking to her.

You walk out that door with him still breathin', you're gonna regret it.

She knew Wade was right, but she redoubled her efforts, lifting the dust ruffle on the bed to look beneath it.

There.

She had to wriggle under it in order to reach the key and when she came up with it, she found Estefan on all fours, head hanging low between his shoulders, blood and mucus a constant drip from his mangled face.

He was still talking, but she just added his voice to Wade's and ignored him too.

At the door she shoved the key into the lock and took a deep breath and a look over her shoulder. Estefan was on his knees now, facing her, glaring at her.

Please. Please let this work...

She turned the key and the lock gave way.

"...over," he said behind her, the words sounding like they were too big for his mouth. "...never be over."

Told ya so...

She didn't answer. Didn't give either of them the satisfaction. She just pulled open the door and stumbled into the hall before pulling it closed with a quiet *click.*

EIGHTY-NINE

MICHAEL, STRICKLAND, AND CHURCH took the stairs as they'd taken the jungle behind them: single-file and quiet.

It was dark but not pitch-black. As soon as they pulled the door closed and reengaged the lock, a strip of running lights illuminated their path, leading them upward. It looked like Reyes had made some upgrades.

But the stairs were steep, carved into the side of a mountain, and mounting them took time and effort. Michael could hear Strickland's breath behind him. He was exerted but not winded. He imagined Church was about the same.

The running lights came to an abrupt end, and he stopped short. "Stop," he said, practically breathing the word. Reaching out, he felt something cool and solid in front of him. The door.

He trailed his fingers along the doorframe, looking for wires. Alarms. Anything that might trigger an alert that would signal their arrival. But there was nothing. Finding the doorknob, he turned and pushed before stepping into a narrow broom closet. He opened that door too, letting himself into a deserted laundry room.

Strickland and Church followed him in, Church closing the door as quietly as possible behind them. The longer they could keep someone from spotting them, the better. He reached into his cargo pocket and fished out earpieces. They each took one and fit it into their ear while he attached their mics to their shirt collars. They were small, barely bigger than the head of a pin, blending perfectly into the dark fabric of their shirts.

"Fancy," Strickland whispered, coming through his comm loud and clear.

The stairs that would take them to the third floor were directly across from the laundry room. "Straight up the stairs," he said softly.

Strickland held up the map and nodded. "Pink pony. I got this," he said as if he'd asked him to pick up his dry cleaning instead of break into the home of a drug lord and take his daughter. The crazy thing was, Michael believed him.

Reaching into the small of his back he pulled his backup piece, a S&W .40 outfitted with a suppressor. He held it out to Strickland, and the cop took it without hesitation. "Just in case," he said to him before turning to look at Church. "Stay together. Get Christina first and have her take you to the Maddox boy and then get out."

For a second she looked like she was going to argue with him. Then she gave a curt nod before lifting her Glock from its holster. "Let's do this, the meter is running," she said, reminding him that he only had her cooperation for so long—if he ever really had it at all.

Michael didn't say anything. Instead he gripped the knob to the door that would lead them into the house and pushed it open, leading them into the hall.

Church took point, leading Strickland up the stairs. Strickland stopped for just a moment to look at Michael, his face saying it all.

Save her.

And then he was gone, disappearing up the stairs along with Church, leaving Michael to do as he promised.

NINETY

Find Leo.

Sabrina thought of him, his pale blond head bent over a stack of strawberry waffles, solemn hazel eyes turned toward her. Watching her. Waiting for her to do something—to get him out of here.

She had to get upstairs. She was almost certain that Christina and Leo's quarters were close to each other and so far, hers was the only bedroom she'd seen on the first floor. Countless sitting rooms, sunrooms, and libraries, but only one bedroom.

The problem was, she couldn't find a goddamned staircase.

She walked faster and faster until she was practically running. Dodging through rooms blindly.

Slow down. You're just getting yourself all turned around now, darlin'. Think about where she took you. What she showed you…

Christina had led her through the house. Taken her from room to room—a meandering route that had taken several minutes.

She'd been trying to show her the layout of the house.

Sabrina stopped moving completely and closed her eyes, watching herself walk from room to room, paying attention to where each of them led…

She was now standing in a formal living room, which Christina had called the Blue Room. Beyond it was a music room and a small paneled "conversation area" that housed a fireplace. They'd walked through it on their way to breakfast. There was another sitting room, one with floor-to-ceiling French doors that opened out on the veranda. On the other side of it was a staircase.

Route clearly mapped out in her mind, she opened her eyes. Standing no more than ten feet in front of her was Alberto Reyes. He had a gun in his hand, and it was pressed into the tender flesh of Leo Maddox's neck.

"I see you and Estefan have been getting to know each other," he said, flicking his flat, dark gaze over her. "Where is he?"

"With any luck, bleeding out on the floor of my room."

Reyes laughed, but there was no humor in the sound. Leo's eyes welled instantly with tears.

"It's going to be okay, Leo. Everything is going to be fine," she said calmly, risking no more than a glance at him before fixing her attention on the man behind him.

"She's lying to you, Leo. She knows that the two of you are very close to dying, and she wants to keep you calm," Reyes said, pressing the muzzle of the gun just a little bit deeper, the pressure widening Leo's eyes, spilling tears down his cheeks. "Tell him the truth."

"The truth…" She looked down at Leo and smiled. "The truth is that this man won't hurt you because if he does, your grandfather will hunt him to the ends of the earth and destroy everything he's built." She looked up at Reyes, her smile dying. "That's the truth."

Reyes glared at her for a moment before he dropped the gun and stepped back, releasing Leo. "Run along now, Leo." He grinned at her. "Sabrina and I would like to be alone."

The boy hesitated, no longer afraid. He looked worried—for her.

She nodded, licking her lips so that they'd move when she spoke. "Do as he says, it's okay," she said. "You're going to be fine. My friend Michael will be here soon." She said it like she was sure of it. The sound of it, her belief in him reverberating in her voice, gave her the courage to look Reyes in the eye. "He's coming for us."

Neither of them watched Leo as he slipped away, bare feet slapping against cool tile as he did what he was told. As soon as Leo was gone, she relaxed her hands at her sides, palms turned in so that when the time was right she'd have a faster draw on the gun tucked into the small of her back.

"So now you believe that *Cartero* will come for you?" Reyes cocked his head, regarding her with the kind of morbid fascination a twisted child would find in a wounded animal. "Or were you just saying that to calm our young friend?"

Sabrina shook her head. "Michael isn't coming here to save me. He's coming here to kill you."

Reyes gave her a quiet smile. "*Cartero* isn't coming; he is already here."

NINETY-ONE

As soon as Church and Strickland disappeared upstairs, Michael moved. At the end of the hall was Reyes's suite of rooms. With any luck, he'd find him waiting there and he could end this quickly. The door would be unlocked. It was the only door in the house that didn't lock at nine p.m.

"I hate it when I can't fucking see. Somebody talk to me," Ben's voice crackled in his ear. "Tell me what's happening."

Michael stopped for a moment, resisting the urge to turn his comm off all together. The last thing he needed was a distraction.

"We've located the Reyes girl's bedroom. Church is picking the lock … We're in," Strickland said, just above a whisper, and then, "Pink pony."

They had Christina.

He allowed himself a moment of relief before he pressed his empty ear to the closed door of Reyes's room and listened before turning the knob. Even without the dim glow of the bedside lamp he could see that the room was empty. "Reyes isn't in his room. I'm heading downstairs."

"Christina has agreed to lead us to the Maddox boy," Church said, sounding slightly disgruntled. "As soon as we have him, we'll head for the boats."

"Keep me posted," Ben said before signing off.

Michael stood there for a moment, trying to remember the layout of the house. He'd take the stair to the first floor—

Something flashed in the corner of his eye. Movement, fast and small, running past him and down the hall. He turned, his arm shooting out to snag the boy, trying to keep it quiet, but Leo had other plans. He dodged fast, spun right out of his grip before knocking into a hallway table, sending a vase crashing to the ground.

"Leo—*stop*," he said, his hushed tone sounding as loud as shout. "I'm here to help you."

The kid stopped and turned. "What's your name?" he whispered, fists clenched, eyes wide.

"Michael. My name is Michael. Your grandfather—"

That was as far as he got before he was interrupted by the sound of gunshots erupting downstairs, followed by a scream.

NINETY-TWO

IT HAPPENED FAST. ONE second she was staring Reyes down, practically daring him to shoot her, the next, Sabrina was the one doing the shooting.

He'd demanded she walk over to him, and she'd refused, knowing the moment she did, her chance to use her LCP would be lost. She'd jammed it into her waistband on the fly; the only reason he hadn't seen it yet was because it was behind her. The second he saw it, her one advantage would be lost.

"I said come here, Sabrina. Don't make me do something we'll both regret," he said, punctuating his demand by thumbing back the hammer of the gun in his hand.

"You're gonna kill me anyway. I think I'll stay right here."

She could see him shift his hand around the grip of the gun—no doubt getting ready to make good on his threat—when there was a noise upstairs. A shattering of glass on tile.

The second Reyes turned his head toward the sound, she reached behind her, the LCP all but leaping into her palm. By the time Alberto Reyes had refocused his attention on her, she was already pulling the trigger.

Three times in rapid succession the LCP bucked her hand as she dove for cover. Reyes returned fire, a bullet catching her center mass, mushrooming against the ultralight vest Courtney had given her.

She fell, landing hard on the tile, her breath stolen as much by the impact of the bullet as by her collision with the floor. She found her feet and started running. If Michael was here, he'd go for Leo first; she had to give him time to secure the boy.

Before she'd taken more than a few steps, something hard and heavy caught her in the back of her head and she fell, landing on the tiled floor for the second time in less than a minute. Her ribs screamed in protest, snapping where they'd been cracked by the shot she'd taken.

She screamed, frustrated and desperate to lead Reyes as far away from Michael as she could. Sabrina flipped over and raised her gun to take another shot, but Reyes was already on top of her. Standing over her. Pulling the trigger.

NINETY-THREE

FOR A MOMENT, NEITHER of them moved.

"He had a gun," Leo said, his words tumbling out faster and faster, chased by fear and panic. "Mr. Reyes let me go and she told me to run so I—" He stopped abruptly, eyes wide and terrified. "I left her."

She. Sabrina. Leo was talking about Sabrina.

He could hear boots pounding down the stairs—all attempts at stealth thrown out the window. Seconds later, Strickland and Church appeared with Christina in tow.

She was older, but he'd recognize her anywhere. Seeing her caused his heart to stutter in his chest, but he held it together, looking to Strickland for help. "Take Leo," he said as he moved, down the stairs. In the direction of the shots.

Strickland scooped Leo into his arms and followed. "We've got to help her, she's probably been shot. Church can—"

"No. We stick to the plan," Michael said, making the landing, running down the last set of stairs. "He won't kill her. Not until I'm there to see it."

"Are you trying to reassure me? Because really, you suck at it," Strickland said, Leo straddling his hip, free hand wrapped around the .40 he'd given him in the laundry room. "I'll go with you as backup—"

"*We stick to the plan*," Michael said, hitting the first floor at a dead run. "You and Church take them and head for the boats!" He moved from room to room, leading them toward the veranda closest to the seawall.

He spoke into his comm. "Ben, Church and Strickland have secured the Maddox boy and are headed your way—" He put his boot through one of the French door's window panels, splintering wood and shattering glass and opening a hole big enough for them to crawl through.

"Got it," Ben said, his voice tight with worry. "We'll be waiting."

He turned to Church. "Keys are in a lockbox in the boathouse. Let me know when you're away." He looked at Christina and tried to smile. "I'll be right back … I promise."

NINETY-FOUR

MICHAEL HEADED FOR THE only place Reyes could be—the place where he'd said yes and started this whole mess.

The double doors leading to the study were closed, but even from here he could hear Reyes talking. "He's coming, Sabrina—can you hear him? *Cartero* is coming for you..."

Michael stood to the side, reaching out to push the door open. It swung wide. He squeezed his eyes shut for a moment, steeling himself against what he was about to see. Trying to quiet the feeling that this time would be no different than the last.

He rounded the corner and stood in the doorway, empty hands held at shoulder level. "I'm here," he said, staring at her; her face was pale beneath the bruises and blood that littered it. "Are you okay?"

She smiled, flashing blood-smeared teeth for just a moment before the effort made her wince. "Never better."

Reyes stood behind her, the barrel of his gun dug into the base of Sabrina's skull. He heard the distinct *clack* of the hammer being drawn back. "Your weapons. Toss them into the corner, now."

He did as he was told without hesitation, pulling guns and knives from holsters and sheaths, tossing them away from him until he was stripped bare. His finger brushed against something small and hard and he rolled it into his palm, concealing it in the web between his thumb and pointer. When he was done he held his hands up at shoulder level, palms out. "That's it. I'm clean."

"Let's play a game, shall we?" Reyes said, surveying the weapons that littered the floor between them.

"Games are a waste of time, Reyes," he said, his eyes darting around the room. Not much had changed. Reyes's wide, heavy desk still dominated the room, a sideboard next to the door housing crystal decanters full of liquor. Behind him was a pair of leather couches facing each other across the low table between them. "Just let her go so you can kill me—that's what you really want, isn't it?"

"What I *really* want is to watch you suffer … and then kill you." Reyes shifted to the side, letting him see his face. "First question: Do you love her?" Reyes said, his voice snaking out from his hiding place behind Sabrina. They stood in front of his desk—or rather, Sabrina stood. Reyes leaned against his desk, using it for support. The arm that held the gun on her was tucked awkwardly against his side. He was wounded. Sabrina's expression confirmed what Reyes's posture told him: she'd shot him.

He nodded, his neck stiff, head jerking as if on rusty hinges. "Yes."

"Would you die for her?"

He thought of crawling in the dirt, covered in blood while his insides spasmed against the poison that coursed through his veins. Of David Song trailing behind him with a scalpel clenched in his fist. Looking at her now, he could see she was remembering the same thing. "Yes."

"You love her more than you loved my Lydia?"

There was no reasoning with him. No explaining that Lydia had been a friend, nothing more. That he'd killed his wife to punish Michael for something he hadn't done. "Yes."

"Then tell her. Tell her you love her."

He opened his mouth to do as Reyes said, but something else came out. "I lied. Yesterday morning... I said horrible things. Did things—"

"It's okay. Trust me; I've done and said worse, the morning after." Incredibly, she smiled at him, tears shimmering in her eyes, electrifying the blue of them until they almost glowed. "But you better not do it again."

Her words did more than offer forgiveness. They told him that she believed in him. That she knew he would get her out of this mess. He smiled back, even though fear was a living thing inside his belly, eating him from the inside out. "I promise."

"I lost my bracelet."

He flicked a look down at her wrist. It was bare. "Somewhere good, I hope."

"Pretty good—Estefan's eye socket." She winced when Reyes tightened his fist in her hair, giving her a little shake.

"Tell her you love her, *Cartero*." Reyes's tone gained an edge.

The moment he said the words, Reyes would pull the trigger and he wasn't ready. Not yet. "The boy Sabrina found in that house—the one that brought me to San Francisco in the first place. He was the nephew of Sergey Filatov. Did you know that?"

Reyes flicked him another glance, this one off-kilter. Wild. "You're a liar."

Michael shook his head. "Lying is against the rules." He paused, waiting for Sabrina to look at him. As soon as he caught her attention, he continued. "Planting a boy matching Leo's description was

432

his idea, wasn't it? Involving Sabrina? But that wasn't his only plan. Estefan killed and practically dumped that kid in your lap so that Filatov would destroy you."

"Estefan is loyal." Reyes jerked her again, and she gritted her teeth to keep from crying out. "He would never defy me."

Blood snaked down Sabrina's neck, a sluggish flow that painted her collarbone bright red. The sight of it did something to him. Grounded him and cleared his mind of everything that he'd been holding on to.

His parents. His team. Frankie and Lydia. Lucy.

They were dead, but it was not his fault.

"He *would* and he *did*. He's been working with Pia Cordova for years now. Estefan set us up to destroy each other," he said, closing his fists, securing the pellet he had hidden there. "He hates you almost as much as he hates me."

"I gave him everything—made him a prince. He has no reason to hate me," Reyes said, but even as the words were spoken, Michael could see it. Understanding.

"He doesn't want to be a prince; he wants to be king." Michael shook his head. "It wasn't my baby Lydia was carrying. While you were off whoring around, Estefan was here—*raping* your wife."

His words did their job, and Reyes roared in response. Jerking the barrel of the gun from where it'd been anchored to Sabrina's skull, he pointed it at Michael.

Like he knew she would, she dropped back on her right leg, driving her elbow back and up, smashing it into his nose. The blow sent his first shots wide, but he pulled the trigger anyway, again and again, and some bullets found their mark.

Michael could feel them punching into his chest and abdomen, shattering his ribs. Stealing his breath.

Sabrina dropped low, using the hold he had on her hair to pull him down with her. Reyes, struggling to stay upright, let go and she rolled away, giving him a clear shot.

He lunged forward, tackling Reyes, sending them both sprawling across the desk. The gun was knocked loose, clattering to the ground, but Michael didn't care. He was going to kill Reyes with his bare hands.

They crashed to the ground, Reyes beneath him, and he wrapped his free hand around the man's throat, squeezing until he opened his mouth to gasp for breath. As soon as his mouth was open, Michael swung, crashing his fist against Reyes's teeth before dropping the pellet inside.

"Ben, blow the second capsule," he bellowed, the heel of his hand slamming into the underside of Reyes's jaw to keep it shut. As soon as he spoke, Reyes went wild, swinging and pulling at his face and hands. Anything to work himself loose.

"You got it," his partner said, loud and clear.

Seconds later, Reyes began to jerk, his eyes rolling back, froth trying to bubble through closed lips.

Michael let go, shoving himself away from the sputtering, convulsing mass beneath him. Blood instantly erupted from Reyes's nose and mouth, spewed into the air, but he didn't stick around to watch the rest. He got his feet underneath him, lurching around the side of the desk to see Sabrina crumpled against the door.

He picked her up and ran, stumbling and bouncing his way down the hall, Reyes's screams fading behind him.

Suddenly, they were outside. He kept moving, lurching across the grass until they made it to the Blackhawk.

He stretched her out on the concrete pad and ripped her shirt open, expecting to find a bloody cluster of holes in her chest. She was fighting him, pushing his hands away. Saying something. "We have to go back. Leo and Christina—we can't just—"

No blood. No holes. Just four slugs mushroomed against the feather-light fabric of an FSS-issued Kevlar tank.

"They're fine. Strickland and Church got them off the island." He looked up, baffled, to find her looking at him. "You're okay."

"I am." She offered him a halfhearted smile while she struggled to stand. "But I'll be a hell of a lot better as soon as you get me the hell out of here."

NINETY-FIVE

THE BLACKHAWK TOUCHED DOWN gently in the dirt, as close as he could get it to the hangar without being a danger, and he powered it off. It'd been years since he'd flown, but it was just like riding a bike.

Some things you never forget.

Sabrina sat beside him, quiet. She hadn't spoken since he'd lifted her into the helo before climbing in beside her. She'd looked out the window, broken hands clutched to her stomach, as if for safe keeping. Her hair was matted with blood, and long rivulets crusted against her neck.

"I love you."

She turned her face toward him. It was dirty and bruised, eyes bluer than the ocean they'd just crossed shining back at him. "I love you too," she said before popping the door open and jumping down from the Blackhawk. She didn't want to hear it: his speech about how she was safer with him gone, that she needed to forget about him and move on. The same one he gave her every time he left her.

He couldn't blame her. He didn't want to hear it either.

Waiting a few seconds, he let her gain a safe distance between them before he followed her across the dirt. She headed straight for Strickland and as soon as he saw her, he turned his back on the conversation he'd been having with Church and met her halfway. They stood close together, talking. Strickland looked at him over her shoulder and, for a moment, he thought he caught a smile.

"He cares for her."

He cast a quick glance at Ben, who'd come up beside him. "So do you."

"You caught me," his partner said with a wide grin. "You really think she's better off without you?"

"I know she is."

Ben didn't answer. They stood there watching Lark pack up his computer equipment and load it onto Ben's Lear while Church carried a roll of duct tape into the hangar. "My father is coming," he finally said, casting an apologetic look between them.

"For me." It wasn't a question.

"Yeah. That's why you're gonna be gone when he gets here."

Michael shook his head. "Nice try, kid, but there's no place for me to go," he said, watching as Sabrina allowed Strickland to lead her into the hangar. As long as Shaw had her, he would never risk leaving. He would do whatever Shaw said. They both knew that.

"Do you trust me?"

It was the second time Ben had asked him that, and he found himself turning his gaze on his partner. He had that look again. The *not*-Ben look that told you he was a totally different person than the one he pretended to be.

Christina appeared in the open door of a plane. Not Ben's, but the one he didn't recognize. Its destination was unknown. As soon as the girl saw him, she smiled and ran down the steps straight for him. He dropped to his knees and opened his arms, and seconds later they were filled with her. His heart swelled inside his chest as he let himself hold her, and when she laid her head on his shoulder he didn't pull away.

"Well? Do you?" Ben said, watching as he stood, arms still around Christina.

He looked down at Christina for a moment before meeting his partner's gaze. "Against my better judgment, yeah, I do."

Ben laughed at him, clapping a rough hand against his back to move him toward the plane. Toward the unknown. "So get on the plane...and stop calling me kid."

NINETY-SIX

Sabrina sat quietly, watching while Church ripped off a long strip of duct tape with her teeth and added it to the several layers she'd applied to her ribs.

"Thank you," she said, the words getting stuck between clenched teeth while pain spiraled through her rib cage to shoot down her spine.

"For what?" Church said, mouth full of duct tape as she did another rip-and-stick.

"For the Kevlar. For the tape." She caught the other woman's gaze and held it. "For not killing Val like you were supposed to."

Church stalled out for a second before she shrugged, looking down at the roll of tape to rip off another strip. "I didn't do it for you," she said, avoiding eye contact while she smoothed the tape in place, pushing just hard enough against Sabrina's broken ribs to make her jerk.

"I still don't like you," she said, waving off another round of duct tape.

Church grinned, setting the roll down on the workbench Sabrina was perched on. "Good, because I don't like you either." She turned and headed out the door, shooting her a quick smile over her shoulder. "See you around."

Sabrina laughed, the pressure of the tape around her ribs making the pain of it bearable. She looked at Strickland. He was leaning against the wall next to the door, and he turned his head when Church strolled past, watching her walk out the door.

"Somebody likes her, though …"

Strickland's head snapped back in Sabrina's direction, a red flush creeping up his neck. "I think one of us dating a government spook is enough, don't you?"

"We aren't government," Ben said from the doorway. "Planes are prepped and ready—we'll be taking off in a few minutes."

Home.

By this time tomorrow, she'd be back in San Francisco. Back to normal…

Back to a life without Michael.

"You mind giving us a few minutes alone?"

Strickland looked at Ben and then at her. She gave him a nod of assent, and he left, exiting the hangar and boarding the waiting plane.

As soon as Strickland was gone, she looked at Ben to find him watching her. She felt time bend, and she found herself back in that dark hospital room, Ben standing in the shadows. Telling her she had a choice to make. That he could fix her life if she'd let him.

"My father's on his way here, so we don't have much time," he told her, moving into the room until he was standing right in front of her.

"Time for what?"

"For you to decide."

440

She looked past him, out the hangar door to the pair of planes that sat side by side on the tarmac. She'd watched Michael lead Christina onto the smaller of the two. Strickland and Church had boarded the other. "Decide what?"

"Where you belong," Ben said.

"I don't understand," she said, even though her heart had begun an uneven knocking against her chest.

Ben smiled at her. "I think you do. My plane is headed to San Francisco."

"And the other one?" she said, looking past him toward the plane she'd just watched Michael and Christina board.

"That plane belongs to a very powerful US Senator who is very happy and very appreciative to have is grandson back... and not too pleased with my father at the moment."

"Maddox?" She looked over his shoulder again, suddenly understanding. "He's going to help Michael."

"Did you know that Montana actually means *mountain*? They wreak havoc on cell phone reception... especially when you're living on an five-hundred-acre ranch surrounded by them without a cell tower within three hundred miles."

Somehow, he'd done it. Ben had managed to get Michael out from under his father's thumb. Relief washed through her, "Thank you, Ben. Thank—"

"Michael is dead." He gave her what she'd come to call his *I'm a very bad man* smile. "He was shot several times by Reyes before crashing that Blackhawk behind me into the water between here and the island. We managed a water rescue for the Maddox boy, but Michael was lost at sea."

"Lark agreed to go along with it?"

"Agreed?" His smile widened. "It was his idea. He also spent the last several hours developing a scrambling program, just in case my father decides to blow his chip for the hell of it. Michael is dead," he repeated, the smile fading into a look that told her just how much it was costing him to let his friend go. "And you can be too. But you have to decide right now, and once that decision is made, it can't be undone. Not ever."

He was making sure she understood. She could have Michael. She could be with him or she could go home. Home to Jason and Riley. Val and Lucy. Whatever her decision, there would be no turning back. Whoever she chose to let go would be lost to her forever. It was a hard choice but it was *hers*—with Ben it always would be. That was the difference between him and his father.

Home ...

Sometimes it wasn't a place. Sometimes it was a person.

She levered herself up from the workbench to stand in front of him. "You're a good man, Ben—and a good friend." She stretched herself, despite the pain, to press a kiss to his cheek. "Thank you ... for everything," she said before walking away.

"Take care of him," he said, and she felt his eyes on her as she left the hangar and got on the plane.

Peggy Coleman Photography

ABOUT THE AUTHOR

Maegan Beaumont is a native Phoenician, currently stuck in suburbia with her high school sweetheart and husband, Joe, along with their four children. She writes take-you-to-the-edge-of-your-seat thrillers and loves action movies and spending time with her family. When she isn't busy fulfilling her duties as Domestic Goddess, she is locked in her office with her computer, her coffee pot, and her Rhodesian Ridgeback and one true love, Jade.

ACKNOWLEDGMENTS

To my husband, Joe: Thank you for always offering me the last cookie in the jar (even though I know you really want it) and for understanding that "I'm almost finished with this scene" translates to "You aren't going to see me for the rest of the day." I love you … I guess. To my always entertaining, sometimes irritating, mostly wonderful children: Finding my balance between writer and mother has been my greatest challenge. Thank you for understanding and loving me, even when I get it wrong. To my ever increasing circle of writer-type friends—Cindy, Holly, Linda, Kristen, Mary, and Susana: Thank you for making me feel like less of a weirdo. With you, I have truly found my people. To my lovely canning wife, Melissa: Thank you for sticking it out with me. Being my friend is a tough job; being my wife makes you a saint.

To Les Edgerton: You were the first person to ever look at me and see, above all else, a writer. For that, I'd open a vein for you … preferably someone else's.

To Cathy Crowley, who has been my hero and my champion from day one: Thank you for your seemingly endless offers of support, enthusiasm and expertise. I thank you, my readers thank you, and most importantly, chapter 48 thanks you. To Mary Lillie, whose eagle-eye and attention to detail keeps me sane: You'll never know how much I rely on you to make me sound like I know what I'm doing.

To my agent, Chip MacGregor: Thanks for looking out for me and for talking me off the ledge when things don't go my way. It's comforting to know I've got you in my corner. To the fantastic team at Midnight Ink—specifically my badass editors, Terri Bischoff and Nicole Nugent: Thank you for the countless hours of hard work and dedication you put in, not just for me, but for all of us. Thank you for being our voice, our sounding board, our advocates, and our biggest fans.

And for you, Annie, who is always last but never, ever least: You were my first and most constant partner in this crazy, unpredictable, sometimes-painful-but-always-worth-it roller coaster we call life. Thank you for forgiving me when I'm being a self-absorbed asshole (which is most of the time) and for being the first person who ever leaned in close and whispered in my ear, *you can do this*. I love you, I do. Forever and ever.

www.MidnightInkBooks.com

From the gritty streets of New York City to sacred tombs in the Middle East, it's always midnight somewhere. Join us online at any hour for fresh new voices in mystery fiction.

At midnightinkbooks.com you'll also find our author blog, new and upcoming books, events, book club questions, excerpts, mystery resources, and more.

MIDNIGHT
INK

MIDNIGHT INK ORDERING INFORMATION

Order Online:
- Visit our website www.midnightinkbooks.com, select your books, and order them on our secure server.

Order by Phone:
- Call toll-free within the U.S. and Canada at 1-888-NITE-INK (1-888-648-3465)
- We accept VISA, MasterCard, and American Express

Order by Mail:
Send the full price of your order (MN residents add 6.5% sales tax) in U.S. funds, plus postage & handling to:

Midnight Ink
2143 Wooddale Drive
Woodbury, MN 55125-2989

Postage & Handling:

Standard (U.S. & Canada). If your order is:
$24.99 and under, add $4.00
$25.00 and over, FREE STANDARD SHIPPING

AK, HI, PR: $16.00 for one book plus $2.00 for each additional book.

International Orders (airmail only):
$16.00 for one book plus $3.00 for each additional book

Orders are processed within 12 business days. Please allow for normal shipping time.
Postage and handling rates subject to change.